FIGHT FOR ME

A QUAKING HEART NOVEL - BOOK THREE

An Inspirational Romance Story

Credits

Edited by Dr. Holly Smit

Cover design by P and N Graphics
Cover cowboy art by Joyce Geleynse
Cowboy Model Jamal Perry

Book layout by www.ebooklaunch.com

Janith Hooper

FIGHT FOR ME

A QUAKING HEART NOVEL - BOOK THREE

An Inspirational Romance Story

6th Street Design and Publishing

Dedication

To my beloved editor, Doc Holly. A heartfelt dedication to you, my dear sister in Christ, for your devotion to *your* work of editing *my* work. Your refinements continue to make my words shine. Despite the constant challenges in your own life, especially in the last year, you have remained faithful to this venture. My hope is that you and I will continue our complementary kinship to augment the world of romantic prose in a way that is pleasing to God, and to my cherished readers.

Thank you, my friend, for your ongoing labor of love, prayer, and support.

PROLOGUE

Coleman Ranch, north of Harper Ranch, Gallatin County, Montana
August 17, 1959, 11:15 pm

Jake Cooper banged the cabinet door closed, rattling what wee bit was left in the cupboard. All he wanted was one measly clean cup for some late night coffee. All he found were three plates and one glass with water spots aplenty. Weary to the marrow and ready to drop from the sweltering work-day, he shifted his gaze to the kitchen sink and stared in disgust. It was filled high with practically every dish they owned.

His eye caught on the mug in the middle of the table, the recurring nightmare of a centerpiece. It was where his *loving wife* placed every note she wrote to him. Were they love notes he'd look forward to them, but nae, not even close. Reminders they were, of her daily needs and his inadequacies; go to the store notes, wash the dishes notes, need hot meals notes, be home earlier notes, and on it went. In essence, they were 'be a better husband notes' and just the thought of viewing today's version made his empty gut knot up. But right now his need for coffee trumped his aversion to the mug, so he wrapped his hand around it, snatched the white paper from it's center… and froze in disgust. The bottom of the note dripped brown liquid—*old coffee?*—onto the filthy dining table. *Drip, drip, drip.*

The frustration he'd been holding back burned up his throat and out his mouth before he could stop it. "*Enough!*" he hollered.

The uncharacteristic roar made Betty jump in her seat. He turned to apologize, but his gaze caught on the crusted eggs from yesterday's breakfast still dotting the rough-hewn tabletop. In the meager glow of their only kitchen light, he saw stickiness from syrup—*when had they last eaten hot cakes?*—spread verra near one of her elbows.

He sucked in a savage breath and tried to rein in his tongue before it got away from him, working it around his mouth to give it something to do. No good. He couldna hold back. "Is it too much to ask for you to do a little housework, lass? I'm bustin' my rump on ranch work, and you seem unmindful of what needs to be done around here."

Betty stiffened in her seat, eyes closed, breath held.

Jake clamped down on the temper that constantly rode under the surface. He didna want to scare his wife. His size alone intimidated most people, never mind the way his black beard obliterated the lower half of his face, leaving only black eyes to reveal his mood. *Lighten your tone.* Betty was nearly seven months pregnant, he reminded himself. "Do you need help? Is that it?"

"All you do is work, Jake," she whined. "I've been waiting all evening for you to come in and make us supper. You never showed. I had to eat *cold* cereal. Again!"

Jake heaved a sigh, wanting nothing more than to jump on his gelding, ride up the mountain, and never look back. He was by nature more suited to a hermit's existence, apparently just like his absentee father. Or so his mum had told him oft enough. Existing as a married man stretched his taciturn temperament past its boundaries every single day. "Listen. Betty. You ken I canna always stop what I'm doing to come in. Cereal will have to do until you make the effort to learn to cook, ye ken?" He glanced at the clock. "What are you doing up at this hour anyway?"

"I need to talk to you."

He pressed his backside into the counter and crossed his arms. Tried to focus in spite of his overwhelming fatigue and disintegrating outlook. "So talk."

"You aren't very receptive."

"I'm tired. Irritated. Hungry. Talk, or forget it, lass."

"*You're* irritated? *I* should be irritated. You're the only one who knows how to cook, and I need more food these days. You're never home."

"Ranch work is relentless. Especially in summer. You ken that. And I used my only day off this month to scrub every crevice in this house. Have you done nothing to it since?"

She ran a hand through her stringy brown hair. It looked like it hadna been washed in days, a true disappointment to Jake. He was a man who appreciated a woman's well-kempt, healthy hair. Betty's had never been that. "You don't even like me, it feels like. I know you don't think this baby is yours, but it is. I need more from you, Jake."

Jake scraped a chair back from the table and dropped into it. He was beyond bone-tired, disillusioned, unhappy. She was right. He'd married her because it seemed the right thing to do at the time, even though he didna believe for one moment the bairn was his. He'd only been with her the one time, the night his Scottish mother died after her five week battle against pneumonia. Betty had found him, unshaven, half starved, just after the coroner took his mum's body away. It didna matter that he'd steered clear of Betty's relentless pursuit until then. Fact was, he'd needed consoling that night, and she'd been more than happy to oblige.

That moment of weakness had cost him. His life, his happiness… his future.

Jake pressed his thumb and forefinger into his eyes and rubbed. He pulled in a deep breath, huffed it out, and stared into her wide-set eyes. "What do you want from me, Betty?"

"I want you to be here for meals. I need *cooked* meals. I need help with the house. I need you to shop with me, for clothes for me and the baby. I want you to get the cradle built. I want you to be here, Jake. Be here for *me*."

As his stomach roiled, he searched his mind for what he could say to her. He should never have married her. Hadna realized women were so needy, or that he fell so far short as a husband. Then again, it wasna like his father had been around to show him how it was done.

As spoiled as Betty was, he still wanted to give her comfort, but he'd never been one to lie. "I canna do that."

She blanched, and he wanted to kick himself. Whenever he spoke, the truth of things always came out his mouth, no matter how callous they sounded. He should have kept quiet until he'd had a chance to explain he didna have enough time in the day to foreman the Coleman Ranch, manage the new project of row crops the owner wanted to try, handle the late deliveries of calves, and plan for harvest. He wouldna be able to manage the household on top of all that, at least not for now.

Before he got another word out, she whisked her sweater off the back of her chair and stuffed one arm in, then the other. "You're hateful, Jacob Cooper. I need someone to take care of me. Someone who cares about *me*. I'm going back home."

Stunned, he watched as she grabbed the keys to the Ford Galaxie she'd come into the marriage with, and slammed out the door.

When the finality of what she'd done reached his muddled brain, he leapt to his feet and raced out of the house after her. Tail lights blurred in a swirl of dust as the car sped south toward Harper Ranch and the intersecting road that went west to the main highway. He stared hard after the tail lights, tracking them for a hundred yards, then blinked. Of all the dimwit, idiot things for him to be doing now, he was making sure Betty made that blasted turn safely. He took off his hat, slapped it against his thigh, and looked away.

Good riddance. Their short marriage was a sham. He'd expected some give and take, a house he could call a haven and a woman he could respect and ken and mayhap even love. For pity's sake, he'd only lain with Betty the one time before they were married and again to consummate it. He'd understood the pregnancy had been too hard on her for him to demand more.

His gaze tracked back to the fading tail lights in the distance. Instead of feeling fury at the sight, he felt utterly hollow. Because where Betty went, the bairn went too. Poor wee lamb, the welcome result of two fools who hadna behaved better. Now the bairn would have a divided life before drawing even a first breath.

Standing in the dirt road, watching the last vestige of his marriage disappear, Jake felt his body vibrate. This day had taken its toll. He was in need of food, sleep, and an impossible sense of peace. It was no wonder he was trembling, though he couldna remember ever having experienced that particular weakness before.

There it was again.

That was a tremor. Not from him. From the ground.

A jolt shook the road with the force of an earth mover. From the light of the full moon, Jake saw gravel bounce and shimmy across the road at his feet.

An earthquake?

He'd never experienced one before, but he'd heard of them. Mostly ones in California, near the coast.

A horrendous sound came out of nowhere and whooshed past him, like a ghostly train on an invisible track. The rumble increased right along with the tremendous vibration, awakening his panic at the same time.

What had he done? *"Betty!"*

He forced his legs into a run, but the ground bounced him around so, it was nearly impossible to keep his feet under him. He may as well have been a puppet on a string. He needed to reach Betty before she got hurt.

It seemed he'd never get to his truck. His legs weakened by the second, doing their best to keep him upright as he scrambled toward the door handle. He stretched forward, then sideways, caught the handle, and held on for dear life. The earth rumbled, quivered, shuddered. The truck bounced on its tires, nearly pitching him off. His feet went airborne. Next he kent, the edges of his boots were digging troughs into the ground, trying to find purchase. He swallowed convulsively. Bile scoured up his throat.

Cyclone winds whipped about. Blast! What was this thing? His hat ripped from his head and spun out into the night. Trembling, vibrating earth, and deafening, wild winds propelled stinging scree into his face with a fury all their own.

Finally, Jake was able to yank the truck door open and doggedly crawl inside. Wrestling the door closed, he straightened behind the steering wheel and watched the mayhem outside. He swiped his hands over his face, clearing his vision. The truck rocked and bobbed. Jake hit his head against the steering wheel, the side glass, then the roof. Sitting a bronco wasna as bad as this. At least he could anticipate which direction a horse might take. This was impossible!

The bairn. Betty. Fear clung to his belly. How could a willful woman and innocent babe survive this demolition of nature? It was his fault they were out there, exposed. He needed to get to them. Protect them. But there was no way he could move the vehicle forward until the quake stopped.

A horrific ripping reached his ears. Glancing out his window, he watched as the earth cracked and split apart just yards away. His gaze followed a crack that made its way toward the fork in the road. *No!* Betty was headed that way. He could only hope she'd already made it to the highway, but his gut told him there hadna been enough time for that.

"Hellfire!" he hollered into the empty truck. He turned the key. The engine roared to life. Stomping on the clutch, he pulled the gearshift into first, but before he eased the pedal back, another shake sent the truck careening backwards. The reflection of the large oak in their front yard filled his rearview mirror, growing larger by the second. He jammed on the brake and clutch. The truck pitched to a stop and bounced some more.

Sweat dotted his forehead, then slipped into his eyes. He swiped it with the back of his hand as he let out the clutch. Just as the gear caught, the quake lurched once more, then stilled.

It was unnatural how quiet it became. The shaking halted, the winds stopped. Debris fluttered unhurriedly to the ground while the moon peeked through, bright and full, as if nothing had interrupted its glow. And what came into his view stunned him. Shredded earth, destruction for miles around.

Guilt and fear seized Jake. He needed to find Betty. Now!

It was slow going, since the road had been shredded. Thank goodness between Coleman and Harper Ranches there was mostly pasture. Jake maneuvered around each torn spot in the road, banging over pits and fissures, driving faster than was prudent.

Finally, he passed the road heading to the highway, and veered off toward their neighbor's ranch. The sign announcing Harper Ranch still swung from its pole, but there was no sign of Betty's car.

His gaze swung across the countryside as he tore along, his heart knocking against his ribs. A faint light caught his eye. On the mountain road heading east from Harper's main house, something shone against the darkness. He stomped on the brake. The truck bucked and complained, until he thought to compress the clutch. Throwing the gearshift into neutral, he leapt out, grabbed his binoculars from behind his seat, and pressed them to his eyes, re-adjusting the focus in the luminous glow of the moon. He scanned back and forth, caught something, forced himself to slow down, then did it again. There. The source of the light. His breath seized in his throat. He re-adjusted the view and squinted this time. He had to be wrong.

A car's tail lights. Her tail lights. The same ones he'd just watched blink out of his life.

Without another thought, he jumped back in the truck, shifted, and gunned it between the timbers of the entrance. Why would she head into Harper Ranch and then take the fork up the mountain and not into the main hub? Did she get disoriented from the quake? Think she could outrun it somehow? But a swift glance to the right told him the reason. The quake had ripped the ground apart across that access. In fact, it looked like the crevice had torn straight down the center of Harper's main camp.

No time to go check on Harper and his crew, he took off toward the small red light. The truck skidded, Jake corrected. Once he got close enough, he ground the truck to a stop and flew out of it.

"Betty!" he hollered at the vehicle.

Slipping on loose dirt and twigs, he nearly lost his balance but regained it and his momentum, finally halting with a smack of his palms to the rear of the car. It was still running.

"Betty!" His lungs burned. "Answer me!" The smell of pine was so strong, it stung the back of his throat.

He clambered around the pointy tail fin for the driver's side, stopped short, and stared. An uprooted pine had crashed into the left side of the car and shattered the window glass. Moonlight highlighted every contour of pine bark and upholstery and window frame in gleaming curves, but beyond that lay only black void. One of the pine branches had jammed the driver's door shut. Jake bent to look inside, the headlights from his truck shining irregularly through the crisscross of splintered branches and needles all around. No one there. Glancing across the front seat, he saw the passenger door was open.

"Betty!" he hollered again. His voice echoed back to him weirdly in the eerie quiet. Was there a new chasm down there? A tremor ran through him, making rubber of his legs. His stomach rolled, his mind avoiding a conclusion he didna want to face. If Betty was gone from the car, and not answering his call—No! He wouldna believe he would only find her lifeless body.

Eyes wide, he backed a step, turned, and circled the back end to the passenger side. Moonlight glinted off paint and chrome and treetops beyond. He slid to a stop at the gaping door. Froze there and listened. There was a trickling of water below, like in a ravine. But he'd been on this road dozens of times before, and there were no canyons, no streams this close. He tried to make sense of what he saw within the ghostly moonlight.

Grabbing hold of the open door's frame, he inched his boots forward until the crunch of gravel went silent under his weightless toes. Had the quake carved a new gulley? Hanging tight, he leaned forward and looked down. A shaft of moonlight twinkled on a redirected stream a telephone pole length down.

Jake couldna take his next breath. His chest ached. He finally gulped air and forced his mind to think. Betty swerved and skidded and braked to avoid the pine. She escaped out the passenger side door, but her right tire had gone off the edge, and—

"*Nae!* No, no, no, no, no," Jake shouted at the car as if the fault belonged to a hunk of metal. Jake dropped to all fours, clambered closer to the rim, and nearly tumbled off the edge.

The truth finally seeped into his panicked brain. Blinking with shock, he felt the blood drain from his face. The car door was open on its hinges to air—only air.

CHAPTER 1

Sacramento, California
May 21, 1960

"All rise. The Superior Court of Sacramento County, State of California, is now in session. The Honorable Judge Theodore Weston, presiding," the bailiff announced.

The two dozen or so people who were interspersed throughout the courtroom complied.

Judge Weston, draped in a black robe—the collar of a white shirt with black tie peeking out from under a double chin and ample jowls—strode through the chamber doors and stepped up the two steps to his wide leather chair. He sat. The court participants followed suit.

His expression was grim. "Miss Harper, please remain standing."

Suzannah's heart sank. It wasn't what the judge had said. It was the expression he wore. She just knew. She tried to rise back up, her skirt juddering against her legs. She'd worn her business suit today, with her hair tied in a knot at her nape in hopes of giving her a sane, composed air. But the tremble in her knees wasn't good. Her dad grasped her elbow to help her stand the rest of the way. He stood erect on her left side, holding steady, and she drank in his strength to stay upright.

Across the massive courtroom stood her nemesis. *Thomas.* The man who had long since crossed over from *boyfriend* to *stalker.* He was sitting now, and she was glad, since the height she once found appealing now locked up the air in her throat. His bristly black beard was gone, too. With those changes, she could do this. Face the man who'd ruined her life, pretend he was someone else just long enough to get through this day.

Except...

The judge would only see that clean-cut façade, too. Still, Judge Weston should be able to perceive the predator within. Thomas could charm an ant at five paces, true, but he was equally possessive and manipulative and dangerous. After years of trying to reject and evade him, Suzannah didn't know what else to do. Any sane person would have given up on her by now.

Obviously Thomas was far from sane.

Then again, maybe so was she. He'd changed her—and now she feared the loathsome change was permanent.

Her life had been on hold awaiting this repeatedly postponed court appearance, for three achingly long years.

"Miss Harper," the judge said. "I'm sorry to say, there isn't enough evidence to bring Mr. Mason to trial for unlawful conduct, or to even allow a restraining order. I suggest you and your young man have a long talk about your relationship. Move on. Court is adjourned."

The brutal thump of her heart against her chest wall was so fierce it hurt. *Your young man.* How could he be so blind?

The gavel struck the sounding block. The finality of it drove a stake straight through Suzannah's chest. It wasn't to be believed. Hadn't the judge seen the smirk on Thomas's face? The leer in his eyes? The raw evil that thrived there?

A deep panic built inside her, threatening to escape in a long, sorrowful howl. Now that she'd finally had her day in court, he had won. She would never be safe from him. Not ever.

She looked up into her dad's face just as her legs did give way. He caught her around the middle and, with mostly his strength, they moved toward the massive courtroom doors. She had just enough pride left to not fall apart in front of Thomas.

She doddered with her dad down the endless stone steps and finally out into fresh air. Sucking in a deep, ragged breath, she found herself hurried forward, again supported by her dad's arm. At the curb, he opened the passenger door of their car and guided her part-way in before hustling to the driver's side door. Suzannah crumpled onto the seat and reached for the door to close it.

"Hold on there, precious," the ominous voice of her nightmares crooned.

Suzannah jumped like she'd been slapped. Thomas stood at the open car door, one big hand on the roof, the other reaching out to touch her face. She smacked it away, fury overriding panic for the first time all day. She thanked God for that small favor.

The creak of the bench seat amplified in her ears as her dad bounded back out of the car. Her jaw clenched until it ached, hands fisted, ready to pop Thomas herself. She glared up at the rotten brute. When her gaze caught the look on his face, his vile expression made her shrink back into the seat, while her stronger side wanted to stick out a foot and shove him on his rear.

She hadn't even noticed her dad move around the hood of the car until he stood nose-to-nose with Thomas. "Back off!" he hollered.

Thomas didn't even flinch. He just turned cold, steely eyes on her dad.

She slid forward, ready to jump up and deliver a mean right cross. But what she saw made her feel like she'd just swallowed tacks.

Thomas was delivering his most charismatic smile, then a chuckle, and the sound spiraled through her, closing off her air passage that much more. She understood that sound, but no one else did.

"Oh sure," Thomas said smoothly to her dad. "I'm leaving. Not a problem." His voice flowed like silk.

She blinked up at the two men, watching in horror as her father's shoulders visibly relaxed, and he stepped back. *Don't buy it, Dad.*

"Now, Suzannah-Anna," Thomas said. "That frown spoils that beautiful mouth of yours." Thomas kissed his fingertips, and laid them on Suzannah's lips before she could turn her face away.

Her dad took a step forward again, but Thomas held up his hands in surrender. "Don't worry, Mr. Harper. You can trust me, can't he, Suzannah?" His eyes rolled toward her, and she would have sworn the blue had turned coal black for a split second. "I'm going now. A pleasure as always, sir."

He rested his gaze on Suzannah then. "Love your hair like that. Such a pretty neck." Then he strode off with a confident gait, whistling *Wake Up Little Susie*.

Suzannah swiped at her mouth with a shaking fist. It wasn't enough. She dug the fingers of each hand into her thighs to try to strangle the tremble out of them.

But after three torturous years, she already knew the only way to stop the furious rattle in her bones was to wait for her adrenaline to drain away. Thomas's veiled threats had progressively robbed her of her confidence, her joy... even her voice.

Her parents talked of a time when Suzannah had been wordy, animated even. She believed them, but couldn't remember any of it. She could practically put all the words she'd said in the last three years on one sheet of stationery.

"Come here, honey," her dad said. He'd gotten back in the driver's side of the car, and now leaned toward her.

She fell into his embrace. He held her tightly as she shuddered. No tears fell. It seemed whatever it was that made tears in her had long since scarred over, right along with her vocal cords, which had been stilted by a permanent lump in her throat. Globus hystericus, one doctor called it; Latin for 'lump in the throat.' It seemed ridiculous to give a fancy name to something that was psychosomatic. Crazy, was what they should call her. Of course, when she said such things her whole family objected, reminding her it was *not* all in her head. Her mom thought it was something a second doctor had suggested: MTD - Muscle Tension Dysphonia, also brought on by a form of anxiety.

Well, she had anxiety all right, and it had a name: Thomas.

"I'm so sorry, sweetie. That judge is an idiot. He should have believed you. I've been praying about what our next move should be if this turned out badly. We're all going to your Uncle Roy's for his wedding in a few weeks. We want to leave you there. For a while. Let this young man see the error of his ways."

"*Error of his ways*, Dad?" Her voice was barely a squeak. From the stress of the trial, or the ever-present lump in her throat, she didn't know, or care. How could her own dad put it that way? As if Thomas would get better. As if she'd have him back if he did.

He felt her stiffen and pulled out of their embrace to see her face.

She frowned and stared back at him.

"Suze, be reasonable. You know what I meant."

"Do I?" Even she could hear the disappointment in her whisper. Did he even have a clue how that comment stung? But she loved her dad. So she would let it go. She turned her mind to the reason she couldn't stay in Montana. "Can't leave them," she whispered, then closed her eyes on a swallow. The lump was much worse today. Blast that Thomas Mason to the devil!

"Listen." Her dad raised her chin up to look him in the eye. "The orphanage can survive without you. I know those babies have become important to you, but—"

She shook her head, hard, to get her point across.

Her dad looked sheepish. "Okay, okay. I know. It's them you're worried about."

A half smile twitched at one side of her mouth. She'd been involved with some of those kids since they were infants.

"But they don't know only you, Suze. They have other caretakers as well." He saw her glare and amended, "I realize you're like a surrogate mother to Lily. That little tyke may be attached. But maybe it's time—"

She slapped a hand to his shoulder, continued her scowl. Dad didn't realize Lily was long past the time she should have had solids introduced into her diet. The staff was too busy to even hold her anymore. They just laid her down with a bottle and went on to the next bed. Suzannah had been there daily. Had brought Lily this far. She wanted—no, needed—to help her.

"I know you love her, and all of them. But maybe time away will be good."

Suzannah grimaced and looked down at cold hands that matched the dread in her heart. She knew her dad thought her attachment would bring her pain in the end. Well, maybe it would, but she'd grown close to little ones more than once, and she'd always gotten over it… eventually. It was the ripping away that was the hardest. And that's what her dad wanted her to do now.

"Maybe it would be easier to pull back early this time. Not wait until she's walking."

Her head shot up. He looked repentant, but determined. She knew he would never have played this card with her if he didn't fear for her. In any case, it was true. She heaved a sigh, thinking how she usually did her own abandoning of these adorable tots when they started to walk, knowing full well they needed someone who could use words to teach them, to have full conversations with them, but mostly to yell to them when they sprinted toward danger.

Like Sarah. The bite of tears burned Suzannah's eyes. Sweet Sarah. Racing across the park on those pumping toddler legs. Chasing a butterfly for all she was worth.

Suzannah had only turned her back for a second. Just a second, to nudge little Jason forward on his swing, but already Sarah was halfway across the field… and headed straight into a high school pick-up football game.

Suzannah tried to yell. No sound came out. It seemed she left her heart where she'd been standing as her feet pounded forward. Everything went black except for the arc of the football above, the wide receiver cutting to the right below, and Sarah's polkadot dress swaying just beyond. Suzannah tried to scream Sarah's name, but the lump in her throat had grown spines she could barely breathe past. The player's hands were up, his eyes skyward, his cleats biting in and churning the turf.

NO!!

Suzannah jumped in her seat, blinking at the tail lights of a car parked directly ahead outside the courthouse. The inside of her cheek hurt. She tasted blood, then let out a shuddering breath. The doctors said Sarah would one day be fine… but the surgeries, the trauma, the scars—inside and out. No. Sarah was not fine, and the blame was Suzannah's.

"Stop it, Suze!" her father's voice broke in. "You have to stop reliving that day."

Her dad never said the words, 'It wasn't your fault, Suze,' because he knew it was. Suzannah felt that familiar sense of loss for Sarah slither down her spine.

"Your mom has already decided to take over for you at the orphanage. She loves Lily and the others as much as you do."

Suzannah looked up at her dad, rolled her eyes. *Mom.*

"She does, honey. I promise you."

Suzannah dropped her gaze to her lap. The deep sorrow of leaving Lily behind sank into her heart. It was always like this. Every time she convinced herself it was time to move on and never go back.

Her dad was still talking, laying out the many crafts her mother was so good at, but Suzannah barely heard. "… lanyard pens and key holders, sewing stuffed animals… cutting and pasting…"

Yeah, Dad. Mom was the talented one. But Suzannah knew her mom was too busy with her other community stuff. She wouldn't go as often.

He brushed his fingers down her cheeks, probably hoping to find tears there. Suzannah knew it distressed him, almost more than her silence, that she didn't cry anymore. His blessed face looked anguished. Each year, new lines formed around his mouth and eyes, aging him beyond his fifty-seven years.

That was also her fault. Resignation trickled in. Getting away from here, disappearing from Thomas... even if she couldn't do it for herself, she would make herself do it for her dad.

* * *

Jake was weightless: arms, legs, chaps, all floating on air—even as his heart and gut scaled his throat. The drift upward seemed endless, the mustang's odd buck paralyzing. Instead of jabbing his legs out behind him, the bronc sprang straight up. Would Jake break his nose? His back? He never thought he'd end up crippled instead of dead.

All four hooves landed at once, folding Jake like a taco. His forehead cracked against the horse's withers. His hat flew off. Before he could suck in another breath, he got whipped upright. Adrift. He flung one arm skyward for balance. The other gripped the bronc-rein tighter. The beast dropped again to the ground—a rigid mass of muscle. Then hurtled into another frenzied buck.

Jake had patiently slaved over this stallion for months. Why hadna the effort paid off?

Another brutal landing and Jake's chin cracked against his left knee, slicing pain through his jaw. His teeth rattled. The new pain seared through the muscles in his ribs.

With no sign of slowing, the horse muscled into another arch. Jake didna ken when the brute would wear down, but then—almost lazily the thought came—did it matter?

Would this be the one? The bronc that ended his life?

It might not be. But for sure, one of the steeds would. Then he could finally give in. Breathe his last. For now, he'd still fight.

A cloud of dust on the road distracted him, enough to give his crazed opponent the edge. Another gut mangled buck. A twist in the opposite direction and Jake found himself flung from the stallion's back. He caught a glimpse of his own legs, black against a blue sky, before reason sought him and he tucked them into his chest. He hit the ground and somersaulted several turns before he tasted sod.

Vicious, the animal would soon be on him. *No time to gather your wits. Look up!* Using the last of his strength, Jake pushed against the turf. He swung his head toward a loud huff and found the feral animal. Saw victory in his eyes. With broad neck bowed and nostrils flared, the massive horse dug in his rear hooves and charged. Jake rolled fast to the left. Sharp hooves landed inches from his face. Too close. He rolled a little farther and up onto his knees.

Shouts from the other side of the corral distracted the mustang long enough for Jake to gain his feet. On shaky legs, he dashed to the fence and vaulted over.

He stood on the other side sucking in air, legs wobbling, watching the furious horse pace back and forth in front of him. The beast snorted and stamped the soft dirt.

Jake slid his hands down his thighs to his knees, dropped his head, and concentrated on pulling in deep drafts of air.

"Hey man, you all right?" That was Pete's voice, coming around the corral. Jake raised his head. Several cowpokes shadowed Pete, who had a bright yellow flag in his hand. The one the cowboy's called the *fury flag*. They only used it when the stallion needed to be distracted. The devil-horse's former—abusive—owners had made a practice of wearing bright yellow, mostly to tease the stallion once they'd learned of his aversion to the color. People like that... well, Jake didna want to think through what he'd like to do to people like that. The abuse the horse had suffered moved Jake to grant more chances than was prudent.

Jake gave Pete a sidelong glance and nodded that he was fine. As his breathing slowed, he stood upright to study the horse. Demon, that's what he'd name him, if Roy would let him. He wouldna though, Jake knew. Roy was a godly man. Demon wouldna be a name he'd want to use. But Demon was a name earned, and Demon this horse would always be called—in Jake's mind.

Jake snorted, Demon answered. They eyed each other across the corral fence. One day Jake would win, or die trying.

Jake straightened his spine, stretching it backwards for a few seconds before turning away from Demon to stride toward the barn. The men trailed after him. He felt his usual discomfort start deep in his gut. He was a man of solitude, especially since the day of the great earthquake in August of last year. Any attention or company from the men annoyed him, even as it surprised him. He didna get why they cared a diddly-dang bit about him. He rarely talked to them. Sure, he helped keep the animals healthy—and an occasional laddie. He had a natural bent for that sort of thing. But beyond that he didna understand his appeal. Mayhap it was some misguided attraction to a descendant of the robust Scottish Highlanders. Whatever it was, someone always seemed determined to cling to him.

Just as he started to enter the barn, the dust cloud that had distracted him enough to get bucked off now arrived in the form of a pale green Ford station wagon with woodgrain side panels. It stopped with its four passengers in front of the main house. Two front and one backseat door flung open. A middle-aged man stepped out from behind the wheel. A woman half a hand shorter and twice as rigid as the man exited the passenger side while another woman—Jake recognized as Jessica's sister, Rebecca—exited from the backseat. Ah, Roy's brother and family, here from California.

Jake fixed his gaze on the remaining passenger, who had yet to step out. Through the side window, he noticed light brown hair—or was it dark blonde—long and pulled over a young lassie's left shoulder. This then was the family's youngest daughter. The one he had yet to meet. Jake took two more steps, planning to disappear down the barn aisle, but couldna quite do it. Something about that shy lassie kept him in place.

When the wee lassie finally stepped out, Jake amended his first observation. Not a little girl. A grown lass—a woman. A petite, shapely woman with rich hair some would call strawberry blonde. That description didna begin to describe the beauty of this lass's multi-colored glory. She was a woman, all right, a pretty wee eyeful in her white shorts and daffodil yellow top.

As eye-catching as she was, something about her reminded him of Gutsy—the runt of the barn cat's new litter. Overrun by her siblings and blind in one eye, the tiny kitten struggled hard to survive anyway. He'd named her Gutsy because she was petite and brave and cute as the dickens, just like the delicate flower his gaze was locked to now. Somehow he knew she was brave, and his inspection had already told him she was petite and cute as the dickens.

As he watched her trying to interact with the men, something protective sprang forth from him. Something he hadna felt in near a year. Something he'd sworn to himself he'd never be in the position to feel again.

The men behind him scrambled toward the car. When they reached it, some shook hands with the older man, others gave a kiss to the cheek of the older woman. Pete and Max, brothers who'd been on Harper Ranch long before Jake arrived, ran up to the wee kitten herself and took turns throwing their arms around her in man-sized hugs. Jake's hardened heart nearly broke when she didna reciprocate those hugs. She just stood there bravely, arms stiff at her sides, letting them do what they must.

It didna take a genius to ken she was damaged in some way. He shouldna care. He'd stopped caring about anything. But against his verra strong will, his severely damaged soul recognized a kindred one, and he felt it reach for hers.

CHAPTER 2

Jake watched while cowboys shuffled to the back of the station wagon and dropped the tailgate down. Two men unloaded suitcases while the others carried them into Roy's home. Rebecca and her parents followed behind them, until they all had disappeared into the house.

That is, except the kitten. She stood stiffly and stared in the direction of the black demon dashing about the corral in a furious lather. Jake followed her gaze and didna like what he saw. The still furious horse had his eyes locked on her, and she seemed equally mesmerized.

A blaring alarm went off in his head.

He saw the well-fed hatred in Demon's eyes, and a determination that made Jake's heart flip in dread. *Her yellow top!*

Demon charged the fence, smashing his chest into it. The posts on either side rocked back and forth. His eyes flashed as he twisted back, loped a full circle, and charged the fence again. A loud crack, another loosened post, and Demon turned away again. Jake wondered if he would settle now. He had to be exhausted—from the training, Jake's ride, the tantrum. Yet, he stood quivering a few yards away, eyes locked on his target. Jake studied him. He ken this animal well enough to know he wouldna give up easily. He was wound tight, more agitated as the seconds ticked away.

Straightening to his full, six-foot-five height, Jake bulked up his muscles so when the horse circled back he was ready. He threw his hands up and hollered, "Whoa, boy!"

The horse tore his eyes off the lass for a brief moment to huff at Jake, then twisted a half-circle and darted to the far side of the corral. The hair prickled at the back of Jake's scalp. Though he looked to have scared him off, Jake kent better. Before his mind could close around a solution, his own legs were in full motion toward the now weakened spot in the corral fence. Jake watched as the stallion's balance shifted to his back legs. His haunches dropped slightly.

Jake's heart climbed to his throat. He kent Demon's next move.

Demon dropped his head, huffed a heavy snort, then dug in his back hooves and tore forward.

Wishing he had his crop in hand, Jake waved his right arm above him and snapped the other to the left, demanding the stallion go in that direction. He whistled the next command. He hoped beyond hope the horse had learned some obedience and would heed his authority.

How wrong he was.

Demon looked right past him to the lass.

Jake twisted on his heels and shot toward the kitten with all he had in him.

The lass's eyes went wide, her rosy cheeks paled, and her throat convulsed as if she were struggling to breathe. She was stiff as a two-by-four, so saving herself was out.

Behind him the sounds of trampling hooves went silent. The animal was airborne. He'd soon land and stampede toward them. Jake didna waste time looking back. When he reached the lass with her frightened eyes pinned on him, he ducked his head and caught her up by her middle. While his legs were still moving, he shifted her farther on his shoulder.

Just as he started to make the sharp turn to the back of the car, he was hit from behind with the force of a freight train and flew forward. He tried to twist so the kitten could land on top of him, but didna quite make it all the way round. They landed simultaneously with a hard *whump*, side-by-side, directly behind the vehicle. No time to check her, Jake shoved her under the car, thankful that he was a big man or the kitten's head would have taken the impact of that blow.

Rolling a few feet away, Jake was just gaining his feet when the animal clobbered him head to head. Pain ricocheted into his skull as he catapulted backward. Making a full body flip, his face hit first before the toes of his boots spiked the ground.

A shrill whistle let loose from under the car. His brain was jumbled. *Was that the kitten?*

A second, even louder one followed the first. *It was her all right.* If he could breathe right, he might have chuckled over her man-sized whistle. As it was, he was face-planted in gravel, not able to move, each breath puffing dust into his face.

And he kent he had to move, had to look up. When he lifted his head, the demon was in full rear. Jake pulled his knees up and shoved, leap-frogging out of the way. He landed on his side, his shoulder taking the brunt of the impact. Out of the corner of his eye, he saw when the black monster's hooves reconnected with ground. Demon shook his head, his black mane spraying in all directions. He snorted, strings of foam blow-blowing from both nostrils. The animal twisted back toward Jake with black eyes ablaze.

He heard the front door crash open with shouts from a slew of men. When the horse's bulky head pivoted toward them, Jake tried to rise to his feet again, but only made it as far as his knees before his head spun out of control and into darkness.

* * *

Jake had scarcely moved his head when a spike of pain shot through it. He tried to wedge his eyes open, but his lids didna function right. He took stock. Pain engulfed his head. He was lying on his back, on something soft—*a bed?*—and with every movement a muscle protested.

He fluttered a blink. His eyelids cracked to a flood of white light. He clamped them shut to find relief in the darkness. A few heartbeats later he dared try again. Not so wide this time. Beneath his lashes, he rotated his grainy eyes, taking in his setting. The last thing he expected to see was a wee fairy standing over him. He squinted up against a supernatural glow that back-lit her saintly silhouette.

Dead, then. He knew his end had been near.

Yet, if he were dead, he shouldna feel pain. And wouldna he have been released from the guilt which had made its home within? In that solemn place nestled near his soul? Emptiness was there too—that infernal yawning loneliness that never left, even though he'd been plagued daily by countless people wanting a piece of him.

The fairy touched him back to wherever *here* was, and he jumped at the snap of electric rush. Static. Had to be. But in his addled mind, he couldna help but think electricity actually flowed through fairies. Or, mayhap it was a connection to another soul?

The wee fairy leaned in closer, and the glow lessened as her face sharpened. His heart did a double beat. *Kitten.* He let his eyes roam over her, from her hair to the slender fingers clasped together nervously at her waist. He glanced back up to that hair. Even with the dirt still clinging to it, he rarely saw such perfection. That same loose braid he remembered, starting at her forehead and falling like woven silk over her shoulder. It swept over the soft swell of her chest to where it disappeared from his view. A bizarre need to ken where it ended gripped him. He wrenched his head over so he could see. Pain shot behind his eyes. He scrunched his lids closed in a grimace.

Kitten patted the hand he had resting on his stomach. His eyes shot open at the same time her palm pushed tenderly against one side of his face. Not because she'd felt a need to touch him. Nae. To straighten his head on the pillow was all. Using her fingertips she circled his temples, round and round, until he felt his grimace smooth and the tension drain away. Well, Heaven couldna be any better than this. If it were he'd be a whole lot surprised—that is, if he were ever good enough to get there. And, of course, he kent he wasna even close.

Not since his mother sang him to sleep as a child had he felt so soothed and all around peaceful-like, as if his life were in her hands, and he could trust her with it. She sure was a better candidate than he. Come to think of it, he couldna remember the last time he'd been careful with his own life. Beyond heedless, he was downright reckless.

She ceased the circles at his temples, but kept her fingertips in place, then slid those soft pads down his cheeks, her gaze following, until they reached his thick beard. At first touch, she flinched back and stared at what her fingers had touched, as if the hair on his cheeks had just appeared.

Trying to understand her aversion to his beard, he looked directly into her eyes and was ensnared by their beauty. At this close proximity, he gazed into blue-green eyes, the likes of which he'd never seen before. The base color was blue, but there were flecks of green circling within. Specks of gold dotted in as well. A dark bluish-green circle encompassed it all, as if its job was to keep the many colors confined.

Inspecting her bonny face, he noted her eyebrows: the color of wheat and straw with a touch of sunshine and burnt ginger woven through. The same color as her hair. The thought was a magnet, drawing his gaze back to the loose braid of shiny locks. He itched to pull the tie off and slide his fingers through, to watch each strand unravel in his hands. He dropped his gaze to her cheeks. A wholesome flush displayed skin so angel-like… so flawless. Her mouth parted, and her pink tongue darted out to give her lips a lick. Full, and now wet, those lips reminded him of succulent peaches. And he wanted a taste.

The pulse at his neck thrummed against his collar. He could view her beauty all day, but if she stayed much longer, the blood might drum right out of his skin before it blinded him with the pain from his head.

He forced his gaze back up to her eyes, and saw… *was that fear?* Did she fear him? Is that why she hadn't spoken?

Just then the doorknob squeaked. Trying not to turn his head too much, he rolled his eyes that direction. The door opened slowly, and Roy peeked in. "Hey, pardner. How ya doin'?"

Jake's attention caught on the stuffed trout over the door and recognized he was in Roy's bedroom, downstairs in the big house. Jake tried to use his voice to acknowledge Roy, but his throat was too dry. Before he could decide what to do about it, an arm went under his pillow and lifted his head. A glass was at his lips, and cool water slid down his throat in welcome relief. When he finished, the kitten lowered him back to the pillow. As she peered at him, her dainty eyebrows knit together. She nodded as if to reach a decision, then scooped her petite arms under his shoulders—which were too wide for her to reach all the way around—and lifted him off the pillow with surprising strength. She cradled him against her chest as she went about fixing the pillows behind him.

Paradise, for certain. Jake didna care what came next. He nuzzled against her softness, breathed in the most intoxicating scent he'd ever had the pleasure of inhaling: a trace of lemon and the kitten's own essence with a hint of the dirt still in her hair and streaked across one cheek. He wanted to wrap her in his arms. Before he got the message to his limbs, she snuggled him back into fluffed up pillows, nodded with a wee smile, then turned and skirted behind Roy, who stood at the foot of his bed.

"Wait, lass. I dinna even ken your—" But the door clicked shut before he could finish.

Roy stepped closer to the bed. "We figure you have a concussion, beings you blacked out. Max knows head injuries. He says you need to sit the fence for a few days."

Jake was still staring at the door. "Who is she?"

Roy raised his chin and frowned, as if he didna understand the question.

"The lass. In here. Just now." Jake heard the agitation in his own voice, but then, everyone was used to that when he actually did speak. This was different, though. The fairy had touched him. Not just his face, but something deep inside.

Roy glanced at the door and smiled. "That's my niece. Jessica and Rebecca's little sister."

"What's wrong that she doesna speak?"

Jake could tell Roy understood just what he meant. "It's a long story, my boy. She doesn't talk much, though she can." Roy sighed. Then his expression became more stern. "Listen. What happened out there? How'd that horse get loose anyways?"

As annoyed as he wanted to be at Roy for changing the subject off the kitten, he ken Roy had a one-track mind. The safety of his family and ranch hands was top priority for him. Jake had realized that the moment he'd stepped foot on this ranch, a shattered man wanting to pack it in, permanently. This old rancher had never let him do that.

Jake pushed himself to a sitting position with Roy's help, then recounted the scene with the demon best he could.

Roy shook his head and stared out the window toward the corral. "We need to put that horse down."

The words stunned Jake, shaking him to the core. "Give up on him? That's not like you, Roy. He's wild, but not mad. There's a difference."

"That's a horse out there, son, not a person. He's dangerous, unpredictable. And I'm not taking any chances with you or my family. Not again."

Jake averted his gaze from the window. Dread crept in at the thought of killing the creature. He should want to, but kent the horse had been tortured. He swung his gaze back to Roy. "How'd the men contain him?"

Roy grinned. "The old man still has a few tricks up his sleeve. I lassoed him round the neck. Pete roped a back leg. A bunch of us pulled 'til he went down. Once the varmint was flattened to the ground we kept him stretched. I sat on his ribs 'til he settled. Took him a long darn time, but he finally did. Pete and Max were able to lead him like a lamb back to the corral after that."

Jake stared at Roy. Finally, he said, "He's fixable, you ken?"

"How so? He just give up this once 'cuz he was wore out, is all."

"Mayhap," Jake said. "But he's fixable. I'm the one who pushed him when he wasna ready. He'd been pretty good on the lead line, moved his feet, obeyed my direction mostly. Shoot, Roy. It was my fault. Let me try again." Even if he did secretly call the horse Demon, Jake felt responsible for the crazed animal. Didna want to be the reason this good man gave up on anything. Roy had never given up on him, which was a first in his life. And if the kind, gentle man thought Jake deserved a second and third chance, so did Demon. It was certain the horse had committed fewer sins than he had.

"We'll see." Roy patted Jake on the shoulder. "You just get better. Don't worry about movin' just yet. Not 'til you feel up to it."

That decided it. Jake moved his legs around until his feet were flat on the floor. No one had taken off his boots or his pants, so he guessed he hadna been on this bed for long. He wasna about to displace Roy. "I'm braw, Roy. Need to see to my work."

Roy squeezed Jake's shoulder until he relented and looked up at the old rancher. "No, you don't. Not today. Test your legs. See how your head feels." Roy let loose and patted his shoulder, then grasped it again as an after-thought. Harder this time. "No work. Hear me?"

Jake looked into the older man's eyes. Eyes that saw everything, understood everything. Roy was a good man, one of a kind. Someone Jake wished he'd been guided by, growing up. Jake's own dad hadna wanted his family enough to stick around. He'd left before Jake was born.

He would do anything not to disappoint Roy. He nodded his agreement.

Roy gave a short nod back, then sauntered to the door. Opened it, stopped, looked over his shoulder at Jake. "Thanks for savin' our girl. No words can say."

Then Roy went out the door, leaving behind an altered man. One whose soul had been prodded back to wakefulness by the need to save a crazed horse. And by the brokenness of a meek slip of a lass.

CHAPTER 3

Suzannah parted her eyelashes and let the early light of dawn filter in. Stretching her limbs like a feline basking in the warmth of the sun, she smiled. She loved Harper Ranch. She felt safe here, like she could breathe again, despite the assault of that wild horse yesterday. She knew the poor creature wasn't really attacking her, especially after Max had told her about the stallion's aversion to yellow. More than once she had seen that same wild look in the mirror in her own eyes. The kind that came from months or even years of torment. She empathized with the big black stallion, in ways she didn't figure anyone else could.

Except maybe the mystery man with the beard, her savior.

She thought back to the moment in Roy's bed-room when the man had opened his eyes. A myriad of emotions had swirled within them, like a pot of hot molasses. In the next instant, he banked those emotions, and she saw nothing more. Just a blankness. An emptiness that only came from past abuse, or self-hate.

She shuddered at how close the man had come to being fatally wounded. The fact that he was injured at all was her fault. Though she felt guilt, she also was grateful. His selfless act had not only saved her, but it had done something unanticipated. She'd been forced to draw near him in order to take care of him. And it felt good. That had been her first glimpse of her true self since Thomas's reign of terror began.

Thomas. He'd so completely disrupted her life. No. More like he'd completely stopped it for three long years. In the process, he'd ripped her true nature from her. She missed that Suzannah, the one who liked to help and serve adults as much as she did children.

She thought again about the mystery man and shivered, remembering those long whiskers. When she'd first dated Thomas, at seventeen, he'd barely had peach fuzz on his face. But as he grew into a man, his beard grew long. It was almost as if the bush had lengthened with the worsening of his dark, demented side.

The beard masked who Thomas truly was.

What was the mystery man masking?

She swung her feet to the floor, threw on her robe, then padded down the hallway to the bathroom. Once she bathed and dressed in ranch duds, she braided her hair to the side as usual and made her way down to the kitchen. There was a lot to get done before Mary and Roy's wedding in less than two weeks, and she'd be sure to do her part to make their day happy.

No one was in the kitchen. She glanced at the dusky light out the window, then at the clock. Just after 5:30 AM. No wonder no one was here yet. To help Mabel, she went about starting the coffee pots. Once that was done, she glanced about, finding nothing else to do for now. Breathing a heavy sigh, Suzannah wandered over to the window above the sink and peered out. It was a clear day, no clouds, just the first phase of a Montana sunrise.

Her gaze caught on a tall gray horse whose reins were looped over the corral fence next to the barn. The mare was saddled and ready to ride, or had returned from a ride. Suzannah presumed the cowhands had left her there. They had probably been up before dawn to begin their day, though no one was meandering around. The black stallion from yesterday was giving the mare a show, dashing majestically back and forth in front of her. Suzannah glanced down at her peach-colored blouse. No more yellow for her, after yesterday's scare.

Curious about the saddled horse, she started for the front door.

"Where're you off to?"

Startled, she twirled back and saw Jessica traipsing down the stairs, a pleasant glow on her sister's happy, but concerned, face. Suzannah gave her a hesitant smile, hoping Jessica wouldn't reprimand her like a child and make her stay inside. Rebecca was overprotective enough. But Jessica… she was downright smothering.

"Sis," Suzannah said, and forced a broader smile.

"It's kinda early for you to head outside, isn't it?"

Suzannah thought a flip of subject was needed. That ploy worked well on Jessica, especially since she'd married that big scrumptious man of hers. She was so content these days, distracting her was comically easy. Besides, Suzannah had questions about her rescuer from yesterday. She took a few steps to grasp one of Jessica's hands and pulled her toward a table. Pushing at her shoulder, Suzannah forced Jessica to sit.

Jessica peered up into Suzannah's eyes, confusion apparent.

Suzannah ignored her expression and turned to the kitchen. When she returned with two steamy cups of coffee, she set one down in front of Jessica and threaded her legs through the picnic bench to settle in. Suzannah closed her eyes a brief moment, took a swallow of hot coffee, then pinned Jessica with a stare. "My rescuer?" she asked in a potent whisper.

Jessica looked confused for a minute, then her face relaxed as the meaning dawned on her. "Oh, that was Jake."

"Tell me about him."

Jessica shrugged. "Something happened to him during the quake. He was a good man, in his own way, before. But now he's sort of… broken."

"Broken?"

"Well, yeah. We've known Jake for years. He worked for Coleman, our neighbor, before coming here. By nature he's a somber man. But since last August, he's been even more melancholy, dark, extra quiet. Unnaturally so. Poor man."

Suzannah raised her brows in question.

"He lost his wife during the quake," Jessica said.

"*What?*" Suzannah's voice pinched on the word.

Jessica took the next few minutes to explain to Suzannah the odd and sad events that had unfolded for Jake ten months prior. Suzannah couldn't believe her ears. To think, Jake didn't know if his wife was alive or not. And the baby… How perfectly awful! She hadn't cried in over three years, but she thought she almost could now. No wonder Jake's eyes held such hollowness.

Suzannah patted Jessica's hand, then rose and headed for the door.

"Hey. I didn't say you could go out there yet."

Suzannah turned back, dipped her head, and gave Jessica a stop-being-a-mother-hen look.

Jessica laughed. "Okay. But be careful, will you? And stay away from Jake."

Suzannah rolled her eyes at her big sister, then turned and escaped out the door, clicking it quietly behind her.

She strode to the mare, hoping she might see the big man. Just as she reached the horse, a figure in the barn drew her attention. She veered toward the open double doors and peered in. Hay and horse and leather hit her nostrils. She inhaled deeply to capture the wonderful smells. A man with extra wide shoulders and a back rich with muscle squatted at the entrance to an empty stall. He had a small striped kitty raised to eye level. *Jake.* He turned the kitten side to side as if he was checking for something. Suzannah was drawn to the way he tenderly held and crooned to that little creature. She tiptoed closer. Saw him smooth the pad of his large thumb across one of the kitty's eyes. A blind eye, it looked like.

She watched for a couple more minutes, but didn't want the man to know she'd seen his quiet, gentle ministrations to a critter most ranch men would have already drowned. After backing out slowly, she turned and made her way back to the tied mare, warmed inside by the kindness she had just witnessed.

"Hello," Suzannah whispered.

The mare turned her head and perked her ears forward.

Suzannah liked talking to the animals. For some reason her voice worked pretty well for them. She approached at the mare's wither and stroked up and down the soft neck. The mare craned her head around to get another look at this newcomer. Suzannah smiled and stroked the old girl's velvety muzzle, with all those sprigs of gray whiskers angling out in every direction.

She giggled when the mare pushed past her hand to snuffle her hair and neck.

"I've been wanting to do that same thing," rumbled a rich, deep voice.

Suzannah inhaled a startled breath and whipped around, flattening her back against the saddle. She raised her gaze to Jake's startled black eyes. He backed up a couple of steps and she thought he might turn and run, he looked so rattled. All she could guess was he hadn't meant to say that aloud. The thought pleased her so, she darted a hand to her mouth to cover an exuberant smile. The mare shifted over a step. Suzannah lost her footing. Jake scrambled forward and caught her arm, tugging her back upright, but too far. She hit the solid wall of his chest and would have bounced off but for his arms encircling and mashing her against him.

He held her there as if letting her go would be like letting her fall from a cliff. Was this man her guardian angel? It was laughable, really. He had such a dark presence about him, yet it surprised her how she had confidence in him. After she'd seen his heart when he saved her, and then again with the wounded kitten when he didn't know anyone was watching, what more was needed to trust someone?

If he was a guardian angel, he was a pretty strong one. His arms were like muscle straps, pinning her own arms to her sides. Trapped with her face to his hard chest, all she could do was breathe, and breathe in she did. He smelled wonderful. Of hay and the outdoors and leather and man. Just plain man. Soap, and his own scent, she supposed.

When she inhaled one long deep breath, he stiffened. He unstrapped those big ole arms like she'd grown thorns and backed out of their embrace. "Sorry. Probably couldna breathe against me like that, eh, lass?"

Then he laughed. A big, boisterous, perfect laugh, like he'd become the butt of a joke and was fine with it. She peered up at him and basked in the wondrous sound. Then watched as his face transformed into a thing of breath-hitching beauty—rugged and handsome and bone-melting—though none of the gaiety reached his eyes.

Then the laugh halted, as if it knew it didn't belong with this man. The remote look returned, his thick brows gathered into a frown.

She looked down at the chest she'd been buried in, then up at him. With the black cowboy hat, black clothes, black hair and beard, all she could think was... *wicked*. Yet, he wasn't. It might be the image he wanted the world to see, but she knew better. She'd witnessed firsthand what he was about, so forever in her mind he would be her kind-hearted, gentle giant.

He stared down at her from where he stood rigidly. Didn't move, didn't say a thing. Though she ached to have him explain what he meant by *'I've been wanting to do that same thing'*, she remained silent. Couldn't seem to make the words she was thinking come out her mouth. Nothing new there.

He didn't look like he was going to move, so she took advantage and peered closer at him. Beyond his height, she noticed the hair under his hat first. It wound in and out of the top of his collar, as unruly as the rest of him. She shifted her gaze to the black beard that looked like it hadn't been trimmed in years, and shivered. She hated beards. Still, she forced herself to examine the hint of chestnut at its frizzy ends. Oh, to see the face under that mask. She forced her gaze upward to his thick brows, black slashes low over his eyes. Black eyes. Dead eyes, they seemed to say. Like his soul had moved on.

Quick as lightning, blood rushed into her face as she realized she'd been staring. She stepped back, ready to turn and flee.

"Dinna be afraid, lass," the towering man said in that rich rumble of a voice.

She wasn't afraid of him. And the plea in his voice stopped her. It sounded so… bleak.

"What's your name?" he asked.

Her mouth opened as she begged her throat to let loose one word. Just one word. But it didn't.

"I willna hurt you," he said.

No words came, but she was able to nod, pleased it would give him some notice she wasn't afraid of him. Not really.

He seemed to sag in relief.

She backed a few more steps with her hand on the mare's rump to alert her she was there.

"Tell me your name," he tried again.

Suzannah pleaded again with her brain. She opened her mouth, inhaled a big breath, but no air could get around the blasted lump in her throat, especially since it grew into a boulder whenever she was near strangers. Frustrated by her ineptness, she twisted on her heels and fled toward the house.

* * *

Jake watched the kitten go. Emotion rustled through him like a breeze whipping into a storm gale. He almost didna recognize the sensation, it had been so long since he'd felt anything like it. She was afraid of him. Did he care? No. He didna. He didna care about anything anymore. But something about her brokenness could not be ignored.

He kent her name was Suzannah—he'd heard it from others—but he'd hoped she would tell him herself. When it seemed she opened her mouth to say something and couldna, that's when something flickered through him. Something vague. Mayhap compas-compassion? Yet it felt more tangible, like if he rubbed his chest he'd feel his heart staggering after her.

Well, it wasna worth his notice. He couldna be trusted with another woman anyway, especially not a wee fairy. Besides, he had his agenda to think about. He scrubbed a hand down his face and over his beard, yanked his hat back down to his brows, then unlaced the mare's reins from the fence. Without using the stirrup, he vaulted into the saddle and took off toward the stream. Once he reached the flowing water, he guided the horse across the low spot the cowpokes used.

In all the time since finding Betty's car overhanging the cliff to the stream, he'd yet to find any evidence of her and the bairn's remains. Anything that would give closure. The folks of Harper Ranch kent he saddled up every morning to go look for her. They also kent to leave him alone with his need to do so. But each day that passed without any sign sent his dark side into a deeper pit. There was a time he feared he'd never recover from those depths. Not long after that, he found he didna care if he did.

Until the gutsy, half-blind kitty. Then the troubled stallion. And now Suzannah. He didna ken how the runt and the horse and the lass kept him from falling eternally into the abyss of despondency. He just kent they did.

Today he would search deeper on the south side of the stream. Betty could have feasibly dropped out of the passenger door of the car and slid down the soft dirt of the new, thirty-foot-high bank. Then she could have crossed the stream, mayhap even made her way south and hit Yellowstone Park. It all seemed impossible, yet he'd found no evidence to the contrary. It was evidence he needed—nae, demanded. Eventually he'd work his way to the Park. He had to try. Right up until the day he found a sign of her, or died of despair.

The mare nickered. Her ears flicked back and forth, trying to catch more of the sound she'd just heard. Behind them. Jake turned her in a tight half circle and combed the area he'd just traveled. Nothing. But he knew the gray mare well. Something was amiss. He slid his rifle from the scabbard and waited.

Just as he decided to head back the way he'd come to see for himself what was haywire, the muzzle of a buckskin horse came through the thicket, then the neck and withers, and then the back with its saddle and rider. *Suzannah*. Puzzled why she'd followed him, he nudged the gray forward until he came up parallel to her, facing the opposite direction.

She peered into his eyes, bravado in her own. Not scared of him then. Confusing, this lass. She sat atop the horse like she kent what she was doing, in snug blue jeans, cowboy boots, and a sleeveless top the color of peaches with big brown buttons rising clear to the hollow of her throat. A feminine cowboy hat sat on her head, barely showing her loose braid.

She squirmed in the saddle before resettling, then blinked up at him.

This time he thought to wait her out. Soon she'd tell him why she'd come. She swallowed, opened her mouth as if to say something, but nothing came forth. Clearing her throat, she dropped her gaze to his thigh.

Fine. If she didna want to talk, so be it. He had things to do. He frowned at her, then whirled back around and continued on his way, figuring she'd turn back, forget about him and his lone journey.

It was rocky where he'd forced his mount to tread, so it was slow going. He rocked side to side as the mare crossed the rough terrain. All he could think of was the lass, when he should be concentrating on finding signs of Betty. The confusion in his own mind made him furious, and fury made him *feel*. He didna want to *feel*. Rousing emotions was like awakening feet from frost-bite. Every numb corner of his mind burned with a deep and throbbing pain. He preferred the numbness.

He heard the kitten's horse picking her way along behind him. Drat the lass! Why was she still following him? He didna want company. This was his time. His business.

Jake stopped his mare and took a calming breath while he waited for Suzannah to come alongside. She didna.

"What are you doing?" he barked over his shoulder, loud enough for her to hear without turning to face her.

When nothing stirred and no sounds came, he relented, reining an about-face. The mares eyed each other across the short distance. One whinnied, the other nodded her head, jangling the bridle. Jake waited for Suzannah to answer him as he stared into those immense eyes. They were pure green today, catching the color of the pines.

The wait was futile. What Roy had said about her floated back to his mind: *She doesn't talk much, though she can.* "Suzannah. Why are you following me?" His tone was sharper than he'd intended, making her jump and her horse skitter to the side.

She gained control of the mare while her brows knit together, never once taking her eyes off Jake. He was baffled. She actually looked... *annoyed*.

She raised her brows in question. What question? Taking a chance, he said, "It's a tight group. Your name came up."

Her brows dropped back in place. Okay, so he'd guessed right. This time. He waited again, to see if she'd voice her thoughts now. She didna. Jake felt a head of steam brewing. The fact she was more taciturn than himself was beginning to get the better of him. He needed to get out of here, away from her. "Go *back* to the house, lass."

This time she didna jump. Far from it, she shifted her horse to the right of his and moved past him. He watched her every move. The lass knew how to sit a saddle, how to handle a horse. She didna seem afraid of him, so why the continued silence?

She turned that sweet face of hers back to look over her shoulder at him. Before long she raised one eyebrow, looking confident and resolved.

He felt a growl coming on, but before he let it out his mouth, he turned his horse to sidle up next to her. In the hope of scaring her back to Roy's home, he caught her chin in his hand, squeezing just enough to get her attention. But the moment he caught that smooth skin in his calloused hand, he kent it wasna right. He almost let go but couldna seem to quit looking at that soft, moist mouth, pushed into a pout by his fingers. For the first time in as long as he could remember, he wanted to press his mouth to soft feminine lips.

Her eyes widened, but she didna try to pull away. Didna move at all. That infuriated him further. Was she too scared of him to move? Getting a grip on himself, he released her chin, then smoothed his fingertips over her jawline, as if he could put her silky skin back to rights.

The flood of wrath setting a course through him, right on the tail of fervent desire, spun fire through his veins. Worried he might succumb to a need as old as time and start with a stormy kiss he had no right to, he spun his horse back toward the main camp. Raking his heels across the poor gray's flanks, the startled mare took off like a shot. When the mare stumbled and almost went down, he pulled up, feeling sick that he'd put his horse at risk.

A quick glance over his shoulder convinced him she was safely following, so he faced forward and didna look back again until he arrived at the barn.

Jake dismounted, led the mare to a stall, and carried the saddle and bridle to the saddle rack. Curry comb in hand, he began to madly groom her. The mare turned her head and butted him. He grunted, then slowed his movements into long, gentle strokes, trying his darndest to do the same with his thoughts. Somehow he kent he was no longer just the Jake who was driven to find evidence of a wife and bairn. He'd been divided right down the middle, and he feared the side that now leaned toward a wee, strawberry blonde lass was about to take control. And deep down Jake kent he'd have to stop that from happening.

CHAPTER 4

The ten-day countdown to Roy and Mary's wedding brought with it all sorts of madness at Harper Ranch, and Suzannah was right in the midst of it. The cowhands were scouring the outside of the premises, while she and the other women all worked on the inside of the ageless two-story house. Johnnie and Rose Marie had just arrived from California, so they were added to the crew hard at work.

Suzannah was already wilting from rising so early to finish a multitude of household chores, so when Rose Marie had greeted her grandma and then followed the other women to see Mary's dress and trousseau, Suzannah quietly bowed out. She wasn't used to so many people, so she made a beeline for her room to gain alone time, and to freshen up.

As Suzannah tied a blue ribbon to the end of her freshly reworked braid, she perused her image in the mirror over the chester drawers. The blue cotton blouse brought out the blue in her eyes. Her eyes did that. If she happened to be wearing green, that was the color they'd reflect. She ran her fingertips down the skin of her face. She'd been blessed with natural beauty—so her family boasted, especially her sisters. Somehow they didn't think God had blessed them with beauty. But He had. Their's came from within and radiated out every pore of their skin. That was so much better than what little her natural good looks offered others, which these days seemed to be only trouble.

She lifted her gaze back to the top of her complicated french braid. It started at her forehead, descended past her left ear and shoulder, and on down to nearly her waist. Proudly, she thought back to how she'd first learned to braid her hair this way. It had taken quite a while to master the complex style on her own. She remembered the long evenings spent at home with nothing much to do except practice the feminine coiffure. She had ceased going out past dark until she was twenty, for fear Thomas might try to capture her. Maturity had changed that outrageous trepidation, but she still believed Thomas capable of anything. The court system, the judge, and even her family thought she'd become delusional. Beyond delusional. Paranoid. Never once did anyone believe Thomas would actually hurt her or kidnap her. She knew better. As cunning as he was, he always made sure to whisper his intentions for her ears only. She knew he'd never give up harassing her, even if he wasn't planning anything worse.

She shivered at the thought of Thomas. She should be thankful, she guessed, that at least she could still *feel*. Even if that emotion was fear. But that unending fear had irrevocably damaged her. Had that been Thomas's intention all along? To imprison her body in her own house and her words in her own head?

Thomas had slain her. It was just taking a while for the burial.

At least for now she felt somewhat safe at Harper Ranch, and actually felt the beginnings of healing taking place within her. Interestingly, Jake was one of the reasons that was so. Though part of her was a little afraid of him—the breadth of him, and the beard that was so like Thomas's—mostly she trusted him. And it wasn't just because he'd saved her from the wild stallion or cared for the blind kitty. It was something more. He carried a mantel of power—and integrity despite being unquestionably wounded. She was indisputably drawn to him. To feel protected, yes. But, also to be his advocate and soothe his hurts.

"You ready to head back down, Suzie?" Mary called through her bedroom door.

Suzannah took one last glimpse at herself, satisfied that her weariness didn't show through. She opened the door to a cluster of happy faces and tried to smile. Once she stepped out to join the other women, Mary led them down the hallway toward the stairs.

Twittering floated up to the rafters of the open-spaced house as the women all spoke over the top of each other. Since the loss of her voice, Suzannah had noticed how much women jabbered and giggled. It was no wonder men tended to escape them after a time, to gain some solace. Whenever she happened on a group of men, she had to smile to herself at how they grunted answers to each other more often than not, in between big drags off cigars or cigarettes that stuck out of the corners of their mouths. She could write the number of words they used most evenings onto one small slip of paper. Maybe that's why she preferred a group of men to women. She just related to them better, especially these days.

The women managed to make their way down the stairs in a clump, laughing, sharing, being the noisy creatures that they were, when the back screen door flew open and Johnnie trod in, a look of hard-working man about him. Before he'd gone back to San Francisco and his work there, he had cow-poked on Harper Ranch. Today, he looked suited for ranch work in his cowboy duds. He strode through the dining area and stopped to peruse their group. Those sapphire-blue eyes skipped from one woman to the next before they landed on Suzannah. He gave her a blinding smile.

Mary walked up to Johnnie. He bent down so she could give him a kiss on the cheek. "How's blue-eyes today?" She looked over his hat, plaid work shirt, jeans, and dusty boots. "You're looking mighty handsome. Sure you don't want to come back permanently? It would make Roy happy, young man. You know how he feels about you."

"Aw, shucks. You're gonna make me blush." He tipped his Stetson at her, then ripped it off his head. "Sorry, Mary. Meant to take that thing off when I came in."

Mary chuckled and elbowed him. "Knock it off. Stop putting on a show for these ladies. Oh, by the way, Johnnie—" Mary reached behind her and scooted two woman forward. "This is Barbara, Pete's girl. And this young lady is Max's fiancé, Anita."

Johnnie gaped at the women. "As soon as I regain my wits, I'll greet you two." He stared at Mary. "Pete and Max's girls, you say. No kidding." Looking back at the young women, he said, "How do, Barbara, Anita." He stuffed his hat back on his head, and gave the bill a hearty pull.

"And, of course, you know Suzannah." Mary turned and smiled at her.

Suzannah was pushed forward by someone, right into Johnnie's path. "Yes, ma'am, I surely do. How are you Suzannah?"

She backed a step, ready to melt to the back of the crowd, but before she could, he lifted her right off her feet into a huge hug.

"Hi, Johnnie," Suzannah whispered in his ear. She was truly happy to see Johnnie. This was one man she trusted implicitly. Of course, it helped that he was a Pinkerton, which only Clint, Jessica, and she knew about. After Jessica's wedding last October, he'd spent some time giving her ideas concerning Thomas. Mostly, those ideas hadn't worked, since Johnnie had suggested the court system was the way to put an end to the man's stalking. Now that Johnnie was here, she'd have to fill him in on how dreadfully that had gone and find out if he had any other suggestions.

Johnnie glanced over his shoulder at the back door Rose Marie had just slammed out of, and sighed. Then he turned back to gaze down at her, studying every line and dark circle she'd just spent the last twenty minutes trying to mask.

"Come, Suzannah. Walk with me. We need to catch up."

Johnnie grasped her hand. She jerked away without thinking, then glanced at him in apology. Not that she hadn't enjoyed a man's touch once upon a time. She had liked Thomas's touch. His kiss. But the bad times had long since swallowed up any good memories. Now that she was away from California, perhaps the bad times would ebb to the recesses of her mind where she could leave them for good.

Suzannah slipped her hand back into Johnnie's and allowed him to pull her out the front door and toward the corral. The black stallion was nowhere to be seen, while Bonnie, the faithful buckskin mare, romped over to them, as friendly as the ranch's beloved Australian Shepherd, Patches. She giggled at the horse's reaction to humans. Some horses were full of personality, and Bonnie topped the list.

Bonnie lifted her bulky head over the corral fence and butted Johnnie's chest. Obviously she had missed the man as much as the people on this ranch had. Suzannah wondered if he missed ranch life, or if his job as a Pinkerton was fulfilling enough.

Johnnie scratched between the mare's eyes and crooned to her in low tones. Before Suzannah realized what was happening, Johnnie had slung an arm around her shoulders and had turned his head toward hers. His hat rim tapped the top of her head, but she didn't look up. She took over stroking the mare, feeling the velvety muzzle under her palm.

"How are you doing, Suzannah? Truth."

"Fine." She was surprised how easily the word came forth.

Johnnie reached for her chin and tilted it up so she had to look into his eyes. "Suze, this is me, Johnnie. You can talk to me, remember? I have no agenda but to help you, you know that. Now, tell me what's going on. You can do it."

She stared into the bluest eyes she'd ever seen. Clear, and open, and not the least filled with scars of his past, though she knew he had them. His eyes gave off truth and healing and kindness. Beautiful eyes. God-honoring eyes.

Yet, ebony eyes were the ones she saw when she closed her own. Eyes that at times were filled with pain and loneliness, but mostly they were empty. Eyes that screamed a need so great, it seemed hopeless they'd ever be filled with something so simple, yet so vital, as love.

Suzannah cleared her throat along with her thoughts of Jake. Johnnie's eyes encouraged her to speak. "I lost," she stated simply. Those words alone made her drop her gaze from his. She stroked Bonnie's muzzle again, for comfort. She didn't cry anymore, but the lump grew larger in her throat. So large it threatened to strangle her.

Johnnie didn't insist she look at him, but he had his head tilted as close to hers as his hat brim allowed. "The court case?"

She nodded.

"Aw, Suzannah." He wrapped her in his arms and hugged her hard. He loosened his arms to look at her. Since she didn't reciprocate, he talked to the side of her head. "I'm so sorry, sweetheart. It's just not right. Makes me want to find this guy myself, and—" Johnnie stopped, but she could feel the tension the anger brought to his body. He sucked in a deep breath then blew it out slowly. "Suze, I promise to do just that, once I have a break in my case load. You can count on it."

Johnnie did lift her chin again after that. When she finally raised her gaze to his, he said, "We'll work together on this, Suzannah. Okay? We'll find this guy and—"

She shook her head, hard enough for her braid to fly over her shoulder to her back.

"Why, no?" His brows puckered in confusion.

She swallowed, then cleared her throat again. "Can't risk your job." It felt like each word had grated a deep trench coming out her mouth. Talking had actually become painful. But there were times it was worth it. She couldn't let Johnnie hurt his career for her. She wouldn't allow it.

"We'll see."

She turned and grasped both his forearms, squeezing hard as she shook her head again.

He just pulled her into another deep hug, then took her by the hand to lead her back to the house. She drug her gaze from the ground long enough to notice a large figure standing at the corner of the house—*Jake*. He was watching them with his usual blank expression. By that impassive look she couldn't discern a thing of what he was thinking. He stood stiffly, like a mighty oak not to be swayed by a gale. And though she had her hand in Johnnie's, the safety Jake emanated by just being near gave her a profound sense of peace.

CHAPTER 5

Jake's mare gave a small leap over a broken tree limb, snapping another in half on the other side. The sun had finally made its way above the eastern mountain range, rising to the clear sky, barely warming his chest in its early morning efforts. The portion of the stream he'd been paralleling today was crisp and inviting with its depth and full eddies. Normally, he'd bring Mabel back a few trout for dinner, but today he'd been out since before dawn, understanding he'd be needed back at the main house for the wedding of the year. Roy Harper was finally going to marry the woman everyone kent he should have married in his youth.

He grunted aloud, aware the sound wouldna be heard by anyone. Marriage. He didna ken why anyone made such a fuss about it. Jake had never been inclined toward marriage, and once he'd been forced to try it, he ken for certain he wasna cut out for it. Some men were not. In his marriage, he'd failed at the two things a man was expected to do—love his bride and protect her. Since he could not handle those two essential requirements, he'd always be a bad bet for any woman.

The mare nickered as she flicked her ears to and fro, alerting Jake to a visitor of some sort. Man or beast? That was always the question out here in the timberland. He'd found an unexplored trail and so had gone farther afield than ever before. As the year since Betty's disappearance drew to a close, Jake's anxiety only escalated. If he didna find some kind of closure, he feared he'd go insane.

Jake reined in and listened. "What is it, lass?" he asked the mare. He bent to pat the horse's sleek neck. Just then the mare tossed her head, nearly smashing his nose, and whinnied.

An answering whinny came through the trees from the northwest. It was terrain Jake had already crossed.

The muscles in his face moved into a deep frown, surprising him. He hadna worn emotion on his face in so long, he wondered how his weathered skin could actually move in such a way.

He'd warned the men not to follow him on these jaunts—not ever.

When the buckskin's nose came round a thicket of spruce, he uttered an expletive. She'd followed him again! Ready to do battle with the wee kitten before he could gain a good glimpse of her or catch a tantalizing whiff of her, he shouted, "Stop right there!"

She rounded the corner into full view, then tugged on her reins, gracefully halting her mount.

He stared into eyes made green by the lush setting and forced himself not to react to the sight of her. He sat rigidly atop the gray and waited for an explanation. None came. He grumbled under his breath. He'd known lots of women in his thirty-three years, but never one who could out-silence him. Before Suzannah, he'd have bet good money it wasna possible. Then he reminded himself it wasna her natural condition. She had a problem, and mayhap his response should be one of compassion. Problem was, he didna quite remember that emotion or how to go about it. At least, not for humans.

Letting the anger drain from him, never mind he wasna able to maintain the strength for it anyway, he snatched off his Stetson, scraped his fingers through his hair, then slammed it back into place, feeling the damp strands at his neck. "Suzannah…" he started, exasperation apparent in his voice. "Why do you keep following me?"

She relaxed the reins and expertly kneed her mare, bringing her closer. Close enough for him to reach out and touch her knee if he'd wanted. He smelled a fragrant lemony scent, fresh and wholesome. She peered into his eyes, not an ounce of fear in hers.

Stunned again by that knowledge, Jake rasped a hand down his cheek and smoothed it over his beard, then tried again. "Listen. I dinna ken why you're following me, lass, but you have to stop." Someone as unsullied as she shouldna be anywhere near a man like him.

She gifted him with a smile. Though it was a small, shy one, it reached inside and rattled his bones, like they were jail bars and she was trying to free him from them. He gulped in air, then bumped through the next breath, but couldna find anything else that needed saying.

She sat looking at him with those big, innocent eyes.

"Go back. They need your help with the wedding, aye?"

She dropped her gaze and pressed her lips together as if she was running through a checklist in her head. At long last she looked up, smiled, and shook her head.

The dratted woman! She was supposed to be scared of him. He was certain she *was* at first. No. That wasna right. He remembered now. It was only his beard she'd feared. Well, she should be scared. Everyone else was. "Suit yourself," he said, then wheeled his horse around and trotted off.

His hope that the kitten would turn back finally did happen after a full hour of riding this new path with no conversation, no acknowledgement of her from him. Mainly he was glad, though a small part wanted her to be tough enough to stand up to him, to keep up with him, to fight for him. He needed *someone* to do that, even if he had always blocked that from happening in the past. No one tried anymore.

A shrill whistle rode the breeze.

That was Suzannah's whistle! He whirled his horse and took off like a shot, fear screaming through his veins for what he might find. By the sound, she was on the trail, a quarter mile or so back. Dread thundered through him.

One last turn and he found her, sitting on the ground. His heart shot up and log jammed in his throat as he yanked back on the reins. The mare snorted her objection, but slid to a stop. Jake couldna get to Suzannah fast enough. He leapt off at a dead run. Reaching her, he dropped to his knees and took stock. Golden hair hung in her face where it had pulled out of her braid. She was covered in dirt and pine needles, reclining with her right leg outstretched.

Jake took hold of both sides of her face, dwarfed as it was in his big palms, and tilted it for her to meet his eyes. He brushed the hair back so he could survey the damage. There wasna any, and she looked... amused? She thought this was funny?

"What the devil, Suzannah? What's so dratted funny?"

Her wee smile flashed to a broad one, then she let out a laugh that was low and remarkably hearty, and so pleasant it exploded into his heart like firecrackers on New Year's Eve.

Once he got hold of his senses, his gaze fell to her legs. "Tell me if you're hurt."

She followed his gaze. He scooted in on his knees. It was a hot June day, so she'd worn shorts, thank goodness. First, he looked over both legs from knee to ankle and saw nothing but a few scratches. They didna look deep. Taking a bold chance, he took careful hold of her left knee with both hands. Surprised she didna flinch at his touch, he risked more, sliding his hands along her leg until he reached her ankle. Then she flinched.

"Hurts?" He brought his gaze to her face and moved the ankle again. She jumped a little. He palpated it, then nodded to himself. "I've seen this on cowpokes who jump off their horses and land wrong. I think I can help, lass, but it's probably not what Doc would do. I can take you to him."

She shook her head, then pointed at him and nodded.

"You sure?"

She nodded.

"It might hurt a mite, but then should be better."

Her answer was a wee smile.

He took her foot in both hands, tugged it toward him until her whole leg was straight, then gave it a solid yank. A loud pop and her sigh of relief met his ears. When he looked up, her eyes were wide. So wide he could see the flecks of yellow and blue mixed with the green. Within two heartbeats, her eyelids lowered and she exhaled a hardy breath. "Should be better now."

She moved her foot in a circle.

This whole situation seemed odd to him. It wasn't a typical injury when you fell off a horse, only when you jumped off. "Exactly what happened, lass?"

He watched her expression shift to uncertainty, then downright nervousness. She swallowed. Coughed. Opened her mouth. Closed it.

Jake sat back on his haunches, hands resting on his thighs. "Okay, Kitten. You dinna like to speak, but I ken you're able."

She jerked her head up, surprised. He waited and watched. Her jaw twitched, she blinked, her lips moved in and out as mobile as Gutsy's when she nursed on her mum, and he wondered—not for the first time—what had happened to transform this bonnie lass into a legitimate mute.

She seemed so fretful as she tried to force words out, he wanted to calm her. Without thought, he raised his hand, ran the backs of his fingers down her cheek. She accepted his touch as readily as she had when he'd examined her leg. So, her muteness wasna from fear of men in general.

He got caught up in the actual *feel* of her skin, rose petal soft. He hadna honestly felt the soft skin of a woman since his wedding night. That second and last time Betty had let him touch her.

He heard a small whisper and realized the kitten had spoken and he'd missed it. "Say again, lass."

She pointed at the horse. "Bonnie…" The word was but a wisp, but he'd caught it all the same. Then she laughed again. That same low, raspy sound, and jumbled emotions circled within him all over again at the melody of it. But he didna get it. What about Bonnie? And, why was she amused?

She leaned forward, grasped the tops of his hands where they rested on his thighs, and tried to pull herself up.

"Whatcha doing?"

She let go of his hands and touched his forearm, waited for him to look her in the eye. With a hand signal she showed him she wanted up.

He shrugged, rose to his feet, and wrapped his fingers around her petite forearms. He tugged slowly until she was up and bouncing on one leg. Settling her injured foot on the pine-needled ground, she shifted to put weight on it. Her face lit up when her smile arrived. Her foot seemed to hold her without pain. She took three steps toward Bonnie, then crumpled. He caught her at the waist. "No more," he barked. "We may have to work on it some more. Back at the house."

She jumped at his harsh command, but didna try to pull away. Catching his eye again, there was a plea there. She grabbed hold of his biceps and pushed to one side, like she wanted him to move with her.

"I do not ken what you want, lass, but you're not to move on that foot just yet." He scooped her up in his arms, clutching her to him. She gave a surprised squeak, then smiled. He shook his head, astounded all over again by the fearless mute. What a mystery this wee thing was.

Distracted by her smile, his mind went elsewhere. To the waif-like face. To the feel of her body. To her scent—earth and pine joined with lemon and woman. *I need to stop this,* he told himself, even as his gaze flickered over each delicate feature: dainty nose, sea-colored eyes, and lips that should not be on the face of an innocent.

He was a fool. She was so far from his side of human existence, it was a wonder their paths had ever crossed. His nostrils flared with a much needed breath, but all he managed to do was fill himself with the scent of her. This helpless state fed a new, ravenous hunger and subsequent anger. He didna have time for this upsurge of emotions. He didna want it.

With an ample growl that startled her and had her encircling his neck, he bee-lined it to Bonnie, who was lipping tufts of wild grass a few trees away. Suzannah was hanging on for all she was worth. He ignored how that made him feel.

Feel. Before Suzannah, how long since he'd even thought that word? The moment Suzannah had stepped onto Harper soil, not only had the wild thrum of his heart obliterated the scars that encased it, but his soul had soared nearly out of itself. *Feel* didna even come close to what was happening to him. And for the first time in his dark life, he *felt* illuminated by her light, his every cell lit like stars on a cloudless Montana night.

Yet, without his usual shield of darkness, terror was sliding in. The terror of finding the evidence he craved. And now that he'd met Suzannah... the terror of finding his wife and bairn alive. And worst of all. The terror of giving his heart to Suzannah, only to risk losing again.

He needed to rush Suzannah back to the homestead and hightail it off Harper Ranch for a while. A few weeks should do it. He could stay in touch with Max. Find out when Suzannah left for California, then return to the homestead. He was long overdue for that vacation Roy had been pressing him to take. In fact, there was that spread of his uncle's down Wyoming way he wanted to look at...

Stop. Think. There was a wedding to get through and a stallion to break. Mayhap the wild mustang would win this time and end all this swelling agony.

Jake lengthened his strides. The faster he moved, the sooner she'd be up on that horse and away from him. But after the first stride, he ken his mistake. Because the faster he moved, the tighter she gripped his neck, bringing her that much closer. Sweat broke out on his body at the point of each contact.

Reaching Bonnie, he started to lift Suzannah to the saddle but she gripped his neck tighter. He stalled, but chose to ignore her silent plea. Trying again to lift her, she slapped her palms to both sides of his face, turning his head toward her. He raised his eyebrows at her boldness. As she held his face for several heartbeats, he thought of how soft her palms would be on his skin if only there were no beard.

Now that she'd forced his attention to her pleading eyes, he thought, a kiss? Is that what the lass wants? Eye to eye now and only inches from that sweet face with those tempting lips, his restraint splintered. He hadna even realized he'd leaned in to kiss her until he heard her breath hitch. Both her hands flattened across his whole face and she pushed him away with unexpected strength; so far and so fast that he stumbled and nearly landed them both in the brush.

"What the—" he said on a livid curse. Once he righted them, he glared down into her face, ready to get after her for misleading him.

Surprisingly, she glared right back.

"Why did you hold my face, then, lass?"

She shook her head so hard in a *no*, he had to shift her in his arms to keep them both upright.

"What *were* you after?" Though he said this as if he kent she'd wanted that kiss, he didna believe it himself.

This time she put only one palm to his face, pushing it to one side and pointing at one of Bonnie's hoofs.

Jake frowned as he noticed the mare was not resting any weight on her front right leg. He picked his way through the rocks and pine cones to a lodge pole pine nearby. After settling Suzannah against the trunk of it, he strode back to Bonnie. He backed up to her and tugged her leg up to hold her fetlock between his knees. Darn the bad luck! She had a small pebble jammed in the frog of her hoof, and him without his pick. He usually carried such tools with him, but today he'd been a dunderhead.

He positioned the hoof back down and glanced around for a firm twig. Something hit him in the thigh and bounced off. He looked down at the object then up at a grinning Suzannah. Picking up the perfect sized stick, he noticed it even had a point at one end. Giving Suzannah an affirmative nod, he went back to Bonnie and soon had the rock out.

Jake set Bonnie's hoof back to the ground, straightened, and turned, nearly knocking Suzannah over. He flung the stick away and caught her to him. She nestled into the hard crags of his body, and he couldn't help but notice how right it felt. Still…

"You shouldna be walking on that ankle," he barked. If he'd swung around any faster and taken a step, she'd have been flat on her back on jagged rocks with more serious injuries than a blasted ankle catch. Just what was it that made her want to be so near him?

Her delicate face stared up at him, not one bit repentant, not one bit afraid. In fact, her hands gripped tightly to his sleeves as his arms supported her torso. If he'd thought her sweet smile had robbed him of half his brain, the broad smile she gave him now made his heart bounce into a bonafide Scottish jig.

He blinked. Their angle was so odd, and they stood so rigidly staring into each other's eyes, they could be a famed sculpture.

His only thought: He had to have her, and that blaring need scared the urge right out of him.

As if he were on fire and didna want her to burn, he whisked her up and onto Bonnie's back. She shrieked in surprise, then winced when her bottom hit the saddle. He gently lifted her right leg over the saddle horn. She took over and settled her foot in the stirrup.

Because of his height, he only had to tilt his head up slightly to look into her eyes. She stared at him questioningly.

"Can you ride?" he said in answer.

She nodded, but took his face in her hands again. Her palms held his cheeks, those soft fingertips touching above his beard. He'd become a blithering idiot if she didna stop touching him. "What is it, Kitten?"

Her eyes widened under raised eyebrows. At what? The nickname? Blast! Her silence was killing him! He needed her to talk to him. When that thought registered full force in his brain, he almost laughed. He could not ever remember a time he *wanted* someone to talk to him. Well, he did this time. He wanted this sweet-smelling, soft-skinned lass to flood him with words.

She wiggled his face, snapping his awareness back to her. "Aye, lass?"

Her stunning eyes beseeched him. Not understanding yet again, he frowned and shook his head in agitation. Her fingers slid into his beard and she jumped, her hands flying off his face like they'd just touched a wad of barbed wire. Instead of giving up, she pressed her index finger to his cheekbone, forcing his face downward. She pointed at Bonnie's hoof and shrugged.

Oh, so that was it. "She's fine, lass. It was a small pebble. You're so wee, she'll never even ken you're there."

Relief washed over her face. She was so cute in her concern, he felt an unfamiliar smile coming on, but kent it would never reach his face.

She blinked in delight, and grinned at him. Had she seen a smile? Certainly not on his mouth. But mayhap his eyes. He didna ken why, but the thought managed to lift his spirits.

CHAPTER 6

Suzannah chewed at her bottom lip while she watched the assortment of people mill around Roy's adorned house. In all the years she'd been sinking into the quicksand of despair over her situation with Thomas, she'd never noticed how much fear could arrive with an influx of people. Roy and Mary's wedding had been beautiful and had gone off without a snag, yet here she was, hiding behind the tall coat rack, prepared to escape out the door at any moment and hoping all the bodies would leave before that had to happen.

How selfish was that? *Get a grip, Suzannah.* It's not *your* special day, she chided herself. Taking a deep breath, she rubbed a hand down her midriff to straighten her rose-colored chiffon dress, smoothed the few loose strands of hair back into her french braid, threw her shoulders back, and took two brave steps forward, right into a wall of muscle. "Oh! Sorry," she thrust from her mouth.

Jake caught her shoulders before she bounced back into the rack, nearly as stunned as she was. While he stared down at her with his mouth agape, her glance bounced from one muscled shoulder to the next and then drank in everything between. A warm blush filled her face at her wayward thoughts, but she couldn't help it. This man was utterly staggering. His dark hair, combed back neatly to show his tanned forehead, spilled over the collar of his black suit jacket. Her gaze fell to his crisp white shirt and the black and silver cravat within the open collar—no bolo tie like the rest of the men?—then to his silver vest, black wranglers, and shined boots. He reminded her of how a wealthy saloon owner must have dressed in the 1800's. Flashy but refined. Boy, did he ever polish up well.

Realizing she'd lingered too long in her perusal, Suzannah's gaze whisked back to his eyes. There was a smirk in those nearly black orbs, but when she glanced at his mouth, the amusement didn't show there. Even so, she yearned to see his face without that beard. Though he'd neatly trimmed it, she would always be put off by it.

Jake cleared his throat, alerting her she'd taken another tour down his exquisitely clad body.

When she caught his gaze again, he said, "Heard two words, Kitten."

"Oh?" she said, then grinned, feeling proud of the normal tone.

He blinked, looking stunned and a bit affronted. In the next heartbeat, he circled his long fingers around her elbow, then escorted her to the front door. Once they were on the other side, he pulled it shut and in two of his long strides and six of her own, he plunked her down on the porch swing, setting it in motion. With one of his knees, he had it under his control before it rocked forward. She figured everyone and everything obeyed him that quickly.

He backed up the few steps to the porch railing and half-leaned, half-sat, his palms braced against it. He stared down at her from his great height, and she thought she'd never seen a more formidable man, so flawless, so... breathtaking.

She wondered at him choosing a seat so far away from her. Was he afraid of her? Afraid for her? But he needn't be afraid for her. She had seen his true self, and trusted him more everyday.

"So, lass. You do talk when you want to. You want to explain that to me?"

Her brows shot up, surprised that's what he'd brought her out here to talk about. She shook her head. How would she explain when she couldn't rely on her voice?

He pressed his lips together, and she thought she might see steam shoot out his ears. All that did was make her want to laugh. And kiss him. She wanted to kiss him, and that stunned her. She hadn't wanted to kiss a man since she and Thomas first started dating.

A brief frown flattened his brows, sinking them even closer to his midnight eyes, then right back up they went, as if they'd never moved. His rising fury was obvious in his bearing, but not on his face. In that moment, her amusement shifted to apprehension. She didn't know Jake well. Maybe he *was* capable of violence, if pushed.

He shoved away from the railing and splayed his hands at his hips. Not in a commanding way. More in frustration. Was he truly angry with her for not talking? Would he understand if he knew why?

Tension seemed to ride his shoulders. Her gaze went back to his hands, so large they nearly touched his belt buckle. She began to study them in the glow of the porch light. They were work-worn hands. Scrapes, scars, and hair-dusted knuckles. She supposed if she turned them over, she'd find callouses crossing both palms.

"Look at me, Suzie—Suzannah."

Her gaze whipped to him. Another nickname? She liked that he did that. Her dad was a nicknamer, and she always thought it endearing. But it was clear he hadn't meant to use it. She wondered why.

"What happened that you dinna talk?"

Suzannah swallowed, hard. Could she tell him? Those she trusted she could speak to. Did she trust him enough? *Try*, she told herself. She swallowed. Men on the whole fascinated her. She related to the lot of them, a whole bunch more than need-to-fill-the-air-full-of-inconsequential-words women. She wanted to find out what made Jake tick. But in order to do so, she'd have to speak.

His brows lifted, and he nodded his encouragement. Almost looked like he was about to smile. But no. It was her imagination. Jake didn't smile.

Suzannah wanted to please him. He seemed to like it when she talked, so she'd try real hard. "Long story," she huffed. "Hard for me to…" Her whisper died off.

For a split second, disappointment flitted across his features. "Never mind," he said. "It's none of my business." She wanted to argue that point, but he dismissed her by stuffing his hands in his front pockets and turning to gaze out into the darkness.

It seemed an eternity before he turned back and looked her in the eye. His chest expanded with a huge breath. "I'm leaving tomorrow."

"*What?*" squeaked out of her mouth as her heart took a plunge. She tried to jump up, but lost her balance. The swing see-sawed back and forth under her, but she finally managed to gain her feet.

Jake had averted his gaze again, so she stood before him, taking that moment to regain her composure. She found herself admiring his rigid profile: strong square jaw, hollowed cheeks, full bottom lip pressed to a top one hidden beneath his mustache.

Coming back to herself, and his painful words, she took the remaining few steps toward him and touched his arm to get his attention, but he didn't move. Bleakness showed in his expression. Reaching up, she sank a fingertip in his beard until it hit his chin. She pulled his face toward her. He let her. She waited until his gaze settled on hers, then showed the question on her face. *Why are you leaving?*

An imperceptible nod. Good. He seemed to understand. But then, there was no answer. His Adam's apple bobbed, and she simply couldn't risk he'd guess wrong. She squeezed his arm, bringing his gaze there. She forced the words out. "Why, Jake?" Only a whisper. Not loud enough.

His head jerked up. He'd heard. He angled his head up to the porch rafters, then back to her, as if debating what to say. "Roy asked me to take some time off, after my row with the stallion. He wants me to stop looking for—" He stopped, sucked in a breath, turned his face away. "Anyway, he said to leave the beast and go."

Suzannah felt panic claw under every inch of her skin. She didn't want him to leave. Where would he go? Would he come back? She circled his forearm again and squeezed hard.

Jake looked down at her hand then up to her distressed face, a wrinkle of concern pressed between his brows."What's wrong, Kitten?"

Suzannah gulped, hoping to spit out her next words with force. "Don't go."

Jake was dumbfounded. The verra person he wanted to escape from, wanted him to stay?

"Don't," she whispered as she shook her head. She leaned toward him, and rested a palm on his chest. She looked graceful in her flowing dress. A vision of loveliness so far out of his realm, he wanted to cut and run from the pain of it.

He plucked her hand off his chest. "Listen, lass. Roy's right. I've gotta go for a while. You'll likely be gone when I get back. It's for the best." With that, he scanned her face one more time, memorizing every delicate feature to bring to mind later. Then he turned and jumped down all four steps at once, taking himself off to the bunkhouse to pack.

Before he stepped inside, he glanced back at the porch. He felt a stab of regret at the sight of Suzannah standing there. Her hand, so recently pressed to his chest, was now resting against her own, her face deep in sorrow. *For him?*

A hollowness overtook him. The thought of going away and possibly never seeing this angel again added to the emptiness already camped in his soul.

He shook his head. It didna matter about him. But she had been hurt by someone. That much he could tell. Somehow, she'd jumbled him up with her past. Probably needed a masculine influence she could trust, besides her dad and uncle.

He couldna seem to shake off the idea that she trusted him.

That's how little she kent of him.

How could he explain to her that he wasna who she thought he was. He wasna good. He'd been wild in his youth, raised by a weak mum and no dad, rejected by his Wyoming classmates because he mixed Scottish words with English ones all peppered with an accent. And, instead of improving when he became an adult, he'd failed in the one thing that mattered most. He had lost his pregnant wife because he hadna been man enough to step up and take care of her needs.

Any woman should steer clear of him. So long as he lived and breathed, he'd keep this innocent away from him.

He entered the bunkhouse, veered off to his bed, and bent to pull a satchel out from under it. Throwing the bag on the narrow mattress, he went to his bureau and grabbed some clean clothes. It would be better for Suzannah when he drifted away. Her confusion over him would clear, and she'd discover how to move her own life forward.

When people got too close to him, their lives just got muddled up.

Jake wondered, not for the first time, how this trip would go with his traveling companion. When Roy found out he was headed to the Cooper Bar-Six Ranch, he offered to keep Jake on the payroll with an added bonus if he'd take Roy's niece Rebecca along with him. The money didna matter to him. He'd lived flat broke ever since Betty drained his bank account at the start of their marriage. And he had no reason to start saving again, seeing as how he didna expect to be on this earth for long.

But Roy's offer—well, it was Roy's offer. And no matter what, he'd never turn Roy down.

Once he was done packing and had changed out of his wedding duds, Jake banged out of the bunkhouse and strode to the horse trailer parked at the side of the barn. When he glanced at the house, he was relieved Suzannah no longer stood on the porch. She'd probably gone inside to enjoy the reception still going on as he heard country tunes and a mixture of voices spilling out the opened windows and doors. Thankfully, flood lights added to the light streaming from the house so he could see the hitch, metal door and hinges, and the tires he needed to check on the old trailer. He reflected on the horse that Roy had asked him to return to his Uncle Cord. That dapple gray gelding had given him two broken ribs, a whole lot of nipping bruises, and a fearsome black eye along the way. Aye, it was time to take the critter back to his owner, now that he'd remained docile as a lamb for several weeks in a row.

Jake ran a checklist in his head, bringing his thoughts to his traveling companion—Rebecca. Out of the three sisters, the two oldest, Jessica then Rebecca, resembled one another in looks and temperament. Which was to say, they were night and day to Suzannah's exquisite beauty and unnerving silence. Over the last two weeks, Jake had observed Rebecca's easy-going personality, though she was plenty talkative. Thankfully, he didna suffer from an acute case of attraction for her as he did for her little sister, Suzannah. So, it should be a simple, relaxing trip. If they left early, it would only take them one long day to reach Sundance, Wyoming, and the Cooper Bar-Six spread. He would avoid an overnight stay at all costs.

Jake immersed himself in the work of preparing for this trip. He stacked gear, filled canteens, gathered supplies, prepared the horse trailer. By the time he had most everything loaded in the truck for an early morning departure, two hours had passed. He had one last task before he could leave Harper Ranch. He sauntered into the barn and let himself into the front stall where Roy kept the gray mare.

"You getting things ready to go?" a pleasant feminine voice asked from the open barn door.

Jake jerked his head up from checking the mare's hock. Ah, Rebecca. He glanced over her sweet face, long brown hair, and ranch garb, then went back to his chore with the horse. "Got your stuff?"

"I think so. I hope so. I have everything I brought with me from California. Uncle Roy says you have my saddle and such."

"Aye, lass. It's over there." He nodded in the direction of the last of the gear he'd stacked on the saddle, thrown over a sawhorse.

She moved up next to him. "What's wrong with Gertrude?"

"Gertrude?" Glancing over his shoulder at Rebecca, he saw her smirk.

"Well, yeah. Gertie. Didn't anyone tell you that was her name?" Rebecca rubbed her hands nervously down her jeans. He had that affect on people.

"Nae. Dinna much call them by their names," he said, trying to ease her tension with conversation, though his own ramped up. He was instantly faced with the fact that he didna like taking a woman on a trip. He didna want a woman around at all. "She just needs rest," he said in answer to her question about *Gertrude*.

Rebecca exhaled a big breath. Seemed she was relaxing a wee bit. That was good for her. Didna matter about him.

"Shall I just put my bag with the rest of the stuff? I'll only have one more in the morning," she said.

"Aye."

"Okay, then. When do you want me here?"

"We leave at dawn."

"Oh. Okay. Thanks, Jake, for doing this. I hope I'll be able to help your uncle and cousins. Cooking isn't my strength, but I'm a whiz at housecleaning." Another glance told him she had more to say. She moved to the other side of the mare to smooth a palm down her neck. "Are you close to them?"

Jake stopped his ministrations and rose to full height. Rebecca's gaze locked onto him, her eyes widening as he straightened, as if she were watching a behemoth rise from the earth. Jake came around the horse to within a few feet of her. She backed a step. He was used to this so, ignoring her reaction, he took the satchel from her and deposited it with the other gear. "Not close. Have'na seen them in over two years."

"Oh. Other than taking me, why are you going?"

"To look at the parcel of land they're offering me."

"Oh… I see… good. Great. Okay… well… I'll see you in the morning then."

He wondered over her hesitancy. He watched her walk away, noting she was Jessica's same size and height. Suzannah must have gotten her looks and wee build, and that beautiful golden hair, from a grandmother or some other relative.

Rebecca pivoted. "Jake…?"

"Lass?"

"Are they good people, these relatives of yours? I have to live with them, you know, and well… I can trust them, can't I?" She wrung her hands together.

Ah, so that's what was bothering her. Understandable. "Aye, lass. Salt of the earth."

She sighed heavily. "Oh. Good. Good. Thank you." With that, she swung back around and scampered out the door.

Jake kicked himself for not asking Rebecca how long Suzannah and her folks intended to stay on at Roy's. But even as Jake fine-tuned his plan to return the *moment* the kitten left, he knew it was the idea of succeeding, not failing, that now burned a hole in his stomach.

CHAPTER 7

When Suzannah closed the front door to the last of the wedding guests at well past 2:00 AM, she noticed her folks sitting at one of the kitchen tables, sipping something steamy. "Tea?" she asked as she approached them. Her mother nodded tiredly as Suzannah leaned down to give her a quick hug, then moved around to do the same for her dad. "Goodnight," she said, and they reciprocated. Then she ambled up the stairs to her room.

As she stopped at her door, she noticed light spilling onto the carpet in the hallway from Rebecca's room. Curious, she traipsed to the door and looked in. Rebecca had her back turned to her and was transferring neatly folded clothing from the bed to an open suitcase. Leaving? But where? Something elusive made Suzannah's stomach flip.

"Where you going?" she asked, her hands gripping her hips.

Without looking up from her packing, Rebecca said, "To Wyoming. With Jake."

"*What?* What do you mean, with Jake?" Suzannah's voice always worked best when she yelled a bit. And right now, her voice worked well. Suzannah glared—full-on glared—at her sister. It was something she couldn't remember ever doing before. What in the world was her sister thinking, to travel with Jacob Cooper to Wyoming? And why? She didn't think her sister had any interest in the man. Did she? Had she missed something?

"Suzannah, don't worry about it. I'll be fine."

Suzannah knew Rebecca could take care of herself. What she wanted to know was why she planned to go with Jake for his time off. Suzannah's blood barreled up her neck and into her ears, then flooded her face to the point she could actually feel it throb. She grabbed Rebecca by the shoulders and spun her around, nearly causing her to fall flat.

Rebecca stumbled, but righted herself. "What the—What's wrong with you?"

Suzannah huffed a deep breath and swallowed, then blurted, "Why?"

"Wyoming?"

Suzannah shook her head.

"Why with Jake?"

She stamped her foot. "Yes."

Rebecca looked annoyed now. It wasn't like she made a practice of answering to her baby sister. She stared at Suzannah for a full minute. Hoping she'd give up these questions and leave, no doubt. Well, that wasn't going to happen. Suzannah needed to know what was going on here, so she waited her out.

Finally, Rebecca took a step nearer Suzannah and sized her up, narrowing her eyes as she looked intently into hers. "Are you interested in that bear of a man, Suzannah?"

Suzannah grimaced at the thought of Jake's beard, then averted her gaze, flummoxed about how she should answer. Was she interested? She trusted him. He was the first man in a very long time that she did trust. Did she like him? He was hard to like, but yeah, she kinda did. He was a protector. He proved that when he'd rescued her after she'd foolishly jumped off Bonnie in order to check her hoof. He was a healer. He'd demonstrated that when he knew her injured ankle just needed a solid pop. He had a heart of gold when it came to animals. And he was magnificent to look at, even if that darned beard covered most of his face.

Rebecca planted her hands on her hips. "Well?"

She brought her gaze back up, peeved that she had to look up since Rebecca was taller. "No." That was a lie, wasn't it? Yet, how could she confess or deny something she wasn't sure of. All she knew was she did not want Jake and Rebecca to travel together. Anywhere!

"Then don't worry about it. Jake is taking me to Wyoming to stay with his Uncle Cord, and his cousins. They're desperate for house help. Uncle Roy felt I could handle this job—that they needed me. In a few weeks, Jake will come back here. Alone."

Rebecca eyed Suzannah again. Watching for her reaction? Well, she wouldn't react. But the thought of those two spending that kind of time together made something inside her snap. "I'm coming!"

She didn't know where that crazy thought had come from. Did she like the idea? Yes. Yes, she did. It was the perfect solution.

Rebecca reared back as if Suzannah had slapped her. Her face flushed red, and she fixed her hands to her hips. "You'll do no such thing!"

Suzannah straightened and took a step toward her sister. "Why not?" For some reason, her distress was helping her fling out words. Without pain. She sucked in a huge breath of air and went for the finish. "You want him for yourself?" Goodness. She was on a roll. Something had changed within and she wanted to fight back. With words.

Rebecca looked stunned, as well she should be. Suzannah hadn't spoken this many words in a good long while. Maybe she could have all along.

When Rebecca was done staring, she cleared her throat. "No, I don't want him. Jake is unattainable. I may well have been interested if he didn't have a don't-anyone-get-near-me sign written across his forehead. He is mighty appealing, if a little scary." Rebecca glanced away and looked deep in thought. "You know, maybe on this trip…" She whispered this, as if for her own ears.

Heavens! What had Suzannah done, bringing Rebecca's attention to Jake? Now, frantic and defenseless, Suzannah paced a few steps away, combed through possibilities in her mind. Maybe she could get her mom and dad to approve of her joining Jake and Rebecca, so that Rebecca was powerless to say no. What reason could she give for wanting to go?

"Go to bed, Suzannah," Rebecca said. "I've got stuff to do. We're leaving at dawn and I still have a few more things to pack." Rebecca straightened, as if she'd just thought of something, strode across the room, and enveloped Suzannah in a deep hug. "I'll miss you, squirt. Take care of yourself." Then as if dismissing her, she went back to her packing.

Suzannah remained in that spot. She wasn't finished, not by any means. Her mom and dad were next. Somehow she would get them to agree. Then she remembered. She was twenty-two, for crying out loud. Plenty old enough to decide her own fate.

Pulling herself up by her bootstraps, she marched out Rebecca's door and on down the stairs, thrilled to see her folks still sitting at the same kitchen table, leisurely drinking from their coffee mugs.

She sashayed up to her dad and hoisted herself over the bench seat. Plopping down, she smiled at her dad, then her mom, who sat across. "Hi," she said.

"I thought you went to bed," her mother said.

"Were you helping Rebecca pack?" her dad added.

She felt her smile slip away and a frown take it's place. *Think, Suzannah. What will make them agreeable so there won't be a fight?* Then it came to her. It wasn't quite fair, considering her mom and dad had been supporting her in her fight against Thomas. It didn't matter they thought her paranoid and delusional, not believing Thomas capable of all she feared he could do. They'd never once left her side. But she couldn't let Rebecca travel alone with Jake. Especially now that she'd awoken her sister's attraction to the man. Some determined beast with a tail of wickedness crowded in on her, and she gave it reign. "I need to go with her," she managed to say.

Her dad twisted on the bench seat to get a good look at her. "*What?* Go with Rebecca to the Cooper Ranch? To work, you mean?" He was frowning, but it was more in confusion.

She shook her head. "Not to work. For the trip."

Her mom scooted in and leaned on her threaded fingers. "You mean, as a little vacation for you?"

Suzannah smiled and nodded.

"No. I don't think that's wise, Suzannah. It's a long trip, and Jake's planning to stay a few weeks. Rebecca's only going because she has a job at the other end," her logical dad said.

Suzannah felt her ire rise. They always babied her. Funny how her appreciation for their support changed so rapidly, but the more she thought of it, the more she realized she had let them baby her. It was what parents did for an impaired daughter. And until now, it was what she had needed. "If she can, I can."

Her mom's face showed a mask of concern. "Sweetie, is this hurting you? Talking, I mean."

She never noticed the pain when anger fueled her words. If she wasn't careful, she'd become addicted to anger in order to talk. *Will this part of me ever heal, Lord? Or, is this somehow my thorn in the side, like what the Apostle Paul suffered?* She knew God could fix anything, but the question was, would He? God's answer to Paul had been, *No*. She'd always thought God's answer to Paul had been the consequence for his original persecution of the Christ followers. Suzannah had never consciously rebelled against God. Still, would He leave her with her thorn anyway?

"I'm fine, Mom. I want to go. I *need* to go."

She and her mom shared a long stare, then her mom nodded and reached across the table to pat her dad on the arm. "I don't think the Cooper men would mind. Another woman around for a short time would mean more work would get caught up on. We should let her go, dear."

Her mom understood then, that Thomas had stripped her of something important, and this was a way to gain it back. But still, Suzannah's anger ratcheted up another notch. She truly was old enough to make up her own mind. "I wanted you to know, is all."

With that she rose and started to swing her leg over the bench when her dad pressed her hand to the table. "Suzannah—"

"No, Pop. I'm going." She swallowed, inhaled, and started again. "I don't have to ask for permission," she said and winced, wrestling with guilt over such cutting words.

She stared into her dad's concerned eyes for a moment, determined not to look away. She wasn't wandering off to Siberia, for crying out loud.

He sighed heavily. "Okay. I get it. Do you need help getting ready?"

She really did appreciate her caring father. He would worry if he couldn't help. "Sure, Pop." She smiled at him then. He gave her a weak smile back.

Once Suzannah entered her room and went about the task of gathering clothes to pack for the trip she hadn't planned for, nerves made her break out in a sheen of sweat. She'd managed to override her parents' concern all right, but did she have the guts to take on Rebecca?

And then there was Jake…

* * *

Jake positioned Cord Cooper's gelding at the gate of Gertrude's stall. He tied him off until he could lead him into the horse trailer already hitched to Roy's truck.

The gelding snorted and shook it's massive head. "In a minute, laddie," Jake soothed. Before Jake got the lead rope tied, the gelding raised his head to Gertrude and pulled his lips back. Jake yanked down on the lead. "Dinna even think to nip her, you skellum! You'll not be slipping back into that bad habit." He shook the lead line again for emphasis.

After staring the horse down for a moment longer, he tied the lead to a stall board in a quick release knot. Just as he finished, he heard soft footsteps entering the barn. Ah, his companion was here. Right on time.

Jake straightened and turned and nearly swallowed his tongue. The early sunlight of dawn barely lit the open barn door, but it was enough of a backdrop to illuminate the wee fairy standing within it. Warmth shot from his chest to the pads of his fingers and toes, as if one look at her triggered his nerve endings to all fire at once. *Suzannah.* In snug jeans, boots, and peaches-and-cream blouse that complemented her skin. She'd slung a satchel over one shoulder and held a good-sized suitcase in her other hand.

In the next instant the warmth in him turned to ice, then immediately back to heat with rage. "What are you about, lass?"

Suzannah lifted her chin, though he was sure he saw it tremble. She added her bag to the stack of gear, then twisted back and strolled over to Bonnie. Just as she opened the latch to the stall, Jake was there, stopping her, holding the gate in place.

"What's this about, Suzannah?" he said to the top of her head, watching her hair stir under his breath.

He was so close he could feel the heat of her body, smell the freshness of her skin and hair. When she was away from him, he could almost imagine his reaction to the lass had been false. Now, as the seconds passed, his desire to wrap her in his arms and breathe her in nearly overwhelmed him.

With a burst of willpower that came out of nowhere, he pushed the gate back into place. The latch chinked loudly, making Suzannah and the horse both jump. Jake tenderly took the lass by the shoulders and turned her toward him. Then, for his own sake, he let loose and backed up a step. He looked down into those eyes, today the color of a Blue Monarch Butterfly, and was rendered speechless. Well now, that made two of them. Mayhap this wee lass and he would have to communicate with body language only. They surely were the two most silent people he kent.

After a few thundering heartbeats, he opened his mouth, hoping the right words came forth. "You're not going." *Too harsh.* "Listen. Lass. I canna take you with us."

The fairy suddenly switched to Gutsy, the kitten who fought for her food, her warmth, and her rights. "I'm going!" she said with surprising force.

She twirled again to open the gate, and Jake let her. But he wasna done with her. Not yet. She could not go on this trip. The need to clasp her against him was far too strong, the hunger to make her his, too uncontrollable. Each minute he spent with her, unfamiliar emotions crashed down on him. He would never be able to keep his head if she were along. He could keep Rebecca safe, no worries there. Taking care of that lass until he delivered her to his uncle's spread would be effortless. But Suzannah? Ever since she had awakened his heart and soul, his old ways were trying their darndest to creep back in. She'd be lucky to get halfway to Wyoming before he'd have her in his arms and ravished until neither one could move.

Nae. She couldna go.

He didna have a right to these new feelings. He sure as heck didna deserve her. It was best if he remained dead to women. This trip was his only chance to reset. Get back to the still waters of lifeless emotions.

Suzannah had put a halter on Bonnie and had her by the lead rope before he came back to himself. He shook his head to clear it, then took the few steps to grasp the cheekpiece of the halter. Suzannah glared at him, but he kept his body between her and his hold on Bonnie. There was no way this wee thing could muscle her way against him.

Her silence forced him to talk, which was the last thing he wanted to do. "Listen here, lass. You are not going, so get that out of your head, right now!"

Startled by his outburst, Bonnie threw her head and snorted. He got the impression she was taking sides with the lass. Jake ran a hand down to her muzzle and stroked. "Easy, lass. Yer fine," he soothed.

Suzannah stamped her foot. It was something he figured she probably did a lot of to bring attention back to herself.

He hauled his gaze back to hers, and got trapped there. "Nae!" he said with vehemence, all the while feeling the ground slip from under him.

"Yes!" she said back, then stamped her foot again.

A strong urge to smile swept over him. He felt his lips twitch.

She stopped all movement, then fluttered a blink. She blinked again as she leaned forward almost imperceptibly, parting her lips and staring at his mouth.

Had he actually smiled? He clenched his teeth and scowled. "Stop it."

Right then, Rebecca decided to enter the picture. Jake was relieved. She'd take control and turn her sister back to the house.

"You ready, Suzannah?" Rebecca asked sweetly.

"*What?*" Jake barked, making the mare toss her head again. Mumbling to himself, Jake turned to the stall, twisted Bonnie's rope around a post, then looked back at the women. He clamped one hand to his hip, rubbed his knuckles across his mouth with the other. "What is this, Rebecca. Explain."

"Oh," Rebecca fluttered a hand at him as if to wave off any concern. "Suzannah's going with us. No problem. She's a better horsewoman than me, Jake. She can help if you have trouble with the horses, or the trailer. It'll be good to have her along."

"Hold on. Who decided this, lass? At the last minute?" He took two steps forward, shifting his gaze from one lass to the other, waiting for someone to ease the ball of tension spinning in his gut.

"Well... um... stop looking at me like that, Jake," Rebecca said as she scrubbed her palms down her jeans. "It's... it's unsettling is what it is."

She sped to the stack of gear, ignoring his question and arranging the last of her stuff with the rest of the gear. The last item she brought in was a knapsack, bulging with some stow Mabel had no doubt sent along.

"Here you go, Suzannah," Rebecca said as she tread over to the lass. "These are for you since you didn't show up for breakfast. Mabel says they're your favorite blueberry muffins." She pulled one of Suzannah's hands out and plopped a brown bag in it, then flitted over to the stall that housed the old chestnut. "Are we taking Bessie here? Or is there another one you would prefer?" She swung around with a questioning look to Jake.

Jake was dumbfounded, by both the idea of Suzannah joining them and the flurry of words coming out of Rebecca's mouth. Never having been around women verra much, he seemed to be unable to move while the lasses were in motion.

He glanced at Suzannah. The lass was unlatching the chestnut's gate. That got Jake's feet moving. He sidled up behind Suzannah to push the gate shut, though this time calmer than before. He took a final big breath and accepted his fate. He no longer wished to ken who'd made this decision, he just wanted to get underway. "The gelding is going back to Cooper Ranch.

There will be no more room. Either the chestnut or the buckskin. Canna take them both." He looked from one lass to the other, awaiting their decision.

Suzannah strode over to the buckskin and patted her rump, then turned to present her choice to Rebecca and Jake.

Both her companions nodded in agreement.

Jake bent to grab some gear in one hand, then treaded through the barn to catch the buckskin, *Bonnie*, by her lead and tug her with him out the door. He made two more trips, gathering the rest of their tackle and suitcases. The lasses were surprisingly helpful carrying their share.

"Get in the truck. The gelding goes in last," Jake said.

"What's his name? And why last?" Rebecca asked.

"He's still skittish. I dinna want to take any chances with the two of you, aye? Dinna ken his name."

Rebecca stopped Jake with a hand to his arm. Her face tilted to one side as she seemed to be studying him. "Now, I know your mom was Scot, Jake. But sometimes you have a brogue, and other times you don't. Some of your words are delightfully Scottish, and others are plain American. And, I've noticed you don't always use the Scottish words."

Jake stared at Rebecca, annoyed. He wondered if she had a question in there, or was just talking to hear herself talk.

"Well?" she said, and cocked her head the other way.

"Well, what?" Jake asked.

"Well… I don't know." A slight pink rose up her neck, and she looked unsure of herself. He had a way of doing that to people, though the kitten seemed immune. "I guess it's not so much a question as an observation."

Not wanting to cause her any more discomfort, Jake nodded, then detoured past her to fetch the gelding.

When he returned with the horse in tow, he scowled at Rebecca, who hadna moved. "I told you to get in the truck."

"Aye, you did, laddie," she said with a smirk and an air of resumed confidence. "I thought you might need help."

"Nae, you didna. You're curious about me, is all."

Rebecca stiffened, eyes widening.

Jake lifted a thick brow and waited. When Rebecca realized he was not going to take the gelding to the trailer until she was safely seated in the truck, she turned and shuffled off.

Jake saw Suzannah peek her lovely face at him from the center of the bench seat as Rebecca rounded the truck bed and hoisted herself in from the passenger side. That meant Suzannah would be sitting next to him for the trip. How was he to keep his wits about him with the lass who scrambled his brains at his right flank?

Jake glanced up, trying to draw strength from the clear blue sky, devoid of even one cloud. He breathed in the fresh morning air. The sooner they started on their way, the sooner they'd arrive at Cooper Ranch and he could be free of the lasses. Then he'd saddle up and ride out for a spell, gain some solitude. He could do this.

With one last purging breath, he strode to the back of the trailer with the dapple trailing on his heels. Distractedly, he led the gelding up the tail gate and into the narrow space next to Bonnie. He wrapped the lead and was about to tie him off to the 'D' ring when Bonnie rumbled a low nicker. Jake raised his head just in time to see the gelding's oncoming teeth. He jabbed a finger into the muzzle just above the animal's protruding lip as hard as he could, considering their close quarters. The gelding tossed his head, and then came back for more. Jake hollered, "Och!" He took hold of the troublemaker's upper lip, giving it a hearty twist. "Old habits, eh? Behave yourself!"

The horse protested Jake's punishment with a loud whinny, then shifted his body to try and smash Jake against the divider. The trailer rocked and the clatter of hoof-strikes against the planks echoed loudly in the small space, but Jake kept his hold on the lip, dodged the horse's brutal efforts, and waited. He wasna going anywhere. Once the horse settled down, finally submitting to Jake's discipline, Jake tied him to the far corner of the trailer to keep him from nipping Bonnie.

"I'd be making you run in circles if I had the time, you son of a she-devil! Thought we were done with all that bad behavior." He ran a calming hand down his own face, then trailed his fingers along the gelding's girth and hindquarters as he exited the trailer. He jumped down and closed the rear gate with a hefty clank. He guessed he'd have some polishing to do on this gelding at the other end. Dang bloody animal!

Huffing with exertion, Jake lifted his hat and ran a forearm over his face. He opened the driver's door, grumbling to himself at their late start, and slipped his black hat behind the seat.

"You okay?" Rebecca said, leaning forward to see him from the far side of the truck.

Jake's head jerked up, at once reminded that he had female passengers to endure next.

"That gelding giving you a hard time?" she asked with deep concern on her face. A glance at Suzannah told him she was worried as well.

If only that gelded brute were his biggest challenge of the day. He glanced at the girls, groaning inside, feeling just devilish enough to assert the same control inside the cab as he had in the trailer. Jake cleared his throat. "Rebecca, switch places with Suzannah, aye?"

Rebecca looked confused, while the hurt look on Suzannah's face speared him in the gut. He busied himself with settling in behind the wheel and closing his door.

"Why?" Rebecca asked. Suzannah's expression asked the same thing.

"Well, now… " *Think fast, Jake.* "See this here gear shift?" Jake gave the knob a hefty pat. "Rebecca, you're taller, so you can straddle it better."

Rebecca laughed. That wasna a good sign. "Suzannah fits just fine," she said on a continued chuckle.

To prove Rebecca's point, Jake guessed, Suzannah scootched her little fanny back and forth on the vinyl and knocked her sweet little knees together, showing they were nowhere near the gear shift emerging from the floor.

"See there," Rebecca said, looking smug and suspicious all at once. "My knees are bigger and would get in your way, Mr. Cooper. Don't you think we ought to get going?"

That sounded a bit condescending even to his uneducated ears, but she was right. Any more talk of this and they would both ken what he was up to. If they didna already.

Reaching up to adjust the mirror, Jake took the final moment to gather his courage. He turned the key and, with his booted toe, compressed the starter next to the accelerator. The truck turned over three times but didna catch. Jake pumped the accelerator then tried again. The engine turned over another three times before catching with a powerful roar. Jake gunned it a couple times, then compressed the clutch and took hold of the knob at the top of the two-foot shifter. He gave it a liberal pull left and back into first gear, and instantly came into contact with Suzannah's inner thigh.

She jumped.

He ground gears.

He hadna done that since he was twelve, when Cord—only eight years his senior and the uncle who refused to discuss his own brother, Jake's father—had first taught him how to drive.

"Pardon," he muttered, feeling a flush of heat rise up his neck. Using his fingertips at the right of the bar just under the knob to keep his own flesh away from Suzannah, he deftly pulled it into first gear. Forcing himself to slowly slip the clutch, the truck lurched a bit but otherwise rolled forward without incident. When a glance in the rearview mirror to the tiny windows at the front of the trailer convinced Jake the ton of horse flesh was riding well, he sped up and shifted into second.

They rode in second gear, and in thick silence, all the way out Harper Ranch and onto the main highway, heading north.

"Where are you going, Jake?" Rebecca asked as Jake turned right on Highway 191.

"Bozeman."

"Why? We're supposed to be heading south to Wyoming."

Jake could barely concentrate on Rebecca's question, thinking ten beads of sweat must have popped out for every shift he'd made between Suzannah's legs. Thankfully, he was in third gear, and done for a tad.

"Have my uncle's saddle to pick up in Bozeman. When that gelding of his threw me at the start of our union, it got tore up pretty good. We'll pick it up in Bozeman, head to Billings, then on down to Wyoming after that."

Jake was relieved when Rebecca let the conversation die off. He let his thoughts drift in the direction of Cooper Bar-Six Ranch, to Uncle Cord's reaction to the dapple grey's bad habits he was supposed to have corrected, to whether he was even interested in the section of land his uncle offered him, to how his six cousins fared. Especially rabble-rousing Bronc. His mind rested there as he wordlessly drove and the sun climbed the east wall of pure Montana blue, shining like a beacon through the passenger window and across the lasses' laps.

Rebecca's voice startled him out of his thoughts—and his covert glances at Suzannah's legs. "Do you think, before we stop to pick up the saddle, we could get some coffee to go with Mabel's muffins? And a personal moment? Especially the personal moment," she said, peering around Suzannah.

Jake glanced over, seeing her sheepish grin, and nodded. Her question was so unassuming—so polite and reasonable. That's what he knew of Rebecca. She'd visited Harper Ranch several times in the past. As the foreman of Coleman Ranch, he'd visited Harper's often enough to have gotten to ken her a bit. Her humble manner was why he got on well with her. It was also why he kent she'd fit in well with his uncle and cousins. His Uncle Cord was a fair man, but he was tough. Without a woman around he'd managed to rub his sons raw. Rebecca was needed. In far more ways than cooking and cleaning. And, something told him she could handle herself amidst all those brash lads.

Aye, he was sure Rebecca could be a buffer between irascible people there, but could she be that for Jake and Suzannah now? Sometime along the way of this trip, the two of them would no doubt need a go-between. As silent as Suzannah was, she was opposite to Rebecca; not obedient, not conforming, and not someone he could push around. And up until now, pushing people around was just an easy form of persuasion for his agenda, without having to schmooze. Because if schmoozing were a class in school, he'd have received an F-minus.

Spotting Bair's Truck Stop, Jake stuck his left arm straight out to signal cars behind him that he was making a turn into the station. He caught hold of the gear shift knob, slowing enough to make a wide turn with his shadowing trailer of horseflesh. He'd forgotten where his fingers needed to go, though, and as he shoved the shifter up to second gear, he slid his knuckles all along Suzannah's inner thigh. They both groaned in unison.

Rebecca choked out a laugh, cleared her throat, then mumbled something to herself. When she finally seemed to gather herself together, she waved a hand toward the station, and said, "Do we really need gas already, Jake?"

The truck and trailer's tires crunched along gravel as Jake pulled in, taking up space in front of two of the pumps. He slowed to a halt. "I'll top her off. You need the lass's room, aye? I'll check on the horses and get the coffee." He nodded toward the truck stop's café.

Rebecca wasted no time jumping out of the truck.

Jake watched as Suzannah extracted herself from the gearshift, proving what he knew all along. Her little rear-end had to be sore from being stuffed into the seat back, trying to keep her knees clear of that darned bar. Why'd she do it? Just to sit close to him?

Suzannah slid across the seat to follow Rebecca. Jake watched until a cheery young man with a *Bair's Truck Stop* patch sewn above his shirt pocket and on his hat bounded around the truck's grill to the driver's window. "Fill 'er up, sir?"

"Top her off," Jake said, then turned his head back to make sure the lasses had gone safely through the door to the lavy. Then he exited the truck for his own duties.

Once Jake returned and the women were settled back in the truck, he handed out coffee in short paper cups. He handed his own cup to Suzannah to hold, turned the ignition key, and compressed the starter. The truck turned over three times, then boomed to life. Jake glared at the shifter for a moment before carefully arranging his fingers where they wouldn't make contact with Suzannah's leg, then shifted into gear.

The pickup rolled forward, carrying them, the trailer, and their cargo out of the truck stop and onto the highway. The late morning sun shone off the hood's red paint, radiating into Jake's eyes and adding to a discomfort he figured would be with him all the way to Cooper Ranch.

CHAPTER 8

Suzannah wondered where her brain had been when she'd bullied her way onto this trip. Though he was kind enough, it was obvious how Jake felt about her. He'd done everything but hang a 'Don't you get it? I don't want to be near you!' sign around his neck. It was Rebecca he'd wanted next to him. He'd shown that each time he'd had to shift the darned truck, and an unwanted caress of Suzannah's leg had caused a clench of his jaw, or an inward flinch. She had to admit his touch was unnerving to her as well. But to him, it was *what*? Did she have scales or something? Weren't men supposed to like touching women?

Once Jake had the truck in third gear and was breezing along the highway, Suzannah gave him a covert glance. With every bump in the road, the truck jostled her against him. Each time, every muscle in his body tensed with the contact, and beads of sweat were now clinging to his forehead and upper lip. How dare he act as if her touch was downright painful. As of right now, she would stop holding her body away from him. It would make him more uncomfortable, she knew, but darned if he didn't deserve a little discomfort. After all, her own efforts to stay out of his way had only earned her a tremendous backache. Besides, she yearned to interact with the man. Even if by touch rather than words.

Jake slowed, getting ready to take a slight turn to the right. He took it a hair too fast. She let her body slide naturally into him. Their hips and shoulders bounced against each other. Startled, Jake's foot slipped off the accelerator momentarily, jerking them along for a few seconds before he recovered. His grip tightened on the steering wheel, turning his knuckles white. When Suzannah risked a glance with a smile, he glanced back to her, only his was an icy glare.

She dropped her smile to copy his glare. *Well, too bad, Mr. Don't-get-near-me! Don't drive so fast then.*

When he turned his gaze back to the road his lips pressed to a thin line and his jaw muscles worked into a ball.

Heavens, the realization that he truly didn't like her touch made her feel ridiculous. She scooted back as close to Rebecca as the gearshift would allow, Mabel's beloved muffins turning to acid in her stomach. She wouldn't be trying such a fool thing again. He'd think she was flirting. Was she? *No. Maybe.* It had only been a test. Sadly, now she wished she didn't know the truth. That he truly didn't want her near him.

Now the trip she'd begged to go on couldn't end fast enough.

Rebecca leaned forward, planting her elbows into her thighs. She twisted her head and leveled a frown at Suzannah. Yeah, she figured Rebecca had noticed. Not much got past her older sister.

Suzannah rolled her eyes at her, heat rising to her cheeks.

Rebecca's gaze wandered off toward Jake. "I hear you were the foreman on Coleman Ranch just under a year ago. What made you decide to take up bronc busting for Uncle Roy, Jake?"

Jake double blinked. Other than that movement, Suzannah would have thought he'd turned to stone. He remained stiff and mute, but Rebecca wasn't deterred. "Jake?"

Suzannah glared at Rebecca, but immediately saw her sister wasn't going to let up. Poor Jake. Nothing ever dissuaded Rebecca when she wanted to know something. Suzannah turned back to Jake, curious about how he'd answer.

His already massive chest expanded more with a deep breath, stretching his black shirt before he released it ever so slowly. Finally, when Suzannah was about to intervene, to somehow let him know he didn't have to answer her prying sister, he said, "It's all I've a right to do."

Rebecca tipped her chin down to look over at Jake with one eyebrow lifted.

Suzannah put a hand to her knee.

Rebecca looked into her eyes with a question in her own.

Suzannah shook her head, and mouthed, "Later."

A frown of confusion lined Rebecca's brow, but she nodded in acquiescence.

Suzannah turned her attention to Jake, waiting to see if he had more to say, and got captured by the view of his profile: strong cheekbones, solid nose—thick at the bridge. It looked like he might have broken it a time or two. Maybe on a bronc? The chin and jawline were sure to be strong under that curly beard. His black hair had been combed straight back and hung in waves at his collar. Currently, those dark brows rode extra low on eyes that were black as night. He looked put out, as well he should. Suzannah loved her sister, but sometimes she interfered where she wasn't wanted. She hoped that would be a good thing for the Cooper men, since she couldn't seem to help herself.

"What?" Jake barked, never taking his eyes off the road.

She'd been staring. He'd felt it. All of a sudden, she knew what she wanted to offer him. Comfort. To let him know she understood Rebecca had meddled. She reached out and patted his shoulder, feeling the warmth of solid muscle under her palm; there was tension there, as well. She understood. He'd been summoned to drive, not only the two horses all the way to Wyoming, but two women as well; one who couldn't speak and blundered at flirting, the other who clearly intruded where she didn't belong.

Jake dipped his brows lower yet, then turned his head. When he caught the look in her eyes, he narrowed his own, then jerked his gaze back to the road.

What did he think he had seen there?

They rode on in absolute silence, except for an occasional cough or slurp of cold coffee. After a dozen or so minutes they seemed to, one by one, relax their postures and enjoy the ride. The landscape was surprisingly flat and sparse, reminding Suzannah of Idaho's terrain, though she knew they were higher in altitude. Since it was summer, the grasses were dry, the land more desolate. There was some greenery along the way, but not what she'd expected. She imagined what it must be like when the snow arrived and the land was blanketed in the sparkling white of winter. A feeling of peace seeped through her as they whizzed along. Or maybe it was how she felt sitting next to Jake in spite of his mood—safe and content. She even thought the lump in her throat had eased a bit.

The sparse surroundings soon gave way to a landscape of buildings here and there. Jake slowed at the outskirts of town, automatically lifting his hand to the gearshift knob. Suzannah stiffened, pushed her backside into the seat, and widened her legs. This time it was to give him plenty of room to maneuver without having to touch her. It wasn't easy to avoid his touch as he shifted into second, but she wanted to shout joyously when the task was accomplished. A glance in his direction conveyed he hadn't given it a thought.

Before long, Jake pulled into the parking lot of Connolly Saddlery, careful to park the rig and trailer along one side and out of the way.

Jake unlatched his door, stepped out, and turned. "Be a few minutes. You lasses need anything?"

Suzannah glanced at her sister.

Rebecca shook her head, then pulled her hair back against the breeze through the open door and looked back down the road. "Well, on second thought, it depends. Are we stopping for lunch after this?"

Jake groaned. "Aye, I suppose." He retrieved his hat from behind the seat and pressed it low on his brow, then shoved the door shut and stomped off toward the saddle shop.

Both girls watched him walk away until he disappeared through the building's front door. Rebecca twisted to face Suzannah. "Okay, give. We don't have much time, and I want to hear it all."

Suzannah frowned, wondering what 'all' meant from her big sister this time. It was a rare moment when she could keep up with everything that crossed Rebecca's mind. She thought of Cooper Ranch and knew Rebecca would need that particular ability to stay ahead of a household of seven men. But for now, Suzannah was her target, and she wanted nothing more than to get off her radar.

Suzannah shrugged in the way she did when she wanted to convey her confusion.

Rebecca lit into her. "You know exactly what I want to talk to you about. Two things really. What was that little game you were playing with Jake, letting your body slide into him like that? Watch yourself around that man, Suzannah. He's... I don't know. Dark, mysterious. Maybe dangerous. I like him, but you're much too innocent to be egging on a man like him. You know?"

Suzannah huffed a breath and glared at Rebecca. Rebecca was the one who didn't get men. She always fell into trouble since she didn't understand the creatures. As for herself, she might be the broken sister, but she got what men were about.

Rebecca ignored Suzannah's response, like she so often did. "And why wouldn't you let me ask him what made him quit the foreman's job at Coleman's? We could have gotten some insight into the man."

Suzannah jumped onto the second question, hoping the first would be forgotten. She was not the least bit afraid of Jake, but she would never be able to explain why she knew he wasn't dangerous. Rebecca wouldn't get it. She thought about how to answer her second question, and then sighed as the sadness of Jake's situation washed over her.

Rebecca was keen and intuitive. By the look in her eye, she knew something serious was about to be revealed. Her calm voice came through. "Tell me, Suzannah. You can do it. What happened to Jake?"

Of all her family members, Rebecca was the best at deciphering how to frame a question for Suzannah to get as much information as possible without a verbal reply. That is, when she wasn't in the mood to force the words out.

"He's obviously had something bad happen to him. Did Coleman fire him?"

Suzannah shook her head, started to try her first word, but as usual, Rebecca plowed forward.

"He hurt someone, then. Beat up a ranch hand?"

Suzannah sighed, and jumped in. "No." It was a good strong sound and hadn't hurt her throat.

"Don't tell me he stole something, because I won't believe it, Suzannah." Rebecca lowered her brows into one of her reprimanding frowns. "I don't know much about him, but I'm pretty certain he's not that kind of guy."

"No," Suzannah repeated.

"No. I don't imagine it was anything illegal. Girl-friend?" Rebecca's gaze centered on the shop's front doors, clearly watching for the man they were gossiping about. "Maybe he's delusional. Seeing wee fairies?" She laughed at that, but when she looked back at Suzannah and saw her sorrowful expression, she stopped.

Then Suzannah saw her wheels begin to spin again. She needed to put a stop to Rebecca's love of mystery. This could go on and on. She rested a hand to Rebecca's face to hold her in place. Whenever she spoke, she didn't want to have to repeat it. "Wife... "

"He probably—" The seat bounced as the news sank in and Rebecca gripped the seat back. "*What?* Jake's married? *Our* Jake? That man in there?" She pointed to the saddle company. "*Married?*"

Suzannah ran a hand down her face, swallowed once, and concentrated. "Was married. Wife disappeared... during the quake."

"What? Oh my gosh, Suzannah. I had no idea. The poor man. How did she disappear? Was she in town shopping or something when it hit? What happened?" Then she was finally quiet.

Suzannah rolled her eyes. This was going to take some doing to explain. She wished she had a paper and pencil to write it out. She inhaled a great breath, letting the air out in a whoosh. "Driving... Jake found her car..." Suzannah stopped, squeezed her eyes closed to the pain, then opened them to a wheezed breath and began again. "Door open over stream... no Betty... no body..." Another big breath. "He looks every morning... at dawn."

Rebecca gripped Suzannah's elbows, turning her in the seat to face her. Her leg caught against the gearshift, but she left it there, and turned as best she could. "Oh my gosh, Suze. The poor man."

"She was pregnant."

Rebecca sucked in a loud gasp, thunderstruck. Jaw hanging, she stayed that way for many agonizing seconds. Suzannah knew how she felt. The same sense of grief had taken her when she first found out.

Rebecca rubbed her palms up and down Suzannah's arms, both in praise for her efforts and in comfort for her pain, as she'd done a hundred times before. "Oh, the poor, poor man. Has he found any evidence yet?" Rebecca continued her caress as she peered into Suzannah's face.

Suzannah shook her head with a twist of her mouth, showing she really didn't know but didn't think so.

"No wonder he's so standoffish. No wonder he doesn't want you touching him, or him you."

That fact centered against Suzannah's heart and tore out a painful chunk. Why hadn't she thought that through before now? Jake was a married man. If he couldn't find his wife, or evidence that she had died, he'd still consider himself married. As well he should. It was no wonder he stayed at arm's length from her. Any honorable man would act as he had. A deep flood of heat filled her face. How foolish had she been?

Rebecca stiffened, grabbed Suzannah's elbows and faced her forward. Suzannah rubbed at the dent the gearshift had made on her leg as she watched Jake come toward them, a shined up saddle fixed between his grip on the cantle and the pommel at his torso.

"Don't act any different. We don't want him to think we've been talking about him," Rebecca said.

Suzannah wanted to laugh at the posture Rebecca had taken, with her back straight against the seat and her hands folded in her lap. Well, if that wasn't suspicious looking, she didn't know what was.

A clunk and small dip of the springs alerted her that Jake had hoisted the saddle into the truck bed. A few more bumps as he shifted his prize into the corner, and then the driver's door swung open. Jake yanked the hat off his head and threaded it through the small space behind the seat. He ran a hand through his hair while he looked them over. Suzannah gave him a smile. His brow twitched, and his eyes subtly narrowed. His gaze passed Suzannah to Rebecca, and then he actually frowned in earnest. Amazing. Emotion. On Jake's face.

"What's up?" he said as he gripped the steering wheel and hoisted himself up behind it.

No one spoke.

Jake glanced at them again. "What're you lasses up to now?"

Astonishing. Could he really tell from one glance they were hiding something? What amazing instincts he had. Suzannah glanced over at Rebecca. Yeah, she looked pretty guilty. And, maybe her own smile had given him the wrong impression, as well. She swung back to look him in the eye, then said, "We're hungry." She was delighted the words had come forth so easily, as they seemed to more and more around this man.

He looked a little stunned, but nodded once and switched on the key. "We'll pick up lunch at a hamburger joint, and water the horses." With a toe, he compressed the starter. Since it hadn't been long since the truck had been on, it started with one turn.

He looked at the gearshift with the expression of one set to take on a rattler.

Suzannah didn't take offense. Now that God had reminded her of his wife, she planned to focus only on helping him discover if the woman was still alive. As Jake reached for the shifter, Suzannah scooted deep into the seat back and stretched her legs wide. Her thigh accidentally touched him and reflex made her slap her legs together. Right on his hand.

He didn't move, like an animal trapped, wanting to be anywhere but here.

She whispered, "Sorry." And, as if moving slowly would keep anything more from happening, Suzannah widened her legs inch by inch, just enough to release his hand. Then, very carefully she situated her knees just so, as if to ensure they weren't going to cause anymore trouble.

Jake's large hand encompassed the shifter and jammed it into first. In his haste, he slipped the clutch. The truck leapt forward and died, rocking the vehicle on its rubber. He cursed loudly and checked the rearview mirror. When he seemed satisfied the horses were fine, he heaved a breath and tried again.

Suzannah studied his profile as he drove out onto the street, noticing his true despondency for the first time. Outwardly, he acted as if he couldn't get out of here fast enough. But could his desire be deeper than that? To perish and be done with it? Is that why he broke horses for Roy? She shuddered at the revelation that seemed to have come from out of the blue. *From you, Lord?*

Her mind had taken her far away, so when Jake spoke, she'd missed what he said. Thankfully, he wasn't used to her talking anyway.

Rebecca took care of it, elbowing Suzannah in the ribs as she said, "Sure, Dairy Queen is fine, right, Suzannah?"

Jake glanced at her, and she nodded. He nodded back, and soon Jake maneuvered the truck and trailer onto a tree-lined street close to the hamburger joint. Jake swung the door open and jumped out. He reached to his back pocket for his wallet, opened it, and retrieved a few bills, just as Suzannah was scooting out the door after him. "Here," he said as he thrust a few bills in her palm. "I'll water the horses and add to their net feed. You get the burgers. No cheese on mine. And a strawberry shake."

He turned toward the back of the trailer and strode off. Suzannah opened her hand to the bills he'd stuffed there and thought, this was the first normal thing Jake had done since she'd met him. A smile came over her as she closed her hand back over the bills and traipsed across the side street to the window of the stand.

"How can I help you?" the young woman with a brown uniform said behind the open window.

Suzannah's mouth gaped. She'd been so caught up in Jake's request for a simple meal, she'd forgotten all about her inability to order it. Anger surged up her throat, threatening to come out in a scream. It wasn't fair, this infernal throat of hers. There was no threat of

Thomas here, so why couldn't she get her vocal cords to work properly?

"Ma'am?" the girl said again.

She wanted to do this. To prove she was a woman capable of handling the small things in life. She would! "Um... " The sound barely registered to her own ears. She cleared her throat and refused to give up. "Three burgers... and... " She'd forced it, making her sound angry.

Rebecca came up behind her. "What are you doing, Suzannah? I'll do this."

Suzannah whipped around and glared Rebecca down until she backed a step. "Okay. It's okay, Suze. Go ahead."

Rebecca stroked Suzannah's back. That calming spirit of hers always helped. Suzannah glanced back at her in thanks, and when she did, she saw Jake across the narrow street at the back of the trailer, standing in a warrior's stance with the bucket forgotten at his feet. He looked ready to take on someone. For her? The girl behind the window maybe? Rebecca?

In that instant, she knew... She had to do this. To please this big, broken man with the small request he had made of her. This man who was willing to plod forward even when he probably preferred to check out and meet his Maker.

She turned back, breathed in and out a few breaths, then speared the young attendant with her determined gaze. "No cheese on one." She swallowed, breathed. "One strawberry mil—milkshake." She smiled, so pleased with herself, she could have soared.

"Okay. Anything else?"

Suzannah dropped her gaze, searched her mind for what she'd forgotten. Yes, she needed a drink... and Rebecca...

She turned to Rebecca, but her sister had already stepped in close so the girl could hear her. "Yes. A coca cola. Suzannah?" She looked at her with one eyebrow raised. "Do you want one?"

Suzannah nodded and breathed a sigh of relief. Good. It was done.

"Your number is thirteen. It'll be about ten minutes."

Rebecca smiled at the girl, then swung an arm around Suzannah's waist and walked her off toward tables set up under a canopy. "See there? You did great."

Great. Yeah, just great. She sat and planted her elbows on the picnic tabletop as Rebecca threaded her legs into the space across from her.

Suzannah grabbed her sister's hands and held them tight. "Help me."

Alarmed, Rebecca dropped her smile of praise. "What's wrong?"

Suzannah pulled together strength from somewhere, and began. "I want to speak. Like... a normal..."

Her sister jumped in, as she always did. "I know you do, Suzannah. You are improving. My goodness, you have talked more on this trip than I've heard in a long time, and—"

Suzannah pulled her hands off Rebecca's and brought them down on the table with a slap, making Rebecca jump. "Stop."

Rebecca looked contrite. "I'm coddling again, aren't I?"

Suzannah nodded, then smiled ruefully. "You care." She patted Rebecca's hands this time, then ventured further. "Jake makes me feel..."

"Flushed?" Rebecca said with a smile. "Sorry. I'll stop. Go on."

"Safe."

"Really? I'd have thought he scared you. I mean, look at him." Her gaze left Suzannah and wandered across the street.

Suzannah looked there too, and saw the cowboy lounging against the truck with arms crossed.

"Him leaning against that red truck reminds me of a black and red viper snake." Rebecca visibly shuddered, then looked back at her. "He's huge, and he wears those black clothes *all* the time. Not to mention his eyes and hair are black as crows. And that beard; Suzannah, it's the same as Thomas's—" She halted, stiffened. "I'm sorry. I didn't mean to bring up the slime-ball."

Suzannah waved off the mistake. "You like Jake, though." She was whispering now, and it was working. At least it worked with her sister.

Rebecca heaved a sigh. "Yes, I do. But he's too powerful for you. In mind *and* body."

Suzannah's hand smacked the table again, making Rebecca focus on her. She jabbed a finger into her own sternum. "I'm not weak, big sister."

A look of regret covered Rebecca's face. "I know. I know. It's just… it's just, I want to protect you."

"Stop that." Suzannah gave her a look of reproof, very similar to the ones she constantly received from her older sisters. "I'm grown. And Jake's not dangerous."

Rebecca took Suzannah's hands in hers and squeezed. She looked her directly in the eye. "Have you asked God for help, Suze?"

Suzannah glanced away, swallowed. "Not lately."

"Why not?"

"I asked. His answer is no," she whispered.

"I know sometimes His answer is *no*. But many times, his answer is *wait*. Don't you think it's time you asked again? You wanted my help. Well, dear sister, my help is this: Ask God again for healing. And if He doesn't grant physical healing, then He'll provide the means to cope with what He deems necessary for you to brave."

Suzannah stared in astonishment. Rebecca's words were so profound. Yet... no, she couldn't risk God saying no. Again. Tugging to extract her hands, she found resistance. Rebecca wouldn't let go. She just locked her eyes to Suzannah's until Suzannah had no choice but to look away.

"Number thirteen," crackled over the loud speaker.

Suzannah jumped to her feet and pulled her legs out from the bench seat, clearing her mind. She hurried forward and picked up Jake's milkshake and the bag of burgers. Rebecca had followed and retrieved the two sodas.

Suzannah stepped off the curb to cross the street to Jake. *Jake*. She had the bag of burgers and Jake's change in one hand, the milkshake in the other, but her mind was focused on the man watching her walk toward him. Rebecca was right. At this moment, Jake did look dangerous as he stood there lazily lounging against the truck with brawny arms crossed and dark eyes inspecting her every move. Though his face resembled a chiseled block of stone, his gaze was wandering up from her boots, past her snug jeans and apricot-colored blouse, straight to her hair. It lingered there, where her french braid began, then seemed to trail every multicolored strand to its end. He never once gave a glance to Rebecca, and that thought thrilled Suzannah.

When she was nearly upon him, his attention shifted ever so briefly to her lips, then snapped back to her eyes as quick as a rubber band.

She stopped when she was toe-to-toe, head-to-chest with him, and tilted her chin up to look him in the eyes. With her heart beating double time, she stretched out the arm that held the milkshake. He wrapped his fingers around the cup, trapping hers beneath, and for a moment her life felt perfectly balanced between the icy chill in her palm and the pervading warmth in his. He closed his eyes, then opened them to their joint hold on the milkshake. He didn't seem ready to bolt, and that surprised her. It was several long moments before he moved, slowly lifting his hand, keeping his grasp on the shake with only his fingertips until she was able to slip her hand out from under his.

She raised her eyes to his, searching for a thread of emotion caused by their touch. It wasn't there in his eyes, but the despondency clearly was. Her heart wrenched for him, this man who nine months after losing his wife seemed to be sinking deeper into despair.

Betty was gone. Suzannah either had to help him find out what happened to her, or help him forget her. She made that vow to herself, along with a vow to work harder on her own physical affliction. Determination sank in, fueled by the man looking down into her face. For him, for her, she would do this.

Then, as delicately as a dove's wings, a whisper of a thought interrupted her own single-mindedness. *You'll need My help*, it said. And, for the first time in over six years—half of which she'd enjoyed Thomas, the other half of which she'd lived in terror of him—she gave it over to the Almighty.

At long last, she acknowledged the truth: Apart from Jesus, she could do nothing.

CHAPTER 9

Thomas scraped back his chair and lowered himself into it. He used to hate these little *chats* his father insisted on having around the kitchen table. But since he'd become an adult, he looked forward to them. Father actually saw him as an equal now, the second in command of the family. He would do anything to keep that hard earned status.

Well, nearly anything.

As if to punctuate his one remaining fear, a whine came from the backyard.

Father glanced to the door and scowled, then refocused on reading today's news.

Thomas's gut twisted. Why hadn't his mother put the yellow Lab back in her kennel? How was he expected to slip away now to do the task when their weekly family meeting was about to begin? Thomas glowered at his mother. She caught his gaze but didn't look the least bit contrite. Odd. She turned her back on him to finish her task. Thomas watched his mother's bony back shift as she made Father's favorite meeting lunch—peanut butter and grape jelly sandwiches—then carried them to the table. With rote movements she opened the cupboard to collect three glasses.

Another whine split the silence. A scratch on the screen door and Thomas nearly wet his pants. *Shut-up, Sally!* Thomas reached tentative fingers up to swipe away a bead of sweat before it slipped away from his temple to travel his jawline. The time his father forced him to hit his dog was never far from his mind. He had just turned twelve. The look on Sally's sweet canine face had nearly destroyed him. It had taken him weeks to regain her trust. He would never—*ever*—do it again, even if his father demanded it. Until now, he'd made sure Sally was in her kennel whenever Father was home. Today his mother had let him down.

Retrieving the milk from the refrigerator, Mother brought that next, along with the three glasses. Her hand shook as she opened the spout and poured each glass exactly one-half inch from the brim, as his father always insisted. Thomas breathed more easily. That was her usual behavior; doing a task to Father's perfection and trembling through it.

Father lifted one of the sandwiches, took a sniff inside, and grimaced. "I told you to get a different brand of grape jelly!" Father barked. "This one doesn't smell right." He slammed it back to the plate, sloshing the perfectly poured milk from all three glasses. "Now, look what you've made me do, you fool," Father yelled at Mother. "Don't just stand there like a worthless statue! Get the dish cloth."

Thomas stiffened in learned reaction, then forced himself to visibly relax before his father noticed. He sent a scowl his mother's direction. From the day he'd turned eighteen, his father expected him to react to his mother as he did. He got praise when he did that, instead of the usual backhand across the face.

"Sorry," Thomas barely heard his mother say as she scampered over to the sink, her limp day dress twisting around her bony hips.

He used to feel sorry for his mother. Not so anymore. Especially when she so blatantly disregarded simple tasks like making sure his dog was safe. Or buying the correct brand of jelly.

Father ignored her for the moment, settling an intent look on Thomas.

Thomas tried real hard not to squirm in his seat. Father didn't tolerate that. "Where's Suzannah, son?" the man said, calm and perfectly collected.

Careful now. You need the right answer. The one he wants to hear. Thomas didn't get slapped as often anymore, once he'd become a man. "Uh…" That was bad. Father hated hesitation. Thomas coughed. "She's gone, Father."

"What do you mean, gone?"

Delaying, Thomas picked up his plate so his mother could clean under it.

"Leave her to that." Father flicked his hand dismissively in the air. "When you help her, she only gets weaker."

For emphasis, Father dipped his chin and scowled up into Mother's downturned face. "You need to toughen up, Margaret. Stop acting so blasted scared all the time!"

His mother nodded, her hand shaking all the more as she worked to gather every drop of spilled milk off the table.

Father's eyes swung back to him. Thomas quickly met his gaze, but not before he'd glimpsed his mother's fingers tighten into a fist around the dish cloth. A small dot of milk squeezed back onto the table.

"Where is your fiancé, Thomas?"

Thomas faltered, caught between his mother's unusual behavior and his father's loaded question. Father thought Suzannah was to be his bride. Thomas did, too, until...

Father didn't know Suzannah had taken him to court. Thomas ran clammy hands down his jeans. If the man ever found out—

Father smacked his thigh, done waiting.

"She's gone to her uncle's ranch for a vacation," Thomas blurted. Then in a smoother voice, he said, "She'll be back."

Father rose out of the chair so fast, Thomas's first instinct was to cover his face. But no. He must never do that again.

Though Father was graying—and had grown a good-sized paunch—the man was still formidable. Then again, Thomas could hold his own now. Physically, at least. He puffed up a little over that thought.

Father leaned in, positioning his face closer to Thomas than was comfortable, though the table still separated them. "For how long?"

Thomas felt his throat close up. He coughed again to loosen everything. "She…"

He didn't know. But he wouldn't let on. Trying his best to sound nonchalant, he said, "Oh, three weeks or so, maybe."

Father narrowed his eyes. "During this conversation, you've used the words, 'uh', 'think', 'don't know', and 'maybe'. What have I told you about weak words, Thomas?"

"Uh…" He flinched, started again. "She went to her uncle's wedding." Thomas found that out when he'd marched into the orphanage where Suzannah volunteered and pressed a meek little co-worker into a closet to extract the information. She sang like a canary.

"Without *you*?"

"Well, yeah—I mean, yes, Sir. She went with her family. That conniving mother of hers married off one daughter to a cowboy, so I'm sure she thought to do so with another." Thomas was still disgusted at Jessica's weak obedience to the woman of that household.

Father's eyes flared, and Thomas realized his mistake. He should have never revealed such a possibility about Suzannah. Thomas did his best to not look away, only to be distracted by the bouquet of drooping sunflowers on the counter beyond Father's left ear. The neglected flowers convinced Thomas he couldn't have seen defiance and anger in his mother's expression earlier. After all, the useless woman couldn't even dump out dead flowers in a vase without being told.

Or get his dog to safety.

At least Sally had settled down outside.

"What did I do, Thomas, when your mother thought to run off on *vacation* ten years ago? Huh, Thomas? What did you see a *man* do about it?"

A quiver went up Thomas's spine before he could stiffen enough to keep it from happening. Thankfully, Father didn't seem to notice. "You went after her and dragged her back."

"I. Went. After. Her. Yes. To bring her back home where she belonged." The man's unrelenting stare was burning Thomas's eyes. But for the first time, he noticed Father's eyes looked rheumy. Was he sick? Nah. Just getting old. One day Thomas would reign. If he could survive the present, he'd have a great future. After he put his mother in an institution. And had Suzannah by his side.

"What are you going to do about Suzannah, Thomas? Be a man, or go back to boyhood? Because if you're going to do that… "

His father raised up the back of his hand, and held it there.

The message was clear. And, he'd never—*not ever*—go back to being a boy. It was one reason he insisted on having a full beard. To prove he was a man. To show he was a man. "I already planned to go after her, Father," he lied.

His father brightened and lowered his hand.

Thomas wasn't quite sure how yet. But he'd learned ways to manipulate Suzannah. He was pretty good at it by now. As long as her old self-confidence hadn't returned. "I thought to leave tomorrow." By then he'd have his plan for dismantling the last of Suzannah's resistance all worked out.

Thomas glanced over Father's shoulder to his mother at the sink. She'd been listening with her head hung low, bracing her hands against the edge. As he watched, she shuddered once, then as if reborn, drew herself upright and squared her shoulders.

Stunned, Thomas almost missed it when a huge smile lit his father's face.

And Thomas loved it when he made the old man smile.

CHAPTER 10

Suzannah watched the large hand grip the gearshift between her knees, as Jake had done for every curve and after each stop for the entire trip. He nudged the shifter over slightly, and, as he pulled it back to third gear—for the umpteenth time—his knuckles raked her inner thigh yet again. The truck lurched, but steadied under Jake's cool recovery. Though he wasn't outwardly overreacting to the intimate touch anymore, his tension had grown palpable. She was sure he'd explode if they didn't arrive at their destination soon.

Blam! The truck swerved. Rebecca squealed. Suzannah slid, bouncing against Jake, then Rebecca, though Rebecca had a strong hold on her. She clung to her sister, trying her best to stay out of Jake's way. Jake muscled the steering wheel like it was one of his wild broncs, using his strength to bring the vehicle under control. Flat tire? Something broken off the trailer? Were the horses safe? Suzannah's mind swarmed around possibilities, all the while wondering if this was the day they would meet Jesus face to face.

Her gazed camped on Jake. They had just left Sheridan, Wyoming, on their way to Sundance where the

Cooper spread was located, so thankfully the terrain was again pretty flat. Jake was eyeing the rearview mirror every few seconds, while at the same time looking for a place to pull over. She saw his gaze lock briefly to a spot up ahead. Following where his eyes led her, she saw what looked like a dirt road leading to a spread of some kind.

When he slowed enough to make that turn onto the narrow roadway, Rebecca piped up. "What happened, Jake? Do we have a flat?"

"Aye. On the trailer," Jake said as he slowly maneuvered the truck down a gradual grade in the road.

"Why aren't we stopping? Shouldn't you look?"

Jake ignored Rebecca's inquiry and continued to follow the dirt road as it dropped down and wound around a copse of ponderosa and bristlecone pines, and then a row of chokecherries. They looked like a windbreak of sorts. Sure enough, as they coasted past them, a beautiful two-story home appeared, nestled amongst another slew of pines.

Rebecca looked to ask more questions. Suzannah stopped her with a hand to her leg. "He knows them."

Jake's head crooked in her direction, a surprised look on his face. She smiled at him, then glanced back at Rebecca and saw the same curious expression on her face. "How do you know Jake knows them?" Her sister leaned forward to better see Jake. "*Do* you know them?"

"Of them," Jake said.

"Huh," Rebecca commented. "How did you know that, Suze?"

"Logic," Suzannah said, and smiled at her sister.

"What do you mean, logic? I swear, you have a sixth sense or something. You always know stuff no one else knows."

Suzannah shook her head. "No talking... observation," she managed in a fairly loud voice.

Jake seemed pleased. That pleased her. "Aye, the lass is right. Stop talking, and you learn," Jake said, his eyes straight ahead.

Rebecca frowned, not one to take criticism well. "I do listen. Just 'cuz you two don't talk doesn't mean it's normal," Rebecca bit out, then looked instantly repentant. "I'm sorry, Suze. I didn't mean—"

Suzannah stopped her with two fingers to her lips. "Can't keep apologizing. I'll get better."

This time both Jake and Rebecca gaped at her like she'd grown an extra nose. Sometimes words came that easily. The truck took a dip and a loud *clank* followed. Jake's attention flew back to the road, but he still didn't put on the brakes.

Once they had stopped bouncing in the seat, Rebecca continued on. She rarely gave up on a thought pattern until its completion, and this was no exception. "Okay. Back to the logic statement, Suze. And since you apparently can talk… do so."

"It's obvious," Suzannah said. "He's driving…" she had to pause here. Swallow. "… to their house."

"So, you're saying he wouldn't drive in unless he knew them?"

"There were others," Suzannah said.

"Others? Like other places to stop, you mean?"

Suzannah nodded and smiled.

"Oh. This one was a little out of the way. I see. A good observation," Rebecca said with wonder.

Suzannah glanced at Jake and saw a crinkle at the corner of his eyes. Was that an almost smile?

"Aye. As we said." Then he turned his head and caught her gaze before he once again looked ahead.

The road leveled out to the private drive of the homestead. Jake pulled around the half circle in front of the house and stopped behind a group of assorted vehicles. Some were shiny new cars, others work trucks. Jake hopped out just as a man of medium height and build, with a crop of unruly gray hair, came from around the side of the house to greet them. His gait was confident, his clothes typical for a ranch hand, but something about his bearing told Suzannah this was the man in charge.

Curious, and achy from dodging Jake's hand at the gearshift, Suzannah piled out after Jake. She came up behind him just as he was shaking the rancher's hand. Jake towered over the man, but it didn't seem to faze the older fellow one bit.

"Mr. Wheeler. Name's Jake Cooper. My uncle has a spread out Sundance way."

The man shook Jake's hand. "Call me Troy, Jake. Have we met before? You seem to know me."

"Nae. Been at a couple auctions you were at, is all."

"Ah. I see." The rancher pulled Jake closer and gave him a hearty smack on the shoulder. "I know your uncle. Cord's a good man. Good to meet up with his nephew. What brings you out our way?"

"Was heading to Cooper Ranch and blew a tire on the trailer. With two horses. Didna want to risk the rest of the drive that way."

Mr. Wheeler—Troy—frowned at that thought, moved past Jake, and bent to look. Jake indicated with a sweep of his hand to go around. Troy rose and skirted the back of the trailer. Jake followed.

Suzannah remained where she was, listening to the muffled masculine dialogue and staring at the gorgeous house before her. It had the most unusual shape, as if they'd started with the main two stories facing the drive, attached a larger two-story unit facing south, and a two-car garage on the other end facing north. The whole of it was unique and beautiful, surrounded by pines and chokecherry trees.

Jake and Troy shuffled back around, still deep in conversation, this time about the horses inside the trailer.

"I'll have one of my men pull her around to the barn," Troy said.

"I'll stay with them. I can fix the trailer. We've a spare tire. Just need a place to unload the horses."

"Jake, my groomsmen can handle the horses. They know what they're doing, son. No need to worry. You and your passengers come join us for supper."

Jake looked uneasy. "The gelding's a nipper."

"The groomsmen have handled biters before, guaranteed." Troy looked to Suzannah then. "And who might you be, young lady?"

He reached out a hand to her. She shook it, and opened her mouth to speak, but Jake interjected. "That's Suzannah Harper, Roy's niece. Another niece is in the cab."

Just then Rebecca marched around the grill and came forward. Her hand was already out, and before she even shook, she said, "I'm Rebecca Harper. It's nice to meet you, Mr. Wheeler."

He cringed and shook his head. Taking her hand, he said, "Troy to you, young lady. Not old enough to be Mr. Wheeler, yet." He gave a hearty laugh. "Good to meet ya. Your uncle is kind of famous. Big spread. Cattle. Now selling some of the best horses in these here parts."

Suzannah beamed at the praise that was really Jake's. She patted his arm, surprising him. He glanced down at her. "Jake…" she started, but couldn't finish. The word had come out raspy. She'd done so well in the truck, she'd forgotten her impairment for a minute. Stupid, stupid. She hated how weak it made her sound.

Rebecca took over as always. "Yes. Jake is Uncle Roy's horse man. He breaks the horses and trains them. Or, re-trains them, as the case may be."

Suzannah wanted so badly to have been the one to give Jake the praise. There was more she would have added. Like how lately he'd been working with damaged horses. Ones people had given up on and would have put down. She'd heard from the cowhands how Jake could never quite give up on an animal. Any animal. The one-eyed kitty came to mind and she felt another warm glow flood through her.

So many men looked the part of clean-cut rancher on the outside. They dressed impeccably, shaved everyday, wore cropped hair and bright colors, and yet could be as black as the ace of spades on the inside. Jake was just the opposite. Black as sin on the outside, good as gold on the inside.

Suzannah pondered that thought, not for the first time. What he portrayed on the outside was how he felt about himself. By his appearance, she figured by now his self-hate ran in deep channels, carved deeper everyday.

"Come on y'all. Bea's been cooking up a storm all morning. Should be one of her best." He spun around and headed up the stone walkway to the front door.

That surprised Suzannah, since today was Saturday, and usually ranchers were busy—and dirty—most everyday but Sunday. Then again, as Suzannah watched Troy leap up two steps to the porch, she finally noticed his clothes weren't everyday wear after all, but seemed to be his Sunday best.

He opened one side of the double front doors and stepped over the threshold. He held the door open for the rest to follow. The moment she stepped in, the glorious smell of barbecue sauce filled her nostrils, making her stomach growl. A look around the vaulted ceiling and the reason for Troy's attire became clear. There were dozens of balloons riding the heavy beams, streamers as their tails, and a multitude of other birthday decorations attached here and there throughout the entire living space. It was light and festive, bringing a smile to her face. She watched Jake carefully, hoping such a celebratory array would coax a smile out of him. It wasn't to be, though, and that made her sadder yet for him.

She would help this man find his smile, if it took the next decade... or two.

"Come on in." Troy swung around, facing the open kitchen. "Bea! Found some guests." He beamed at the busy woman in the kitchen, her gray hair bobbing with a nod and her frail hands drying off on a ruffled apron that was wrapped twice around her stick frame. She smiled, eyes twinkling, and went about setting more places at the decorative table. A huge cake sat in the center, a bucking bull etched into the icing and a *Happy Birthday, Looney* written across the bottom in bright red frosting.

Three men banged through the door and filled the kitchen's remaining open space. They had to be Troy's sons since they all resembled him and looked to be in their twenties. Maybe Bea was their grandmother?

"Boys," Troy said. "I'd like you ta meet Cord Cooper's nephew." He swung a hand in Jake's direction. "This here's Jake." He turned toward Suzannah and her sister. "These two are Roy Harper's nieces. Suzie was it?" Suzannah smiled and nodded, not able to correct him anyway. "And her sister, Rebecca."

The three men stepped forward and shook Jake's hand, one by one, giving their names along with the shake. Suzannah immediately forgot their names since her focus was on Jake's face. Likely just being cordial, his face had managed a friendly look. Almost pleasant. He repeated each name back as they shook hands. They were all dressed in their cowboy best, and each one was handsome in their own way, Suzannah thought. She wondered why none of them sported wedding rings or made mention of a spouse, or girlfriend for that matter.

Suzannah and Rebecca nodded at the men, but didn't offer their hands. Rebecca asked, "So, whose birthday is it?"

"Bill's here," one of the men said. "He's the baby of the family. Finally hit that whoppin' twenty-one-year-old mark. We'll be going drinkin' tonight, for sure and for certain."

Troy seemed on the verge of discussing the matter further, then just shook his head and dipped his hat toward the gray-haired woman. "This is our cook, Bea. She practically raised these boys. Couldn't of made it without her."

That statement made Suzannah think of her sister's new arrangement. She'd be walking in where a beloved cook and housekeeper had been for as many years as Bea had probably been here. Even as a young woman, Rebecca would be expected to take over and keep seven men happy. Suzannah's chest swelled with pride in her sister. It would be a difficult task, but if anyone could do it, Rebecca could. Though time would only tell how successful she'd be.

Once the older Wheeler had shown his guests to the bathroom to wash up, they returned to the main living room. Suzannah was now enjoying a splendid view of the grounds through extra large windows at the back of the house. Green lawn was surrounded by a hedge of tall, lush trees.

"Come, everyone. Sit," Troy announced.

As the four men parked themselves in what Suzannah figured was their usual spots, the rest of them found an empty chair and settled in.

Troy picked up a platter of spareribs drenched in barbecue sauce, took two, and passed it to his right. That seemed to be the signal for everyone to reach for the bowl or platter before them. They helped themselves first, then passed their particular dish to the right, the same as their dad. Jake, Rebecca, and Suzannah followed suit, and soon everyone was enjoying a delightful meal and casual conversation, mostly about cattle, horses, or hard work. Suzannah noticed that Jake didn't talk much, as usual, but did interject with mostly one word answers when asked a question.

After they finished their meal, Bea brought in a knife to cut the cake.

"Wait," Rebecca piped up. "I must know, I assume Bill here is Looney? There's a story behind this bucking bull on your cake. Confession time, Looney." She arched an eyebrow in challenge and smiled at the young man.

While Bea cut the cake and added a scoop of ice cream to each plate, Troy grinned. "Well, son?"

Looking a bit sheepish, Bill—Looney—merely dropped his eyes to his plate and dug in to the extra large chunk of cake.

"He's not gonna tell you, so I will," his eldest brother said. "Little brother here is a bull rider in any and all rodeos he can talk Pa into letting him enter. He's pretty good, but since he's been riding anything with four legs around here since he was two, we nicknamed him Looney way back. It stuck. It should, since he's crazy enough to ride the impossible ones now."

They all laughed and elbowed him, or knuckled his hair good-naturedly.

"Not only that," Troy said over a chuckle. "He's big on bringing strays home. Every kind of animal you can think of. Even a skunk once."

They all laughed again.

"Even stray women," the eldest son said around a chuckle.

Another of the sons piped up. "I remember that woman. Near a year ago now. She snuck in the back of his truck."

"We thought he'd lost his mind for sure that time," the eldest said.

"All the way from Sheridan. Crazy fool. Never even saw her in the bed," another supplied, then jammed an elbow in Looney's side as they jostled him back and forth.

Troy nodded. "Come to think of it, poor thing ate like she was half starved even though she was a chubby little thing." Troy's smile dropped off, and he looked disturbed all of a sudden. "I still don't get why she up and left before dawn that next morning. I told her we'd help her out."

"She snuck into my truck bed when I was paying for gas," Looney said. "And, she wasn't fat, Pa. She was pregnant."

Jake's chair slid back, screeching loudly against the wood floor. All eyes swung to him. He sat ramrod straight against the chair back. He didn't say a thing, but his tanned face had blanched nearly white.

"What month?" Jake snapped.

"What?" Looney asked, looking mighty uncomfortable under Jake's scrutiny.

"What month was it you picked up this lass?"

Looney shifted in his seat, ran a hand down his face. "Same month as Montana's big earthquake, I think. I don't know. When was it, Pa? You remember?"

"Heck, all I remember is her leaving a note of thanks in one of our coffee mugs. Right in the center of our table where Looney's cake is now."

Jake jumped to his feet so fast his chair crashed backwards to the floor and slid two strides away. Suzannah had never seen such emotion on this man's face. His body seemed to have doubled in size, and his face had distorted into a mix of agony and hope all at the same time.

Suzannah leapt up with him. She knew beyond doubt Jake thought this woman was his wife. Her heart went out to him, wanting to calm him, soothe him, all while it wrenched at the thought he might find her and Suzannah would never be more to him than an awkward acquaintance.

But if her word were true, the time had come to show her mettle. To help him find his wife, or at least an ending of some sort so he could move on.

Without thinking, she grabbed his forearm. He couldn't go like this. He looked half out of his mind. What was his plan? For sure he shouldn't drive in this state.

He wrenched out of her fingers and turned for the front door, Suzannah on his heels. He was out the door before she could stop him, talk to him, help him devise a plan calmly. She hesitated for only a moment at the front door as she watched him chew up the ground with long strides in his need to get to the truck. She glanced back at the table of stunned onlookers, then took out after him. She felt a definite twinge with her first step down, then slowed her pace, not daring to re-injure her ankle. Instead she limped after him.

She didn't know what he was planning to do, where he was planning to go, but for sure he was *NOT* doing it alone.

CHAPTER 11

Betty's alive! After what he'd just heard, Jake kent it was true. Frantic hope left him quaking, just as the the earth had done over ten long months ago.

He raced across the grounds, hoping his truck was still unhitched from the trailer so he could bolt after Betty. Where he would start was obvious. Her folks lived in Gillette, probably only fifteen minutes from here. How would they react to seeing him so long after she'd disappeared? He'd called them right after the quake, sure. But he'd never taken into account she could have made it to their house days, or even weeks later.

The barn's huge sliding doors were open. As Jake drew nearer, he couldn't miss his red truck parked off to the side, while the empty trailer was up on jacks right smack in the middle of the way. He charged up to the man who was on one knee next to the trailer. Looked to Jake like he was either jacking it up or down. It had better be down, he thought, or he would take over and do exactly that. "You 'bout done here," Jake's voice rumbled, startling the man.

The man twisted his head to one side and gave Jake a nod. "Done." He ignored Jake then, and went about his business.

Jake's insides were on fire, lightning striking off every nerve ending. He paced, ran a hand down his face, then around his neck and squeezed. "Listen, laddie, I need my truck, so I'll help you push this thing wherever you want to store it."

"Huh?" the man said dumbly, making Jake's head explode.

"Aye, ye hackit bampot! I said—"

Jake stopped short when a warm hand touched his arm. He kent it was Suzannah by the sweet hint of lemons before she'd even sidled up in front of him. He looked down into her wide eyes, her wee chin jutted out so she could look straight at him. As he stared down into those blue-green depths, he read her thoughts as clearly as if she'd stated them. And she was right. He needed to leave off. Wait two minutes for the man to finish his work—the work he should have been doing for himself.

Jake huffed out the pent-up breath, looked up, and dug his fingers into the back of his neck. As he scanned the rafters, like they alone could calm his frenzied body, his mind went to the wee scamp. Nobody in their right mind would enter Jake's space—especially when he was riled. This wasna the first time he thought this wee wisp of a lass had nerves of steel. Even so, his admiration was nowhere near strong enough to overcome his irritation.

"Why are you not back at the house with Rebecca?" he ground out. "I have to go. Be back in an hour. Tell her."

Suzannah didna move. Instead, she took a half step closer. Her blouse brushed his buttons, and he could feel her warm breath at the V of his open collar. It smelled sweet as she did. Jake felt stirrings flock in, like bees to their hive. Stirrings he couldna escape when she was this close to him.

He backed a step, glared. "Go back."

"No," she said, utterly unruffled.

"Suzannah, I'm warning you." Jake backed another step.

They were gathering a crowd now. Three cow-pokes had left stalls they'd been working in to come forward, plus the man who'd just finished the trailer, and all were watching. Jake glanced up when he heard snickers. One of the men didna try to hide his mirth as he stood with a huge grin on his smug face.

Growling low in his throat, Jake grasped Suzannah's elbow and headed for Roy's pick-up, boisterous laughter at their backs. Turning her around, he used his fingertips to push her into the driver's door. Leaning down for her ears only, he softened the look he gave her, and called on what wee charm he possessed. "What are you doing, Kitten?"

"Going," she said under a frosty stare.

A laugh stirred inside him, but he stifled it easily. He'd already used the only laugh he'd had stored up on this gutsy lass. He wouldna do it again.

"Nae. I'm going alone. Return to Rebecca."

If he thought his usual commanding tone would see him done with it—and her—he was woefully mistaken. She stamped her foot and glared. Then before his next breath, she twisted away from his fingers, shot under his arm, and dashed to the other side of the truck. Once there, she swung the passenger door open and jumped inside so fast, he wondered how she managed such a thing with her wee body.

Fine. No time to waste. He turned to the group and shouted over their laughter. "Tell Troy Suzannah and I will be back in an hour or so." He opened the driver's door and hoisted himself inside. As an after thought before he closed the door, he hollered, "Tell him I apologize. Same to Rebecca."

Jake turned the key, pumped the gas, then stomped the starter. The truck turned over four times before Jake stopped, then repeated the process all over again. The engine roared to life on the second try. He pulled down into first and took off out of the barn and on up the drive to the highway.

The only time Jake had been to Betty's folks' house was the day she'd told her parents she was pregnant and was marrying Jake. They hated him the minute they'd set eyes on him. The whole evening had been a disaster, and the only other time they'd come near him was at the courthouse where he and Betty had been married before a Justice of the Peace. He hadna seen them since, and hadna planned to…'til now.

Once Jake had his plans set, he glanced at Suzannah, quiet as—well, as Suzannah. She was so far against the door, if it unlatched she'd fall right out. Roy had warned him that door was tricky. "Crowd over closer."

Suzannah's head jerked in his direction so fast, her braid whipped to her back. Her eyes were wide. "Why?"

"If that door happened to open, you'd fly right out, lass."

She turned and scowled at the door, as if it was plotting to do just that, and scooted her backside over a length. "Thanks," she said.

Jake glanced at her in surprise. Her words seemed to come easier lately. He figured traveling with him would have scared the lass into more silence. Instead, it seemed she'd improved.

In his peripheral vision, he noticed her watching him. Kent something was on her mind. After a long silence, she touched his bicep. He barely felt it, but kent she was about to speak. He tuned in.

"We'll find her," she said, and her words couldna have surprised him more. He heard her deep intake of one breath, then another, and kent she wasna finished. "I want to help."

She wanted to help him find his wife? "Why?"

"Not… your fault," she croaked.

It was his fault, but his heart softened in spite of himself. This time when he glanced at her, he caught her eyes with a question in his. "Why do you care about this, Kitten?"

She touched his arm again. This time her touch lingered. "Jake… earthquake. Not you."

Instant rage sent heat into his cheeks. "You dinna ken what you're saying, lass. You werena there."

"Tell me."

They were coming into the town of Gillette, so Jake slowed, then shifted into second gear. It hadna escaped him that two of the least talkative people he kent, himself and Suzannah, had managed to talk— though sporadically—the whole trip to town. Comfortably at that, though the topic itself was anything but.

Ignoring her last request, he focused on where he was going. If he remembered correctly, he was to take a right at S 4-J Road. As he came upon an intersection that looked familiar, he slowed again, checking the street sign. Aye, that was it. He made the turn, shifted again, and sped down the street. Betty's folks lived close to the highway, on a street with the name of a bush. He remembered that much. Within a few minutes he came across W. Juniper, and kent that was it.

A warm hand came to his thigh, making Jake's foot jerk on the accelerator. The truck bucked, and he cursed. He'd have to explain to the wee innocent about such things as touch, right after he explained how there were other ways to gain someone's attention.

"Where we going?"

He peeled her hand off his thigh and placed it in her lap. "Betty's house."

Jake heard her swallow, then inhale a deep breath. "Didn't she… live with you?"

Her question was so direct, it stunned him. Then he remembered, her words were precious. She couldna waste them when saying them was such a chore. "Aye, she did, before the quake."

To the left was Humphrey's Bar. He remembered that, so he was in the right place all right. Continuing on down the road, he saw the commercial area give way to residential. He slowed as he saw the house he remembered, right before a sharp curve in the road. A squirt of adrenaline streaked through him, speeding his pulse.

Jake, with eyes glued to the residence, pulled the truck to a stop and turned off the key and the lights. It looked the same: flat-topped, run-down, in dire need of a new coat of paint—and a new set of owners. He ran a hand down his face. If he continued down that line of thinking, he was sure to get no answers from in-laws who already despised him.

The acid in his stomach heaved, sending a blistering burn of barbecued ribs and cake up his throat. What kind of man was he? So caught up in his own guilt and grief that he had never given these people a second thought.

What was he thinking, to do this?

He reached forward and turned the key back on. Just as he was about to press the starter, Suzannah grabbed hold of his knee to keep him from it.

"Jake?" she said, with a deep scowl that did nothing to diminish her sweet face.

Okay, now was the time to tell her about touching him. She had to ken such a move would land her in trouble one of these days. "Listen, Suz—"

"No!" she snapped, and tugged his leg away from the starter. At the same time she reached for the key, turned it back, and yanked it out of the ignition. She leaned toward him and stuffed the darned thing in her jeans pocket.

"What are you up to, Suzannah? Give me that!"

"No!" she said again. "What's wrong?" This time she looked into his face, searching it for answers.

He didna have any. He just kent he'd never given Betty's folks any regard concerning their daughter. What sort of rat did that? He couldna face them. He'd find another way to look for her.

Fixing an open palm under Suzannah's nose, he tried again. "Give me the key, Kitten. We're going. This was a mistake."

"Why?" she said, batting his hand away. Once again he wanted to laugh at her lack of fear. This fairy. This Gutsy kitten. He wished he could turn back time, before the earthquake, before he'd met Betty, before he'd managed to derail his life, and see what a track toward an angel would have gotten him.

Okay. She'd asked. He'd see how quickly the lass would run from the snake he'd become. "Because I was never involved with her folks after she went missing, that's why." He shifted toward her in the seat, grabbed Suzannah's wrists and squeezed, his eyes penetrating hers.

She caught on a breath, but he kept squeezing. "Dinna you get it, angel? I called them when she first disappeared, to see if she showed up here somehow. But I didna bother to call them again. In all this time, when I couldna find her, when I wrestled with whether or nae she was dead, believing she was, I never bothered with them at all. Not to confirm. Not to say I was sorry. Nothing!"

Suzannah twisted her wrists enough to grab his own. Her fingertips made soothing circles on the inside of his forearms. The tender look in her eyes tried to soothe as well.

He averted his gaze. "Now," he went on. "I'll drive you back and we'll find you and Rebecca another ride to Cooper Ranch, since I'm sure you won't want to be anywhere near me, aye?" He flung her wrists away from him and turned a glare on her as added emphasis, waiting for her to agree and scoot back too close to that hazardous door again.

Her eyes misted over, and the sweetest look of compassion tangled with the flush of her skin.

He pushed back against his door and stared, watching for the sudden change that was sure to come. It didna. Instead, she leaned toward him and reached a hand to his face. To the beard he was sure she despised. When her hand connected, he jerked, not knowing what to expect.

"Oh, Jake," she said in her raspy voice, as she smoothed her hand across his face not once, but over and over again, like she was petting that wee kitten he'd taken to.

Then, when he thought she couldna surprise him anymore, she lifted her other hand, and the two brushed against his beard, and now into his hairline, until he thought he'd go mad.

"Suzannah," he said around a thick lump in his throat, understanding for the first time what it was to have pain with speech like this brave lass did. He thought his dead heart would break for her, and thrive for her all at the same time.

Slowly, her fingers curled in, entwining his beard until they brought a stinging bite. "You must," she whispered with force. "You have no choice."

He reached up, placing his hands over hers, to pry her fingers off. But once his hands touched her skin, they seemed to move on their own accord, caressing the backs of hers. He let one hand wander to her face, and cupped her jaw. So soft. So fragile. So feminine. He stroked the angel's skin.

Her mouth parted on a wee intake of breath. Instead of moving away, she stilled, and blinked. All he could do was stare back, so poleaxed he couldna move even a fraction. When she rubbed her cheek along his calloused palm, staring into his eyes with affection in hers, a window opened in his mind, letting in a gust of awareness. *Think laddie! You canna have her.*

With renewed vigor, he pried her hands free of his beard, reached behind him, and grabbed the door handle. The door swung open, nearly landing him on his arse. He grasped the door frame, holding himself in place until his legs were under him.

"Stay here," he roared, thrusting his trigger finger at the seat.

The hurt on her face nearly undid him, but he forced his thoughts back to Betty. He was a married man, with a wife and baby missing, and he thought to sit here and soak up the warmth of another lass? Gad, how low had he sunk? He didna even ken a bad enough word for the skellum he was right now.

Jake grabbed his Stetson from behind the seat and shoved it on his head, the force of his stare keeping Suzannah in place. He flung the door shut, turned, and strode toward the house. His trepidation had been replaced with anger at himself. At least the force of it would get him to the front door.

Stepping close, with his middle knuckle he rapped three times. Waited it seemed a five full minutes. Heard someone shuffle up to the door. They didna open it, like as not looking through the peephole instead.

A sound a lot like a bairn's cry resonated into his head, shaking him to the core. *She's here. My gawd, she's alive.*

Jake pounded this time, and would soon rip the door off its hinges himself if they didna answer.

Just then, the door cracked open. Jake tilted his head to hear better. No sounds returned to him. Did he imagine what he wanted to hear? Through the crack in the door, he saw the television, a black and white cube positioned on a small table. It was turned on, but to what? He didna ken or care, except to wonder if he'd heard a bairn crying on a program.

"What are *you* doing here?" the gruff man he remembered as Betty's father said.

Jake pressed his fingertips against the door. "It's best we talk inside."

The man hesitated, but ultimately relented, letting the door swing in.

Jake pushed past the man to the interior, stood on a warn rug in the center of the living room, and looked around. If she were here, if the bairn lived here, there would be signs. There were none that he could see, but that didna mean anything. "Harold," Jake said, then removed his hat and held it in his left hand, reluctantly offering his other to his father-in-law.

The man scoffed at it and him. "What do you want?"

Jake dropped his hand, swallowed hard.

He took a step closer to the kitchen, darted a look in there. "Heard from Betty?"

The man's eyes turned bleak. He ran a hand over his mouth, then glared up at Jake. "Is that supposed to be a cruel joke? Even for you, I can't imagine… "

Pressure built in Jake's head, blinding and throbbing, as he glanced around the house again. "Is she— was she here?" He fingered his hat, turning it round and round in his hands.

The man's eyes filled with tears, and Jake knew the answer already. "You just now comin' here to look for my girl? *Your* wife!"

There was no reason to cover for himself. He deserved all the wrath Betty's father wanted to heap on him, so he decided not to tell him he'd spent the last ten months scouring Harper Ranch for her. Had he been in that much despair that it never crossed his mind she might hitch a ride somewhere else? Had she wanted away from him so badly that she'd been willing to risk hers and the bairn's lives?

He felt like a leper. He wanted her father to lambast him. He wanted to lambast himself. "Where is she, Harold?"

"She's dead! You should already know that! She's dead," the man said, choking on the last word.

Jake stepped forward, grabbed the man by the shoulders, and shook him. "How do you ken? Tell me, old man, how do you ken she's dead?"

The man was like a rag doll, flopping in Jake's hands, like he had no will left. But his dark glare never left Jake's eyes, penetrating straight to his soul. In that moment, he kent what the man said was true. Blood pounded in his ears, drowning out his own word. "How?"

Jake still had a hold on the man's shoulders, instinctively aware if he let go, the wee man would collapse. "When she *left you*, she came here. Gave birth too early, died in childbirth."

Hot tears burned Jake's eyes. Something he hadna experienced since he was a wee child. "And the bairn?" his voice cracked.

The man stiffened in Jake's hold. He yanked away from him with restored strength and turned away. Not looking back, he said, "Gone."

It couldna be they were both dead. She'd been at Troy's while he'd been wasting his time scouring the area around Harper's. Then, when he'd heard that sound behind Harold's door... he'd hoped... he thought mayhap the bairn...

Jake trembled where he stood until a last gasp of denial crashed into him. "Wait a minute. You said gone?"

"Gone! Departed! But for your neglect, they'd still be alive. Now get the hell out of my house!" The man drew up, strode forward, and shoved Jake in the chest.

Jake had nothing left. The shove easily moved him. He stumbled a few steps back, but caught himself, an overwhelming flood of grief drowning him.

"Nae..." he whispered. He staggered to the door, and slammed a palm onto it. He stood with head hanging, bracing against it, as if he alone held up the Rockies themselves. "Nooo!" he shouted this time, trying to batter this new reality to dust in front of him. But the door remained intact ahead, and the cold, slippery horror of his guilt slithered like a tangle of snakes up each leg and around his chest.

Finally, when he found the strength to shift his feet once again, he backed a step, stuffed his hat back on, then turned an agonized face toward the old man. He said nothing more, but threw open the door and strode out.

All he had left now was anger. Jake stormed across the street. He flung the door open and hurled himself inside the truck.

"Jake?"

He barely heard the small voice through the sound of blood whooshing in his head.

Jake glanced at Suzannah, and she gasped. The look in his eyes must have been lethal.

He ignored her, turned the key she'd already put back in place, and stomped the starter so hard it belched, then erupted with a vicious roar. He didna care. He wished with all his might he could leave Suzannah on the curb and take off for the hills, never to be seen again. Since he couldna, the next best thing was that bar he saw back a piece.

He stomped the clutch, threw the truck into second, and gunned the engine, spinning the wheels hot until they caught and threw the chassis forward. The truck fishtailed as he spun them in a U-turn and headed back toward the bar.

Suzannah's wee body nearly somersaulted as it crashed into the passenger door, and one of his worst nightmares unfolded before his eyes. The door swung open on impact and all Jake could picture was Suzannah landing and breaking her neck. Her raspy scream filled the interior.

"Suzannah!" Jake hollered on a curse. Letting off the gas and clutch at the same time, he barely caught hold of her front jeans pocket, just before the back of her head smacked pavement. Jake held fast.

The truck bucked several times before it died. Jake hardly noticed. He rotated, using his other hand to grab her waistband and tug her by her pants only until her rear was flush to him with her legs straight up in the air. He wrapped his arms around her flailing legs, knocking his hat to the floorboard, and held tight. The anguish he'd wrapped in anger ripped free. First one sob tore him in two, then another, and another, until a flash flood of unused tears streamed from their hidden tomb.

CHAPTER 12

Suzannah was flabbergasted at Jake wedging his face into the backs of her calves, murmuring apologies and heaving sobs.

Was this the same Jake she'd known for this past month? Self-controlled Jake? Taciturn Jake? The intimidator-of-all-within-shouting-distance Jake?

He sobbed against the backs of her legs—big, racking sobs—until Suzannah felt the perma-lump in her throat swell even more, stopping up her windpipe. She needed to sit upright, catch her breath, but Jake had locked what felt like steel bands around her knees. She stroked him on the shoulder. Nothing changed. He was breaking her heart with the assault of tears and sobs. She was desperate to embrace him, to take his pain away in whatever small way she could.

Still flat on her back, she shifted both legs as best she could off to one side, giving her access to a bit of his head. She moved her fingers into his surprisingly silky hair. She threaded her fingertips through it and through it, over and over until he finally raised his head, and pressed a cheek to the side of her leg.

She peered at him. A shell of a man gazed back at her, eyes blacker than ever, shimmering like onyx with more pent-up tears. That ravaged face. Those weeping eyes. Seeing the broken man before her, she felt them come—long overdue tears that burned the backs of her eyes as if they were acid instead of salted water.

Jake saw, and froze.

What a vision they must make, the two of them. Jake with a death hold on her legs, Suzannah bent in half with legs lapping over one of his shoulders, and her own hand stroking Jake's disheveled hair. If it wasn't so tragic, it would be comical.

"Oh, Suzie," he said, the new nickname tearing from his mouth, sounding pinched and painful. He pulled his head back and turned her on the seat, allowing her feet to drop to the floorboard. But he wasn't done with her yet. With those massive hands of his, he took her by the waist and raised her to her knees at the side of him. Her heart raced at his touch.

"So sorry, Kitten, to risk you like that."

So tender was his apology, it seemed to come from a secret place deep within. She already knew he was a tender soul, but this—this was different.

Nothing more came forth. He slipped those muscled arms around the curve of her hips and stared into her eyes. Just stared. Soon, he looked as if he wanted to say something but couldn't quite spit it out. She knew exactly how that felt.

He finally managed to say, "They're gone, Suz—"

She was sure he'd meant to say Suzie or Suzannah, but a sob caught in his throat. She stroked his hair again, and with her eyes, encouraged him to try again.

"Betty and the bairn. They're—"

Comprehension arrived. She shook her head at him, imperceptibly at first, then with such vigor, he grasped her face to stop her. Her face contorted in agony for him. He didn't need to say the words. She knew. Saw it in his eyes. The torture, the guilt. Would he ever be whole again?

"Aye. They perished." Once those words passed through his lips, the torrent let loose again, filling his eyes, and spilling over onto his cheeks, then disappearing into his beard.

He ducked his head and buried his face in her stomach. She didn't hear them then, those heart-wrenching sobs, but she felt them. His shoulders rose and fell with every broken sob and lost hope.

It was her turn to wrap him in her arms. She pulled his head in deeper to her heart, trying her best to shield him from any more torment. With one hand she held his head tight to her, with the other she stroked his hair and what she could reach of his back, up and down, trying wordlessly to soothe his spirit.

After what seemed like hours passing, when only minutes were possible, he tugged his face away from her and gazed up.

She looked down into that devastated face, so unlike the powerful Jake she knew, and her own tears began to arrive, one following the other. The very ones that had long since dried into a lump of fear and dread in her throat.

His thick brows drew together, his own eyes still glistening. "Nae, Suzie. Dinna cry for me, lass." He stroked the small wisps of hair back from her face with one hand, then added the other. He locked their gazes together with black eyes that had been so empty and now seemed to churn with emotion, like storm clouds before a twister.

And then, just like that, his eyes iced over. He dropped his hands from her and slid back under the steering wheel. He tromped the starter. When the engine turned over, he muscled it into gear and took them smoothly forward. He was a man back in control of his world.

Suzannah twisted in the seat and sat back, subtly sliding nearer the door, feeling dismissed. How could he turn off emotion like that? Especially when she knew it was emotion that had been locked inside him probably since he was a small child. She didn't know what to do, or say. At least he would not expect her to talk, so she could be silent without him thinking anything of it.

Abruptly, Jake rotated the wheel to the right, going way too fast for a turn. Suzannah screeched as her body took off across the seat and, but for the gearshift slowing her momentum, would have slammed her full body weight into Jake. As it was, she was practically on top of him anyway.

As if nothing untoward had happened, Jake pushed the gearshift into neutral, turned the key, and yanked it out. Once he had his door open, he dropped to the ground, wordlessly turned, and reached under her legs for his hat. Stuffing it on his head, he gave her one long glare, as if she were responsible for the rise of emotion that had just ambushed him.

Twisting on his heels, he plowed forward to the front door of Humphrey's Bar and Grill. As Jake crashed through the front door, Suzannah wondered how that was received from the patrons within. Would he be thrown out right off the bat?

Suzannah swung out the driver's side of the pick-up, pushed the lock button down before flinging the door shut, then trailed Jake inside, worried how he'd conduct himself after such devastating news.

The place was busy. She saw Jake winding his way through the throng. Some squeezed together in a corner, dancing to the loud music; some ate at tables. He stood head and shoulders above everyone else, the only one all in black, so tracking him was simple enough.

She followed but hung back to watch Jake with the barkeep, staying close enough to hear his request for a shot of whiskey and a beer. Once he'd paid, he grabbed the two glasses, turned, and nearly trampled her. He reared back just in time, beer sloshing over his hand. "What the he—heck, Suzannah!" he yowled as he transferred the beer to the hand with the shot, shook his hand, and sucked the alcohol off his fingers.

Jake's eyes were red-rimmed, and only she knew it was not from drinking. It made her want to pull him back to the truck for more time to sort through feelings that he needed to *feel*, not deaden with booze.

Something shifted in his demeanor, as if he just this second remembered his plight. Suzannah saw the despair in the slump of his impressive shoulders when he skirted around her. She turned to watch him meander through the crowd, a dozen or so females eyeing him like he was fresh chocolate rolling by.

When he reached a small round table with two chairs, he set the whiskey and beer down, then sat himself. He caught the other chair with the toe of his boot and slid it out for her. Not entirely chivalrous, but a good effort considering the circumstances. She hurried forward to take him up on his offer.

Jake was slumped in the too-small chair, a distant look clouding his eyes. He sipped at his whiskey, then took a drink of beer. At least he wasn't downing them in gulps, as she feared he might do. He didn't once look at her, and she wondered if his gentlemanly gesture had been a natural impulse only.

Minutes ticked off as Jake finished his drinks, only to rise, gain another set, and sit back down with Suzannah. Maybe he wanted her there just to hold his place each time he vacated his chair for more numbing liquid. His eyes never found hers, and he never offered her a drink, food, or conversation.

After an hour crawled by, Suzannah felt her ire enter the ring, boxing full rounds with first her compassion, and then her anxiety. She was so far out of her comfort zone, surrounded by strangers, she expected to see hives flare up all over her body. Why was it okay to make her sit here and watch him anesthetize himself when she was more than willing to offer comfort in the privacy of the truck? Or back at Troy's? Ignoring her completely was getting them nowhere. Wanting to get a rise out of the man who appeared too busy drowning his sorrows to care if she were made of wax or flesh and blood, Suzannah jumped to her feet, catching the back of her chair with one hand before it flew backwards into the crowd. She glared down at Jake, who was still oblivious to her and her angry outburst. She knew he was hurting, but oooh, the man could be so aggravating, not letting her in.

Fine. It was time to amuse herself. She squared her shoulders, took a deep breath, and scooted her chair in so as not to trip anyone. Facing the crowd, she bull-dogged her way to the bar. Because of her size, the crowd seemed to swallow her whole. After squeezing her way through, practically elbowing people out of her way, she jammed the heels of her hands against the wood counter. She swiped a hand across her face, then smiled to the man behind the bar. He was young and attractive and instantly attentive. Well, good. At least she'd be able to get service. His face split with a glorious smile, showing straight white teeth, and with them came an overwhelming charm. "And, what might I do for you, beautiful creature?" he said, widening his already ample smile.

She pointed to the whiskey bottle he'd been peddling to Jake. The young man didn't waste a moment, but splashed a measured amount into a shot glass and pushed it toward her. As she reached for it, he wrapped his hand around hers and added a leer to go along with his smile.

Annoyed, Suzannah's nostrils flared with her quick intake of breath. Trying to extract her drink along with her hand, the grip on hers tightened. The barkeep leaned in, as if to deliver a message just for her ears. The second he came to within a foot of her face, he jerked back to his place, his eyes centering on something over Suzannah's head. His fingers flung off hers like they'd been sent a bolt of electricity. Backing up, he turned and hustled to the other end of the bar.

Interesting, she thought, frowning in confusion. Making a face to herself over the weird scene, she plunked money on the counter, nabbed her whiskey, and turned... straight into a wall of muscle.

"Oof!" Whiskey sloshed over her glass, onto her fingers, and all over—

She peered up and cringed. All over Jake. She licked her fingers, then tried to brush off his waterlogged shirt, awaiting an explosion.

What met her gaze instead were those desolate, black eyes.

Jake wrapped his fingers around her elbow and steered her away from the bar. The crowd backed away like the parting of the Red Sea. When he got her back to her seat in the corner, instead of sitting down, he ventured back to the bar.

The same dozen women marked his every step. One brazen girl slipped in front of him. Suzannah watched him skid to a stop and tilt his head down—probably to give her a scathing stare. Soon the girl backed out the way she came in, and blinked after him as he continued on his path. Her heart went out to the girl when she saw the shell-shocked expression left on her face. Many times in the past, Suzannah had received that same get-the-blazes-out-of-my-way look he'd no doubt given to her, and had experienced the same humiliation.

When Jake returned, he had two shot glasses full of amber liquid, and another beer. Dropping into the chair, he set all three glasses in front of himself then dug right in. First with the beer, then the whiskey, and on it went.

Dare she try to stop him? But how?

A slow song came from the jukebox and filled the air: Paul Anka's *Put Your Head On My Shoulder.*

Abruptly, Jake rose to his feet, surprisingly steady, captured the hand Suzannah had circled around the base of her drink, nearly spilling it, and pulled her into his arms.

If shock alone could kill a person, she'd have been dead as door nails right then. Her heart beat so fast she was sure he'd feel it through the thin fabrics of their combined shirts. He held her so close, every beat of his powerful heart vibrated through his chest and into her ear. That heart still beat strongly, though he probably thought it had died along with the news of his deceased wife and child. Just the memory of that news brought Suzannah in closer. She gripped his hand a little tighter, raised her left hand up higher on his arm until she clasped the roundness of his shoulder.

Jake's splayed hand at her back held her firmly against him as he danced them to the center of the swaying crowd.

Thank you, Lord, for this chance to remind him he's not alone. When she had a moment, she would explain that God had him in the palm of His hand, and if Jake would only accept that truth, he could rest in God's comfort for his grief.

Suzannah was jolted out of her musings by Jake's tighter grip at her back, and his sudden twirling of them, round and round in circles. Those on the dance floor began to shuffle off, some still dancing at the outskirts, but most had stopped to watch them. She clung to him, this magnificent man, this gentle giant, her feet naturally following the path he was leading. It was exhilarating! She hung on and let the moment flow through and in and around her. His ample body became lithe as moving fluid with every note of the music, and hers followed like she'd been created for just this purpose—and for just this man. They were breathing in unison now, legs entwined in an intimate ballet of movement and emotion as if it were Swan Lake instead of a folk dance to a rock-n-roll pop song.

Jake's breath tickled her hair at the crown of her head, his chest heaved in and out with the exertion, his heart beat hard in tempo with hers, his booted feet moved along the wooden floor with the grace of Fred Astaire himself. Who was this man? Where had he learned to dance like this?

In the next instant, Paul Anka ceased, and Bobby Vee began with *Take Good Care of my Baby*.

Jake stumbled to a stop, sucking in an agonized, ragged breath Suzannah felt clear to her toes. He went rigid, right there in the middle of the dance floor, Suzannah entrapped in his embrace. The patrons of the cozy bar-and-grill froze as well, some watching with curiosity, others with irritation.

Suzannah, still panting, peered into Jake's eyes and saw the wall to his emotions had again fallen. She knew what was coming next if she didn't get him off this dance floor pronto. She wrenched out of Jake's arms, took hold of his hand, and turned toward their table. When he still didn't move, she gave him a sharp tug, waking him from the nightmare the song must have caged in his head. He followed her, zombie-like, back to their seats. Though the music kept playing, no one moved for several heartbeats, until finally Jake and she were forgotten and the floor filled as if the previous scene had never occurred.

Suzannah shoved Jake into his seat and pushed his two drinks up to his stiff fingers. Poor man. She wondered if the song had a particular meaning for he and Betty, or if it was strictly the words that had him reeling. Whatever the cause, Suzannah wanted to get him back to the truck where they could talk about it before it was stuffed somewhere inside his head alongside other loathsome past experiences.

"Jake…"

He didn't look up, and she knew she would never be able to converse with him over the top of this deafening music. She put a hand on his, startling him. He glanced up, looking visibly soused. She pointed to the door, and waited for his response. Sighing heavily, he dropped his gaze back to his drinks.

Okay, so she would finish her drink, but immediately changed her mind when she remembered she'd have to drive, and was already feeling the effects of the sips she'd taken. She sat through two more songs, both by Bobby Vee, and had finally had enough. Rebecca would be worried. Jake was getting more drunk by the minute, so moving him could be a challenge. And Troy, their involuntary host, was meshed in this drama whether he wanted to be or not.

Enough was enough. She glanced at the clock over the bar. Admiring the new 1960 white Corvette surrounded by palm trees on its face for a brief second, she noted the time. Nearly ten o'clock! They'd been gone four hours instead of the promised one. They needed to move, now!

Before Suzannah could act, Jake downed his last gulp of beer and got to his feet, probably headed back to the bar. "Oh no you don't... Mr. Jake Cooper," Suzannah whispered to herself. She rose along with him, circled the table, then his waist, and used his momentum to turn him toward the exit.

He was drunk enough to let her lead him, yet surprisingly stable on his feet. His body was probably used to alcohol. That thought made her sad for him all over again. He'd been through so much in the last year.

She opened the bar's front door, and the cool breeze filtered in, filling her lungs with much needed fresh air. Just when she was sucking in another great gulp of air, Jake stumbled on the threshold. Both his arms shot up and locked onto the casing, securing the two of them in place. She glanced up and snickered at how they must look with her clinging to his waist—not much good she was doing him there—and him filling the entire doorway like a bouncer tasked to keep people out.

Suzannah peered at his face. His eyes were wide with the look of spinning terror that too much drink and unsteady legs brought. She snickered out loud this time. Her laughter made him drop his gaze to her.

She grinned up at him, and it was clear he didn't know what to make of it. "Come, big man," she said while tugging him forward, away from the door. His hands grappled, then one caught hold of her shoulder. He clung as if she centered him. "Move," she said. "Come on."

She tugged forward again, and he took a couple of steps. The door swung shut behind them, leaving them in the dimness of the night. A light breeze was blowing, ruffling the damp hair that peeked out from under Jake's hat.

Her hair had long since pulled out of its rubber band, and her braid was unwrapping in the intermittent gusts. When one of her strands of hair circled upward and slashed across Jake's face, he flinched in surprise, but caught the tendril between his fingers.

His boots dragged to a halt. He tightened the one arm surrounding Suzannah's shoulders and, with the other, fingered the hair in his hand. Though he swayed like a willow in the wind, his focus remained on that piece of hair. His gaze followed the strand to the roots of her hair and then to her face, and as if he just figured out who held him securely, he whispered, "Suzie... Kitten."

His countenance was so dear. The severe lines that normally were visible around his eyes had relaxed. Even in the darkness, his eyes glittered. Not with anger, not with malice, not with unshed tears, but with something tender, almost affectionate. She wanted to camp right there, and gaze back into those magnificent black windows of a careworn soul.

They stood. They stared. Until Jake's fingertips came up and, with a slight tremor, slid through her hair, stopping when he caught on a clump. He groaned deep in his throat, his eyes glued to the unraveling of her braid. He combed through it again. Once her hair was set free, he pulled his fingers back only to comb them through again and again.

The sensation was so gentle, so soothing, Suzannah almost forgot she was the one who needed to do the soothing, and to see this hurting man home. "Come," she said, catching his hand before he could slide it through again. She pulled his arm more tightly around her shoulder and turned them toward the truck.

Jake submissively ambled along beside her.

Keys. I need the keys. Should she bring it up, and have him fight to keep them, or should she sneak them out of his pocket? Sneak them, she thought. Which pocket? Running back through Jake's actions when they'd arrived, she remembered he'd stuffed the keys in his right front jeans pocket. Guiding them to the passenger door, Suzannah backed him against the truck bed. He teetered, but stayed where she put him.

Burrowing down into his pocket as fast as the tightness of his jeans allowed, she fingered the keys, stuffed harder, and grabbed hold. Just as she was about to pull them out, he flattened his hand over hers.

She was good and trapped and felt the rise of heat up her neck and into her face.

CHAPTER 13

Suzannah needed to think quick. Jake's brain had to be muddled up with booze, so brain power was the only way she could outmaneuver him. She glanced around, looking for something—anything—that brought an idea. Her gaze caught on the door lock. It was up. That's right! She'd only locked his side in her rush to follow Jake inside.

Still trapped in his pocket with his hand over hers, she stretched to her right and depressed the door handle button, yanking the door open.

"Wha—?" Jake said, looking down at his hand still over hers in his pocket.

"Forgot," she said. Swallowed. "To lock it." Suzannah smiled up at him. She shuffled over a step, barely moving the bulky man as she tugged. He did forget the hold on her hand, though, so she snatched the keys out of his pocket and pushed on his shoulder, turning him toward the door. "Get in."

He stood staring at the seat with his brows knit together and lips in a grim line.

"I'm driving," she said, giving him another push.

He jerked his head toward her, and tried to glare. Looking a little cross-eyed, he rocked back on his heels and blinked, his hand snaking out to catch himself on the door frame. He dropped his head and puffed through a few breaths.

Suzannah thought at first he might be sick, but soon he lifted his head, then his leg up to the running board. Once his foot was planted, he pushed upward, miscalculated, and slammed his head into the top of the door jam—effectively popping off his hat and knocking him back down. His hat flew backwards and hit the ground as he staggered in place, groaning and rubbing his scalp.

"Try again," Suzannah said. This time she pushed his head down and in. Along with his own thrust, he went sprawling across the bench.

He lay there for several seconds face down. "Hat," he said into the seat.

"Got it."

He worked, and twisted, and finally got his body into a sitting position, all the while looking like he might lose the three beers and four shots of whiskey he'd ingested. Truth was, he'd be better off if he did, since tomorrow's hangover promised to be a doozy.

Suzannah threw his hat in and pushed the door closed when his head lolled back against the gun rack. Hustling to the driver's side, she unlocked the door and hopped in. Once the seat was adjusted for her, she started them up without a hitch and was off toward the Wheelers' ranch and her sister.

Jake snored the whole way there. She was grateful he could lose himself in slumber. She didn't look forward to the pain she'd see in his eyes tomorrow, pain that had nothing to do with a hangover.

Suzannah made the tight turn onto the dirt road Jake had navigated with a flat tire this afternoon. Under the Wheeler Ranch sign she drove, wondering how hours could so quickly feel like a thousand lifetimes. Winding down the road toward the ranch house nestled between mature pines, she remembered how beautiful the place was. How in the moonlight, the trees surrounding it reached into the low clouds before her like a living wall meant to keep calm and peace within its boundaries. She couldn't wait to pull up and dive into its slumbering tranquility.

When she arrived at the house, though, every light seemed to be lit and loud music poured out the windows and open front door. Here she was concerned they'd be worried about her and Jake when it was apparent Bill's twenty-first birthday party was still in full swing.

Rebecca was standing at the big picture window in the front. When her eyes locked onto the pickup, Suzannah watched as she disappeared from view just before seeing her dash out the door and on down the pathway.

By the time Suzannah had emerged from the vehicle, Rebecca was there, grabbing her up into a huge, desperate hug. "Oh my gosh, Suze! I've been so worried. Where have you been? Why are you driving? Where's Jake?"

Suzannah grasped Rebecca's face in her palms, forcing their eyes to connect. "There." She pointed at a slumped-over Jake, his head wedged in the corner of the cab. "Drunk."

"What?" Rebecca swung Suzannah out of the way and peered in at Jake. "Why? What is going on, dear sister?" The fear in her voice had been replaced by confusion and annoyance. Suzannah understood.

As was their norm, Rebecca finally settled into a listening mode, knowing full attention was needed for Suzannah's difficult delivery of words. She leaned against the truck bed to listen, a breeze ruffling her beautiful chestnut hair across her face. She captured it in one hand and held it over one shoulder. "Go ahead, Suze. I'm listening."

"His wife and child—" Suzannah swallowed, breathed. "—are dead," she began, and stammered through the rest of the story to a teary-eyed Rebecca.

A sob that must have been stuck in Rebecca's throat through the telling escaped her now, and with it came a few tears down her cheeks.

Suzannah swiped at matching tears of her own. She pointed at Jake. "Needs to... sleep it off," she said, sounding as if she had gravel in her throat—from her own speech impediment, or the retelling of Jake's tale, she didn't know for sure. It mattered not. All that concerned her now was to help Jake recover from his drunken binge, and then ultimately to help him heal from his harrowing news.

Suzannah opened the passenger door to Jake's snoozing body. She tapped him on the shoulder, hoping that would be enough to wake him. Of course, it wasn't. Gripping his shoulder, she shook him. "Jake."

He snorted once, shifted his head towards her, and was off again to slumberland. This time she took hold of one shoulder and, with the other hand, grasped his knee. She shook again. "Jake."

He stirred, opened his eyes, and she watched as he tried to focus on her. She grasped his face this time, folding her fingers in his beard until she felt the hairs tug against his face.

Jake thrust toward her, probably trying to free himself, and bonked her on the head. That woke him, and left her a little dizzy. But she wouldn't stop to rub her head, not when she had him awake, sort of. "Come."

Just then, two of the Wheeler sons exited the open front door and jogged down the walkway toward the truck. Suzannah and Rebecca both sighed in relief.

"Hey there, gals. We'll get him." Each man took an arm and hoisted Jake out of the truck. When his feet connected to the ground, he grunted and tried to stand straight. It looked comical, like someone had removed his bones.

"Where do you want him?" the birthday boy, Looney, said.

"You tell us," Rebecca said. "It's your home. And we're interrupting your birthday party. Sorry."

Looney waved off her concern. Each man slung one of Jake's arms over their own shoulders, one of them catching hold of the back of his belt, and headed toward the house, half-dragging, half-walking him. "He's a heavy one," birthday boy said.

The effort was so great getting him inside, the two men gave up the idea of taking him upstairs and veered off toward the formal living room, which happened to be free of any party patrons. They unloaded him as if he were a sack of potatoes onto the couch, then shooed Rebecca and Suzannah out while they stripped Jake down to his skivvies and covered him with the afghan from the back of the sofa.

When Suzannah saw the men leave the room, she left Rebecca to the party and came back in to check on Jake. She knelt on her knees by his head and brushed his hair out of his eyes, then smoothed out his beard. The poor man looked ravaged even in a drunken stupor. Lines marred his closed eyes, at their edges and under his dark lashes. She rubbed at the pucker between his brows. The fact that he was frowning in this state reminded her of the news he'd received tonight. To think, he had spent nearly a year looking for his pregnant wife, to this end. It was heartrending.

After several minutes of Suzannah soothing his face into a more relaxed expression, Jake opened his mouth as if to speak. It closed, then opened again to whisper a word. Suzannah hadn't caught it. She leaned in close. "Again?"

"Annabelle…" he rasped.

Suzannah pulled in a large breath and expelled it on a sigh. "It's Suzannah."

"Nae," he countered.

"What?"

"Annabelle," he said again.

"Who?" Suzannah said, none to sweetly, feeling the rise of jealousy.

His eyes were shut, and his breathing eased into a regular rhythm. She guessed Annabelle would remain a mystery. At least for now. Pulling the afghan up to his chin, she leaned over and gave him a kiss on his forehead, loving the feel of his warm skin under her lips.

He jerked and opened his mouth again. "Annabelle."

This time Suzannah didn't respond.

"If it was a girl, I would have named her Annabelle… "

Shock and sorrow hit her simultaneously. Suzannah sat back on her heels and stared into his bleak face. Though his eyes were closed, he was awake. He had to have been to coherently share such a thing. She felt her own aching heart reach out to his broken one, wanting to soothe and stroke it back to whole.

"Oh Jake…" was all she could say before her lump thickened and took her voice completely. She did the only thing she was able to do. She stroked the side of his face, over and over again. The poor, suffering, dear man.

As she watched and waited for him to drift off again, she saw when the tears squeezed out from the corners of his eyes, one by one, and slid down into the hair at his temples.

As her heart broke for him clean in two, right then and right there she vowed again to herself, and to God, that Jake would not be alone through this tribulation. Because Suzannah Marie Harper would stay by his side until he healed from this horrific wound.

She put her face to within inches of his, knowing he had nodded off again. Mustering up all the power she could to speak full sentences, she whispered, "I will fight for you, Jake Cooper. You will never be abandoned again."

* * *

A loud crash of metal against metal jolted Jake awake.

First thought: Where am I?

Second thought: Kill me now!

He opened eyes that felt as if they'd been scraped and battered in a bad sand storm. As a morning person, the unusual grogginess had him confused. Every cell was bursting in his head along with the symphony of, *what*? Pots and pans, he guessed, when he finally tuned in past the throbbing in his head. A rush of memories swept into the mix of pain and confusion, reminding him why he felt as though he'd been trampled by a raging bull.

Another crash. Were the possessors of the noise trying to jar him awake, or was this his penance for drinking too much? He didna like this feeling—this hangover. He'd been anti-social his whole adult life, and adamantly against drinking alone, so drunkenness had never been added to his list of personal sins.

It was about the only one that hadna. Well, now even that had changed.

Without opening his eyes further, Jake rolled to his side—and straight off to the floor. *Whump!* Groaning in double pain now, and lying with his face wedged against the cold floor, he risked prying his eyes open. He stared cross-eyed at the wood floor, his stomach convulsing. Cramming his eyes closed, he waited until the dizziness subsided.

Wee bit by wee bit he lifted his head, peered around him. He was in a house. Had been on a couch.

Out of the blue, a door opened and cool air whisked over his bare skin. His gaze crept down the length of his body. Someone had been daring enough to liberate him from his clothes. Left him in only his drawers, though an afghan was tangled about his legs.

"Ah, so you're awake." He kent that voice. From yesterday. Troy Wheeler.

Jake peered up with gritty eyes at the man. The man who looked work-worn, yet carried a wry grin on his face. Troy started to laugh, clouting more spikes of pain into Jake's head.

Jake groaned and dropped his head to the floor with a bang, then groaned again. "You wanna just kill me now, aye?"

"Nah. Guess it's time we hoist you up and ply ya with some coffee. You missed breakfast, dinner, and supper," Troy said, and laughed some more.

Jake wanted to punch the man. But, besides a show of bad manners to the man who helped them out, he didna think he could lift the weight of his own arm to do the job. Then his comment sank in. He'd been asleep all day?

Troy reached down and grasped Jake by the armpit, hauling him to his knees, then thrust him onto the couch. The man was stronger than he looked.

Sitting upright, his head pounded, his stomach churned, his gritty eyes ached, and his limbs dangled like limp noodles. How the hands at Harper Ranch did this every Friday night, he would never know.

"The girls have been ready to go all day. We'll do our best to get some grub down ya, then send ya on yer way."

"It'll have to wait," Jake said.

"Why's that?" Troy asked, looking truly confused.

"Canna drive just yet. Give me an hour or two, if you dinna mind, Troy."

"Oh that." Troy slashed a hand through the air. "Ya don't have to fret. The women folk have it covered. They'll do right fine."

"Nae!" Jake barked, then winced. He straightened his spine, bringing another wave of nausea over him. He forced his stomach to obey, then stumbled to his feet. He stood, wavering a wee bit, closed his eyes, then when that seemed a bad idea, snapped them open again and focused on the fireplace. After a few sturdy breaths, he carefully brought his gaze to Troy's amused face. Again he wanted to slam a fist into the man's jaw.

Why would any reasonable man put himself through the torture of hangovers? On purpose?

"Stop worrying, my man," Troy said on a chuckle. He stepped forward and patted Jake on the shoulder. Each pat drove a stake into his brain. The older man was getting a kick out of this, and Jake couldna even let his anger rise, since that only brought more throbbing and more daggers.

Besides, it wasna Troy Wheeler's fault Jake was in this sorry state. They needed to get out of here before he embarrassed himself further. It wouldna take much for him to throw up on the bear rug in front of the cold fireplace.

Troy brought Jake's clothes to him. The effort it took him to lean over to situate his jeans, socks, and boots was enough to convince Jake going naked would have been a better plan. Once his shirt was nearly buttoned up, Jake ambled into the kitchen, searching for a much needed cup of coffee. He hoped his stomach could endure, since he wasna giving it an option.

"Here you go, Jake," Bea said, handing him a cup of black coffee. "Sit down on the bar stool there."

Just the name 'bar' made him shudder. A wave of sadness followed right after, reminding him why he had new holes in his heart.

"You don't look like you take anything in it. Do you?"

"No, ma'am," Jake managed. He sipped, then downed half the cup. Waited for the revolt. Was grateful it never came.

Bea handed him a dry piece of toast. Didna look verra appetizing, but she probably kent best. He munched on it slowly. It did seem to calm the nausea some. She handed him a second, and by the time that one was gone, he felt better. Not grand, just better.

Next Bea brought him two aspirin and a tall glass of water. "You don't look like the hair-of-the-dog kind of fella, so take this instead. Drink all that water. Then you may survive this thing." Bea smiled with empathy.

Just then the front door swung open, then slammed shut. Jake felt it vibrate clear down his spine and right back up to his head.

Rebecca popped into the kitchen, smiling wide. "Finally! You're up!" she said. "We're ready outside. Do you think you can ride okay?" She stopped talking and looked him over more carefully. Her brows knit together. "Maybe we should wait a bit longer."

"Nae, lass. I'm ready. But, I'll be driving, aye?"

Rebecca's smile changed to something sly. Jake had a bad feeling about this.

"Come along, Mr. Cooper. You'll be just fine." She grabbed hold of his hand and tugged until he started moving. Then she let go and hurried toward the door. "Just fine," he heard her repeat, though she was already on the porch and heading down the steps.

Jake took one last swallow and handed the cup off to Bea, who'd followed them to the door. "Bye, now," she said, and turned back to her kitchen.

Troy saw him out and shut the door behind them.

The alcohol had melted Jake's bones, he was sure of it. How he'd get them working well enough to use a clutch was a concern, but he'd done worse things in his time. They needed to get to Cooper Ranch before it got too late, and though it was slower going with a trailer full of horses, it should only take them an hour and a half, two tops.

Dusk had settled in, making shadowed silhouettes of the many trees surrounding the ranch house. Jake shook his head in disbelief that he'd slept the day away, and immediately regretted it when his head hammered. Shouldna the aspirin have done its job by now?

As Jake approached the truck and trailer, horses already loaded, he saw Suzannah sitting pretty as you please in the driver's seat. Ah nae! Now he'd have to argue to get her to move, and he was pretty sure he'd throw up in the middle of their fight. Not to mention his legs were flagging with each step, his lungs panting, his head pounding.

People were plumb mad to put themselves through hangovers.

"Come on, Jake. In you go," Rebecca called to him.

He strode up to her and put a hand out in a gesture for her to go first. Once she was in, he'd go to the driver's side and lift Suzannah out before she could protest.

"No can do, Jake. I already tried. My knees are right in Suzannah's way. Yours will be longer and will reach farther past the gearshift. She can shift between your legs."

Darned if he didna see a twinkle in Rebecca's eyes. He tried to roll his eyes at her and immediately wished he hadna. Steadying himself with a hand to the door frame, he dropped his gaze to the ground and blinked, then stuffed his eyes shut—opened them and blinked again. Bile came up his throat. He grimaced and swallowed. Ah rats! He was going to lose his toast and coffee. Sure enough, sweat broke out as he felt it coming. He dashed around Rebecca on rubbery legs, hitched an elbow on the truck's tailgate, and proceeded to lose his only meal behind the truck. While he gained his breath with his head still hanging down, feeling somewhat better from emptying his stomach, he studied the tongue of the trailer, and the job done to hitch it up. Looked good. Everything in its place. The men had done a fine job. But, he was sure-fire not going to let Suzannah drive this rig. If she thought so, she had another think coming.

Jake straightened slowly, tugged his kerchief out of his back pocket, and wiped his mouth. "Gad, just kill me now and get it over with. What do I have to live for anyway?" he said to himself.

Someone touched his back. He got a whiff of her before he saw her. Lemons, fresh air, woman.

"A lot to live for," Suzannah whispered at his back. Putting her tiny hands at belt level, she turned him slowly around and handed him a stick of Dentyne gum. He took it and popped it in his mouth. The juices from it soothed his throat and settled his stomach some. Suzannah swung her arm around his waist. He in turn laid an arm across her shoulders, and a sense of home came over him.

She started back toward the passenger side of the truck, but he shuffled them to a stop. "Nae, lass. Driver's side." He kent Suzannah could drive the truck, since she must have last night, though he didna remember a dang thing. But pulling a loaded horse trailer? Nae.

She ignored his plea and kept moving him in the same direction. He didna ken if it was his own weakness or the fact he couldna deny her anything that caused him to obey. When they reached the opened door, he used the last of his strength to climb in.

His left knee banged painfully against the dash board, and then so did the right. He cussed, then doggedly scooted toward the middle. Suzannah must have moved the darned seat all the way up. By the time he'd lifted his leg over the gearshift and had his knees spread enough to fit, he wondered how he'd ride this way for five minutes, let alone ninety.

Rebecca and Suzannah simultaneously bopped into the truck and closed their doors. The bounce of the seat jarred his stomach, and the smiles on their faces made him want to hit something. He shut his eyes. Nope, wrong thing to do. Back open they came.

"Do you ken what you're doing, Suzie?" he asked, partly to give himself a distraction.

Rebecca jerked a glance at him. "Suzie, huh? Cute. I like it, coming from you. How do *you* like it, Suze?"

Suzie ignored Rebecca, and so did Jake. He really wanted his question answered. "Have you ever pulled a loaded horse trailer before?"

Suzie shot him a glare, then turned the key, and trounced on the starter, bringing the truck to life. She grabbed the gearshift with added gusto and yanked it toward her, on down his leg, and into first gear. He jumped, trying to scramble out of her way. Not an easy task. "Easy, lass."

"Who do you think backed this baby into the barn, hitched it, then loaded up?" Rebecca said on a laugh.

Jake looked back at Suzannah, astonished. "Did the gelding behave?"

Suzie smiled, a ridiculously smug smile, and said, "Absolutely."

"She knows how to handle horses. Didn't I tell you that, Jake?" Rebecca added.

Jake shook his head in disbelief. That reminded him to look straight forward. What he didna need to do was begin gagging, forcing Suzannah to come to a sudden stop for him to puke again. Jake settled his head back against the gun rack to wait things out. An uneasy sort of coldness came just before a welcomed numbness. Good, he could travel numb.

Through slits in his eyes he watched as Suzannah made the swing around the barnyard, then headed out of Wheeler Ranch and on up the winding road to the highway. She was surprisingly competent, the lass was, able to handle the vehicle and trailer no less steady than he would have. But then, why should he be surprised? Everything she did, she did with absolute ease.

Except talking.

One of these days, he'd have to get her to tell him about her affliction; how it happened, why it happened, and when she expected it to be cured. It wasna right that a lass like her should be so afflicted. She had her whole life ahead of her.

Unlike him.

CHAPTER 14

Suzannah shifted down as she took the turn into the Cooper Bar-Six Ranch. Rebecca had followed the map Uncle Roy had stashed in the truck, so they didn't have to wake Jake. Suzannah was thankful for that, since by now she was a little beside herself at her intermittent gearshift strokes to a sleeping Jake's sturdy thighs. Now she understood fully what he'd had to endure while driving. At this point, she either wanted to escape this vehicle and cool off in the open range breeze, or shove Rebecca out the door and bound into Jake's lap to act on her own overactive imagination.

Good grief. She'd never had such consuming fervor for a man. But then, Thomas had been the only other man in her life. Now that she had seen the difference between Thomas and a real man, well, it was like comparing a malicious mule to a disheartened stallion. And this disheartened stallion seemed to constantly stir something vital in her—something besides sympathy.

After last night, something had drastically changed. About him, about life. He'd been hurt, made vulnerable. He'd exposed deep, raw feelings to her, shed unmanly tears, clung to her. And that had broken her and healed her all at the same time.

Deep in thought—beams from her headlights bouncing as she rambled over the rutted dirt road—Suzannah didn't see the ranch house until she was nearly on top of it. But, someone from the house had seen them coming since the expansive home's exterior flood lights popped on. She tromped on the clutch and the brake a little too zealously, jolting Jake awake. Without glancing in his direction, she gave the gearshift one final push to neutral, turned the key to off, and hopped out.

As she shoved the door closed, she saw Jake crane his neck to watch her head off. She only went as far as the rear of the truck, stopped, and lifted her face to the breeze, flaring her nostrils to take in an extra large breath of fresh country air. What was happening to her?

Jake. Jake was happening to her.

When she regained her composure, she'd go back and help Jake out of the truck, make sure he was all right, get him settled in his uncle's house. Then she'd take care of the horses. Making plans always seemed to settle her. One final deep breath and she was ready.

Just as she was about to turn back to the cab, she felt a hand to her shoulder and near jumped out of her skin.

"Easy, lass. It's just me," Jake said, his warm breath fluttering the hair at her crown.

"Jake… " she said on a whisper, but didn't turn around.

"Seems you got us here in one piece."

She whirled around, instantly incensed and ready to take him on. "You doubted." It was a statement, one she planned to argue with Jake about, vocal problems be hanged.

"Nae. Well, mayhap some."

Was that moonlight glancing off his onyx eyes, or a twinkle of amusement she saw there? Her annoyance drained away as her hand went up to steady his face, to get a good look. She'd done it automatically, the touching of his face. She was used to touching people's arms and faces, and those who knew her put up with this little idiosyncrasy if it helped her communicate with them. But, now? Right now, she had to admit to herself, she'd used it as an excuse to touch him.

He stiffened in response, but didn't move away.

Her hand drifted down his soft beard, stroking it over and over again. It came to her then; his beard didn't remind her of Thomas's anymore. "Stomach better?" she rasped.

He nodded. His hand came up again, the width of it covering her whole shoulder. Warmth spread through her at his touch. "I didna thank you, Kitten. I mean to do that now."

Confused, she frowned up at him. "For driving? Told you I could."

Through the furry beard, she thought she saw a ghost of a smile. "Nae. Not the driving. For last night. I wasna so drunk as to nae remember. Ye saw me through... well, I thank ye, lass."

Those words, sounding so charmingly Scottish to-day, melted something deep inside her. Who would have thought Jake Cooper, of all people, had such a soft side? "Aw, Jake. How that must have... I can't imagine..."

Shoot. They were bonding here. She wanted to say so much more. The ability to speak to Jake had gotten simpler, but she still couldn't make her voice box get through more than one short sentence at a time. She wished he could read her mind. Find out how her heart ached for him.

She did the only thing she could. She reached up with both hands, and placed her palms on either side of his face, trying to express with her eyes how she understood what he must be going through. The loss of something so precious—be it a wife and child, or the ability to speak—should never be borne alone. Suzannah needed Jake to know she was here for him.

More importantly, God was here for him.

She knew that fact like she knew her own name. Then why couldn't she incorporate that truth into her own situation?

For now, she needed Jake to understand. As she gazed into those black eyes, ones that were more expressive tonight than she'd ever seen them, she feared what he saw in return from her might be the wrong message. She wanted him to know she wouldn't leave his side as he worked through his ordeal. What she feared came through was how drawn she was to him, especially after seeing his vulnerability last night.

Suzannah had been so busy conveying her message through her eyes, she hadn't recognized Jake's stillness beneath her palms. Suddenly he was a statue of granite. In the glow of the outdoor lights, her gaze took in his eyes, his face, then dove to his stiff body, arms rigid at his sides with fisted hands. Jerking her gaze back up she now saw he looked stricken, like a feral cat trapped in the corner of the barn—no way to pass, and no means to disappear. He didn't want her touch. Why hadn't she remembered that? Last night had been different. He'd been devastated and drunk!

Blood pumped into her face in a flash flood of heat. Her hands dropped to her sides like they'd been put in irons. Her own embarrassment flipped the switch of girlish swoon to womanly fury. She shouldered Jake out of the way and whizzed to the front of the truck and around it toward Rebecca.

Standing at the passenger door and seeing the mortified look on Suzannah's face, Rebecca opened her mouth to say something but didn't get the chance. The extra large oak door opened, and a man in wranglers and blue work shirt strode out of the house, all loose-hipped brawn and man-in-charge confidence. As he came closer, Suzannah was reminded of Jake—towering good looks blighted by an expressionless face.

Suzannah watched Rebecca catch sight of the same attractive creature coming toward them, her eyes twinkling with appreciation. Forever the greeter of the Harper family, her sister didn't hesitate to move toward him. Her neck slowly tilted back on her spine as they neared each other. If he towered over Rebecca like that, he was exceedingly tall. Her neck was stretched now in order to gaze up into his face, her long chestnut hair hanging nearly to her waist at her back.

He halted within two feet of her. The man stood and stared down into her upturned face, his brows in a knot and lips pressed together, looking mighty uncomfortable, while a sweet, compassionate look was plastered all over Rebecca's face in return. Only Suzannah knew that look of her sister's. The one where Rebecca read a need in someone and had already begun formulating a personalized rescue.

They stood like that for what seemed full minutes before the man spoke. He reached out an unsteady hand to Rebecca and said, "Trevor Cooper, ma'am."

Rebecca started a bit at his gruff voice, but recovered quickly enough to meet his shake. Suzannah noticed bunged up knuckles and healing wounds on his work-roughened hand as it engulfed Rebecca's. Her sister never took her eyes off Trevor's face. Suzannah didn't blame her. He *was* pretty darned eye-catching.

Finally she said, "Rebecca Harper. I'm your new cook and bottle washer." She smiled up at him as he stared back grimly. His silence gave Suzannah the impression he didn't know what to do next.

Jake moved forward, breaking the stare-down between the new housekeeper and the first son of Cooper Bar-Six. "How ye been, Trev?"

Trevor seemed relieved as he withdrew his hold on Rebecca and grasped Jake's outstretched hand. "Good to see you, cousin."

Business was always the first thing on Jake's mind. He plunged in with, "Uncle Coop here? Brought his gelding."

Trevor dropped Jake's hand, using his own to rub across his mouth, hiding some kind of emotion— discomfort, amusement? He coughed, settled his gaze on one of his boots, scraping something off its side, then sighed in resignation. He looked up, meeting Jake's eyes.

"Dad's, uh... well, Dad's gone to Cheyenne. He, um... he's got some business there for a couple months. Left me in charge."

Suzannah almost laughed. Trevor clearly was keeping something back about his father.

Trevor glanced away from Jake, twisted a half-turn, and his eyes landed on her. "And who might this young lady be?" He sounded more animated, she was sure, by the need to change the subject about his dad than by his own reaction to her. He smiled, and she and Rebecca took in a breath in unison. He was already a handsome one, but whew, that smile was downright knee-flagging.

Rebecca's big sister shield went up as she stepped toward Trevor. "That's my little sister—"

Trevor put a hand up, stopping her words. His brows nearly touched as he frowned in puzzlement at Suzannah. "Cat got your tongue, sweet thang?"

Suzannah wondered if it was as obvious to Jake and Rebecca how awkward that charm—or attempted flirtation—was for Trevor. For a man who only moments before seemed vigorously comfortable in his own skin as he'd strode toward them from the house, he now had a circle of sweat in the hollow at his throat, as if the effort to speak to a woman was distressing all by itself.

She wondered briefly if her one word answer would pass over the lump in her throat—he was a stranger after all—and was somewhat mollified at his uneasiness. She straightened her arm toward him as he did toward her. They shook hands while she strained, gulped, then tried, "Suzannah." Though the word sounded pinched, she was grateful she'd gotten it out.

Out of the corner of her eye she noticed Jake's glare, as if she'd kept the word from him all this time and had now decided to grace another man with it; which was ridiculous, of course, since she talked more with Jake than anyone else. Yet, the thought he might be jealous made her want to giggle and whoop all at the same time. The little red devil sitting on her shoulder nudged her to crank her grin brighter for Trevor. The man stiffened and blinked, but didn't say anything more.

As she gazed up at Trevor, he finally seemed to come back to himself and released her hand. He tapped his hat brim, strode by her to gather up two of Rebecca's suitcases that Jake must have unloaded from the bed of the truck, and tromped off.

Jake, understanding the unspoken language of men, reached down for two others, bounced a particularly stern glance at Suzannah, then followed on Tre-Trevor's heels. When they both had disappeared through the front door, Rebecca's mouth dropped open. She turned to Suzannah and, seeing the amusement in her eyes, let out an unladylike snort and burst out laughing. Suzannah started with a small chuckle, then, always tickled by Rebecca's laugh, followed into a side-splitting one of her own. Rebecca leaned forward to grasp Suzannah's arm and bent to laugh some more. Pretty soon they were hugging each other while they howled.

"Whew-wee!" Rebecca said, wiping tears of mirth from her eyes. "That man is jeee-alous! I've never seen anything like that from Jake before now. What would he do if you were actually serious about another man, do you suppose? Might turn him inside-out, eh?" She snorted a final laugh. "To tell you the truth, I hadn't noticed his interest in you until this very moment."

Rebecca stilled at her own words, and peered at Suzannah. She tilted her head to one side, studying her. "Do you... do you have feelings for Jake?"

Suzannah waved a dismissive hand in the air, not about to tell her overprotective sister that she had struggled not to, but after last night she had unequivocally fallen for the man.

She turned away before Rebecca could catch her expression of longing. Standing on tiptoes, Suzannah dug around in the bed of the truck for her own overnight bag. Once it was slung over a shoulder, she rummaged for her other larger bag, pulling it noisily over the metal side before it dropped to the ground. She got a better hold, then headed after the men. She heard Rebecca behind her, gathering the remainder of her own belongings.

Welcoming light streamed through the front door, beckoning Suzannah in a way she couldn't quite describe. Maybe it was that the house was comprised of hard-working cowboys, usually known for watching out for their women folk. Or maybe it was that even though Thomas intended to hurt her when he found her, she didn't think he'd walk into the midst of a group of gents like these. At least at one time he wouldn't have. Either way, she felt safe with Jake's family, filled with warm fuzzies as she stepped over the threshold. The clip of Rebecca's boots followed Suzannah's onto the wood floor of the expansive entry way. Suzannah glanced over her shoulder at her sister, curious if Rebecca beamed with the same contentment she was feeling.

But no, it wasn't contentment on Rebecca's face. Not even close. Her sweet face was twisted in pale horror. Suzannah spun back around to see why.

What she saw made her stomach flip. First, she noticed a bundle on the floor that appeared to be mud-speckled wranglers and a plaid shirt, a white undershirt peeking out from inside the flannel as if it was all tugged over an impatient man's head. The pile lay on the throw rug connecting the kitchen and the living room. Bits of dirt and lumps of mud were scattered around the heap like fallout from an explosion.

Suzannah felt her mouth drop open a little more as she continued her perusal of the room, noticing scraps of newspaper, more clothes, more mud, empty bottles of beer and pop, two cowboy hats on the floor, plates with day old—or maybe week old?—remnants of gravied food, two knives embedded in the flooring as if a knife contest had ensued, more underwear draped on corners of wall pictures, and a few more on the lantern-fashioned lamp hanging from the middle of the pine slatted ceiling. Last but not least, her gaze settled on the two men splayed across a couch that faced a square TV, where a boxing match ensued.

Suzannah's astounded gaze fixed on the nearer of the two. He was slouched so far down the sofa it looked painful, with knees bent and feet flat on the floor, wearing jeans and filthy socks. The other held a beer bottle on his flat belly, just above the waistband of his once white skivvies. His hairy legs were stretched out and crossed at the ankles. Both men were equally brawny, both had a couple days of stubble on equally pleasant faces. Wait! Suzannah volleyed her gaze from one man to the other. Not just *equally* attractive faces, but *identically* attractive faces. No one had mentioned to Suzannah that there were identical twins in this household, but then, no one told Suzannah much of anything. It was as if her silence made her invisible.

A loud snore erupted from the mostly naked cowboy. Suzannah couldn't help but stare. Heaven help her. After several long moments, she turned back to Rebecca, her face heating.

"Maybe we should head to the kitchen," Rebecca whispered behind her hand. Suzannah couldn't tell if Rebecca was smothering a laugh or covering her nose to stifle the smell.

She nodded and hustled after her sister.

Once in the kitchen, Rebecca dropped the rest of her gear on the floor and scraped a chair back from the table. She dusted it off with one hand, then plopped into it as she pulled another out for Suzannah. Suzannah dusted hers too, not knowing if it needed it or not, and carefully lowered herself into it.

"Well, now, these men really do need a keeper," Rebecca said with disdain.

Suzannah sighed, and gave Rebecca a sympathetic smile.

"It's not going to be easy, considering they're bachelors. I thought Maria had gone back to Mexico to help her family just over a month ago. How could they wreck a place this fast?"

"Our brothers could," Suzannah reminded Rebecca, and smiled again. This time with meaning.

Rebecca smacked both hands over her mouth and snorted into them. "You're so right. They could do it in a day!" She matched Suzannah's smile then, noticeably less stressed. "Okay. Let's get settled. I'll just have to make the best of it. At least you don't have to stay." Rebecca laughed outright then. Suzannah joined her, enjoying the pain-free sensation a laugh always gave her.

A crash came from the next room. The sound of breaking glass was followed by a male bellow that could have roused everyone the next county over. Suzannah jumped to her feet, heading in that direction, Rebecca at her heels. As soon as she'd gone through the door of the kitchen to the living room, Suzannah saw Trevor standing over his brothers, face bulging with fury.

Both men had jumped to their feet. The one who'd been snoring earlier swayed a bit, his thumb and forefinger rubbing at his eyes. His beer bottle lay in a heap of broken glass at his feet.

The other twin stepped forward and yelled profanities back.

Trevor glared at the nearly naked brother first. "There are women here, Brand, you scuz bucket. Go get dressed!"

The twin's shocked gaze took in both women at once. Suzannah glanced away so as not to embarrass him, while Rebecca, seemingly unaffected, scanned the floor, no doubt figuring how to best clean up the mess.

As if his brain sprang back to life, he leapt to the right of his brother and dashed toward the back door. A huge yelp, then hardy curse filled the room as he limped the rest of the way out the door, leaving it thrown wide as he disappeared into the darkness.

They all watched him go as he left a trail of blood behind him.

"Trevor. He's hurt!" Rebecca cried as she strode up and poked him in the chest. "I'm sure Suzannah and my sensibilities would have survived his unclothed state just fine, but now the poor man cut his foot on broken glass. Which, by the way, is all your fault!"

Rebecca's body practically vibrated with hostility. Her compassion was her biggest asset as well as her biggest failing when it came to times like this.

Everyone in the room froze and stared at Rebecca. Suzannah got the distinct feeling no one in their right mind had ever spoken to Trevor Cooper that way before. She braced herself, because the man looked ready to explode.

Suzannah's eyes grew wide in fear for her sister. The one sure outcome was Rebecca would never back down, which could lose her the job before she even started. Suzannah had to rescue her. But how? She couldn't intervene with words. She'd need too many. But she could...

Suzannah sucked in a huge breath and threw a hand over her face in a melodramatic swoon, as if she were Scarlett O'Hara herself. She let her legs wobble as if she would fall, knowing full well that the couch would catch her.

She should have known better.

Before she even finished the attention-getter, Jake was there, whipping her into his arms—a down-right exceptional version of Rhett Butler—and whisking her off toward the front door.

At that moment, everything seemed to slow down, like a 45 record being played at 33-1/3 on the phonograph. As Jake twisted to fit them both through the door, Suzannah watched three sets of eyes swing toward her, three mouths go lax, and one shouting match go silent. She congratulated herself, until she realized Jake was still wrestling her past the crooked screen door and into the night air.

He'd be furious if he knew she'd faked the whole thing. Nothing more for it but to follow through with the smokescreen. She lolled her head against his shoulder and moaned, then opened her eyes and stared up at his face. Jake looked down at her with eyes the color of night, swirling with dark intensity. And, like an old crack in a clay pot, something broke loose inside her. Warmth tracked through her veins as she stared back at him. His solid body against hers made her feel safe and alive. All remnants of her past fears seemed to be gone in that split second, and it felt good. Really good.

She swallowed, and for the first time in three years, couldn't feel the lump.

Joyous, Suzannah looped her arms around his neck, pulling herself in closer. To help him carry her, she told herself, though she knew he wasn't having any trouble doing that. His neck was warm and a little damp. She leaned in and fit her face where his shoulder met his neck, feeling his rapid pulse against her nose and enjoying his scent of man and a remnant of whiskey. She breathed in a deep breath—a full breath— without restriction. No lump in her throat, no anxiety constricting her lungs, no sudden need to escape, no compulsion to try and speak—Jake was the king of reticence, after all—and no reason to ever leave his arms again.

So this was what euphoria felt like.

Jake stopped before the porch swing at the corner of the house and seemed to have just noticed how she'd wrapped herself up in him. His eyes widened and he loosened his arms, making her slip down a notch. She clung harder so he wouldn't drop her. Could their responses be more opposite?

Within two long strides, he arranged her on the porch swing, accidentally thumping her head on the wood when he let loose too quickly. He straightened and backed away. Stood there staring down at her while the swing danced clumsily, back and forth. She couldn't tell what he was thinking since his usual impassivity was back in place, but the word 'poisonous' came to mind.

The muted porch light winked past his black silhouette with every forward swing. The entire light shone over his shoulder when he finally yielded and leaned in to examine her.

She stuck out her hands to stop him. No way was she going to be considered poison to this insufferable man. Embarrassed—*again*—and burning to flee, she slid her feet to the porch boards, thrusting the swing into a wild thrash as she stood. It slammed into the backs of her knees crazily, tumbling her back into it again. Now sprawled and even more embarrassed, she covered her face with her hands in an attempt to hide from him. The act was so childlike she wanted to yell profanities, scream lengthy sentences into his face, anything to show she was an adult and not a darned child, or an irreparably damaged victim!

Her temper rose, as did her body out of the swing. She glared at Jake, pushed against his chest to move him out of the way, then ran down the porch steps and into the black of night. By nature she wasn't a runner, as her sister Jessica had been, so her desire to flee from Jake surprised and disgusted her. Maybe love had changed her nature? No. She had an impulsive side. This was it. She groaned as she fled.

She dashed along the curved dirt road and didn't stop until she'd come to the big, rambling barn. The moon shone large in the clear evening sky, illuminating the small door to the right of the main barn doors. She noticed their horse trailer backed in on one side of the barn, the truck parked next to it. That meant the horses were inside. Good. *Bonnie.* She was what Suzannah needed right now to calm her down. She depressed the latch, then pulled the side door open on its hinges. Just as she entered, to the right she saw a string hanging from a lightbulb. It swung back and forth on the breeze from the open door. She grasped it and pulled downward. The small bulb popped on and lit a surprisingly large area of the cozy interior.

The barn was immense inside, at least two stories to the rafters. Inhaling the familiar and wonderful scents of hay, horse, and even manure, Suzannah felt her tension drain away. The breezeway narrowed to a path that passed in front of each stall. Though her embarrassment had eased, she still wanted to hide out here for a spell.

A pleasant nickering came from the first stall on the right. Bonnie. The horse had already thrown her head over the stall and had her muzzle stretched in Suzannah's direction.

"Hello, girl," she crooned to the mare, shocked at how easily the words slipped out. She strode to her and rubbed the backs of her fingers against the soft velvet between her nostrils. There was nothing like the feel of a horse's muzzle. It offered her peace, calmed her emotions, gave her a connection to another live, voiceless creature. She felt her muscles relax another degree and stepped in closer. Bonnie threw her head up, startling Suzannah. Before she could leap back, the horse relaxed her head over Suzannah's shoulder. She pulled Suzannah forward, capturing her in the crook of her neck, then nickered at her back. Suzannah giggled, thinking this was an equine's version of a hug. She stroked what she could reach, which was the downy soft fur under Bonnie's mane, and whispered, "Cuddly, aren't we?"

"Look who's here," came a deep voice from the shadows.

CHAPTER 15

Thomas? Suzannah jerked back as a lead ball seemed to drop through her stomach.

Alarmed, Bonnie banged her jaw against Suzannah's head as she flinched back herself. Suzannah grunted in pain, then whirled, fumbling with numb hands against the stall door for a nail or loose board… anything to arm herself with against Thomas if he came any closer. Out of the darkness a shadowing figure moved. He stepped into the lightbulb's halo of light, and Suzannah released a quivering breath of relief. It was only the Cooper twin who'd run out the back door, half-naked. Her heart thudded less by the second as she pushed her stalker memories down and assessed the cowboy.

The twin took two more steps toward her. She began to wonder why he wasn't limping.

"What are you doing out here?" he said. He sounded ill-tempered, demanding, possessive, just like Thomas, but with an even deeper, gruffer voice.

The twin leapt forward, grabbing hold of her arm. She sucked in a sharp breath, glancing down at the hold he had at her elbow. Fear stabbed into her, a cold, burning pain that intensified the lump in her throat. Her thoughts tumbled toward a distant memory, a deep horror frozen into a corner of her mind, but no sooner was she upon it than she sped past it and back to the fingers clamped on her elbow.

He isn't Thomas! Show strength, Suzannah. When she lifted her chin to glare at the twin, the most magnificent, yet unnerving, hazel eyes glared back at her. They almost moved in waves of changing color as he stared at her with mischievous intent. "What's your name, little girl?"

That ruffled her big girl feathers in a way this scalawag could never understand. Her fear evaporated. It came to her then that she had misread this man. With twins, there was usually a strong-willed one who dominated, and a sweet one who was compliant. This one wasn't limping, he was fully clothed, and definitely not submissive. He was the one who'd taken on his older brother, bellowing in his face.

The dominant twin. Not the one who'd run out of the house half-naked with an injured foot.

She yanked at the hold he had on her.

He let loose, but barked, "I asked you a question."

"Her name is Suzannah, and you'd best get back."

Both she and *dominant twin* wrenched their heads around toward Jake, who towered in the doorway. If she thought this twin looked menacing, she need only look into Jake's eyes to see true venom. It surprised her every time Jake showed emotion. But there it was, brewing like a thunderstorm about to erupt.

His cousin stood mesmerized, watching Jake as if awaiting an avalanche he could not hope to escape.

Jake was upon him before Suzannah even blinked. He grabbed his cousin by the collar and hauled him up to his tiptoes in one smooth move. "Do nae ever— *ever*—talk to her that way again. Aye?"

No comment.

Jake shook him. "Bronco?"

The hypnotized look vanished, and Bronco's sneer tightened back into place. He didn't speak. He stared though, until Suzannah thought the two would burn each other to death from the fire in their eyes.

This was wrong. She needed to intercede. Bronco hadn't harmed her, and he was Jake's cousin, after all. An old cliché zipped through her mind: Nothing like a woman to come between two men. Well, she wasn't going to be the cause of a family war.

But, this was Jake. It would take great skill to calm him.

"No," she said, but could barely hear it herself. Her voice failed her. No surprise there. She had no choice. She'd have to touch. She ran up next to him, reaching out an arm. The second her fingertips touched his upper arm, he jerked toward her with a raised fist, then halted mid-breath.

Bronco took his opportunity and shoved Jake hard. Jake back-stepped as fast as he could before losing his balance and hitting the dirt. He somersaulted backwards, crushing his hat, then came to rest in a sprawl, flat on his face.

He raised his head and shook it, then scrambled to his feet in a fit of fury.

Suzannah's breath froze. *Jake is going to kill him!*

Jake grabbed the smashed hat off his head, threw it to the side, hunkered down, and charged. He hit Bronco square in the stomach.

Bronco took the hit with a loud grunt as they shuffled backwards together. Coming up against a row of hay bales, Bronco's heels caught. He flipped backwards over the bales, hard. Jake managed to spin sideways to keep from crashing over the bales himself. A loud crack and holler of agony sent both she and Jake tearing forward. Bronco had broken something. Suzannah prayed it wasn't his neck.

One glance at Jake, and a shiver of dread spiraled down her spine as she visualized a wounded Bronco being pummeled by a raging Jake.

A scream rose up and out Suzannah's mouth before she could think otherwise.

Jake slid to a halt, twisted around, and sped to her, a look of fear overtaking the rage on his face. "Suzannah!"

He reached for her, started with her face, gripping it in his big hands—checking for injuries she supposed. His hands traveled over her—her shoulders, her arms to her fingers, his gaze doing the rest, examining every inch of her down to her boots. Then he ceased his inspection. She watched as the cloud of worry lifted, leaving behind something quite different. Under the veil of his lashes and below the slash of lowered brows, his gaze shifted back to hers. All she saw was rage.

She cringed and backed a few steps.

Jake followed, ready to... what? Finally he asked, "Why'd you scream?"

Just then a loud groan came from behind the bale. Suzannah gestured toward Bronco then pled with her eyes, hoping Jake would get the picture why she'd had to stop him any way she could.

* * *

Jake vaulted over the bale and came to Bronco's side. "Where'd that crack come from?" His words came out rough, fury still running a hot path through him. He was barely holding it together.

"You son-of-a—" Bronco cursed at him.

That just made Jake want to pummel him some more.

Suzannah crawled over the bale and squatted down next to Bronco, running her small hands over the arm he was favoring. This topped it. Of course the kitten was going to concern herself with his injuries, big-hearted as she was.

A surge of jealousy merged with the fury, mixing him up. What was he doing? How was he to act around the lass now? She'd seen his weakest self, last night. He didna remember all of it, but he remembered balling his eyes out like a silly bairn against her legs and then her belly. Gad, he should skulk off to the deep woods and live as the hermit he was meant to be. He sure as Hades wasna fit for human folk. Especially not her.

"Jake…" Suzannah said, smacking him on the arm to get his attention. "Broken, I think."

"*What?* Nae!" He cursed. Jumping to his feet, he cursed some more.

"Get something…" She used her hands to show they needed splints of some sort.

He nodded, and hurried off to the tack room where he knew his uncle kept riding crops for difficult horses. Grabbing two short, thick ones, he also found some cotton rope. He rushed back to his kitten and a sputtering cousin. Bronco was groaning and sweating with his injured arm nestled in Suzie's hands.

"I'll hold it," she said. "You splint."

Jake peered into her confident eyes and nodded. He was the healer. He knew what to do, but was surprised she did. Amazed at Suzannah's calmness while she held Bronc's arm as still as possible, Jake dropped to his knees next to her.

"We need to secure it first." He untied his kerchief from around his neck and wrapped it around Bronc's arm. He tied it snugly as Bronc grunted in pain, then placed the two crops on either side of the forearm. Suzannah held the splint in place as he dug for his pocket knife. After slicing the cotton rope in three short pieces and one longer one, he tied one at Bronco's elbow, forearm, and wrist. The longer length he made into a sling, placed it, tied it, and then sat back on his haunches to examine his work. "That's all we can do. Off to the hospital you go."

Suzannah also inspected his work, and nodded. She still didna look happy, but then, he'd been pretty brutal with his cousin. Suzannah surely would oppose such behavior. He did too, but kent he'd do it all over if his cousin crossed the line with her again.

"Come. Up with you." Jake rocked back and stood up, then pulled his cousin none too gently to his feet.

"What's going on in here?"

They all looked to Trevor, who was silhouetted by moonlight in the doorway.

"Our *cousin* here decided to give me a vacation from ranchin'," Bronco said.

Trevor flipped on the overhead lights. "What are you talking about?"

Jake gripped Bronco's good arm at the bicep and walked him toward Trevor. Suzannah followed a few feet behind. "He needs his arm casted. Do you want me to take him, or you?" Jake said.

"What the devil happened, Jake?"

"We dinna have time for this." Jake moved as if to round him to the open door.

Trevor stopped him with a hand to his chest. "What, happened?"

Suzannah snatched Trevor's hand away from Jake's chest and shook her head. "Hospital first."

Trevor stared. Jake would have laughed if he were doing that these days. Trevor had to be astounded that not just one, but two Harper women had taken him to task in the span of as many hours. Little did he ken that his life was on a path toward total transformation once Rebecca got settled in to cook, clean, and control these Cooper kinsmen. Good. Jake had watched these decent men flounder for years without a mother for moral guidance. Mayhap they would finally gain some ground with a respectable woman in their midst. One who would be hard put to keep her nose out of their business.

He would be darned if he'd feel sorry for them, though, since the wee kitten had done the same with him since the day he'd met her. He'd yet to find solid ground. Apparently that was the course of all men when a good woman stepped into their lives bent on staying.

It seemed they were going to have a stare-off, his kitten and the eldest Cooper son. Finally, Trevor nodded, backed out of the way, and said, "My truck's in the drive. I'll take care of it."

"Maybe we should bring my nurse with us," Bronco said, waving his good hand toward Suzannah, and giving her a wink.

"Mayhap nae," Jake said back, giving the bicep he still held a firm squeeze. "I'll go."

"Ow! Let loose," Bronco said, yanking his arm out of Jake's hold.

"What the heck, you two. You haven't seen each other in two years, and you're right back at each other's throats." Trevor motioned to the twin's arm, then glared at Jake. "I think it's best I take Brand with us."

Trevor glanced around the barn. "Where is he anyway? He still needs patching up. Trailed blood everywhere. He may need stitches."

"Have'na seen him," Jake said.

"Blasted! Now I have to track him down."

Jake went for his hat and plucked it off the ground. "I'll find him," Jake said, guilt pounding at him. He needed to help his cousins while he was here instead of cause more work and worry. Mayhap back off Bronc as well. He reshaped his hat and stuffed it back on his head. "Come on, lass. I'll walk you back to the house."

He watched as the kitten lifted her hand to give Bronc a pat, caught herself, and clasped her hands in front of her. Her shoulders were stiff, breathing controlled. She'd just touched Bronc for the splint out of compassion, but now? Would she have an aversion to men from now on? Or mayhap she already had an aversion to aggressive men.

A lead ball dropped in Jake's gut. *You're an aggressive man.* He worried over that for a few seconds, until he remembered her usual behavior around him. He was certain she harbored no fear of him. A deep intuition told him this had to do with something that happened to her in the past. Somehow he'd have to get her to open up about it.

Bronc winked at her again.

Jake snarled under his breath. If Jake popped him in the nose, Suzannah would never speak to him again. And here he'd just decided to back off with Bronc. He ran a hand over his thick beard. Well, he'd still try. As long as Bronc didna come anywhere near the kitten again.

Taking Suzannah by the elbow, he delicately extracted her from her rigid stance and escorted her out the door. He held firm, surprised Suzannah didna squirm away from him as they made their way back to the house along the curve in the drive.

Jake gripped the ranch house's front door knob, trying not to notice how cold it was in his hand compared to the soft warmth of Suzannah's arm in his other. He gave the knob a twist. The door swung slowly inward, revealing first Rebecca on her knees and then Brand seated opposite her on a kitchen chair. This time, Brand was combed up and fully clothed, except for his bare feet, one of which was resting on a short stool with Rebecca applying some sort of bandage to it.

"So, that's where you are," Jake said.

Brand cranked his neck around. "Where'd you think I'd be?"

"Trevor just came from the house. Didna ken where you were."

Brand turned back to Rebecca. "Yeah, well, he was so ticked, I stayed clear until he left the house. Thought I'd bleed to death before he got out of my line-a-sight." He snorted with indignation.

"Criminy, Brand. Fool thing to do," Jake said, circling Rebecca to see Brand's wound. "It didna need stitches, eh?"

"No," Rebecca said while she worked. "I'm taping it tight. Should be fine. But he'll have to keep it up for a while."

Suzannah started for the front door.

"Where're you off to, lass?" Jake asked.

"To tell Trevor," she said, pointing to Brand.

He didna want her anywhere near Bronc again. Not Trevor either. "I'll go. You stay and help Rebecca."

She shrugged and walked back to stand behind her sister.

Jake made his way out the door and up the drive to where his cousin's truck was parked, grumbling to himself the whole way. Once he'd discovered Betty and the bairn had perished, he'd acted as if Suzannah's comfort could make all well. Hardly. He'd have to work himself to the bone here to pay the universe back for his guilt. And now he'd compounded that guilt ten fold.

CHAPTER 16

After watching Rebecca patch up Brand, Suzannah meandered up the drive to the barn to see how it was going with Bronco. Trevor had brought his truck near and was now helping Bronco in it. Jake was there, but it looked to her like he remained on the outskirts, a deep scowl riding his face.

As she strode along the dirt road toward them, a gentle wind rustled the leaves of a nearby oak. She focused on the base hum that filled the air around her, teasing away the lapping symphony of insect sounds to hear the lowing of distant cattle. The evening's peace soaked into her. She breathed as much of it in as she could, fortifying herself before once more facing a fuming Jake.

Trevor shut the passenger door for Bronco and strode over to Jake. Since Trevor faced away from her, Suzannah could only hear part of what he had to say. "… hands full… go back… angry…"

Jake's lips were pressed together, his jaw muscles working. Finally it was Jake's turn. Before he even started in, she saw the impact of Trevor's words in

Jake's posture. "So, that's the way of it, aye? You want me gone."

What? Trevor was kicking him off the ranch? Because of the fight, and for breaking Bronco's arm? It was an accident, but if anyone were to blame, it was her. Her feet carried her forward before she could think better of it. Jake wouldn't be happy, since he'd told her to stay at the house with Rebecca. But no way was she letting him take the full hit.

Jake caught sight of her as she came around the truck bed toward him. He held up his hand to stop her. "Nae, lass. Go on back."

Trevor turned toward her, looking determined, yet remorseful.

Blood drained from Suzannah's head, and her heart felt heavy. Poor Jake. One more thing. All of the sudden a thrust of fury hit her, then another, as if she were caught up in a whirlwind. No! She would not let Jake take the blow alone.

She strode straight up to Trevor and pushed at his shoulder. "No! Why?" was all her throat would allow. She hoped her face said it all.

Trevor ran a hand over his mouth. She'd seen him do that before, just before he'd kept something back, or lied, about his dad.

"Don't!" She pierced him with her best glare.

His hand fell from his mouth. "Don't what?" he tried, then instantly relented as if he knew he was found out. He rolled his eyes, then shyly met her gaze. "Fine."

Trevor turned to Jake then. "Listen. You brought Rebecca and the gelding. Dad won't be back for two months, so you can't see him. Bronco is hard enough to manage on a good day. Now, once his arm is fixed up and he thinks on it for a while, he'll give anger the lead. Anger at you. You really should go."

Suzannah watched with horror as Jake's shoulders slumped, his eyes drooped, and his fisted hands relaxed. She thought if a seat were close by, he'd drop into it.

Lord, help me help him, please!

The prayer echoed back to her as if from an empty well, but still she urged her plea heavenward. With every fiber of her being she prayed, until the lump in her throat lodged in her soul as well. She fell silent inside, waiting through one heartbeat... and another. And then the answer came.

* * *

Jake turned away from Trevor and strode into the barn, Suzannah's light footfalls registering behind him. Barely able to breathe, he needed some space to figure things out. Going back to Harper Ranch wasna an option. Not now, anyway. Roy had practically kicked him off the spread. What would Roy say when he came back from this bloody *vacation* too soon? Seemed he wasna welcome there either.

Troy Wheeler came to mind. Mayhap he had a bronc or two Jake could conk heads with. It was all that was left to him again, the dark nothingness of waiting until an instant of brutal pain put him out of his misery for good.

Jake closed his eyes. He'd been on the cusp of living again, all because Suzannah had begun to pry apart the bars around his heart. Now it seemed like the last several weeks with her hadna happened at all.

The kitten. What would he do with her if he bunked out at Wheeler's for a spell? He could leave her here and come back for her in a couple weeks. Aye, that could work. He rubbed his chest. An ache formed at the thought of leaving her anywhere near Bronco... or Trevor for that matter... or leaving her at all. He pushed his hat back and swiped at the beads of sweat on his forehead. What choice did he have? Besides, Rebecca was here and could watch out for her. She'd be fine. She'd have to be.

Just as he was about to turn back to tell Suzie as much, he felt her small hand at his back. That same, soothing stroke she'd gifted him with last night. He took comfort in her touch until the biting reality of having to leave her behind returned. He pivoted to face her, nearly clobbering her with his elbow. He managed to lift his arm over her head in time, but trapped her snug against him when his arm dropped into place.

Suzannah peered up at him. She was warm and soft and beautiful and… so preciously fearless, Jake found himself sinking into the depths of her lovely eyes. This close, he could see the yellow and green flecks scattered at random within the rich blue. His hat sheltered them, cocooned them, and time halted. It was he and the kitten. No one else existed. Their breathing synchronized, breath for breath, sweet and warm. The animal sounds around them ceased, the barnyard smells faded. Stillness surrounded them, and his good sense drifted away. When he finally wedged open that door to his emotions, true affection flowed out from him, reaching for her.

His palm came up to cup Suzannah's cheek. It was so large, his hand, it practically swallowed up her wee face; dark against her fair skin, rough against her smoothness. He stroked her cheek once; the silky sensation of it started in his palm, tingled up his arm, and shot straight into his unsuspecting heart, rendering him motionless. When he could move again, he glided the pad of his thumb over that beautiful mouth. Then, just the bottom lip, tugging it down as the tip slid along the moist warmth inside. Full… soft… inviting.

The universe shifted.

A sliver of his old self tried to burrow in. Suzannah had only been trying to soothe him, he told himself. Only… it was too late.

He bent to her mouth, all the while tugging her into his embrace. She didna resist. If she had, this farce would be over. Instead, she arched in, and his lips touched hers. In an instant, night turned to day, day to night; the earth stilled, it rolled; his heart froze, it galloped; it was cold, it blazed hot. His head spun, everything shifted, rose, fell, sped, slowed, until finally… finally, he focused on the kiss itself. Sweet, tender, a brush of lips. Then, he couldna hold back from the mouth he'd become so aware of. The contact felt like Heaven itself. She was the angel, and he was…

What am I about? He should move away from her; the sight of her, the smell of her, the feel of her. But by degrees, her eagerness, her heat, and the demand from his own deprived body won out. Sliding his fingers into her hair, he angled her head so he could indulge himself more—taste her, drink her in.

A wee voice broke through his fervor. *Stop. Now.* But it was his own conscience, not Suzannah's voice, else he'd have obeyed it. In the next instant, she wrapped her slender arms around his neck and pressed in. This was no chaste meeting of lips. Nae. This was a woman's kiss, and the offer was all he needed to shut the door to his conscience. He rubbed his palms up and down her back, so slender, yet woman-soft all the same. For the first time in years he allowed himself to feel—truly feel.

On the heels of that long-forgotten sensation came the war. It broke out deep within his soul. He ignored it, plowed deep, slid farther into her space, pulling her supple body into the hard angles of his own.

All the while the voice of despair scratched at his mind, reminding him how worthless he was. *Wake up, Jacob Cooper. A knob like you shouldna ever be allowed to lay one finger on an angel like her.* That thought whizzed through his brain, caught hold, and carried back his reason. His lips halted against hers. They lingered, still starved for her.

Release her. Back off.

Finally, he took hold of her upper arms and straightened his, pushing her back. Her breathing was erratic, as was his. She wobbled, so he kept his hold. The hurt on her wee, angel face was breaking his heart.

"Lass," he said, taking a deep breath and huffing it out.

Her big eyes widened. Had she guessed what he was going to say? "No, Jake," she said.

"No?"

"No. Don't you dare say the kiss was a mistake."

Sidetracked by her long sentence, proud of her that it sounded so normal, he shook his head to regain his focus. The kiss *was* a mistake, purely because he'd wanted it for so long, and just plain took it. Now, he'd given her the wrong impression. "Lass."

She glared, like she was going to reprimand him again. He wanted to chuckle at that, but didna. "I'm going to head out. Mayhap to Wheeler's for a bit. You stay with Rebecca. I'll pick you up in a couple weeks."

He released her arms, since she seemed stronger now. Indeed, she was heating up, her face flushing pink. She brought her hands to her hips, looking indignant, ready to explode.

He felt his mouth curve up on one side.

She fluttered a blink. Her mouth gaped, and the flush slipped out of her cheeks. She cocked her head to one side and looked at him as if he'd just changed faces.

That made his other side lift as well.

She blinked harder and her jaw came unhinged. She looked like a baby owl ready to feed.

This time he couldna help himself. It could have been the cute expression on her face, the warmth of her closeness, the nourishment of that kiss. Who ken? And who cared? All that mattered was the fact his lips had parted into a liberating, beaming smile.

Her knees wobbled, and he thought she might fall. Grabbing one of her elbows, he held her snug, his smile flitting away like it was glad to be off.

A disappointed wee sound escaped her. She lifted a hand to his face, and with all four fingertips, rubbed it across his now closed mouth. "Beautiful," she whispered in awe. "Do it again?"

And, lo and behold, her adorable quest brought it on again. He smiled in full.

She blinked, smiled right back at him. The sight was a blazing sun to his cold soul, warming him from the tips of his ears to the pads of his toes.

He wondered at his own smile, why she would even want to see it again. It felt so unfamiliar on his face, he thought it must look absurd. Especially since it was surrounded by the full beard he hid behind. Still, it pleased him that it pleased her.

They stood there like two teenage kids, staring and smiling and probably looking outlandish.

"What are you two doing?" Rebecca said, cutting in on their mutual admiration stalemate.

They each took a step back from one another, but still didna look away. Jake couldna seem to tear his gaze away from the lass's glorious, smiling face, though his own smile had fled once again. Slowly, hers did as well.

Suzannah made a half turn to glare at Rebecca. Jake almost smiled again at the kitten's anger over her sister's intrusion. He felt the same way. Who knew when they would ever have a moment like this again.

"What do you want?" Suzannah said, plainly.

Rebecca started at Suzannah's clarity, but gathered herself and went on. "Trevor has long gone with Bronco to the hospital. So, why are you two still out here?"

"None of your business," Suzannah said, with a stamp of her foot. "Go back."

Rebecca came forward, frowning and studying Suzie closer. "What's really going on, Suze?"

The kitten slammed her fists on her hips. "Why do you need to know?"

Once again, Rebecca looked stunned. Suzannah was having a clear conversation with her, and she was baffled. Frankly, so was he.

Rebecca glanced at him, then back to Suzie. "I'm just concerned, is all."

"About what?" Suzie said with a little louder voice.

"Well… about you. Being alone out here with Jake, if you must know. Come on back to the house."

Suzannah glanced at Jake with a worried expression, no doubt thinking Rebecca's words had insulted him and he would bolt. Frankly, he was enjoying this.

"No!" Suzannah said.

"What do you mean, 'no'?" Rebecca shot back.

"I mean, no. Jake and I were just discussing our plans to…" Suzannah stopped and coughed. Apparently, a dozen words was her max. Still, it was much better than normal. Or, so it seemed to him.

"Your plans to what?"

Jake's brain kicked in just then. He'd been so intent on Suzannah's delivery, he hadna listened to what she implied. He strode forward. "I was telling her that I would be leaving. She's staying here with you."

He felt Suzannah's glare.

"What are you talking about?" Rebecca said. "I thought you were staying for a week or so, then would be taking Suzannah back with you." Rebecca scowled directly at him. These Harper lasses sure had a way with wordless exchanges. "Why have you changed your mind, Jake?"

"Trevor changed my mind," he said, as the old melancholy crashed back in. Anger, despair, futility, they all demanded a spot in his conscious mind.

Suzannah stepped in front of him, facing her sister, as if to guard him from her. "Jake and I are going to Wheeler's. He'll work... with horses, and I'll... I'll clean."

It was a pretty good idea, he thought. But, he couldna let her come. He was still wrestling demons. She would want attention. It wasna a good mix.

While he was pondering how to let her down, she whirled to face him, her shiny braid flying over her shoulder to lie upon her chest. She stood two steps away, yet he could feel waves of heat from her wee body, could still smell the citrusy fragrance that always enticed him so. Her angelic face peered up at him. Her well-kissed lips were pressed together and drooped slightly at the edges, her eyes pleading soulfully at him. How could he tell her 'no'?

Nae. He couldna.

He eyeballed Rebecca, over Suzie's head. "Aye. Suzannah and I will be leaving soon."

The elated smile the kitten gave him was worth anything he had to do. It set off a burst of joy inside him, like pinwheels on the 4th of July. He was a stone-cold sucker for this lass, aye? And, to his surprise, that was okay by him.

Rebecca's mouth gaped and then her voice gobble-gobbled like a flustered hen, but Jake didna hear another thing she said. He leaned near Suzannah's ear and said, "I better give ole Troy a head's up, aye?" Then he slipped a gentle hand down her hair, because he had to. Gave her a wink, and moved around both lasses to exit the barn for the house.

* * *

Suzannah's heart pounded against her chest as she watched Jake disappear into the night. That tender touch and wink had meant more to her than his extraordinary kiss. And he was going to take her with him! Hope, freedom, love, all swirled within her. Besides that, something deep inside ached at the thought of him ever being away from her. He needed her. She needed to watch over him. *Oh, Lord. I want to help him. To be near him. Please, let there be work for me.*

Now, to deal with her sister. She took two solid breaths, then turned back. "Why did you come out here, Rebecca?" She knew her sister didn't deserve her bitter tone, but she'd had enough babying.

"I told you why. And what do I find? I find the two of you staring into each other's eyes like pie-eyed lovers! With grins on both your faces." Rebecca shook her head. "Come to think of it, I have *never* seen that man smile before. My goodness, it appears good looks run throughout all the Cooper males. But, Suzannah, I warned you to be careful around Jake. It's a dicey situation. He's dangerous."

"And I told you he's not!"

"You're not going off with him by yourself. I don't care where."

Older sisters! "First off, I'm not your responsibility. I'm my own person. Secondly…" She cleared her throat. It was so darned frustrating not to ever be able to finish a thought out loud. *Please, Lord, fix my throat,* she begged for the umpteenth time.

Rebecca waited, God bless her. She worked hard at understanding Suzannah's annoying affliction. Suzannah took a step closer, softened her voice. "… we'll be around people. At Wheeler's."

"Are you going to Wheeler's for sure?"

"Jake went to call," Suzannah said, turning to follow him back to the house.

"Wait."

Suzannah turned back from the barn door.

"Why are you doing this, Suzannah? What is Jake to you?"

All she could do was ease Rebecca's mind. Suzannah gentled her expression as she strode back to her. Her sister meant well. She'd had to watch over Suzannah off and on for years now. "Sis. I know you're only worried about me." She took the final step to her, laid a hand on her shoulder. "Trust me. Jake is good." She wanted to say more, if only she could. That Jake was trustworthy, his heart was gold, he'd never harm Suzannah even to save his own life, and he cared for her as she did him.

Rebecca's face softened as worry left her.

"If we leave you?" Suzannah raised her brows in question.

"Me? Pfft. I'll be fine," Rebecca said, waving a hand at her little sister's concern.

Suzannah looped an arm through Rebecca's and turned her toward the open barn door. She switched off the lights, then tugged the door closed, Bonnie's low nicker sending them off into the night.

Neither opened their mouths as they moseyed up to the Cooper Ranch house. It seemed bigger than ever, appearing more mansion than house in the glow of the rising moon. It had a homey feel to it, even with its oversized rectangles of lit windows flaunting exquisite ranch-style furniture inside.

Suzannah dropped her arm from Rebecca's as they approached the front door. Through the glass she saw Brand lazing in one of the bulky couches with his injured heel up on a foot stool. Probably where Rebecca had left him. Suzannah pulled the front door open. Both of them hustled through it. Rebecca pulled the door closed behind them then veered off to the living room to check on Brand.

Jake took the telephone receiver from his ear and placed it back in its cradle just as Suzannah strolled into the kitchen.

Suzannah caught Jake's eye. "How did it go?"

Jake smoothed a hand over his beard. "Aye. There's work. He's glad for both of us. Tonight even. He'll leave the porch light on for us, all night if need be." Then he grinned. Again! The sight tumbled her insides. Oh, but she could get used to that smile. She wondered if he had cheery brackets around his mouth, or even dimples. She had already seen the gentleness behind the scowl. Now she wanted to see the true face behind the beard.

Jake's grin slid away and his brows knit together. "Will Rebecca be all right if we leave her so soon?"

Suzannah grinned, pleased he cared what befell her sister. "She's the tough Harper."

Jake nodded, then slid a palm over her hair, watching his own hand bump over the nubs of her braid. Next time, she'd let her hair go free, so he could finger each loose curl. Oh, how that would feel.

He stroked her hair once again, but stopped at her cheek, and stroked it with his thumb as he gazed into her eyes. She thought she could stand right here for the rest of her days and let Jake stroke and stare and love her.

Yes. Love her, as she loved him. And she did. She may have only known Jake a few short weeks, but she'd never been more sure of anything in her entire life.

Lord, if You agree, my prayer is to make this man mine. Truth was, she only wanted God's will for her. She'd made the mistake before of forcing a relationship without consulting God. She'd seen the signs early on, but chose to ignore them. Besides, she had to leave Jake in God's hands. Jake's own relationship with Him would have to come first. God was his only hope for true healing from everything that plagued him. Without genuine healing, he'd never be able to move on with his life, plant a new relationship, and watch it grow.

"We should go. Get our bags. Be on our way, aye?" This time he gave her a closed mouth smile, full of tenderness.

Her knees trembled a bit, right along with her racing pulse. The word 'we' sounded so perfect on his lips.

She raised her chin to him and matched his smile, nodding with absolute agreement.

CHAPTER 17

Jake glanced over at Suzannah. She was quiet as a snow fall, cloaked in contentment, so opposite his own state of being. Since the moment they'd driven off Cooper Ranch towards Wheeler's, remorse had mushroomed inside him mile by mile. What had he been thinking to act so rashly with the kitten?

As much as he wanted her near him, it was foolish of him to think long term. She was from a good family. If he were a father of a lass, a man like him who'd already failed horribly at marriage to the doom of his wife and bairn wouldna be allowed on his property, let alone near his daughter. He came from a broken family with a non-existent father. She was an innocent lass, and he was a brazen good-for-nothing with no future. He had not kept his wife and bairn safe. In fact, he was the one who'd caused them to die. That meant Suzannah would never be safe with him, and his desire to protect her would never be enough.

He couldna lash her to himself. It wouldna be right.

He felt bad, real bad, that he'd kissed her. Not that he didna enjoy every second of it. He had, more than any kiss he'd ever given a woman. But, if she felt the same way he did, well, she'd be wanting more, and he already ken he wouldna say 'nae' to anything she asked of him. His only hope was to stay away from her. He'd be able to do that at Wheeler's, but on the ride back to Harper's... well, he'd think of something.

Jake slowed the truck, shifted down, and entered Wheeler's property. A quick glance at Suzannah disclosed a smile, bright and beautiful, like sunshine breaking through at the end of a thunderstorm. That unfettered smile made his breath hitch. Ah, he was a fool if he thought he could keep her from affecting him. Still, he would try. It was the proper thing to do.

As they pulled up to the front of the oddly shaped ranch house, Troy came rambling down the walkway toward them, the glow of the house lights at his back. He swung Suzannah's door open and smiled cheerfully at her. "Welcome back, youngsters. I hear you're gonna clean up for us cowpokes, eh, SuzieQ?"

Jake frowned. *SuzieQ?*

"We couldn't be happier than pigs in a teeming sty, but I'm afraid, dear girl, we bachelors live in a sty of our own makin'. You done such a fine job of cleanin' up after the party this mornin', I'm embarrassed to show ya what we done to it already." He smiled sheepishly, and offered her a hand. "You might oughta look closer before you decide for sure. Come on in."

Suzannah shadowed Troy up the walk and into the house, Jake trailing behind. One step over the threshold, and by the rigidness of *SuzieQ's* stance, it was bad. He glanced around, but couldna judge, having just seen a whole lot worse at his cousin's place. Looked to him it was a bit untidy, was all. Closing the door behind him, he gave her a wee shove from behind, loosening her tense legs. She gracefully moved forward with a smile on her face, covering her poor reaction to the clutter. That made him proud. Suzannah wasna one to make others feel bad. She'd find a way to make Troy relax about this.

When Jake noticed her wee hand touch Troy on the forearm, the older man considered her face and visibly relaxed. Jake couldna see the look she'd given him, but knew it had convinced Troy everything would be fine.

"Well now, I ken there's nothing Suzannah canna handle," Jake said, to save Suzannah's voice.

She smiled up at him, an affectionate glitter in her bonny eyes. His heart tripped, but his mind reminded him of his promise to himself to keep his distance.

He averted his gaze, bringing it back to Troy. "Shall I find your foreman, to meet the bronc needs fixing?"

"No, Jake, it's late. We'll get you all set up on the morrow. We're up with the chickens round here. For now, I'll show you both to your quarters."

Jake turned to head for the front door.

"Where you going, son? We have plenty of room in the house for the both of you. Follow me."

"Nae, Troy. Put Suzannah up here. Bunkhouse is fine by me."

Troy frowned. "I won't have it. You may be in my employ for a week or two, but you're also a guest. Enough. This way." Troy pivoted to the stairs.

Suzannah looked back at Jake with a question on her face.

He heaved a sigh. "Aye, lass. It's fine." He kent she wanted to follow his lead. She'd been doing that since his news. His gut clenched at the memory of Betty's father charging him with neglect. This time last year, he'd have wagered his best cutting horse against anyone who'd thought him capable of such a thing, protector that he believed himself to be. But Harold was right. The memory of his words still burned Jake's insides. He would never be deserving of a lass's love again.

The lass stood, watching his face as if she could read each thought as it whizzed by. Wanting to calm her concern, he slowly ran a hand down her hair. When his hand reached her shoulder, he took hold of it and turned her toward the stairs, giving her a wee thump on the rear before he thought better of it.

He needed to put his brain in gear; keep his hands from setting off on their own. Space was his only hope of doing that. So, he waited two heartbeats before dawdling behind.

"Here's SuzieQ's room," Troy said, holding the door open for her.

She squeezed past, then smiled in delight at the particularly feminine room. Turning toward Troy, she gestured with her hands and shrugged.

Troy looked confused. Jake jumped in. "You should know, Troy. Suzannah has a wee speech problem. She can talk, but with difficulty. If you can figure what she needs, it's best she save her voice."

Jake had come to stand by her, so he was close enough when the jab in the ribs came. "Oof, lass!" Jake said, rubbing his side. "Troy needs to ken why you dinna speak up when he talks to you, aye?"

She blushed to the roots of her hair and averted her gaze to the window.

Jake decided to save her embarrassment by bringing them back to the first topic. "She likes this room. Wonders why you have such a frilly room in your bachelor pad."

Suzannah shot Jake an amazed look, her eyes twinkling, the corners of her mouth doing a slow rise until her honeyed lips were chock full of straight white teeth.

Sunshine, is what Jake thought. "Aye, lass. Took me a while, but I'm catching on."

She touched his arm tentatively and glued her gaze to his. He'd learned, this was the time to shut-up and pay close attention. "You're talking more, too," she said, then smiled again.

He snorted a quick laugh. "Well, one of us has to, my wee lass." Then he smiled at her, because he knew that pleased her and would make her smile some more.

They stood grinning at each other he'd thought for only a second. Apparently not, since Troy cleared his throat. "Um… Jake. You wanna come with me, son?"

Jake started, then felt a deep flush rise to his face. He hoped his beard hid his boyish reaction. "Settle in. I'll get your bags," he said to Suzannah, then followed Troy.

To his dismay, Troy took him straight across the hallway. The room was plain, unlike Suzannah's, and decidedly masculine. Still, he was uncomfortable to be in Troy's house, let alone so close to the kitten. He ran a hand down his face and over his beard as he glanced around. Mayhap a week or two at Wheeler's had been a bad idea. It sure ramped up his need for people skills, which he had none of; not to mention his dodging skills, of which he had plenty—except when it came to Suzannah.

Well, nothing could be done about it. He'd make due. "We appreciate this, Troy. I'll be up by dawn to get started."

"Now, son, don't be too hasty. We get up at dawn, all right, but to go on down to breakfast. Oh! That reminds me. I'll need to show SuzieQ around her kitchen. Have her come on down when she gets herself settled in." He gestured toward her room. "Hope she's a good cook."

Jake stiffened. Had he missed something? He took a step toward Troy. Troy was several inches shorter than Jake, so he hoped his size spoke more than what he was about to say. He kept his voice low. "Thought you said housekeeper, not cook. You already have a good cook. A great cook. We were looking forward to her meals."

"Yeah. Well. I didn't want to scare the girl off, you know? Truth is, Bea had an emergency in her family." He must have seen Jake's panic, since he amended with, "She'll be back in a few days. Don't you worry none, son. If the girl can't cook, we can some."

Jake blew out an uneven breath, then nodded. "Better let me break it to her."

The older man nodded as well, then twisted back to the hallway. Jake heard his steps thunder down the stairs, just like his heart was doing in his chest. How would Suzannah take this news? He had no idea if she cooked.

It took him just two strides to reach her door. Too short a distance. His dreams were sure to drift right over to her every night. He gulped down a wave of foreboding. Could he even make it through one night, let alone two weeks?

Suzannah looked up the moment he leaned against the doorjamb. He folded his arms, trying his level best not to show his nerves. He'd noticed that lately. The lass had him all tied up.

She smiled a greeting as if she hadna just seen him, and his tongue tripped, stopping up his words. What he wanted right now was to close the door, wrap his arms clean around her, kiss that bonny mouth, and walk her backwards to the bed.

And that wayward thought alone gave him the strength to rein his passion to a sliding halt. He'd rise early, work his bones to dust, and fall into his own bed for an exhausted, dreamless sleep. It was his only hope for survival. And, aye, he kent now, he wanted to survive.

He felt his whole face relax as he smiled back at her. Pushing off the jamb, he straightened to full height and planted his fingertips casually on each hip. "Tell me, lass, can you cook?"

Her smile shifted to a cute pout of puzzlement, her brow pleating. "Aye," she said, making him bark a laugh. He loved how she constantly surprised him.

It took him a minute to regain his seriousness while sheer delight ran rampant through his system. But, oh, how good that felt. "It seems Troy is without a cook at the moment." He waited. Watched for her reaction.

Her fingers shot to her mouth. "What happened to Bea?"

"Dinna worry, lass. Bea is fine." He didna need to worry her about the emergency. "She'll be back in a few days."

Suzannah studied his expression for a moment, then waved a slender hand in the air. "Pfft. No problem."

"No problem? You cook back home?"

She smiled again, and he drank it in. "Aye," she said, then giggled.

It was like her smile triggered his own now, since he felt a goofy grin split his face almost without his say-so. He couldna remember a time when he'd smiled this much in twenty-four hours. Criminy, he'd barely smiled since birth.

He cupped her cheek, his hand covering the side of her face. "Troy will be pleased, lass." He stroked her skin, so velvety soft, and had to pull back before he again took more than he was entitled to.

"Come." Jake took her by the hand and led her out of the room. He kept hold of her hand as he descended the stairs with her close on his tail. "Troy wants to show you around *your* kitchen."

* * *

Suzannah loved her small hand being gripped by Jake's big paw. It made her feel safe and normal and feminine, and finally ready to take hold of life. She skipped along behind his long strides to the kitchen where Troy was pouring a cup of coffee.

"Freshly brewed," he said as he held up the cup in offer.

Suzannah shook her head.

"Thanks," Jake said, and probably only took the cup since Troy had gone to the trouble of brewing a pot so late.

Jake pulled Suzannah around him to the kitchen counter to face Troy, then peeled his hand away from hers before settling into one of the vinyl kitchen chairs.

"So," Troy began, "you're okay with being Bea for a few days?"

Suzannah scrunched her face up.

Troy looked confused.

"She's worried about Bea," Jake explained.

Troy shook his head in awe at Jake's ability to read her. So was she. "Bea's fine. Had to see about an emergency in her family."

Suzannah kept her eyes on Troy, waiting for an explanation.

Troy looked to Jake.

Jake chuckled. "That one seems obvious, Troy. She wants to ken more."

The older man swung his gaze back to Suzannah, and shrugged. "Don't know. Can you cook?"

Suzannah wrinkled her nose at Troy, annoyed he didn't care to know more about poor Bea. "Aye," she finally said.

Jake grinned at her, another chunk of his grief seeming to fall off him and their bond cinching tighter.

Suzannah relented and gave Troy a smile.

"Good. That's very good. You don't know how you're saving us," he said, then laughed. "Here's the pantry, refrigerator is full of our favorites... " He droned on. Suzannah half listened, knowing she'd figure out everything on her own. Cooking was a love of hers. If the Coopers had realized that, they would have wanted her rather than Rebecca.

At this moment, her mind wanted to camp on Jake and his staggering smile. She'd only seen it once before in Montana, briefly, and couldn't quite believe it was so magnificent. It seemed to show up when she smiled at him. That made things simple. She'd smile the melancholy right out of him, help him release his guilt and truly live again.

It was sure that her speech problem was improving around Jake. She didn't know if it was because of her deepening affection for him, or that she felt safe with him. Either way, she could actually see a future in which she was normal again. And she wanted that future with Jake.

Turning her head to glance at the object of her thoughts, she caught him drinking coffee and... inspecting her rump? When he saw she'd caught him, his face flamed red through his beard, and he nearly choked on the gulp he'd taken.

She couldn't resist teasing him. All indignant-like, she shot around and wagged a finger at him.

He winced and looked so adorably sheepish, she burst into laughter, low and hoarse, but hardy nonetheless. Then she winked, further inflaming his face, and turned back to Troy who was eyeing them both with a question in his expression.

She shrugged and twirled a half circle, an arm outstretched showing the kitchen layout.

Once again, Troy looked baffled.

"She understands about everything you showed her," Jake said from behind her.

She twisted around and gave Jake an adoring smile. He gave her a small lopsided grin back.

"Now, how'd you know that, son?" Troy asked, shaking his head in wonder.

"I just do."

"You just do?"

"I speak Suzannah," Jake said, then grinned again at her.

Good grace, but all they seemed to be doing in the last day was smile at each other. His smile was warm and attractive and downright comforting. All she wanted to do now was curl up in his lap and snuggle in until his legs fell asleep. Was that so bad?

"Well," Troy said. "If I have trouble communicating with SuzieQ here, I know who to ask." He smiled at them both, then headed across the kitchen to the back door. He put a hand on the doorknob, then spoke over his shoulder. "Get some rest, young'uns. Tomorrow will be a big day." Then he was gone, probably to do one last circuit through the barn.

Jake leaned forward and caught her by a hand, tugging her toward him. "Come here, *SuzieQ*," he said, ribbing her. He drew her near, then tugged harder. She had nowhere else to go but onto his lap. Right where she'd imagined being.

He stroked her hair once, then pulled her braid around and released the rubber band at the tip. Ever so slowly, he unwound the braid all the way up to her forehead. Her breath caught when he drove all ten fingertips from her hairline on back until he'd freed knots and could comb through the entire length. She heard a small groan in the area of his Adam's apple and matched it with a moan of her own.

"That's all I've thought about doing since the first day I met you."

"You have?" she asked, reaching up to remove his hat, then doing the same thing back to him. His hair was surprisingly silky, and black as a panther's. It fit him, that hair color, just like the black clothes and hat he wore. Not because he had a wicked soul, for she knew he didn't possess one. But because his heart had been blackened, gouged, utterly mauled by the events of his life, until all hope seemed to have burned to ash.

But there was still hope. Because there was One who could resurrect life out of the ash. Jesus, the Savior who would willingly carry all of Jake's burdens. Like her favorite Scripture—Matthew 11:28—reminded her daily: *Come unto me, all ye that labor and are heavy laden, and I will give you rest.* She had leaned on this truth since the day her voice had been stolen from her. It was what had helped her endure from that moment's terror to this moment's exquisite bliss.

Jake groaned in earnest now, and closed his eyes. His breathing had become ragged, and his nostrils flared with each intake of breath. "Suzie…" he murmured under his breath. Then he stiffened and his eyes popped open, but he didn't look at her. "Nae. Canna do this, Kitten. Much as I want to."

She dropped her hands from his hair to his shoulders and gave a push, making him look her in the eye. "Aye, we can."

His smile was short-lived. "Lass…" He sighed, then frowned.

"You start… you stop," she said.

"It's just…"

She sighed as well. "Just what?" She took in the room with a brief turn of her head. "No one around."

"Nae. That's not what I'm worried about."

He stroked a palm down her hair, then fingered a curl, letting the lock slip off his fingers little by little. His eyes caught hers again. They were apologetic, and she feared what he'd say next.

He opened his mouth to speak, but she jumped off his lap instead. "Gotta go to bed. Making breakfast early."

She turned and hustled to the stairway, scurrying on up to her appointed bedroom. She flew through the door, closed it, and leaned into it as if she could keep all thoughts of Jake's rejection on the other side of that door. Why did he keep doing this to them?

A fleeting awareness tore through her, and she knew it was a reminder from God. *The news of his wife and baby is still raw. Be patient, Suzannah.*

Her groan bounced off the walls. She wasn't a patient person. Not anymore. Since Thomas had put her life into an interminable holding pattern, she tended to jump into what she could control. She wanted to comfort Jake, yes. But more than that, she wanted to help him heal. That was the only way he'd let go of his past and have any chance of a future with her.

Then she thought, shamefacedly, if God were in his life, that spiritual healing would be so much better than any temporary comfort she could offer him. It was what Jake needed no matter what happened with them.

She reflected on how it had been for her. She didn't know if God would ever remove her physical affliction, but she knew without doubt that her spiritual life was intact—that she trusted Jesus with this life, and the life after this one.

She fluffed two pillows on the bedspread, then sank down amid ruffles and lace. She must do her best to follow Jake's lead. Give him space. Wait until the man wanted more from her, and only then be ready to give it.

So what if they found each other irresistible? Now was not the time to explore those feelings. For now, she would get up early, work hard at cooking and cleaning, then fall into bed, weary, for a dreamless sleep. She could do it. She had to, for Jake's sake.

CHAPTER 18

Jake was up with the chickens, all right, but also the cowhands, the cattle, the horses, and every other two- and four-legged creature on Wheeler Ranch. It was like a trip to the county fair. No one slept past dawn, and all were full of energy for the coming day.

Jake dragged his worn out body out of bed, threw on his work clothes, splashed some water on his face in the bathroom down the hall, then chugged down the stairs. He hadna slept well last night, his mind betraying him with dreams of Suzannah. Today would be a different story. He had sixteen hours to make himself exhausted. It would work. It had to.

Glorious smells of bacon and something with warm cinnamon reached his nostrils. A large growl rumbled from his famished gut as he strolled into the kitchen.

One look at the kitten at the stove and he froze dead center.

Her back was to him, so he took his time in a thorough inspection. She was in her snug blue jeans with her hair in its usual sideways braid. But it was the enormous men's blue shirt she wore that got his full attention. It came down to her knees, leaving only her denim clad calves and hot pink keds showing. A man's belt was wrapped about her waist—twice—and the sleeves were rolled up so many times, it looked like she was wearing children's inflatable armbands for swimming. Her outfit was so comical that anyone else would have looked ridiculous. Not so, Suzannah. The growling in his stomach quickly changed to a different kind of churning as he envisioned her wearing his own shirt at breakfast… in their own home.

Their own home. What a dream that was, and nightmare all at the same time. He wasna any good as husband stock. Didna he already prove that?

She must have sensed his presence, since she twirled around, saw him, and grinned with all those lovely teeth of hers, instantaneously prompting his own need to smile. But, he didna. His reaction to her only proved his need to get on with the day.

The sooner the better.

"Suzannah," he said, wishing he hadna sounded so cold.

Her smile dropped off her pretty mouth like it had been erased. That soured his stomach a wee bit more.

"Jake," she said, matching his tone, her brows bunched up in a confused and hurt expression.

That broke his heart, but it couldna be helped. He averted his gaze to the cinnamon rolls still steaming on the counter. "Just coffee for me. And mayhap one of those," he said, nodding toward her sweet smelling confections.

He heard her sigh, but still didna look her way, afraid he would lose focus.

The coffee pot perked its last gurgle, just in time. He strode to it, grabbed a cup she'd so carefully stacked near the pot, and reached for a roll. "Thanks," he mumbled, as he walked past her to the back door.

Jake's whole body felt out of sorts as he headed for the barn. Hurting the kitten destroyed him. But it was the only thing that would save her. And that was all that mattered.

Entering the barn, his eyes took a moment to adjust. Troy's son, Looney, strode toward him, a grin a mile wide on his youthful face. "Hey ho, Jake. Glad to have you join us in tryin' to break the meanest bronco this side of the Himalayians."

Jake felt a grin coming on, not quite making it to his mouth. "Himalayas are in Asia, Looney," Jake said, wondering if his name actually applied for a different reason than was originally given.

"Oh, righto. I meant the Alps."

"Europe," Jake said, this time with a half-grin.

"Oh, sure, sure. Well, ya'll know what I mean."

"Aye. I do. Appalachians, I think you mean." Jake gave him a slap on the back. "So, where is this devil horse?"

"Come on," Looney said, speaking over his shoulder as he ambled along. "He's out back, probably givin' old Charlie a hard time. That's our foreman. Charlie, I mean. Not the horse. The horse doesn't have a name yet. Probably a good thing, since we maybe have to put him down, Pa says."

Jake ground his teeth at the thought of destroying a horse, and he hadna even seen it yet. For the last year, he'd thought he broke these horses in hopes they'd somehow break him. Since Suzannah, he'd come to realize he'd only wanted to help the creatures. Give them another chance to live correctly, like Roy was doing for him. And now because of Suzannah, he did want to live, and to live honorably. "I need a lead rope, and a driving whip."

"Sure. I'll fetch the stuff in a minute." Looney opened one last gate to a small corral that contained a pure white, agitated horse. At second look, Jake saw it was a stallion. Figured. Couldna the male of any species behave itself once in a while? He grunted his irritation.

"Where'd Troy get this horse? Could be an Arabian. But, looks more like a Morab Tennessee Walking Horse cross. Reminds me of Lone Ranger's Silver." He chuckled. "Kinda rare, at least in these parts."

"Pa picked him up a few months ago out California way. A beaut, ain't he? Ornery as all get out, though. No one can stay afloat. Story is, the owner hated him. Didn't like his looks, mostly."

The stallion flew up to the fence, crashing into it, then twirling to run off. Looney sidestepped, fidgeted. Jake caught Looney's gaze. "Why didna they just sell the poor creature then? What'd they do, beat him?"

"Don't think so. Just taunted him, I'm told. He don't like people." Another crash rattled the fence. "A'tal!" Looney yelled.

Jake huffed a curse. "Makes our job harder. How'd you get the halter on him?"

"He came with it. No one can get near enough to take it off."

"Well, that's something, anyway. Hope it's not rotted through by now. Do you run when he charges you?"

"Well yeah! You would too."

"Nae. I wouldna. You better watch. You'll be doing this next."

"Me?" Looney backed up a few steps. "No. Not me. Maybe Charlie. Not me. No. Couldn't. That horse is nuts!"

"Looney, listen up," Jake said, keeping his voice even. He always had to calm and coach the owners before he could train the horses. "You can do this. Someone will have to keep at it after I'm gone."

Looney backed away and turned to run. "I'll get your gear. Be right back," he said, over his shoulder. "And fetch Charlie."

Jake stood to the side of the gate, watching the horse's show of dominance as he crashed into the fence in front of him again and again. Jake didna move. He thought about the black devil at Roy's and pondered both these horses; one white, one black, and both considered to have black hearts. But, nae, it wasna their hearts. Both horses had been mistreated, so they didna ken proper behavior, was all. Horses, by nature, wanted to like humans. It was respect, then trust, they needed to be taught. But, just like the abuse that makes a human go bad, so it was with animals. He'd see what he could do for this one, then get back to the black stallion at home.

Home. Aye. Now that he was away from Montana, he missed it. He missed Harper Ranch. He was appreciated there, admired... feared. He grimaced. Och! He'd have to change that last sentiment. It wasna right to allow them to misunderstand him as he had.

Before he could finish his reminiscing, Looney slid up next to him, the items he'd asked for in hand, eyeing the stallion nervously.

"Good," Jake said, as the stallion charged up to the fence once again. He handed the long rope to Looney. "Hold this for me. It will be a while before I can get close enough to hook it to the halter."

"What? Uh... outside the corral, right?"

"Aye. Stay right there until I tell you."

Looney's eyes went wide. "Then what?"

"You bring it to me."

"What? No—"

But Jake was already studying the gate. Too risky to open it now with the stallion grandstanding his power. Jake had remained frozen to one spot, not reacting, giving his own stance of alpha male.

Now it was time to move. Jake climbed up and over the fence, landing with a puff of dirt on the other side. He pressed his hat down tight to his brows, then slapped the whip against his thigh. Just as the stallion started to charge him, Jake took out after him with arms spread wide, the whip in his right hand swinging hard round and round until he got near the horse's bum. He whipped behind the backside to put him on the run. The key was to move the feet while staying in control, until the horse stopped reacting and started thinking. He kept up his efforts until the white devil turned to charge once again. Jake took out after his backside again, pointing with the other hand in the direction he wanted the steed to go.

The stallion ran one turn around the corral then skidded to a stop. With eyes round, the horse pinned back his ears and reared. Far from being surprised or kowtowed, Jake lunged forward, pointing and whipping, forcing the horse to move around the fence line again. When the horse stopped, he moved in to reverse his direction. Back and forth, clockwise, counterclockwise, and on it went.

Finally, the horse slid to a halt, just a few yards away, and eyed Jake. When he faced Jake fully, Jake turned his back and walked away slowly.

The cowboys on the other side of the fence went wild, shouting grave warnings. Jake patted the air, trying to signal their silence. They instantly stilled.

Jake turned back then and saw the horse had come a little closer. No sooner did Jake turn than the stallion dug into the loose turf with his front feet, spraying bits of dirt behind him as he charged again. Jake spread his arms, shouted, ran forward, whipping the leather strap round and round again, surprising the steed enough to send him careening around the corral again. Jake slapped the whip continuously while standing in the middle, only moving his feet. He glimpsed the wide smiles of the dozen or so men on the other side of the fence.

Again, once the horse slowed and looked full-faced at Jake, Jake gave him his back and strolled slowly away. He glanced over one shoulder at the stunned the horse. The stallion stood stiffly, not quite sure what to make of Jake. This was typical. Confusion as to what a human was about was a big part of getting these steeds under control.

Once again Jake turned back to another show of dominance by the horse, though not quite as aggressive. Good. He was slowing down, the submissiveness Jake was after peeking through. A few more trips around the corral and the horse, frothed with sweat, slowed. The animal was nearing exhaustion.

Worn out himself by now, with the horse showing signs of submission—the lowering of his head, the chomping of his lips—Jake halted, motionless, and waited. Minutes clicked by. His eyes remained locked to the steed's. When the horse hung his head subtly, Jake walked toward him. Not exactly slowly, but not fast either. Just confidently. When he drew near, Jake caught a look in the stallion's eyes. When the devil raised his bulky head, Jake didna wait for a stomping. He began hollering, pointing, and whipping the ground once again, sending the horse into a frenzied run once more around the corral.

Another half hour went by before Jake stopped again and waited.

This went on two more times before the exhausted horse finally gave up and turned to face Jake. As usual, Jake turned and walked away. But when he turned back, this time the steed lowered his head and stood on trembling legs. He didna move. Finally, submission.

Jake trudged forward on his own tired legs, coming to within a few feet of the worn-out stallion. He'd be flat exhausted himself by the end of the day, just as planned. Jake rubbed the stick part of the whip between the stallions eyes, up and down in a steady, soothing stroke as he gained another step. Then another.

"Bring me the rope, Looney," Jake said carefully over one shoulder.

"Charlie will," Looney said.

"Come on, Loon, you can do it, aye?"

"Ahh, why you pickin' on me, Jake?" But Jake heard him scramble over the fence and come up behind him.

"Come here." Jake pointed at the ground. "Stand by me."

Looney did as he was told, probably because he didna want to speak this close to the stallion.

"Take this and keep rubbing between his eyes, then up and down his neck. Slowly. Calmly." He handed the crop to Looney.

Jake took the rope from Looney and stepped closer. The horse's ears were forward, he was licking at his lips, his head hung. He was done. Once the rope was tied to the ring at the bottom of his halter, Jake handed it to Looney and took the crop back. He rubbed the stick in a soothing motion across the sweaty back. The stallion's blue eyes dimmed, the lids dropped a bit, and Jake ken he had reached an important pinnacle.

The Wheelers could actually take over at this point with a little training of their own by Jake, and do fine. This big, white stallion was not mean-spirited. He'd be okay now with a lot of work and some lovin'. That was a whole different situation than with the black devil back home.

Once the horse stood submissively for a few minutes, Jake dropped the stick at his feet and used his hand to rub the steed's head all over. Up and down, from his forelock to his muzzle, to his cheek, around his eyes, his ears, watching as the animal almost looked like he'd close his eyes and sleep. A verra good sign.

"Good, laddie," Jake said. They were the first words he'd spoken to the horse that hadn't sounded crazed. "Easy now. You're fine, big fella."

Jake picked up the stick. "Guide him back to the barn and put him in a stall. He needs a scrub down that he will enjoy right about now. Dinna put it off. Right away. Understand?"

Looney looked scared to death, but nodded.

"And calm down. You'll rile him again otherwise. He'll be fine. Trust me."

Looney took a deep, hardy breath, then nodded again, looking a bit more relaxed.

Jake strode back to the fence. Once he was over the top and had landed on the other side, the group of twenty or more cowhands began a swell of cheers. Hats flew in the air, claps landed on Jake's back, the crowd surrounded him like floodwater around a tree, as if he were some sort of champion.

Aye. Sure, a champion, a hero. What would each man think if they ken Jake had killed his wife and bairn? He wanted to curse at them, but held his tongue and stalked off toward the house. He had to get away from the crowd. The horse wasna the only one who didna like people.

As he stormed toward the house, a desire to see Suzannah powered his steps. He needed her. To ground himself. To get pampered a wee bit. To see her smile, and mayhap bring on one of his own. His vow to stay clear of her flew off with the meadowlarks he disturbed from the tree as he stamped by.

Hoping no one else was around, Jake crashed through the back door, adrenaline speeding his heart. Suzannah was nowhere in sight. She'd be cleaning. Upstairs, mayhap. He threw off his hat and raced to the bottom of the stairs, then took two at a time until he was on the landing. Feeling frantic all of the sudden, he flew down the hallway, listening for her as he searched each room. No Kitten.

Something fretful clawed through him and grabbed him by the throat. Where was she? What would he do if he didna find her? More importantly, what would he do if she were nae in his life?

He rushed back down the stairs, the strike of his boot heels echoing off the walls like gunshots.

Just as he approached the kitchen he heard the back door snap shut, and there she was.

His Suzannah.

His Kitten.

Sunshine had just walked through that door, and she sported a huge smile. Relief flooded him as he rushed forward, peeling off his hat and throwing it haphazardly aside as he went. He gathered her up in his arms, straightening to bring her to eye level, her wee arms wrapping around his neck.

"Where were you?" Was that his voice, sounding so desperate and alarmed?

Her smile practically split her face. "Jake," she said with a soothing tone, stroking a hand over his tousled hair. "You all right?" she asked, as if having her feet dangling at his shins with his face right in hers was an everyday occurrence. He had plumb lost his mind this time for sure.

She smoothed the rest of his hair back in place and then held her wee palms over his bearded cheeks. "You were wonderful!"

What was she talking about? All he wanted to ken was where she'd gone off to long enough to scare him out of his mind. "*What?*"

"Out there." She nodded toward the kitchen window. "With the stallion. You were wonderful," she repeated.

"You were out there watching me? I didna see you."

"You were busy, silly man," she said in a wee voice with a swat on his shoulder. "Jake, you were amazing. And, kind."

Hadna she seen his whip connect a few times? He frowned at her assessment.

She read his mind. "When he reared, or kicked at you... you had to use *some* force. He's deadly otherwise."

This was why he'd come in search of her. She understood him—she was ointment for his wounds, salve for his soul. He needed her. To Hades with his vow. He wanted her near him. Every single day. "Aw, Kitten," he murmured, before he leaned in and pressed his lips to hers. When he tilted his head to deepen the kiss, he heard heavy boots clomp up the porch steps. Mo Chreach!

He grudgingly pulled back from Suzannah to look in those jeweled eyes before he had to let her go. Their kiss had barely been a peck, and she looked as disappointed as he felt. Holding her tight with one arm, he used the other to bring a fingertip to her cheek, then on to her chin, and finally her throat. Her skin was soft, silky.

A rough pounding at the door startled Suzannah. She pushed away from Jake's chest. He released her and her feet met the floor, shakily. Jake held her elbow for a moment, to steady her. She drew a quick breath, smoothing her shirt back into place. Another round of knocking boomed into the kitchen. Suzannah headed for the door.

"Nae, Suzie. By the sound of the boot falls, it's a man. You stay here."

Suzie twisted her lips and raised a brow, telling him she was perfectly capable. He ken that. Just couldna help his need to protect her when he could.

Jake strode to the door and swung it open.

Stared. Then gaped.

The man at the door seemed to be doing the same.

The silence grew as the air filled with tension. "Jacob?" the man finally said.

Jake didna believe his eyes. It couldna be.

The man looked uncomfortable, as well he should. Slow, escalating fury pumped through Jake's heart. Jake's gaze slid over the man's physique, surprisingly solid and much like his own. The man wore black jeans, but had on a white shirt rolled at the sleeves. Jake's gaze slid back up and landed on black eyes under thick black brows. The hair had been solid black once as well, he figured. But, now it was laced with gray. The face was the same as that in the picture his mum had kept, though older now, and lined. The man looked like someone who'd lived a rough life. That ratcheted Jake's rage a notch higher. It should have been Jake who'd put those lines on the old man's face.

"Jake…?"

It was Suzannah. Standing by his side.

Her presence gave him courage to finally speak. "What do you want?" he barked at the man. His voice was harsh, gravelled by years of hatred for a father who didna have the courage to raise his own son or take care of his own wife.

And, just like that, the truth bowled him over. Like father, like son.

He felt Suzannah grip him round the waist. She held tight for such a wee thing. Was he wobbling?

The man on the porch staring back at him seemed to be having the same trouble. Without releasing Jake, Suzannah reached out and grabbed the man's hand, bringing it to the doorjamb. He braced himself there while she brought her hand back and rested it on Jake's abdomen.

For big men, it amazed him how much the two of them needed this wee female to right them. It would be hilarious, if it wasna so sickening.

"Come in," Suzannah rasped at the man. He noticed her voice was not as strong when it wasna just the two of them.

Crivvens, what a wimp he was. She was the one with a life-altering affliction, and here he was, falling apart over his father—*nae, his sire*—showing up on his doorstep. Or rather, Troy's doorstep. He'd come to Troy's. Why? To find his only son? At least, he thought he was the only son. What good could possibly come of this?

Suzannah pushed with her hip against his upper thigh, moving Jake aside. She was strong. Bossy to boot. She was the only female he ken who could be bossy without words. And had the courage to boss him. That amused him, calming his anger a nick.

When the sire didna move, Suzannah dropped her hold on Jake and stepped up to the man. She took a good hold of the hand braced against the jamb and, while looking him in the eye, got him to release his stiff-armed lock. Jake hadna seen the look she gave him, but the man's had softened, and a wee smile was now lurking. *So, that's how you look when Suzannah looks you in the eye.* Goofy. Smitten. Like he'd do anything she asked of him. And sure enough, he would.

"Come," she said, and tugged on his sire's hand. The man came through the door willingly, glanced once at Jake, then trailed Suzannah.

Jake threw the door shut. It rattled on its hinges. He stood and watched it vibrate, thinking that's how he felt; rattled, and vibrating with rage and confusion.

After multiple deep breaths and many long minutes, he turned and followed after the two. When he reached the opening to the kitchen, he saw them both seated at the table with a cup of something in front of each. Suzannah was smiling, and his *sire* was rattling off his very proper name of Dodge Jacob Cooper. Then he asked for her name in return. Her voice didna even crack when she recited, "Suzannah Marie Harper." And that's when she gave him that sunshine smile of hers that was supposed to be reserved for only Jake.

Jake closed the distance between them, scraped a chair out as annoyingly as possible, flipped it backwards, and then straddled it. Their two sets of eyes followed his every move, while both mouths remained closed with flattened lips. Good. He had their attention. He laid one arm atop the other across the back of the chair, and locked black eyes to the other identical set. "Why are you here?"

Dodge's Adam's apple dipped down. "Well, son—"

"Do. Not. Call me son. Not ever."

The older man frowned, but held his tongue. He was surprisingly calm. Nae. Deadpan. Whenever Jake applied his intimidation skills, people shuddered. He glanced at Suzannah, and the poor thing was cringing. He gave her a quick apologetic look, then swung his gaze back to the old man, and hardened it.

He waited.

Finally, his sire spoke. "I've come looking for you. Trevor hoped I'd find you here."

"Why?" he shot back.

"I've been away for a while, so—"

"*Away for a while?* Is that what you call not showing up to raise your own *son?*" Jake flung his arms out. "Or take care of your *wife?*" The sting came, but he forcibly swatted it away.

Unable to sit there and look at this man anymore, Jake stood so fast, the chair slammed into the table, splashing coffee. Half a cup's worth doused Suzannah's hand. She flinched and brought the hand to her mouth.

Jake winced, but he didna have time for apologies. He paced to the door, then back to the kitchen. "Why show up now, eh? A wee bit late, dinna you think?" His voice had risen a level. "Mum is dead. Your *wife* is dead!"

The man took the blow badly, his face blanching. Good. Jake had finally made him feel some pain.

"I know," his sire said on a whisper. "I'm"—he gulped—"sorry about your mother. More than you know."

Jake laughed, an evil, cold laugh. "*Sorry?* If you were at all sorry, you'd have come home before the poor lass—"

"I was in jail."

Jake stilled. *Jail.* Didna that beat all? Jake's gut twisted in such a tight turn, he thought he might need the lavvy. Instead, he burst into another round of vicious laughter to rid himself of the tension. "That just figures."

"I was unjustly accused."

Jake barked a laugh. "Of course you were."

"Jacob. Listen to me, son—"

"I told you to never call me that!" Jake shouted, surprised the man dared do it again. No one came up against Jake when he meant business. No one!

He took two long strides until he stood over his father. He stared down into eyes the color of onyx, doing his best to make the man cringe. "You did not earn the right!" he shouted, puffs of air stirring the hair at the edges his father's contrite face.

"Now, Jake," Suzannah's whisper barely penetrated the sound of the swishing blood in his ears.

He turned to glare at her. "You want to leave us?"

"Nae," she said. And for the first time since his father had arrived, he wanted to soften. But he didna.

"*Suzannah!*" he barked.

She flinched, then raised her chin, defiant, and didna move. "You need me here," she said.

She was right about that. He did need her. In more ways than he cared to examine right then.

"Fine," he said with less vigor. He turned the kitchen chair back around, then dropped into it. "Just dinna interrupt." He stared into those big eyes of hers, so full of concern, and felt like a complete jackass.

His father turned to her. "Are you married to Jacob, Suzannah?"

Jake was all set to laugh at his father. Tell him he'd gotten it verra wrong. Wasna as smart as he thought. Before he opened his mouth to do just that, he glanced at the wee lass. The smile she'd given his father earlier didna compare to the one she graced the old man with now. When she turned it on Jake, his legs trembled at the sight, and his mouth went dry.

It took him a moment to put his brain back in gear. Back to the question his sire had asked. Could it be she liked the idea of being married to him? To Jake, the man most men feared? To Jake, the man who fell so short of husband stock that his wife and unborn bairn had died under his care? To Jake, the man who even God would not want? To Jake, the sourpuss who scowled at the poor lass more than he smiled at her?

Ah, but that part was changing. Was it possible there was actually hope for him?

"Nae," Suzannah said to Dodge, snapping Jake out of his musings.

"Are you Scottish as Jake's mother was?"

"No," she said, and giggled. He loved the fairy-like, tinkling sound. "Picking up... some words."

His father's brows bunched in the middle. Jake kent that look. That frown was confusion. He couldna let Suzannah be embarrassed, so he jumped in. "Suzannah has a condition. She can only say a few words before it becomes difficult. It's sort of a permanent lump in her throat she has to speak past."

Before anyone could think another thought, Jake's father reached forward and grabbed Suzannah by the throat.

CHAPTER 19

Suzannah's heart practically flew out of her chest. Dodge pushed his fingers harder against her throat, his other hand braced behind her neck. She was too stunned to fight back, barely breathing now past the lump and the extra pressure. Black dots swam in her vision, carrying with them something from her past. A memory. *Thomas*. His fingers at her throat, just this way.

Jake was on his feet, peeling his father's hands off her.

It was surreal. Her mind was sifting through memories faster than she could recount them. A baby-faced Thomas, smiling at her as he pushed her in a swing. A slightly older, tuxedo-clad Thomas, opening a car door for her, and her in a pretty turquoise prom dress. Thomas, with stubble on his cheeks and tired eyes, helping her carry her books to Psych class. And finally, the ravaged-faced Thomas, snarling and… strangling her.

Her mind circled that memory as if it had been caught in a stream's eddy. Swirling round and round until it dove deep into the remembrance. She watched it replay before her as if she were a spirit floating above, unable to change a thing. She could only watch and feel, and then shudder deep in her bones.

"Where were you tonight, Suzannah-Anna? Huh? Didn't I warn you to stay away from other men?" Thomas's spittle landed on her face as he shouted past his rage. He looked so evil. How could someone so handsome turn so hideous? She thought of how the Bible talked of Satan as the beautiful angel before his fall. That's what she saw right now, just inches from her. The fall.

Thomas backed her up, shoving her around the brick corner of the pharmacy. She'd gone in to retrieve the prescribed antibiotics for her roommate's strep throat. The pharmacist's assistant was a young man.

Thomas had seen her talking to him. *Talking to him.* That was all. Thomas's jealousy was past insane. It was time to end this farce of a relationship. For the last year it had gotten awkward, and negative. She never saw Thomas smile anymore. All he did was scowl.

He was scaring her now. His body pressed harder into hers. The bricks at her back bit into her skin. Blood swished past her ears from a frantic pulse. "Thomas. You're hurting me!"

"Hurting you? Hurting *you?* What about me, Suzannah? Don't you think you're hurting me when you flirt like a Ninth Street whore? You want hurt? Eh? I'll show you hurt!" He slammed her head into the bricks with his fingertips digging into her throat. Pressing, pressing. Stars floated in her vision, she couldn't breathe. "Thom... as," she barely choked out.

He didn't let go, just pressed until she heard something pop. An eruption of pain corked her breath.

Her eyes rolled back. A flood of darkness washed over her.

"Suzannah!" Jake's voice. "There she is. That's my lass."

She rotated her eyes back and forth beneath her lashes. She was lying down. Why?

"Get back!" she heard Jake shout. "Have'na ye done enough damage?"

"Move out of the way, Jacob. Let me see to her."

Scuffling. The men had become physical. She forced her eyes open so she could see them. Jake shoved his father, but Dodge gave as good as he got.

Jake must think Dodge hurt you. She needed to stop them. She always seemed to be the reason for family strife. Clearing her throat, she prepared herself for as loud a sound as she could muster. Taking a deep breath, she spouted, "Stop!"

Dodge had a handful of Jake's shirt, the other hand had a grip on his shoulder. Jake had hooked an elbow and forearm around Dodge's neck, and both had stilled like they were a snapshot in Wrestling Revue. Their eyes were trained on her.

"Jake." She tugged at his Wrangler's hem. He released his hold on his father and dropped to one knee next to her. When he looked her in the eye, ready to listen, she whispered. "Dodge didn't hurt me. Only scared me. Brought back a memory… that I hadn't recalled… before now." Not able to go on, she swallowed painfully. She scooted up so she could press her back against the table leg.

Jake took over, grasping her upper arms to help her straighten. "What happened back then, lass?"

Jake's concern warmed her heart. She knew she would always be okay with him around. "Water, please."

Jake craned his neck up to his father. "You heard her. Get water."

"Please," Suzannah said for him. It would take time for Jake's inner wounds to heal. She knew that. She would make sure he settled down long enough to listen to his father's explanation.

While they waited, Jake stroked her hair and watched her closely. She smiled at him, not able to stop herself. He was so attentive. So un-Jake-like, as far as the world saw him. But she knew better. Oh, did she know better.

He frowned all the more. She guessed now was not the time for that glorious smile of his to show up.

Dodge handed her a water glass, then dropped to a knee next to his son.

Jake glanced at him with a scowl so heated, she wondered if his beard would burn up in a fiery blaze.

"Now, now. Let's get along like good little boys," she managed to say perfectly.

Both gazes swung to her. Dodge gave a shout of laughter. Jake actually lifted one side of his mouth. Good. That was a start.

"Tell us about Thomas. What did he do to you, exactly? Give us every detail," Dodge said.

Her eyes widened. She glanced at Jake, who looked equally expectant to hear the story. She shrank back, and slipped off her support. Jake caught her. With a swift heave upward before she could protest, he had her at the sofa.

Once she was sitting with both men kneeling at her feet, she gulped and began anew. "How... how do you know about Thomas?"

"When your memory took hold, you whispered parts to us," Dodge said, patting her hand. "Start from the beginning. Don't leave anything out."

She wondered briefly if he had been a lawyer. He sure sounded like one. Jake astounded her in his submissive state, letting his father take the lead.

Suzannah took her time and, through many sips of water and periods of rest, she got through bits and pieces of Thomas's attack. "Before today, I didn't remember… that he had tried to… to strangle me." The utter helplessness she'd felt that night crested before her now, a terrifying tidal wave poised to crush her all over again.

Jake took her hand, caressing his thumb over the back of it.

Dodge moved closer. "May I? I'm sorry I didn't ask before. I didn't mean to frighten you. I was only trying to check your hyoid bone."

"My what? Why?" she asked.

"Let me give you a bit of background first. Then you'll understand. I was studying to be a doctor when I was accused of murdering a patient during my residency. He was the son of a wealthy businessman. The man had a team of attorneys. There wasn't much of a trial before they threw me in jail. Life sentence." He glanced at Jake and gave him an apologetic look. "Your mother was pregnant with you at the time."

Jake stiffened, and inadvertently squeezed her hand.

Suzannah squeezed back, and when he looked at her, she shook her head in warning. Thankfully, he remained quiet.

"I'm afraid she didn't believe I was innocent. She never came to my trial, never visited me at the jail—" Overcome by emotion, Dodge ran a hand down his face. He cleared his throat. "Since I'd nearly received my Doctor of Medicine degree, my jailers thought to use me to treat some of the inmates' injuries. A lot of their injuries are to the throat. Same reason as you." He shook his head. "Which brings us back to you, Suzie."

Jake shot daggers at his dad for using the nickname.

Suzannah smiled gently, first at him, then at Dodge. "Go on."

"I've seen many a damaged hyoid bone with strangulation, or when thumbs were pressed into it. And, when you said Thomas pressed his fingers just so…" He demonstrated on Jake's throat. Jake's nostrils flared. It didn't seem to faze Dodge. He dropped his fingers and continued, "he may have damaged one of the horns, or torn the whole bone away from its position. You see, the hyoid is the only bone in the body that isn't attached to another bone. It's considered a floating bone, although it's surrounded by cartilage, ligaments, and muscles, and is very close to the larynx. You aren't the first person I've seen who has trouble speaking after such an injury. The fact that you heard something pop… well, I personally think he injured it. Have your doctors x-rayed it?"

Suzannah pressed her lips together, a reminder of the humiliation she'd experienced at each doctor's appointment. "No. They called it psychosomatic. Globus Hystericus, or MTD - Muscle Tension Dysphonia."

Dodge patted her shoulder. "Those anxiety disorders could have added to the problem. Especially when you found you couldn't speak and were told it was all in your head. But you don't seem to me a person prone to psychosomatic issues. I don't know you yet, but if you can control this giant beast," he nodded toward Jake, "you must be tough as twice-baked leather." He laughed outright.

* * *

Jake fumed. What did Dodge ken about his son? The idea of him acting so... familiar, made Jake want to smash something—with his fists. The old man's jaw would do. He growled his displeasure.

Both Suzannah and his sire ignored him. His rage rippled hotter. He ground his back molars, trying hard not to interrupt what could be important information for the lass.

"Do you mind?" his sire asked, his fingers hovering over her throat.

She nodded her consent.

Dodge used his thumb and index finger, starting at the edges of what must have been the hyoid bone. He pressed, moved his fingers inward, and pressed again.

"Does this make the feeling of the lump in your throat worse? Or this?" He changed the position of his fingers over and over again.

She mouthed the word, *No*.

"Here?"

Her eyes widened, and she nodded.

He stopped his probing, then asked, "Do you ever experience pain, Suzie?"

Jake's scowl deepened. "Her name's Suzannah," he barked.

"Jake..." she said.

She may as well have added, *Behave*, since that's how she was looking at him now. Jake shot to his feet and stomped to the kitchen, reining in his tumultuous emotions. Dodge and Suzannah kept up their conversation, while he poured himself a cup of coffee and sat at the table to brood.

Lost in thoughts of what his life might have been with a father in it, he didna hear anyone until he heard the front door click shut and felt a hand on his shoulder. He jerked his head up to see who had dared touch him. *Suzannah*. Relaxing a bit, he brought his hand up to lay across hers, and gave her as good a smile as he could muster. Must have looked like the grimace that matched his mood, since she frowned back.

"You feeling better, lass?" he asked.

She nodded, then came around and sat next to him at the table. "Your dad helped. He's gone back to his motel."

Jake glowered and averted his gaze.

Suzannah leaned forward and put a hand to his face, turning it toward her. The feel of her palm on what wee skin was exposed warmed him clear down to his toes. Her beautiful eyes scanned his face, then came to rest on the hand she had on him. She stroked his beard, like he was a furry animal, instead of a flesh and blood man. At this moment, he hated his beard. How would it feel to have that wee hand on his smooth-shaven face?

Time to stop hiding. Time to shave the dreaded thing off.

Jake covered Suzannah's hand, then slid it down to his lips. He kissed her palm, then gazed into those eyes—eyes that divulged anything he wanted to know. Like right now, she wanted him to kiss her. So, he would. He leaned in.

The back door burst open, stopping him cold. A combination of male voices sailed in ahead of a half dozen men, one after the other. Two of them were in a heated conversation about ranch work, but the other four tromped up to him.

"That there spirit horse is a down-right lamb now," a lanky cowboy with not one bit of extra hair on his face said as he slapped Jake on the back.

A full-bearded man elbowed in. "That's right. Reckon you know what yer doin', Captain. Looney's not afeared of him anymore." Jake studied the two men's faces as he shook their hands, and wondered why he'd let his own beard grow in as thick as this last man's. It really made the poor sod look like a man hiding behind a daft bush. If Jake wasna convinced before, he sure was now. Had he gone completely numb before Suzannah?

Two more men gave Jake praise, then behind them came Troy and Looney.

The back door slammed shut. "Hey! What'd I tell you about slammin' doors, son," Troy scolded Looney.

"Sorry, Pa." Looney sped past his father to face Jake. "You can't believe it. Whatever you did to that rascal horse, well, he's never gonna be the same, ya know? I mean he's quieted down completely. Reckon anyone can walk up to him now. He acts like he's been trained for years already. It's somethin' to see. I mean, I think we can put a saddle on him already and he'd let anyone ride him. He's—"

"Enough!" Troy said. "Gall darn it, boy. You re-mind me of your mother—God rest her soul—couldn't shut up for one minute." He blinked at his own words and seemed to deflate ever so slowly. "Course, it had been all right by me," he said, on a quieter note.

"Sorry, Pa," Looney said again. He looked back at Jake. "Anyways, the Wheeler ranch hands are grateful to ya. Boy howdy, it would have taken us forever to train that crazy horse." He glanced at his father out of the corner of his eye, then must have decided he'd better be done talking.

Troy squeezed Jake's shoulder, and sat down next to him. "Get us some coffee, Loon," he said, then watched to make sure the boy walked over to the pot. He looked back to Jake. "We really appreciate all ya done. We thought that horse would have taken months to train. You're a gosh darn miracle worker with horses, my boy. I think we got it from here."

Jake's jaw went slack, right along with the sinking feeling in his gut. Yet another rancher wanted him gone? He guessed he'd always be a temporary fixture anywhere he went. Heck, he'd even been a temporary husband. The reason his jailbird father could up and topple his life with one swing was simple enough.

Jake had no idea *how* to put down roots.

He'd been duping himself with Suzannah, telling himself she could be a permanent feature in his life. So much decency versus so much rubbish. Who was he kidding? He didna belong anywhere.

Troy must have read into his expression, since he said, "You can stay on if ya want, o' course, we've got plenty to do."

Jake rose, clapped Troy on the back, and silently strode to the back door, clicking it shut behind him.

CHAPTER 20

"How do, Mr. Harper," Thomas said, careful to smile and exude charm. He'd been vigilant to dress in gray slacks and a starched white shirt with a bow tie, to impress. "I'm told you are short an accountant."

The older man reached out a hand to him. "Call me Roy, son." They shook hands. "Now, where'd you hear about my bookkeeping needs?"

"Sorry, sir. I didn't mean to sound like I was prying." He gave one of his brilliant smiles. The kind Suzannah never could resist. Before. When she knew her place. "I was in the West Yellowstone Bank today, asking after a job. They didn't have any, but mentioned you might be looking for someone. I have a degree in accounting." That wasn't exactly true, but he'd taken plenty of classes in accounting, before he quit college in order to keep a better eye on his wayward girlfriend.

"That so?" Roy said. "Happens my foreman and myself keep the books, and Clint is out of state with his in-laws just now. Won't be back for several weeks."

Yeah, he already knew that. Had found that out before he'd swung east to Montana. He grinned to himself. He'd honed his skills in surveillance years ago, and Suzannah's family was one of his regular marks.

Roy sized him up with a quick head to toe. "I could maybe test you out a bit to start."

Thomas knew before he'd asked for the job that Harper would jump at the chance. He practically laughed out loud at what country bumpkins these people were. All he needed was a reason to be here so he could grab that disobedient girlfriend of his and disappear. He wouldn't go home either. No, he'd take her on the road with him. Try his hand at slapping her around a little. Make her sorry she'd escaped him, finally teach her submission before he took her back to show his father he could handle his woman just fine.

"Yes, sir. Anything would be acceptable." He glanced around the vicinity. "Where is everyone? Looks pretty sparse of cowhands for a big spread like yours."

"Ah. A few of them are on the road. Some are out of state. The rest are movin' one of the herds to another pasture. It's usually pretty quiet until mealtimes." Roy looked behind him at the big house. "Come on in. I'll introduce you to Mabel, then we'll get you settled in the bunkhouse."

"On the road?" Thomas said, hoping to get some news of Suzannah.

Roy started toward the house. Thomas caught up and stayed at Roy's side. Roy glanced over and said, "My bronc buster took my nieces to Wyoming. One of them was needed for cookin' and cleanin'."

Which one, Thomas wanted to ask. "Is that right? Your nieces?" Roy was the talkative type, he could tell. Making casual conversation would eventually get him what he wanted. He was plenty patient when he needed to be. "You look too young to have nieces old enough for cookin' and cleanin'."

"Ah, shucks. You flatter me, son. Truth is, I just got back from my honeymoon, so I'm feeling pretty young and spry again. Had to cut it short, though, since Clint's father-in-law lost two of his cowhands, and Clint had to go help on the farm out California-way. It don't matter none. As long as I'm with my bride, I don't care where I'm at, ya know?"

Thomas grinned at Roy, thinking how grand it was going to be when he and Suzannah got married. She'd see reason soon enough.

"Anyway, Suzannah and Jake will be back 'fore ya know it. " Roy smiled, then turned to go up the steps of the ranch house.

And, just like that, Thomas got what he'd wanted, though the old man's mention of Suzannah traveling with that—what'd he call it?—bronc buster, ate a trench through him. He glared a hole through the fool's back as he followed him up the steps.

* * *

Suzannah raced out of the house after Jake. She hadn't believed her ears when Troy had pretty much dismissed him. Was poor Jake destined to be sent away from every job he put a hand to? She knew Uncle Roy hadn't really discharged him, but he had sent Jake away all the same. It seemed shovelfuls of Jake's self-worth were continually being dug out, reshaping the trustworthy, talented man she knew him to be into something he probably didn't recognize anymore. Probably hadn't for some time.

Jake was right in front of her, headed for the barn, every muscle in his body swollen with tension. His steps were bold, determined, a man on a mission. It worried her what that mission might be. She wanted to holler his name to get him to stop and turn around, to soothe his torn pride once again, but the sound would only make it past a few feet. Resigned, she jogged behind at a distance. Knowing him, he was after a horse that needed breaking. He'd let the bronco buck the stuffings out him or kill him in the process.

Suzannah had just reached the barn door when she saw Jake speaking to Troy's foreman. She lingered back, waiting to see what he would do. The last thing she wanted was to embarrass him further by being a tag-along female interrupting a male conversation. Once he was done, he set out along the many stalls on the south side of the barn until he reached a surprisingly gentle-looking steed a few stalls down.

Suzannah hurried forward and caught the fore-man's arm before he ducked into his office. He turned back at the contact. "May I ride with Jake?" she asked.

"Sorry, ma'am. What was that?"

She cleared her throat, thrust her chin up, and tried again. Tapping her chest, she said, "Suzannah."

"Charlie," the man said.

She nodded a greeting. "I'd like to ride with Jake." There. That should do it.

"Sure. I'll saddle up old Zeke for you. He's a gentle gelding, old as the hills."

Suzannah frowned and shook her head. "I can ride. That one," she said, pointing to a gray speckled mare just behind the man.

He turned to look, as if that was necessary to know what horse she meant. "Ah. That Appaloosa is a bit high-spirited. I don't think—"

"Perfect," she said. "Saddle, please. Her name?"

She knew her words sounded rude to someone who didn't know why she used so few, but she had no choice. In this case, she figured it would only help her cause.

"Name's Misty." He eyed her warily, but then nodded. "I'll get the saddle."

Jake came up then, reins in hand, the buckskin gelding following leisurely behind him. "What are you doing, Suze?"

Though he sounded gruff, she knew it wasn't her. He'd been broadsided once again, and he just needed to get away. But not without her. "Going with you."

He opened his mouth to object. At least, that's what the look on his face said. It immediately softened. He nodded, his whole countenance fallen. "I'll be out front."

She'd take her time getting the saddle on Misty. Give him a few minutes to collect himself. She actually looked forward to escaping with him for a while. He'd been through so much in the last week.

Once the foreman helped Suzannah get Misty bridled and saddled, she led the horse out of the barn. Jake was leaning on the corral fence, his forearms propped on the top edge with reins in one hand, a booted foot on the first rung. His eyes were on the vast land before them, filled with hard grasses and natural vegetation that led up to tree-lined canyons, his look contemplative. He was sure a fine figure of a man; tall, widespread shoulders, hard muscle lining his frame. She could stand here all day and gaze at him, but he needed her to do more than that.

One more minute of admiring the outer man, and she'd be ready to ease the anguish of the inner man.

She came up even with Jake and placed her hand on his bicep.

"Suzie…" he said on a breath, his eyes remaining on the view before them.

"Come, Jake. Let's ride."

He turned his head and gave her a brief, sad smile.

No. No sadness! With one hand, she caught hold of his beard before he could turn away and held him in place. "It'll be all right, Jake. Everything. I promise."

"Aw, Suze. You're one of a kind, you ken?" He turned away from the fence and stroked a hand down her hair like he was prone to do.

She smiled up at him, then gave one last playful tug before she released his beard.

"Yow," he said. "I think it's time I get rid of this thing."

"Yes!" she said, beaming at him.

He chuckled. "Okay, okay. I get the hint. I'll shave it next week."

She shook her head.

"After dinner tomorrow?"

She shook her head again.

He sighed. "Before I shower tonight?"

She nodded and gifted him with her brightest smile.

He gave her a lopsided smile back, shaking his head. "Come on, Kitten. Let's ride." He leaned down and gave her a quick, tickly kiss on the forehead, then turned to his horse.

She looped the reins over Misty's head and used the bottom rung of the fence for a little help to reach the stirrup. She was up and mounted before Jake had even gotten his reins in place.

"Smart aleck," he said on a grin.

Suzannah was thrilled Jake was loosening up, smiling again. She turned Misty toward the gate, lifted the rope off the post, and pushed. The gate swung open. Giving Misty a squeeze with her knees, the horse leapt forward and trotted off. Before Suzannah even thought about halting as Jake refastened the gate, he appeared at her shoulder, sitting his buckskin's trot smooth as butter under a summer sun. Even so, she noted how rigidly he looked straight ahead, like a caged beast bent on escape. This man needed a pounding ride. Misty wanted to run. Suzannah set her jaw and loosed the reins.

Under the wide blue sky and amid the open spaces, Suzannah laughed aloud at her sense of freedom. She pulled the rubber band from her braid and let her hair uncoil in the wind. Tears streaked into her hairline, muscles awoke with activity. The anticipation alone, of time with Jake, made her want to whoop with pure joy.

She turned her head to give Jake a beaming smile and found the man of her thoughts keeping pace with her, watching her with a look of admiration. She wanted to leap out of her saddle and into his arms. Show him he'd never have to feel alone again; he deserved to be regarded, respected, praised, enveloped in a love that, while there was breath in her, she would grant him day after day.

She slowed her horse to a walk, and Jake followed. Turning Misty into his mare, she leaned over to get a good hold of Jake and pushed off her horse. Shock registered on his face, but his arms were already reaching for her, lifting her out of her saddle and onto his lap before she could fall. The entangled horses faltered for only a few paces before they slowed to a stop, dropping their heads to what little grass they could find.

"Foolish lass," he tried to scold, but his voice gave him away. It was low and husky and full of longing.

"Shhh." Suzannah kissed the exposed skin on his face, smoothed his beard, and gazed into hungry eyes for several heartbeats before she pressed her mouth to his. "Jake…" she whispered, then kissed him again.

He wasn't kissing her back. She leaned away, saw the hesitancy in his eyes. Then, as if he could no longer battle the urge, he took over. His hand cupped her face, speeding her heart, reminding her this man was her home. She wanted nothing more than to live out her days in his arms just like this, with his walls down and emotions freed. His hand slid to the nape of her neck, bringing her lips to meet his. The kiss started gentle, but then he angled his head and deepened the contact. "You taste so sweet, smell so good," he said, releasing her and tilting his head the other way, only to seize her mouth again. "You're mine, lass. Mine," he murmured so quietly against her lips, she knew he hadn't planned on her hearing. But, she had. And, she *was* his. Body and soul.

He ended the kiss, wrapped an arm around Suzannah's waist, pulling her snug against his chest, then nudged his mare in the side. The horse tore out one more tuft of grass, then raised her head and perked her ears forward as she started off in a trot. He gave a short, shrill whistle for Misty to follow. Suzannah wasn't surprised the horse responded immediately, trotting up behind them. People and animals alike seemed to obey Jake's every command.

Jake guided them toward a grouping of trees a mile from the house, Suzannah soaking up Jake's warmth. If only they could run off together, away from treacherous horses and threatening people... and loss... they would be able to find their way together. *Lord, I know this is what I want.* She took a breath. *But Your will alone be done.*

Jake reined his mare around a poplar tree, then stopped, still holding Suzannah firm. He looked deep into her eyes. He dropped the reins onto the horse's neck, then used both hands to smooth her hair back on both sides. His fingertips slid into her hair, unwinding what was left of her braid, untangling the knots. He slid his hands through it and through it until she thought her breath would slow to a stop. For such a gruff man, Jake's touch was so gentle, it was almost graceful. Her eyes slid closed, her scalp tingled, her breathing grew erratic. Pure bliss.

She felt him kiss her on the forehead. Opening her eyes to his, she beheld the emotion stirring in the inky depths. Was it love?

With one last stroke of her hair, Jake lowered her to the ground. She backed up to let him dismount. Her heart was all aflutter, her legs jittery. She wondered if Jake experienced any of those effects. He looped the reins over the head of his horse, grabbed up the reins from Misty, and snugged both to a tree, taking more time than usual to tie them up.

He finally turned back to her. Her heart sank at the mask that was back in place. Where had all those wonderful emotions skulked off to?

"Suzie…" Jake said on a exhalation of breath.

"Nae, Jake. I always have to stop you."

His brows puckered in the center. "Stop me?"

"From saying the kiss was a mistake."

Jake's eyes softened. "Lass. As much as I want to, I—"

"Stop it! Just stop." Sticking out her chin, she also stamped her foot. Just once she wanted to be able to scream!

Instead, she closed her eyes and counted to ten. *Listen to him, Suzannah.* The tender thought slipped through. She knew it was the Holy Spirit. Knew how often she tuned Him out while she was busy feeling sorry for herself. She rarely quieted her mind enough to hear. *Okay, Lord,* she responded in her head. *Help me to do that.*

She slid her eyes open. Jake looked so downtrodden. She was supposed to be the comforter here. She wasn't a narcissist. Why was she acting like one? "Forgive me. Go ahead with…"

He opened his mouth to speak, but didn't. He blinked, inhaled, exhaled, dipped his head, raised it up, shifted from one foot to the other. This time she wouldn't jump in to force things to go her way. She'd wait, as he always waited for her in her struggle to speak. He may not have trouble getting words out his mouth, but maybe words were hard for him to formulate correctly. Hmm. *Did that come from you, Lord?* Amazing what wisdom came to her when she'd only listen.

A full minute must have gone by before he raised his eyes to her. Proud that she'd actually waited, she smiled. It seemed to shake him, that smile, and she wondered why.

He took a step closer, but they still stood a good half dozen feet apart. He pulled his fingers up into fists, squeezing until the knuckles turned white. Suddenly, she didn't want to hear what he had to say. If she grabbed her horse and bolted, he'd never be able to deliver the hurtful words. And somehow she knew they would be hurtful. *No. You're not a runner. Stop running!*

"Listen, lass…"

Her heart sank to her stomach, and her legs wanted to give out. She stood firm, though, willing her body to stay put.

"I need to ken what happened to you. About your affliction. The story behind the attack."

She exhaled a breath, not realizing she'd been holding it. This wasn't at all what she'd expected him to say. It made her wonder how many times she'd missed important comments from people due to her impatience. Now she had to decide. Did she want to tell Jake about Thomas? She'd only just remembered some of it when Dodge felt her throat. Did she want to bring Jake in on her nightmare?

Yes. And, no. She didn't want him to believe he needed to do something about it once he'd heard. But, if she had any hope of convincing Jake they should be together, she needed to be upfront with him. Starting today. "Okay," she said, then glanced around for a place to sit.

"Hold on. I have a blanket."

Once he brought the rolled blanket from the back of his saddle, he laid it out and offered a hand to help her sit. Such a sweetheart, this man.

He settled in next to her, propping himself on one arm while the other draped over a bent knee. "Tell me from the start."

It was hard to begin, but once she'd begun the telling, even amidst the breaks to rest her voice, the wretched saga of Thomas's shift from childhood sweetheart to threatening stalker poured out of her like discharge from a lanced abscess. Little by little, she felt the darkness drain away and relief settle in.

Jake leaned in to rub his thumb across her cheek, and frowned. "No tears, lass?"

The concern on his face made her wish she could cry. It would sure seem a more natural reaction. But she hadn't cried over her situation in a very long time. She would have long since thought her tear ducts had calcified if it hadn't been for the night she'd sobbed with Jake—for Jake.

"Cried buckets at first. Not one tear since."

"Except for me," he said, and smoothed the thumb over her skin again.

"Except for you," she agreed.

He smoothed his palm over her hair clear down to the tips, then re-settled his arm across his knee. "So, you reckon that bone in your throat got broken?"

They would need to discuss his father next. But first things first. "Dodge thinks Thomas may have broken my hyoid bone, yes."

"Your doctors didn't find that?"

She shook her head, her lips turned down at the edges. "I passed out. Heard later that Thomas dropped me off at the hospital." She breathed in, swallowed. Though raspy as always, her throat was doing surprisingly well. "It's why I couldn't get a restraining order."

Jake's expression was one of confusion.

"He's charming. Convinced the doctors I tripped and he caught me by the neck. Accident."

"And you couldn't change their minds?"

"His word against mine. Couldn't talk to... give my side. Attorney lousy."

"But, you talk so well now. Have you noticed how easily your words have come?"

"Aye."

He chuckled. She loved the sound. "It appears I'm turning you Scot, eh, lass?"

Smiling, she said, "I'm comfortable with you, Jake. Dodge says stress makes it worse. Lots of people around makes me so..."

"Aye. They make me 'so' as well."

She smiled. The tension inside her eased. That's what he did for her. It's what she wanted to do for him. But she knew the next subject would tie him into a knot.

It couldn't be helped.

"Jake... your dad—"

"Dinna ever call him that again, lass. Hear me?" He came up on his knees and got right in her face. "He hasna earned it. He doesna deserve it."

Should she fight him over that? No. She tried another tactic. "Jake…" He edged downward, bringing his nose to within inches of hers. She stuck her chin up. This was too important to him for her to let him buffalo her. "Hear me," she said, looking him straight in the eye.

He softened his glare and sat back on his heels, turning his elbows out to grip his thighs. Always considerate of her plight, she knew he'd remember it was hard enough for her to talk, let alone argue. "I promise to listen."

She sighed in relief. At least he'd hear what she proposed. Whether he went for it or not, only God knew. *Please help me to say the right words, Lord.* "Your father—" She put up a hand in apology before he could react. Then started again. "Dodge was in jail, but he didn't do anything wrong." The look on Jake's face was anything but believing. He tore up a clump of dead grass and started ripping the blades into tiny pieces.

She ignored it. "They let him out because there was new evidence. Otherwise he'd still be there." She came up on her knees to grab his shoulders. That stopped his agitated fingers and made him freeze in place to listen. God bless the man, his sensitivity. "He'd been sentenced to life, Jake. Life!"

Jake averted his gaze from her. His eyes roamed the countryside, while his mind apparently roamed the new information. She knew he was a fair man. She hoped this was all she'd need to say to move him down the path he must go.

His eyes centered back on hers. He waited, perceptive that there was more.

"Jake… for me… please hear him out."

CHAPTER 21

Jake groaned, and scrubbed a hand down his face. Somehow he kent in his gut what Suzannah was going to propose. They were often on the same plane ever since he took up watching her gestures to help her communicate with others. But, he'd had enough of his so-called *father*. He refused to be in the same room with the man let alone hear any more tall tales.

Playing the injured card was his only hope, since he wasna capable of saying nae to the lass if she pressed. Gad, he was a smitten fool. "How can you ask that of me, Kitten?"

"I do it *for* you."

"*For me?*" He glared daggers at her. "For argument's sake, let's say he was in jail, unjustly accused, all of it. Has he ever heard of paper? Pencils? Stamps? Why didna he write and tell us this, aye?"

Suzannah's expression was woeful. He had a bad feeling about this. Had forgotten about the time Suzannah had spent in Dodge's company while he, himself, had been moping in the kitchen. She put her hand over one of his and squeezed. Automatically he stilled and looked her in the eye. She sighed, looking apologetic. "He did."

He did what? Write? Couldna be. Mum would have told him. Jake snatched off his hat and spun it by the brim, breathing through an updraft of anger. "You claimin' he wrote and mum never bothered to tell me? Nae." He stuffed the hat back on his head. "Nae!"

He pushed to his feet and tramped to the horses. Animals always soothed him. He stroked a palm down the neck of Suzannah's mare. It didna soothe him like caressing Suzannah's silky hair did, but it helped.

"Jake, he sent money too. Haven't you wondered how you lived?" She coughed, cleared her throat. "Please talk to him. Let him explain everything." Her voice petered off, but he'd heard her well enough.

If he believed what she was saying, he'd have to blame his mum. He didna want to check one more loved one off his list, and his mum had been his only ally. They had hated his father together.

He heard Suzannah come up behind him. If she tried to convince him his sire had been in the right and his mum had deceived him, had allowed Jake's hatred to continue, well, he could end up hating Suzannah, as well.

Before she reached him, he ducked under her horse's neck to reach his own. He whipped the reins off the low branch and was up and onto his horse within a few seconds. "Go back to camp," he said, then gave his horse a good kick. Poplar branches whipped past his face. Then there was only wind over the flatlands and the pines beyond.

* * *

Max strode to the east end of Harper Ranch's main barn, aiming to fix the slat at the bottom of Bonnie's stall while the mare was in Wyoming. This was when he missed his younger brother, Nick, the most. His brother's construction skills were a far sight better than his own—and double that again compared to Pete's, whose only real gift lay in surviving his own daily mayhem.

Max hefted the pitch fork in his hand and shook his head wryly. He knew enough at least to do things in order. Site preparation. Otherwise known as mucking all the straw and manure out of the stall. He had no shortage of experience in that department. When he reached the end of the aisle, he unlatched Bonnie's stall door. It swung open on creaky hinges. He'd have to remember the WD-40 on his next pass through. Max squatted, resting his forehead against the pitchfork's handle as he compared the length of the damaged wall board to the pile of 2x8s they had in the wood shed.

"Need help?" a male voice called from the barn's breezeway door.

Not recognizing the voice, Max craned his neck around to see who spoke.

The man came toward him. "Howdy. I'm Tom Mas—uh—that is, I'm Tom Mattison, new kid on the block." He chuckled and held out a hand.

Max rose, knocking over the pitchfork, tines up, but ignored it to extend his hand for the shake. "Didn't know Roy hired anyone. Where you from, stranger?"

"California-way," Tom said, trying to sound like a cowboy, but falling way short as far as Max was concerned.

"Kinda far from home, ain't ya?"

"Oh, not really. I been traveling about the countryside. Need to see the good ole U. S. of A."

"That right? Well, what's Roy got planned for you?"

"I'm an accountant. I'll be helping with the books."

"You replacing Clint?"

The fellow laughed. "No. No, just doing some of the menial tasks. Taking some pressure off them, is all."

Max immediately distrusted this stranger. This was not like Roy to be so unquestioning. Especially with the books. Newlyweds. Bah. Max sure hoped he'd keep a few more brain cells after he was married. "I see. Suppose a welcome is in order."

"Roy says it's good timing that I'm here now, since Clint had an emergency, and Roy himself has business out-of-state in a few days." The man gave a huge smile.

Max's chest tightened. This one was too slick. Didn't Roy see that? He'd keep an eye on him, for sure. Fraud came to mind…

"Where is everybody?"

Odd question. "What d'ya mean, everybody?"

"You know. The bronc buster, the ladies."

Max frowned. "How do you know about them?"

"Roy told me," the fraud said as he glanced around the barn nonchalantly.

Pete caught sight of the two talking outside Bonnie's stall and strode up the barn aisle with his hand out. Tom took a couple steps toward him. "Hey there, pardner. Who are you?"

"Pete, watch the—" Max started, but, it was too late.

Pete's boot landed on the pitchfork's tines, and up the wood handle shot. With a mid-air twist, it whirred right past Pete and straight into Tom's cheekbone. The man cursed like a sailor, and swiveled to hit Pete.

"Hold on there, mister," Max spouted, stepping between the two. "Got a short fuse there, hey?"

Tom immediately released his fist and laughed. He ran a hand down the now growing lump on his cheek and said, "Just fooling with ya. I wasn't going to hit him."

"No. You weren't. Why don't you go on back to the house and see what Roy wants you to do."

Tom's mouthed twitched in anger. He masked it quick enough, sure, but not before Max saw it.

The rogue smiled. "Sure enough. Nice ta meet you both." Tom turned and was gone.

"Nice shot, Pete," Max said.

"Who's the one what put that thing there?" Pete hollered, taking a few steps toward Max.

"Settle down, crazy man." Max nodded toward the barn door. "What do you make of him?"

"Don't know. Didn't get a chance to check him out. Why?"

"I don't know. Just a gut feeling, ya know? Don't like him. Too far from home. Asked too many questions."

"Questions. 'Bout what?" Pete matched Max's frown.

"About Jake, Suzannah, and Rebecca."

"Called them by name? Does he know them?"

"No. Called them by *the bronc buster*, and *the ladies*. I don't like it. Why would he need to know anything about them?"

Pete scratched his head. "After the trouble we had with Brad and his horse-thieving friends, I got no interest in any kinda repeat."

Max huffed a humorless laugh. It just figured. His first stint as temporary foreman while Clint was away, and he had to keep his head on a swivel because of some no good stranger. "Jake called this morning. Didn't stay on the phone long, just said he was leaving

Cooper Ranch, heading to Wheeler's to pick up Suzannah, then on home." A wedge of unexpected relief levered itself in between Max's shoulder blades. "When Jake gets home we'll see what he has to say about him. He knows how to read people." Max dipped a glance to Pete's mouth. "On account of him being so quiet. Something you could learn, my man."

"Who's the one talkin'?"

"Just help me keep an eye peeled, Pete. I think that hombre's up to no good."

Pete turned toward the stall. "You got it, master," he said on a laugh.

"Watch out—" Max started, but it was too late. Pete had once again stepped on the tines of the wayward pitchfork. It shot up, twisted, and zipped straight for Max. He caught it with a slap to his hand, then burst out laughing. "You are a menace, little brother. If only we could find a way to utilize that talent of yours." He waved a hand out in front of him. "You go first. I'll follow several paces behind."

Pete's loud protestations filled the barn.

Ignoring the noise, Max turned back to watch Tom enter the main house. He found his gaze locked on the front door long after it had slammed closed.

CHAPTER 22

Suzannah rose long before the rooster crowed or the sun graced the sky. Only dim light filtered into her bedroom, and with it, the same dread she'd felt the night before. With barely enough energy to pull on her jeans and sleeveless blouse, she slinked about the room, trying to muster up the desire to prepare this breakfast spread for Troy and his crew. She hoped it was the last, but agonized over the real possibility it could be the first of many more to come until someone besides Jake came to fetch her.

As she tugged on her boots, she stared at the red plaid flannel shirt she'd draped over her vanity chair. Jake had given her that shirt after seeing her in one of Troy's her first morning in the kitchen. Men's shirts made great aprons, so she'd always worn one of her dad's. Now she had Jake's. She picked it up and slid her arms into the rolled up sleeves, buttoned it, then slipped her arms around herself, letting the fuzzy feel of the fabric and the slight scent of Jake wrap her up in warm thoughts. She didn't belt it, just left it to hang to her knees. The enormity of the shirt perfectly matched her feelings for the man. It was a symbol. A keepsake.

A reminder that the Jake she knew and loved would return for her.

Wouldn't he?

Her fingers shook so much as she braided her hair, she almost gave up. But she didn't. And she would never give up on Jake.

Even when…

She stared into the mirror, but all she saw was a dark blank screen, and then a replay of last night's wretched parting. Jake crashing through the front door after midnight, the thud of his boot heels against the wooden floor halting to within a foot of her, his masculinity and masked vulnerability laid out before her. And then his words. His mutilating words.

I am leaving.

The statement was still alive and growing barbs in her head, abrading her already raw emotions until she wanted to scream. No matter which way she looked at it, he hadn't said, *We.*

And then he'd left. Hadn't told her why. Or if he'd be back. Just whirled about and disappeared into the night. Gone.

Had he truly abandoned her? Or would he be back?

She scrubbed her hands down the flannel, blew out the breath she'd been holding, then let herself out the bedroom door. Reaching behind her to pull the door closed, she stared ahead at Jake's room. Just a couple of steps, and she would know if he'd taken all his stuff.

No. She wouldn't look. Instead she turned to go toward the stairs. Took two steps. Stopped. She spun around before she could talk herself out of it and stalked back to Jake's open doorway. She stood frozen in the open space as she glanced around. Neat as a pin. Bed made. Dresser clean of Jake's new shaving gear.

No satchel. No clothes. No trace of Jake at all. He'd taken everything with him. He didn't have to return.

Except he must return. For her. Her chest tightened so much, it threatened to suffocate her from the inside out, even without help from the aching lump in her throat. She closed her eyes and concentrated on taking the next breath in, slowly. Out. In.

Once her breathing evened out, the only thing to do was go downstairs, fix the hardy meal, and hope it was the last because Jake would come for her. He would. She was sure of it.

Suzannah yanked the cast iron frying pan out, placed it on the stove, then retrieved the sausage from the fridge. For the next several minutes, she settled into the mixing up of Grandma's recipe for cinnamon rolls, beating the eggs in a bowl for later, setting out orange juice, apple cider, condiments, starting several more pots of coffee, boiling the water in a dutch oven for mush, and finally unwrapping the bacon to fry after the sausage.

A half hour slipped by with Suzannah mindlessly preparing the meal when the back door banged opened. She flinched, glanced over. The cowboys filtered in, one by one. They were boisterous today. Unruly. Loud. So loud. Her back tightened. She pasted on a smile as each offered greetings while passing by her for the table. She scraped the sausage out of her frying pan onto a platter, and stilled when she heard the front door open and close. Turning her head sideways she felt her pulse beat hard in her neck as she waited to see who it might be. Hoping to see her gentle giant walk through that door. *Please be Jake.* But no. Looney. Her heart flipped a few unsteady beats as she turned back to the bacon she'd carefully laid in the frying pan.

A vehicle slid to a stop outside. A door slammed. Grease popped, and she yelped when it hit her hand. She cursed the bacon. Turning the heat down, she forced herself to concentrate on flipping each strip until they were cooked and on a platter. She thrust the bacon into one of the cowboy's hands as he passed through the kitchen, smiling wanly up at him. He nodded back and took the platter from her.

What had caused Jake's thunderous scowl last night? It had practically vibrated the air around him. She refilled a pitcher of orange juice and donned a pair of oven mitts. The kitchen timer dinged. She moved almost unconsciously, a puppet on strings obeying the chime. The oven door was heavy in her hand. A blast of hot air whooshed past her face, burning her gold cross against the notch at her neck.

She hefted the pan of cinnamon rolls, butter bubbling along each edge. Vaguely she heard hoots and hollers from the monstrous dining table behind her. It *did* smell good. She inverted the cinnamon rolls onto the last platter in the house and drizzled icing on top. Jake was going to miss the rolls while they were piping hot. He loved them while they were still warm from the oven and wafting cinnamon smells throughout the house.

Jake would show up. He knew Suzannah had to get back to Harper Ranch. That she had planned to go back with him. He was never irresponsible. His entire identity centered on him being utterly dependable.

The thought stunned her.

That was why he rode every morning for an entire *year* searching for his missing wife and child. That was why he hated his father so. She deposited the steaming platter of rolls at the end of the table with leaden hands. That was why he looked so murderous last night as he dictated his own departure. Because, in his mind, she had become just the latest person in his life to take the other side. To abandon him.

The lump in her throat grew claws. She swallowed past it, blinking through the dry burn in her eyes. *No, Jake. I didn't abandon you. I never…*

Her gaze flitted toward the front door again, until the claws that had lodged in her throat turned to ice.

The cowboys were rising from the table, one after another, taking their plates to the sink, each thanking her as he strode by. Some patted their stomachs, others grinned and nodded, one burped, another scolded him. How long had she stood here?

Troy was the last to drop off his plate and head for the door, a hearty thanks on his lips. She stopped him with a hand to his arm. When he turned back, she asked, "Where's Jake?"

"You didn't know?"

The lump swelled, stuck hard in her throat. She swallowed. Had to get the words out. "Know what?"

"He left last night for his uncle's ranch. Said he needed to pick up the horse and trailer before he headed back to Harper's." Troy patted her hand, then turned to follow the last of the men out the door.

Yes, she knew that. But, where was he now?

A ball of lead seemed to have dropped from the lump in her throat and land hard in her stomach.

She'd done it. Had crossed the line. Had passed from concern into meddling where she had no place. She knew why Jake didn't want his dad in his life. He hadn't been there while Jake was growing up. And, had it been his father's fault, she might've agreed with Jake, and let him imprison his black thoughts of the man in the place where broken dreams were kept.

But that wouldn't heal his soul, would it? The un-forgiveness would eat him up, bit by bit, like a vulture devouring a dead carcass. Maybe that's why, when she'd first met Jake, his eyes had looked so lifeless. And now she had compounded the abysmal grief in his life and turned around and heaped it right back on his head like hot coals.

Before Troy closed the door, he peeked back in. "And, Suzannah, since Jake should be rolling in anytime now, I probably won't see you before you leave. Thanks for the great meals. We'll all miss you round here."

When the impact of his words registered that Jake would be back, a groundswell of relief washed over her. But, behind that swell came the wave of doubt. Troy hadn't seen how Jake had been with *her* last night.

Once the kitchen was put to rights, Suzannah trod up the stairs to pack her things. *Please bring Jake back to me, Lord.* She didn't care that it was a completely selfish prayer. She had to believe Jake wanted her in his life. At the very least, that he would do the dependable thing and give her a ride back to her uncle's.

Once she was packed, and Jake had yet to return, Suzannah decided to do a last cleaning of the house, to occupy her mind. Why hadn't Jake returned yet? Would he? Her legs trembled with every squat and stoop she did to gather up Wheeler household clutter. By the time she finished putting the house in order, it was time for the men to arrive for lunch.

She and Jake should have long since been back on the road toward Harper Ranch by now. She ignored the meal downstairs since the Wheeler men knew to fend for themselves from here on out. Embarrassed and confused by Jake's absence, she stayed upstairs and took her time thoroughly scrubbing the upstairs bath-room, then cleaning each bedroom.

Finished with her job, she glumly trudged to her own room to wait and pray when a bold male voice filtered through her window. *Jake's voice!* A sudden spike of elation shot up her spine, but in an instant turned to ice. Why was he shouting? She ran to the window and pushed back the airy curtains. Sure enough, Jake was in some cowpoke's face, shouting profanities for all he was worth. She'd never heard him swear like that. What could be wrong?

Suzannah flew down the stairs and out the front door, pure joy making her steps light, but dread turning them to lead by the time she arrived at the scene. Looney had a good hold on one of Jake's arms, another man had locked elbows with his other. Even so, Jake dragged both men across the dirt drive as he bulldozed toward a cowboy who was backing as fast as Jake gained on him.

"What's happening?" Suzannah asked one of the watching men.

"Bobbie there ran over a bunch a' raccoons, is all," the man said, scratching his head in bewilderment.

Jake's entire body seemed to pulse with rage. His neck was bright red up to the beard he still hadn't shaved. His breathing was ragged. His thigh muscles bulged against his jeans. Did he really care so much about the coons? Or did he just want to beat this fellow period, as if that would grant Jake payback for all the wrongs done him in life?

The cowboy next to Suzannah looked down in her face with a question in his eyes. "I said, Bobbie there ran over some raccoons on the road."

"I heard you!" Suzannah said, then choked on her own yell as Jake yanked his arms free and launch himself at the man. "Stop him!" she screamed as she raced forward, planning to do the job herself if need be.

Just as she reached Jake, she got knocked out of the way by a swarm of men joining Looney to stop Jake. She stumbled backward but caught herself before landing on her backside. She backed out the of the way then and watched, ready to run forward again if Jake needed her.

"How?" Suzannah asked of another man who observed the squabble. Her voice was low and husky, but still working.

He seemed to understand what she meant by her question, thank goodness. "Goofin' round. They can be kinda a menace, so he probably tried to run over 'em. On purpose like." The cowboy turned away and sauntered off, as did most of the other men.

"Stay right there, Bobbie," Jake said, stopping the whole group with his command. He marched to the barn while no one moved. Bobbie's eyes grew large when Jake returned with a shovel in his hand. The man turned on his heels, ready to flee, but Troy had come up to stand a few feet behind him. Bobbie slid to a stop when he saw the boss. With shoulders slumped, he turned back to face Jake.

"Go bury the mother and her dead bairns." Jake's voice was deadly calm.

"Yes, sir," Bobbie said, then scurried over to the dead carcasses and the wheelbarrow another man had rolled up.

Jake pointed at a greenhorn half-hidden within the crowd. "You! Where's the kit that survived?"

"It—it's in a box," the young man began, "over there." He gestured toward the barn. "I th-think they're planning to drown it."

"Bring the kit, along with some cat food. Dog food, too."

Jake glanced at Suzannah in the dispersing crowd, but shifted his attention to Troy. "You got some fruits and greens, mayhap some nuts I could have?"

Troy lifted his hat and ran a hand over his graying hair, then replaced it. "That mother must have been moving the kits. Unusual for 'em to be out during the day. Let me take care of the last one. Don't concern yerself."

Suzannah knew Troy would just drown it, since it was too young to make it on its own. Besides, she knew Uncle Roy hated the pests. Troy probably did too. But not Jake. She was sure of it. Of him.

"If its all the same to you, let me take it," Jake said.

Troy frowned. "If you're sure."

"Aye," Jake said. "I'll get it out of your hair. Can I grab some of your fruits and vegetables? It can be old stuff."

Jake turned his head and caught Suzannah's gaze fleetingly. "Suzannah can help you with that."

Suzannah's sigh of relief was probably heard all the way to the barn. Thank goodness he planned to take her with him. Or, at least she thought so…

"Whatever you need. But Jake, it probably has ticks, and who knows what else."

"Who's your vet?"

"Doc Willows. In Gillette."

"If you'll draw me a map, I'll go there before heading to Roy's." He nodded his thanks to Troy, then blew out a steadying breath. The fierce crimson burn faded from Jake's face, leaving only the rugged tan every cowboy sported. He turned to face Suzannah. Really face her—for the first time since he'd left in a huff the night before.

Troy and the remaining few wandered off for the barn, but Jake remained solid, staring into her eyes as if he could pluck out a truth of some kind. "Are you ready to go back home?" His words were salve to her soul, but cool all the same. Maybe he'd meant home to California, not Montana. As uncomfortable as his incriminatory stare was, she would not look away. He would know by her unbroken gaze that she was with him in whatever he decided to do. Always.

His sable brown eyes looked black in that moment. A lifetime of emotions locked up tight behind their inky wall. If she had to, she'd stand here and stare into them until the sun went down in order to prove she was with him.

A full minutes must have passed before she noticed the tension in his neck and chest relax, his shoulders rounded a bit. Would he forgive her? Understand she wanted only what was best for him? She didn't know what else to do but wait him out.

His gaze finally skirted away, as if he remembered an important fact. He scrubbed a hand down his face, smoothing his beard. "If you'll start gathering the greens and such, I'll be right in to help." He glanced around. "I want us out of here before Dodge comes back from town."

The lump in Suzannah's throat doubled in size. She nodded, unable to speak. *Us.* He may have chosen to reject his father, but he had not rejected her.

CHAPTER 23

J ake tried to quiet his thoughts, wanting nothing more
than to put the last day out of his mind. As they
bounced over the ruts in the drive on their way out of
Wheeler Ranch, he glanced at Suzannah. She was
cooing to the young raccoon, wrapped as it was in a
cotton towel on top of her lap. Jake had tried to convince her the kit should stay in the box they'd brought
along, at least until the vet could check it for stowa-
ways. But Suzannah being… well, Suzannah, she'd
stubbornly insisted it was too scared to be left unat-
tended. She was right, of course. It would likely have
scurried around in the box, making itself sick and
leaving excrement everywhere. He was secretly glad she
had a heart for animals. But then, from what he'd seen,
she had a heart for every living thing.

After all, she'd seen something worth saving in
him.

Or had she?

His thoughts turned dark when their disagreement
the day before crashed back into his mind. He'd relived
that bitter betrayal a hundred times since then. Of all

people, he never thought Suzannah would jump ship. But she had. She'd taken Dodge's side against him.

Another quick glance told Jake the bairn was enjoying Suzannah's soothing sounds. It had peeked it's wee black nose out at first, to sniff her breath. Now, it had it's whole head out of the protective rag to more readily hear her voice and stare at her face. He didna blame it. Her raspy voice delighted his senses every day, and that face... well, it was the verra essence of sustenance to him.

Or had been.

"You enjoying that critter?" Jake said, cringing inwardly at how gruff his voice sounded. His disappointment in her still gnawed at him, and it showed.

He glanced at her, unsure how she'd react. But she just smiled, oblivious, and nodded. "We need to name it."

We. That had a lovely sound to it. Just that smile and her willingness to speak closed off his aggravation and lifted his spirits. "What would you name it?"

"Maybe Bandit." She lifted it to speak into its face. "Are you a boy?" Settling it back in her lap, she said, "Female... hmmm... don't know. You should pick the girl's name."

Her statement hit him like a wallop to the gut, leaving him breathless. Betty had given him that same option. He thought of the name he'd picked out. *Annabelle.* Thoughts of an Annabelle, who would be about eight months old now, floored him. He could almost picture a dark-haired angel with her mother's blue eyes.

"Well...?" Suzannah's voice cut through his thoughts.

He cleared his throat. "Um… well… how about Coo?"

"Coo? For raccoon, you mean?"

Nae. For the lilting cooing sounds you make to it, he wanted to say but held back. "Sure."

Silence. Then, "Okay. I like it."

Of course she did. Back to her pleasing ways. Without intending to, he'd rattled her last night; or mayhap he had intended to. Either way, she would have agreed to name it Bunny if he'd suggested it. He wasna proud of the way his behavior brought about her meekness. But he wasna going to let her maneuver him into believing his sire's lies. Or, into forgiving him.

Jake watched for the veterinarian's office, then made the turn into the parking lot. He threw the truck's gearshift into neutral, set the brake, and jumped out to round the bumper. He opened the door for Suzannah and the raccoon. A band tightened around his chest. She had the kit re-swaddled and held by one arm like her own wee bairn. He threw off the image they made and helped her to the ground while she gripped the wee thing to her chest. Lucky critter.

They introduced themselves to a young Doc Willows. The doctor was a pleasant enough fellow, the kind of man Jake figured women would find appealing if they had a hankering for blue-eyed intelligence and close-cropped tidiness. They all stood in a room that smelled of alcohol and included a long, metal-topped table. The doc took one look at his patient and smiled with a hint of amusement. Jake caught that amused smirk, and wanted to throw Doc Willows out the compact window.

Suzannah gave the doctor a beautiful smile. Jake ground his teeth together.

"So, what do we have here? A raccoon kit?"

"Aye," Jake barked.

The doctor ignored his sour look. "What happened to its mother?" He took the now squirming creature from Suzannah's arms.

"Run over," Jake said.

The doc looked up and studied Jake for a few seconds, then looked back down at the kit and nodded. "I see."

What did he see? That Jake was enraged someone had purposefully run over a family of helpless critters? That he was waiting to be laughed out of the room for bringing vermin in for an exam? Or mayhap that he was jealous of the smile Suzannah gave the doctor.

It didna matter which one. They all stuck in his craw.

The doctor looked to Suzannah. "Help me unwrap your little package. We'll first find out what gender it is, and then determine how old it might be."

The doc's calm practicality only ramped up Jake's temper. "It's eyes and ears are open, so we figure over a month old. Given the size, closer to two."

The doctor smiled at him, amused.

Jake wanted to grab him by his white lapels and growl in his face. What an arrogant fool.

The doctor was silent as he checked the gender—a female—checked it for ticks and parasites, and then teeth, for age. When he was done, he re-wrapped the kit and handed her back to Suzannah.

"Okay, folks. She's over two months old. Already weaned, or pretty close, I'd guess. The mother took really good care of her, since she's free of ticks and any other crawling pests. Their den must have been spotless. A good sign, since I'm not going to worry she might have rabies. I'll give her some drops for possible internal parasites, then she should be good to go. If she's already so comfortable with you, Miss Harper, I'd say she'll make a pretty good pet. For now."

"For now?" Suzannah said as her first words.

"Well, you will have to introduce her back to her natural habitat, eventually. She is a wild animal, Miss Harper, and therefore unpredictable. Plus, she can carry roundworms that harm *you*. Use the dewormer regularly, practice good hygiene yourselves. For now, she'll be fine with you. I'll give you some special meal. Later, you can give her cat food, but not too much. Too much protein for too long and you can give her gout. Fruits, vegetables, nuts. Those are all good. Raccoons are pretty easy to please. They eat often. But because she'll eat all the time, don't over feed her."

One look at Suzannah innocently taking in all the doctor said, and Jake was finished. "Got it, Doc." Jake had been taking care of animals his whole life—wild and domestic. There wasna much the doc could tell him he hadna already experienced. Didna the man see he was overwhelming Suzannah? She didna look overwhelmed, but he was sure she must be.

"What do we owe you?" Jake said.

"You can settle with my receptionist." He patted Suzannah on the shoulder, then turned to give Jake a handshake. Jake took his hand to give it a quick shake, but the doctor held tight. "Not many people would have bothered to save her. I'm honored to meet you both. And your little coon there."

Jake was amazed. So, the doctor hadn't been making fun of them to himself. "Thank you, Doc. And, for treating Coo here."

"Coo?" The doctor smiled again, and Jake realized he just had an easy smile and disposition. He hadna recognized it, since he didna own one himself.

"Aye. It's what we decided to name her if it was female."

"Oh. Fine. Fine. Good name," the doctor said, then gave a pat to Jake's back when he turned to go.

Jake followed Suzannah and Coo to the door.

Before they exited, the doctor stopped them. "Wait a minute, folks."

Jake and Suzannah turned simultaneously. "Aye?" Jake said.

"Listen. It's late. Why don't you leave Coo with me tonight? The de-worming is kind of unpleasant if you're traveling, and when Troy called to make your appointment, he said you were headed to Montana. Pick her up in the morning."

The doctor came up to Suzannah and took the bundle out of her hands. The raccoon squirmed against the doctor's chest.

"No. That's okay—" Suzannah started to say.

"Thanks. Good idea, Doc—" Jake said at the same time.

Jake smoothed a hand down Suzannah's braid. "It's fine, lass. He's right about the de-worming. Trust him."

She was peering into his face like a worried mother. Her beauty in that moment was so irresistible, it seized the breath in Jake's throat.

"She'll be fine, Miss Harper. I have a nice cage with warm blankets for her. We'll have her all cleaned up for you in the morning."

Suzannah slid her arm under Jake's to wrap it around his waist. His heart hammered at her touch, so hot and insistent through his shirt. One glance her way and the hammer shrank to a pin tip. Suzannah stood rod-straight, shadows thrown by her clenched jaw. She just wanted reassurance that the wee kit would make it through 'til morn. He pulled her in close, feeling her warmth spread like syrup along his right side, and tried to reflect back as much comfort as he could muster without a word. The feel of that link between them stole his voice away. He found he could only nod his heartfelt thanks to the doctor before turning for the door.

They held each other's waists all the way to the truck. Jake opened the passenger door for Suzannah, then gave her a kiss on top of her head, breathing in the scent of her hair, unwilling to let her go. Finally he helped her into the truck. "She'll be fine, lass. Dinna worry."

"I know," she said as she settled in the seat. She sighed and the sad sound touched him. "Where will we go?"

"Motel. Get a couple of rooms."

Suzannah sighed with relief this time, and Jake almost laughed. As much as she enjoyed his kisses, she was probably worried it might go further. With that silky hair of hers, and her soft skin and inviting curves, he sure thought of it often enough. But tonight, her angelic smile eased him back from the idea of reckless passion, because she was so much more than silk and curves and lovely smiles. She was the only woman he'd ever known who, simply by listening to the unspoken, could reach in and soothe his wounded soul.

His mum had never been still enough to hear, and his wife had never been quiet enough to care. But Suzie... she was a giver. And he drank up her care like the empty vessel he was.

As he drove them around Gillette, he finally decided on the Mustang Motel. Nothing fancy, and not expensive. God ken, he wasna a rich man, yet he was honor-bound to get them two rooms.

Once they'd said their goodnights and Jake had settled in, he tossed and turned in the too soft, too short bed until his thoughts centered on the woman next door. Staying in a motel with just the kitten wasna the smartest thing he'd done. Yet, all he had to do was get through the night without allowing his passions to stir. Suzannah in the room next to him eased his need to protect her, but he was surprised to find it did more for him. It soothed him, healed him. Just having her near quieted his mind.

When the first light of morning slipped through the gap in the motel's heavy curtains, he awoke with a deep breath and languid stretch. Was that contentment he felt? He couldna remember the last time he'd slept so well. He threw off the covers and swung his feet to the floor. First he'd take a shower. After that—

He straightened with the realization he'd been scratching his bearded cheek. He ran his palms down both sides of his face and fingered the hair along his throat. The beard felt itchy, hot. Claustrophobic. He didna want to hide from the sun anymore. Not when the sun's rays were right next door.

By the time Jake stepped out of the shower, the mirror was entirely fogged with steam. He swabbed it clean, then wrapped the discolored motel towel around his hips. He studied his face, turning it from side to side. One of the many reasons he'd grown a beard was to be able to stop glaring at himself in the mirror everyday. Somehow escaping his reflection helped him to live with himself.

Now it was time to stop hiding. For Suzannah.

He took one last look at the black mask he'd been wearing, then tore into the satchel he'd carried to the bathroom with him. At the bottom, he found the Rapid-Shave cream, razor, and small scissors he'd bought weeks ago. He hefted them in each hand, remembering when Suzannah had seemed afraid of him because of his beard. With his lips pressed into a thin line of determination, he plunked the cream and razor down by the faucet, and used the small scissors to trim the bulk of the curly hair. He snipped away, a steady downpour of jet black bristles falling to the sink in layers. That done, he loaded his safety razor and twisted it shut, shook the can of shaving cream, and then squirted it in his palm. He hadna done this in a verra long time, and now he wondered if he'd end up with nicks all over his face. Well, there was no hope for it, so without more thought he worked up a good lather, spread it on his face, and tackled the job—verra slowly.

When the blade rasped its last sweep against his skin, he rinsed his face, patted it dry, and took a good look in the mirror. The man staring back at him was a stranger. At first, all he noticed were black eyes with black slashes over the top of them, and pale skin below. Then his nose seemed too long. His lower lip too full. His chin too square. He cocked his head and dared himself to smile. Sure enough, the dreaded things had not left him. Creases that dipped in enough to be called dimples. He felt his blood ratatatting against his eardrums like a machine gun spitting bullets.

Ahh, what had he done? How could he keep the respect of rough and tumble cowhands with these senseless things plastered on his face? He'd hated them in his youth, and now he remembered why. They looked foreign on the face of a man who scowled a thousand times more often than he smiled.

He inspected himself for a minute longer—wishing he could stick his beard back on—turned off the water to the sink he hadn't remembered leaving on, and inhaled a deep breath. He just hoped it made Suzannah happy. If not, he'd grow the dang beard right back.

A pounding came on the connecting door to his motel room. Had that been going on for a while? Dread gripped him. *Suzannah!* Jake flew out of the bathroom, unlocked the deadbolt, and cranked the knob.

As the door slammed open, Suzannah was already talking, shaking her head, hands and eyes skyward as if beseeching the heavens for a little help trying to get through to Jake. "Geez, Jake… I've been standing here… knocking and knocking, and—" Her gaze dipped enough to take in his mostly unclothed state, and she stopped cold. Then her gaze drifted from head to toe—stirring his already burning libido—and toe to face.

And camped there.

She tilted her head, took a step forward, and studied some more. "Jake…" she said in a wee voice.

"Aye?" His voice came out warbled and thick, like a drowning man expelling his last breath underwater to call out to her.

She took another step toward him. Then another. When she was within a foot of him, he became aware of his shifting towel. He grabbed hold and re-tightened it around his hips, noticing for the first time how it barely fit. He gulped.

Suzannah hadna noticed, thankfully. Not the least bit shy, she reached up a hand and, with the backs of her fingers, smoothed them down his clean-shaven face. "Ahh, Jake." Did her voice seem huskier than normal?

He puffed his cheeks as his last lungful of air escaped through tight lips. He was unraveling fast. Before he could excuse himself back to the bathroom where his clean clothes awaited, she pressed both her palms to his face. Up and down she slid them, feeling his skin. Problem was, he could feel her skin, too. He was in trouble here. *Move!* But, not one muscle obeyed.

Then she ruined him altogether with that irresistible smile of hers. Today he would resist. He must. He pressed his lips together so hard they ached, and aimed for a scowl. However he accomplished it, he'd make sure she never saw those useless, ugly dimples on either side of his monstrous face.

"Jake. You're beautiful." She sounded awestruck.

He felt the blush. It started at his chest, moved straight up his neck into his naked cheeks, and didna stop until it reached the tops of his ears. *Beautiful. Great.* That was the last thing he wanted to be.

She must have seen his face flame red, since her brows tilted up in the center and she pouted those full lips into a sensuous little coo. Just like she'd done for the blasted raccoon. Sweet little *oh's* of sympathy whispered up her throat.

And, just like that, he was undone.

He stood like a darned besotted beggar, ready to traipse after the wee fairy anywhere she wanted to lead him.

CHAPTER 24

Suzannah had never seen a more striking man in her life. She'd thought Jake good looking before, but now...

His face was beautifully chiseled by the Master himself. Strong chin, angular cheekbones, hollowed cheeks with sexy creases along his mouth on either side. And, that jaw. Square, with just a hint of black stubble since his beard was too coarse to eliminate the color entirely. Her gaze dropped to his lips. The top lip was thinner than the bottom, now that she could see them both perfectly. She wanted to nibble on that bottom lip. A grand passion welled up inside, her draw to him so strong it was like falling into the grip of gravity.

Male perfection on the outside that flawlessly matched the big heart on the inside.

The only thing missing was his smile. Somehow she knew it would be perfection, too. And, she knew just how to coax it out of him. She stepped back a pace, taking the pressure off him. He sighed in relief, but she wasn't done. Slowly, with all the dramatics of Elizabeth Taylor herself, she let her smile start, then expand, and finally beam.

He winced and closed his eyes.

Oh no you don't, Jake Cooper. "Jake?"

He pressed his lips together—as if that alone would prevent the smile—and refused to open his eyes.

"Jake?" she said, letting amusement tingle at the edges of her word.

He barely opened one eye, and said, "Aye?"

She didn't want to play this game anymore. She needed to see that smile. "Jake Cooper! Smile for me, you stubborn ole mule!"

She'd only wanted him to smile, but instead he burst into laughter. *Laughter?* She watched while he laughed, one bout after another. What in the world? Nervous energy maybe? Or was it the futility of a woman demanding something from a man like him?

Then she stopped frowning and noticed it. Really noticed it. The open-mouthed smile that went with all that laughter. Jake's teeth were nearly straight, white and appealing. His eyes twinkled when he laughed. *Actually twinkled!* And then… her attention latched onto the creases at each side of his mouth. They'd become full-fledged dimples—deep, and oh-so-adorable. Oh heavens! He probably hated them. But there they were. Glorious little craters where God must have tested him to see if he was done. She nearly laughed herself over the silly thought.

But no. She fought to rein in this new round of joyful laughter. The last thing she wanted was to discourage future laughter from Jake. She wanted him to smile all the time, and she'd be content just to stare. Like she was doing now.

In an instant his laughter died, a choked death right in front of her. She watched as embarrassment took over his expression, and a deep flush colored his cheeks. No! He'd never show her again if she let that happen. *Distract him.* "What's so funny, may I ask?" she said, sounding put out, though she was anything but.

He double-blinked, and his mouth parted slightly. Good. He was thinking over her question.

"Well?" she said.

He cleared his throat. "I um—" He stopped and glanced down at himself, as if he just realized he was mostly naked. He put a hand to her shoulder, effectively turning her toward her room. "Go. I need to get dressed."

When he let go to close the door, she turned back. "Jake?"

"Aye?" he said, holding tight to one side of his towel, looking so delectable with his hair-dusted chest, tummy, and legs.

She wished they were married and she could eat him up right then and there.

Shaking off the splendid daydream, she smoothed a hand over her own jaw and chin to demonstrate. "I like it. Really like it." Then she smiled at him, and turned to bounce off as Jake closed the door after her.

* * *

They were finally on their way back to Harper Ranch, the only place Jake felt he was needed. Though, as quickly as Roy had shooed him out of there, he wondered about that now.

In the last few weeks, Suzannah had been his only mooring. If he hadna tied himself to her, he would be adrift by now, lost in a hopeless hell.

He glanced over at the lass. She delighted his ears, and at the same time his heart, with her delightful cooing to the young raccoon. Coo had already joined her own wee heart to Suzannah's, connecting in a way only one who'd lost its sanctuary could do. And Suzannah, in turn, had yielded her own heart to the motherless creature. A heart so full of love and giving, he wondered how anyone could ever abuse it. And yet, someone had.

As Suzannah babbled to the wee creature, Jake's mind circled round the incident that happened to Suzannah long ago. He couldna fathom a man abusing a woman at all, but to harm someone as beautiful inside and out as the kitten… well, if he didna keep in check, he'd find himself on the road to California to search out the bastard who'd tormented and maimed her.

"Do you think she should eat again?" Suzannah's raspy voice floated to him.

Jake glanced over with a smile, thinking how easily his smiles had been coming of late. At least smiles for Suzannah. Here she was, asking him if the bairn should eat, when she already had an instinct about it, handling two of the feedings perfectly already. A natural mother, she was.

"What do *you* think?" he said.

She looked down at the coon in her arms. "Yes." She nodded. "Yes, I think she's hungry."

Jake smiled at her again, letting her ken without words she'd decided correctly.

Contentment rolled over him. A family was what they were: his kitten, the wee coon, and himself. At least until the coon was a few months older and they'd have to turn her out to the wild. But he could visualize a bairn or four of their own in the future, and that made a goofy smile come upon him. No one had ever told him smiling was so good for the soul. He could actually feel his soul swell with every smile he shared.

He drove along, quiet deep in his soul, listening to the sounds of nurturer and bairn. Suzannah was feeding Coo cat food and bananas, and the bairn was grasping pieces in her wee claws to nibble away each bite. Then came the water from a bottle the vet had given them. It all came so easily to Suzie, and she seemed to enjoy every minute.

Once Coo was fed, she snuggled her nose into Suzannah's chest for a snooze. The kitten stroked the coon's back, and continued her delightful cooing.

After a while, a hush fell over the two, and Jake felt unexpectedly bereft. For so long he'd been alone, with only the sounds of nature surrounding him on those long treks in search of his pregnant wife. Today, the grief and guilt were somewhat lessened in the company of the one who not only nurtured the wild animal, but who settled the wildness in his own being. For the first time he could ever recall, he needed to fill the silence.

"She seems to have taken to you, Kitten," Jake said.

Suzannah smiled at him. Jake glanced over to get a full view of that sunshine, though brief, and smiled back.

Once he'd looked back to the road, he still felt her gaze on him. "What?"

"Just admiring the view," she said, shocking him.

Blood rushed into his face at her words. When he thought how exposed he was and that she'd see his flush, more blood came rushing into his head until there was a swishing sound in his ears. He cleared his throat. "Uh… we'll be home in three to four hours. I'll stop in Billings and pick us up some lunch and get gas."

"Jake… I don't miss the beard."

That statement sent even more blood rushing everywhere. Part of him regretted shaving away his only hiding place. But another part of him enjoyed Suzannah's approval. More than he should.

He pressed his lips together, trying to keep the ugly dimples from showing up. The thought of arriving at

Harper Ranch with the darned things exposed turned his gut. No one would take him seriously now. This whole episode with his beard proved Suzannah had made him into a different man. Now, he had to decide if he was okay with that or not. And he needed to figure that out before he parked the truck in front of Roy Harper's ranch house.

"Jake, I need to talk to you." The one sentence every man dreaded to hear made all that blood drain out of his face. His only hope was Suzannah sounded apprehensive as well. Amazing how he could be so content one moment, and the next want to be a dozen counties away.

"Aye, lass. Go ahead."

"Your… *Dodge* is coming to Harper Ranch."

He whipped his head toward her and scowled. What had she done this time? "Why?" He glared back at the road.

"He wants to be near you, Jake. Get to know you."

"Suzannah, I warned you. You need to stay out of this." He set his jaw so hard, he imagined cracking a tooth.

"Jake. Since you wouldn't listen to him, may I tell you what happened to him?"

"Nae! I dinna want to ken. I dinna care." He shot her a glare. "Drop it."

"But, he'll be there, Jake. What will you do?"

"Why is he going there, Suzannah? Did you have something to do with that?"

She was silent. When he glanced at her, she was stroking the wee coon and looking straight forward. Dread roiled within him. He didna want to allow his hatred for his sire to affect how he felt about Suzannah, but darned if her meddling wasna already pumping poison through his blood. "Lass?"

She swallowed so hard, he could hear it where he sat. He thought of the lump in her throat, which could only be growing bigger as the seconds ticked by. New guilt mixed with the old fury inside him. But this wasna his fault. He ran a hand down his face, wanting the feel of soft beard to calm him, and instead feeling the scratch of new growth. He hated it.

"Where's Bonnie," Suzannah asked.

"What?"

"The horse. Bonnie. Why didn't you bring her with the trailer?"

She already ken the answer to that. "Rebecca wanted to keep her while she was there. Dinna change the subject."

"How did it go with Bronco?"

Jake slammed an open hand on the steering wheel. Suzannah jumped, and the wee coon flew out of her arms. The little thing shot up the seat back, scurried along the top to his shoulders, and wrapped it's wee body around the nape of his neck.

"Och!" He bent his head forward as far as he could without taking his eyes off the road.

"Whoops!" Suzannah scooted over and reached up. "Here, let me see if she'll come back to me." She coughed her last couple of words.

Her prodding only made Coo dig her claws more deeply into his neck as she tucked her nose under his collar.

"Stop," he said to Suzannah as calmly as possible. "She's scared. Digging into my skin. Let her calm down first." They'd just arrived at the outskirts of Billings, thank goodness. "I'll stop for gas here and peel her off me."

"Okay," Suzannah said.

Jake heard a small noise escape her. He couldna look, since he was turning into the gas station, and his neck had to stay in one position. He heard another wee sound. Pretty soon, he deciphered it. Suzannah was trying her darndest to hold back a laugh.

As he slowly leaned forward to downshift and maneuver the pickup and trailer into a gasoline bay, Suzannah snorted, as heartily as Rebecca ever had. Then came another snort. By the time he was stopped and could view her out of the corner of his eye, she was roaring with laughter. As she laughed and laughed, he found he couldna stay angry any longer. He kent it must look pretty funny with Coo draped around his neck like an old lady's fur. He smiled. Then when he turned and saw Suzannah's whole face beaming with delight, it tickled him so, he ended up joining her for a good laugh. What made it funnier was how still he had to be while doing it.

A tap to his window interrupted the lightness of the moment. Just that noise alone startled the coon and made her scramble against Jake's neck. This time she shot across to the steering wheel and onto the dash. She bumped her head into the windshield several times, not realizing glass was keeping her from the great outdoors.

Suzannah stopped laughing and began cooing to her. Not only did it calm the wee coon, it calmed Jake as well. Nothing like a woman's ability to soothe rattled nerves, aye? Coo stared at Suzannah, listening to the musical sound of her voice. Jake found himself doing the same thing.

The tapping came on the window again, snapping Jake out of his rapture. This time Coo didna flee. She actually came forward and let Suzannah take hold of her, snuffling her all over her face. Jake envied the wee bairn. All the same, he rolled the window down half a foot.

"Fill 'er up, sir?" the young man at his window asked.

"Sure," Jake said. "Get the windows, as well."

"Please," Suzannah added, and smiled at the young man.

A stab of jealousy hit Jake's chest. He didna want the kitten to give away those smiles to anyone but him.

The young man smiled back at Suzannah, then said, "Yes, ma'am." He scurried off.

"Yes, ma'am?" Jake said with irritation in his voice.

"Well, I did say *please*," Suzannah said as she stroked the bairn back to sleep.

"Fine." Jake squinted toward a drive-in hamburger joint next door. "While your little friend there fills us up, I'll run over and get us some burgers."

Suzannah nodded.

"Any requests?"

"Whatever you like is fine with me."

Jake was amazed, as he always was when Suzannah said such things. Betty had never been agreeable that way. Even when he tried to comply, it never made her happy. He'd often wondered why she manipulated him into marrying her if he could never please her.

"Jake?" She tapped him on the shoulder, snapping him out of the past. "Where'd you go off to?" Suzannah said with a concerned look on her face.

He ran his fingers through his hair. "Uh. I'll go get us the burgers. Coca cola?"

"Sure."

Jake scrambled out of the truck, forgetting all about his hat. He was glad for the few moments he'd have to himself. As much as he loved having Suzannah near, he also felt like he didna have a bit of control over himself. He shook his limbs, one after the other, as he walked to the burger stand, then rubbed his neck where Coo had scratched him, bending as he went to see the blonde behind the window. Why did they make these wee windows for ordering so dang short? "Four burgers. Two Coca Colas in bottles—loosen the caps, but leave them on."

Reaching into his back pocket, he retrieved his wallet and handed the gal some greens. The young lassie was staring at him, but hadna moved. Had Coo left blood on his neck? He wiped at it, bringing his hand to his face. No. No blood. What then? "Uh... that's all," Jake said.

"Oh. Oh, sure. Okay. Yes. I got it. Sure. It'll be a few minutes. Is that okay? Uh. You can sit right over there." She pointed to a few picnic tables under a canopy. "Will that be all right? Your number is twelve. I'll call you when it's ready. Is that okay?"

Jake stared, dumbfounded. Mayhap the owners should rethink hiring lassies who were so fidgety. He wondered what had rattled her so. He nodded to her, gave her a forced smile, then straightened to full height.

The lassie dropped her pen, then her pad. Before he'd moved to the table, she peeked her whole head out the window.

"Aye?" he asked.

"Ohh, you're Scottish. Right? Or Irish, or something. Do you live around here?"

"Scot. Montana." He paused, half waiting for another barage of words to hit, then thought better of it. He pointed vaguely toward the tables. "I'll be over there," he mumbled before speeding away.

When the lassie finally called his number, she opened the stand's side door and brought the meal to him personally. The wee thing stood a good foot shorter than him, but it didna stop her from boldly gazing up into his face. He grabbed the paper box out of her one hand, grasped the bottles between his fingers from her other hand, and nodded his thanks. Turning, he started toward the service station.

"Will you be coming back around sometime?" she called after him.

"Nae," he called over his shoulder, then hastened his steps. He'd never been through anything like that. What had gotten into the lass?

Suzannah had her lips pressed together when he entered the vehicle, yet he could see amusement in her eyes. "Now what?" he asked.

"See, I'm not the only one who likes the new you," she said, then chuckled.

"What are you talking about?"

"That girl. Captivated by you."

"Nae. She was just a wee lassie. I'm an old man compared to her."

"Face it, Jake, without the beard… you're one mouthwatering cowboy."

Shocked by her boldness, it took him a minute to realize she was still talking. Glancing back at the burger lassie in spite of himself, Jake smiled ruefully and returned his attention to Suzannah's chatty voice. He took a burger out of the box and rolled down the paper for her. Handing her the burger, he asked, "Suze. How's that lump in your throat?"

Suzannah instinctively swallowed. Then swallowed again. Turning her head toward him, she smiled excitedly. "Better." Then she swallowed again. "You know, Jake, it's always better with you, so I think the doctors were right. All in my head."

"It's not all in your head," he said, annoyed.

Jake took the second burger out and fixed it for himself, but laid it back down to pay the gas station attendant. Then he started the truck and merged back on the road toward Bozeman. Once he'd finished shifting, he picked up the burger and took a big bite. He chewed for a few seconds, then said, "I lodged the colas in the corner of the box. The lids should pop right off."

"Here, I'll get yours," she said. She set down her burger and lifted the wee coon to put her in her box with one of Jake's undershirts, then went about serving Jake. Once he had his cola, chugged it, and rested the bottle in the V of his crotch, he noticed she'd picked up her burger again. She was careful not to touch the burger itself, but just the paper around it. He hadna thought of how she'd probably want to wash her hands after touching the coon, but she hadna mentioned it. He didna ken any lasses who would not have complained about having to eat without washing their hands, but for some unknown reason, that thought pleased him.

They ate, drank, and chewed in companionable silence. Jake was... perfectly and profoundly content.

"We should talk about your dad," Suzannah said.

Jake's peace shattered. His hand cramped into a fist on the steering wheel. "Nae. We will not."

"You're a captive audience, Jake. I'm going to tell you what happened to him."

"Suzannah!" he barked, but not as loud as he wanted since he was conscious of the bairn at her feet. "What is your obsession with the old man? It's none of your business."

He glanced over with the scowl he used when he meant business, but her hurt expression penetrated his shield. The anger whooshed out of him faster than air from a popped balloon. Even so, he tried to keep up the façade.

"It is my business." She was tougher than he thought.

He glanced at her again. This time her eyes requested something of him. He frowned, confused. What was that look?

"God has made you my business, Jake."

He stared at her, caught up in the plea in her eyes and what she'd just said. He looked back to the road only to see a curve dead ahead. Jumping on both brake and clutch, he downshifted, hoping the trailer could handle the sudden deceleration and turn at the same time. Thank the Lord Bonnie hadna been in the trailer.

Thank the Lord? Since when had a sentence like that ever entered his mind? It was Suzannah. How the lass could trust God even after what she'd been through humbled him. And made him ponder the idea of God.

Once the rig was back under control, he put a hand out to the kitten. "You all right, lass?" he said with a light stroke to her arm.

She inhaled a big breath, exhaled, then leaned over to check on Coo. "She's still asleep. How does she do that?"

"Getting used to us, aye?"

"I suppose."

Should he continue the conversation she'd started? He wasna sure exactly what she'd meant by him being her business, but he wasna entirely sure he wanted to ask. He let the sound of the truck's engine fill the silence.

"He was in a fellow intern's car."

"*Suzannah…* "

She ignored him. "Your dad and the man were both bone tired from working an extra shift at the hospital."

"I told you, I dinna want to hear it." His voice was low, menacing, meant to make her back off.

"Jake. Be reasonable. I will tell you, then you can think about it." She patted him on the thigh. "It'll be all right. God's got you."

That thought knifed through him. *God's got you.*

Did He?

Her stare penetrated the side of his face as she awaited his permission to continue. That hand of hers rested on his leg, unsettling him. What was she doing? Demanding he hear about a sire he didna want to ken? Mayhap if he let her get it off her chest…

"Go ahead," he said, curtly. Though he wouldna promise to actually listen.

She rubbed his thigh reflexively as she spoke, and he felt sweat pop out at his hairline.

"The fellow intern—Joseph, I think his name was—ran over someone."

That statement pulled Jake straight out of his scattered thoughts and directly into the subject. "He *what?*"

"He ran over an older man walking on the sidewalk. Joseph fell asleep at the wheel, veered off, and hit the man." Suzannah rested her voice for a minute, then cleared her throat and went on. "Your dad forced Joseph to stop. He wasn't planning to, since he was close to finishing his last year of school and didn't want to lose everything he'd worked so hard for." She swallowed. And then again. "But when your dad got out to help the man, Joseph took off, leaving your dad to pay the price."

"Wait a minute," Jake grumbled. "You telling me he was convicted of a death when he wasna even driving the automobile?"

"Exactly."

"How?"

"Something about Joseph going to the police straight away and fabricating a story." Suzannah coughed, swallowed. Took a few sips of her cola. "Said your dad was driving. That he had to talk your dad into stopping. That he, Joseph, was the one who got in the car to go for help. The man Joseph hit died."

Could this be true?

"Your dad was convicted of involuntary manslaughter. And Joseph convinced the authorities Dodge would have driven off… if Joseph hadn't taken the car to get help. So, that complicated things."

Jake felt the stirrings of righteous anger for his sire. Only, he didna want that. Didna want to believe his mum had never told him any of this. "No more! Rest your voice."

Suzannah must have understood enough was enough. She patted him on the thigh once more and calmly scooted back to check on Coo.

He thought he might be sick. The hamburger and cola and stomach acid rolled around each other in his gut. A slow burning anger—the kind that could burn through metal and rock and bone—pushed the nausea aside. *I have to get out.* An open meadow came into view. He downshifted and let off the accelerator until they came to a rolling stop. The fingers of his left hand were knotted at the steering wheel, the right, squeezing the gearshift knob.

"Jake?" Suzannah said, startling his fingers from their attachments.

"Stay here," he commanded. He threw the truck into neutral, leaving it running at the side of the highway, and slid his feet onto solid ground.

Walking a few paces into the meadow, Jake splayed his hands on his hips and hung his head. Pulling in great drafts of air, his body started to relax. He kent what he needed. Suzannah had taught him that, but would God have him?

God's got you. Her words repeated in his mind.

Finally, as if without his approval, he heard himself say, "I do not ken you, God, but Suzannah does. If you—please help me. I canna do this alone anymore."

CHAPTER 25

Suzannah watched as the big man in black walked away and halted in the open field. Late blooming wildflowers stood all around his feet, like a stage built by God Himself to support Jake as he slumped his shoulders and dropped his head down in abject brokenness. And, wasn't that what they all were? Broken pots of clay that only a Savior—Jesus—could piece back together? It was certain this life would beat them all to a pulp if it wasn't for Jesus. She'd never have made it this far with her wits about her if it hadn't been for Jesus carrying her while Thomas stalked her.

Poor Jake. Once again life had offered up another punch to his gut. She had no idea how hatred for a father felt. But Jesus understood, and only He could help.

Please God, be with Jake right now. Help him to know you, and know only you can understand what he's going through. Give me that deep understanding, as well, so I can help him.

Suzannah kept watch, and prayed, all the while stroking the little coon who'd awoken, wanting more food. She peered into the little one's face, and thought what an awesome God they had. What else could she call the One who knew the number of sparrows in the air, the number of hairs on her head, and the number of days little Coo would live.

Just as Suzannah placed Coo on Jake's undershirt in the box, Jake opened the cab door. Silently, he settled himself behind the wheel, put the truck in gear, and pulled them out onto the highway.

Many minutes went by before Suzannah dared to speak. When she couldn't hold back any longer, she said, "Are you all right?"

"Aye. I am."

"Anything I can do?"

Jake glanced over at her, surprising her with a glorious, two-dimpled smile. She sucked in a breath.

He looked back at the road, but reached out a hand, palm up. She looked at his hand, then up at his face. The smile barely lingered on his closed lips, but it was there when he turned to her once again and nodded. She nodded back and slid her hand into his. He closed his fingers around hers. They stayed that way for the better part of an hour, until Jake had to pull away to downshift before some tight turns. The loss of his hand in hers left her bereft of his warmth. His connection. He didn't offer it again.

"How's Coo?" Jake asked much later, as they bobbled down the road toward the ranch entrance.

"I'll check," she said as she leaned forward to inspect the raccoon.

Jake downshifted, then made a tight turn, taking them between the two timbres that supported the sign for Harper Ranch overhead. Big piles of dirt still sat along the road between newly erected telephone poles, repair from the earthquake ongoing.

The truck made a sudden lurch to the right. Suzannah's head whacked into the dash hard enough for her to see stars. She pushed herself back as Jake steered them back onto the narrow road.

Jake was cussing heatedly into his rearview mirror. "Who was that?"

Suzannah regained her equilibrium, then twisted to look over her shoulder at the vehicle that had just shot past them. All she saw was a huge cloud of dust swirling along the road they'd just come down. "I didn't see them, but that's one of the ranch trucks."

"Well, whoever the devil that was, they'll get a piece of my mind if they come back. Son-of-a—" Jake slammed the heel of his hand against the steering wheel. "The fool near exploded himself in a sinkhole before trying to ram us into the ditch."

"Male, female?"

"Male."

"What did he look like?"

"Och, I dinna ken. Mayhap your age, light brown hair, scar on his left cheek."

Suzannah froze. Couldn't be. That was a complete coincidence. Besides, the scar she'd given Thomas must have faded by now. But even as she thought it, she knew that wasn't true. She'd sliced him pretty deep with her fingernails. One spot had scarred. She shook her head. No. She was imagining things.

"The fellas will... will know who he is," Suzannah said, chewing her lip.

She heard a scrambling in the box. The sudden pitch of the truck must have scared Coo awake. Suzannah leaned over and tried to grasp the coon. The critter took the opportunity to claw her way up Suzannah's arm. Suzannah yelped. Coo shot to the back of the seat and onto her favorite place, wrapped around the nape of Jake's neck, with her nose under his collar.

"Och," Jake complained as he tilted his head forward as much as possible. "Why does she always go there when she's scared?"

"Because you're so big and warm and protective. All females know that about you," she said, teasing him.

He flushed several shades of red, but didn't say a word.

Jake drove up next to the large Harper Ranch house, then backed the trailer into its spot next to the barn. "We're here," he said, shutting off the truck and sighing deeply.

"Aye," Suzannah said, feeling sad that their private time had ended.

Jake graced her with a small, lopsided grin. She smiled back. Their gazes locked and her heart sped. Jake...

A knuckle to Jake's window startled them both. They both looked at the head and hat taking up the view. Max was bent over, staring into the cab at Jake. The expression on Max's face was comical. He was glancing between Jake's face and neck with a mix of shock and confusion. He leaned closer to the window and squinted.

Jake cracked the window and smiled at Max. "Aye, it's a raccoon. Go get the cage from the tack room, if you please."

Max reared his head back and guffawed, so heartily, Suzannah thought he might burst something. She'd nearly forgotten the men around Harper Ranch only knew Jake as taciturn and grim-faced. He'd certainly never smiled for any of them. And then she remembered. He'd shaved his beard, so his dimples would be showing. Could that be what Max was laughing about? If so, she had to stop him from teasing or Jake would grow the darned beard back overnight.

Still laughing his fool head off, Max strolled into the barn.

She scooted over as close as the gearshift allowed and reached up to peel Coo off Jake. She started her baby-talk to the young coon. "Come on, cutie. You're all right. Come to momma." Her arms were wrapped around Jake's neck so she could get a good grip on the front claws first, trying to keep Coo from taking a layer of Jake's skin. She noticed Jake's hair behind his ear stirring while she talked to the coon, she was so close. She almost laughed. This was sure a different form of whispering sweet nothings in someone's ear.

Jake had stiffened. He was barely breathing. That was helpful, how Jake held real still so she could get the task done. Her arm brushed his chest as her own chest pressed against his arm. It was so intimate that if it were anything but retrieving an animal, she wouldn't have had the guts to do it.

"Come on, sweetie," she cooed, and peeled. "You're okay," she said, then peeled again. The darned critter really liked Jake. She was sure Coo felt safe, at the very least. But she'd never untangle her if Coo refused to let go.

Jake turned his head just then, nearly knocking noses with her. She should let go of Coo and scoot back, but she didn't want to. So close, she saw Jake's eyes were now jet black. His nostrils flared with each intake of breath. His gaze settled on her lips. He parted his own.

She froze. Was he thinking of kissing her? She didn't have to wait long. He twisted his body a bit more and leaned in, catching her lips in his. Her arms were already draped around him, so she pulled herself closer. His hand found her face. With his thumb at her cheek, fingers at her nape, he tilted her head enough to deepen the contact. Her pulse sped.

Jake broke the connection, but lingered at her lips. "Kitten," he breathed against them.

Just as Jake pressed against her lips again, Coo took that moment to dig in and launch off his neck. Coo scurried up Suzannah's arm and into her hair. Suzannah jumped right out of his arms and yelped.

"Blasted coon!" Jake said, reaching up to lift the creature off Suzannah's head. Its claws hung on to globs of her hair.

"Wait, Jake. She still has a hold." Suzannah added her hands to his, and finally loosened the coon enough to lower the kit into her lap, several long tendrils still attached to the claws. "Ow! Crazy girl. Let go!"

Max returned with a large cage in hand, rags in one corner of it. He took one look at the two of them and bit the side of his lip, clearly trying not to laugh again.

Suzannah saw the glare Jake gave him. "Back up so I can get out," Jake said through the small opening at the top of his window.

Max backed a few paces and set down the cage. Jake opened his door and turned to reach back. "Give me Coo. I'll put her in the cage, and we can be done with her for a spell."

Suzannah chuckled, seeing the frustration on his face. She scooted closer and handed the baby over to Jake. Coo squirmed, but she didn't have a prayer of getting free with those massive hands cradling her. Jake squatted down, opened the cage, and put her inside. She scurried toward the rags and buried herself in them.

Standing again, he said, "Give me the undershirt, and her food."

When Suzannah handed those things to him, he glanced up to her eyes and winked with an adorable one-dimpled half grin on his face. Her tummy fluttered. Then worry slid in. Would they have time together, now that they were home? Or would Jake slip back into the life of solitude he had before?

Lord, please don't let him get lost again.

* * *

Once Coo was in the barn, cozy in her new bed with food and water at her disposal, Jake helped Suzannah carry her bags to the house, leaving her there as well before setting off for the bunkhouse. With each footfall toward his previous life, he felt the absence of Suzannah, a gaping hole, widening with every step he took. How would they carry on from here?

When he came back to the barn, he searched Max out. The cowpoke was picking one of the gray mare's hoofs. "So, Roy put you in charge." Jake kent it sounded curt, but the men on this ranch were used to Jake's gruffness.

"Yep. Johnnie and Clint are both gone."

Jake nodded.

"Nice to have you back, Jake. Roy will be happy."

Jake scoffed. He questioned that. "Aye… That black beast needs taming. Listen. We passed some fool on our way in today. Had to veer off the road for him to pass like his tail was on fire. Who the devil was he?"

Max dropped the hoof back to the dirt and rose to full height. Other than Clint and Johnnie, he was the only other man on Harper Ranch who stood close to Jake's height. Looking him straight in the eye, Max said, "New man. Sent him to town for supplies. Roy hired him a few days after you left."

"What do you mean a few days after. His honeymoon was two weeks, I thought."

"Nope. Clint was called to Harper West in California. Jessica's dad is short-handed at the moment. Clint and Jessica went to help. So Roy came back early. Too bad, really. But he says as long as his bride's with him, he don't mind."

Jake grimaced, wondering why Roy didna just call him back early. Here he'd been, wasting time at Wheeler's place when he could have been helping out. "Back to the fool."

"Name's Tom Mattison. Come from California. And, I gotta tell ya, Jake, I don't trust him. He tries too hard, if ya know what I mean."

Jake felt a stab of sadness on hearing Max's last phrase. Those words were something old Walt used to say. Jake hadna kent Walt well before he'd passed on, but he admired the man greatly. Come to think of it, that admiration didna proceed so much from the man himself as from Walt's unquenchable, almost infectious love for God. Jake hadna seen the truth of that before, but there it was, in plain sight.

Jake shook the tangent thought away and met Max's gaze. "Why does the name Tom ring a bell?" He frowned. "What'd Roy hire him to do?"

"Accounting, mostly. The fellow says he has degree in it. I'd bet my best gelding against that being true." Max picked up another of the gray's hoofs, and got to work. "Help me watch him, will ya?"

"Count on it," Jake said, still pondering the name.

A cloud of dust floated into the barn. Tires rumbled to a stop, and the sound of an engine cut out. He'd be having a talk with this Tom fella, right about now. Jake strode out to the piece of road between the barn and house, and saw an old beater truck out front. Not Tom, then.

Jake stopped short when he realized who was about to exit the cab. *Dodge.* Suzannah said he'd be coming here.

Should he turn and run, before his father caught sight of him? Part of him wanted to. To continue living with hate and darkness instead of truth's blinding light. But he couldna crush Suzannah's heart like that. He seemed frozen to the ground anyway, legs locked up, heavy as lead. The predictable acid dumped into his belly and started its churning. All the while, he could hear Suzannah's voice reminding him of Dodge's innocence.

Along with another voice—God's.

Once Dodge had his feet planted on the ground, he glanced around, saw Jake, then strode slowly to him. He wiped his left hand across his mouth as he stuck the other out for Jake. Jake looked down at it, and back up to Dodge's face. Finally he took the proffered hand and shook it. His father's eyes glistened.

"What are you doing here?" Jake asked.

"Didn't Suzannah tell you? It's time we get to know one another, Jacob."

Hate had thrived in Jake's veins for this man, for a verra long time. Jake turned away, but his boots re-mained rooted.

Lord, help me. How do I forgive this man after all this time?

The same way I've forgiven you, his inner voice seemed to say. Or, was that the Holy Spirit people talked of, the unseen Spirit that guided believers in this life?

Jake closed his eyes and sucked in a vital breath. His head spun with the truths he'd heard about Dodge: unjustly accused, sent letters, provided money, tried to save a man someone else mutilated, took the blame, paid the price. *Jesus took the blame for all mankind, paid the price* he could hear Suzannah saying. And one of her favorite Scriptures about Jesus came next: *The thief comes only to steal and kill and destroy; I came that they may have life, and have it abundantly.*

Here Jake had nearly given up on life because of losing a wife and child. But Dodge hadna given up. This man—his own flesh and blood—could have long since thrown up his hands and wallowed in bitterness. The poor man had spent half his life in jail for something he didna do. His own wife rejected him. His only son hated him. Yet, he'd never given up hope.

Shame flooded through Jake. This man—*his* father—had more character in his wee finger than Jake would ever possess. *Thank you, God, for making me see.*

He turned back to his father, shaking his head. *I canna believe I'm thinking this way. After all the years of hate.* The bitterness had seeped into his whole life, he now realized. No wonder Betty was so unhappy. She had reason to be.

It was him.

It had been him the whole darned time.

"I owe you an apology, Dodge—Father."

His father's eyes widened, then filled with tears. Jake watched as he rubbed a hand over his eyes and swallowed back emotion. Jake's own eyes welled up. Both men stood glued to the spot, both reacting much the same way. Jake suddenly yearned for all the days he'd missed with his father.

That poignant longing shifted his grief over feeling abandoned by his father to fury over being manipulated by his mother. Jake lowered both hands to his sides and pulled them into fists.

"Don't do that, son. Don't blame your mother."

How did this man ken that's what he'd been thinking?

"You're wondering how I know what you're thinking. I can see it on your face. I recognize it, because I was there once, many years ago. For a long while I hated your mom, for not believing in me, for keeping you from me. I would have gone on hating her if I hadn't been introduced to Jesus Christ by a fellow jailbird."

Dodge wore a sad, but resolute smile. He scrubbed a hand through his hair, thick like Jake's own with a touch of gray. "I don't regret going to jail, Jake. I learned that hope is found in genuine humility. *Humble yourselves, therefore, under God's mighty hand, that he may lift you up in due time.* You'll find that in I Peter 5:6. You see, Jake, God had to contain me, bring me to the end of myself, before he could bring me hope. Now I can love freely, forgive readily, give God control of my entire life. Now, God has given you back to me. I'd like nothing more than to get to spend time with you. The son I sired, but never got a chance to know." He lifted his brows in question.

Suzannah strode up behind Dodge, circled to the front of him, and gave him a strapping hug. How long had she been out there listening? She looked up into Dodge's face, and nodded. "He'd be delighted."

Jake just blinked at her. Shouldna he be angry she'd answered for him? But he felt his face screw up into an altogether foreign expression. Wonder—at her, at his father, at the God who seemed to be standing at their backs. Then Jake nodded and said with absolute, dawning sincerity, "Delighted."

Suzannah released Dodge and spun on her toes to Jake. With one of her sunshine smiles for him alone, she jumped into his arms, wrapped her beautiful legs around his waist, and kissed him all over the face. He laughed while she giggled, and Jake thought he'd never experienced a happier moment.

Before that thought had even seated itself in his besotted brain, a vehicle came speeding in. That idiot in the ranch truck skidded to a stop just outside the barn door, blanketing it with dust. Jake scowled at the culprit.

He gave Suzannah a quick kiss on the lips, then set her on her feet. "I need to take care of this."

"I'm going with you," she said, with a look that made him want to whoop with glee. She was so darned headstrong, in a cute sort of way.

"Aye. I expected you would." Jake took her by the hand. "Come on, my kitten."

"So, it's *my kitten*, is it?" an angry male voice said from the other side of the truck.

Suzannah stiffened next to Jake, dragging them to a stop. Jake looked at her fear-contorted face, then at the man who was taking his time strolling around the front bumper of the truck.

"Who—" Jake started, but never got a chance to finish.

CHAPTER 26

Panic would have seized Suzannah if it weren't for the protective hold Jake had on her hand. It gave her a strength she'd never had before in Thomas's presence.

"Why…?" She'd wanted to know why he was here, but could scarcely get the one word out as her grip tightened on Jake's hand.

Thomas, nowhere near as formidable as Jake but turning out to be stupidly bold, came a few strides closer, a bizarre smile plastered on his face. Jake was already answering Thomas's smile with his own notorious scowl, which didn't seem to be fazing her ex in the least.

"I'm here to take you home, Suzannah," Thomas said. "I'll wait while you gather your clothes."

Her eyes opened just about as wide as her rage. "Never!"

He strode closer, and pierced her with the stare that always made her knees knock. "You will, bitch! Now go, before I decide you don't need your things."

Jake pushed Suzannah behind him and took a step forward. "If you dinna want to find your backside meeting that filthy mouth of yours, you'll be on your way. Now!"

The cock of a rifle sounded behind them. In unison, they all turned to see Jake's father holding the weapon on the intruder. "You need to do as he says," Dodge said.

"Fath… Da… "

"Don't worry, son." The smile Dodge gave was downright wicked. Before now, Suzannah had only seen kindness in the man's face. Dodge's current expression, she had no doubt, was the one he'd had to polish to remain unscathed in jail. "I won't mind going back to jail. Not at all."

It was just the thing Suzannah needed to hear to unleash the full measure of her wrath. If she didn't deal with Thomas herself, right here and right now, it would never be over.

She turned and bolted toward Dodge. Grabbing the rifle out of his hands, she turned on Thomas. Using her most intimidating face—the one she'd learned from Jake—she strode forward a couple of paces.

"That's my lass," she heard Jake say for her ears only.

Thomas burst out laughing, and her stomach plummeted. Her resolve was fleeing, right along with her dignity. She couldn't let that happen. Not this time, or she'd never be whole again.

Please, Lord, help me!

Then, something wonderful happened. A renewed confidence poured in, filling her with unflinching strength. Suzannah felt the fear leave her. Her legs stopped trembling, her hands tightened their hold on the lever action 30-30, and one side of her lip lifted in disgust.

This man would not ruin her life for one more second.

Thomas raised his brows high, a disbelieving smirk on his face. He sucked in a huge breath and let another stint of laughter reach the heavens. "You've always been such an idiot, Suzannah-Anna. That's why you need me."

It was that last wave of laughter that turned the tide. What Thomas clearly didn't know was, as a farm girl, she wasn't just used to shooting rifles. She was the most accurate shot in her household.

Suzannah cocked the rifle for effect, kicking out an unspent round, her penetrating gaze never leaving Thomas. The rifle remained at her shoulder.

A small flicker of doubt was there and gone on his brow. Then, a broad smile took over. The one that used to make her swoon. He ambled toward her with malice in every muscle.

"Stop!" she shouted, thanking God her voice had roared so. Then, in a low, calm voice, she said, "Not another step. I *will* shoot you."

Thomas seemed momentarily stunned. Then, he shook his head and looked around to the group of men who'd gathered at a short distance. "Silly girl," he said, as if they would all agree.

No one said a word; they only stared. Max was in the doorway of the barn where Thomas couldn't see, shotgun in hand. Suzannah was grateful the Harper crew was allowing her to handle this herself for now. Confidence grew within her as she awaited Thomas's next move. She knew exactly what she would have to do if he stepped closer.

Thomas froze in place, as if he'd read her mind. But, egotistical as he was, it was only a matter of time. A light breeze ruffled loose strands of hair about her face, cooling the perspiration on her neck. Puffy clouds pushed across the sky, dimming the sun as each crossed beneath it.

Still, no one moved.

"Leave, Thomas. Go back home to Daddy."

Thomas sneered. He looked around once more. And, as if his own arrogance had duped him into believing the group would stand with him, he nodded once, then leapt forward to grab for Suzannah.

She squeezed the trigger. A loud *boom* split the quiet.

Thomas yelped, grabbed his thigh, and hit the ground a split second later. "You crazy bitch! You tried to kill me!" He writhed around a bit, until he realized no one planned to help him.

Suzannah calmly stepped closer. "That's just a graze. If I'd wanted to kill you, you'd be dead." She took another step forward, now looking straight down into his face. If she yelled a bit, her voice would work longer. Gathering her might, she went on. "Be thankful I have a God who's bigger than you, Thomas, whom I love, and who wouldn't want me to take vengeance into my own hands... or I'd have killed you outright." She blew out a breath then swallowed. Not wanting to show her weakness, she pushed through. "If you ever come near me again, I will be the last person you ever see." Her voice sounded menacing, when in truth, it was losing strength. *Please God, let it hold up.*

"You are nuts!" Thomas glanced up at the cowboys who'd circled around him. "These hillbillies have made you loco!"

Suzannah nodded at the few who stood closest. "Fetch his car and send him on his way."

They moved so fast, Thomas gulped in fear. "Ow, ow! Easy. You're crazy, every last one of you!" he yelled as Max drove his car up and they threw him in it.

Jake stopped them before they could slam the door. He untied the kerchief at his neck, pulled one out of his back pocket, then knotted them together. Thomas eyed Jake like he was a bull deciding when to charge. Instead, Jake swung Thomas's injured leg out of the car and cinched the kerchiefs around his thigh.

Suzannah was conflicted by what she saw. Why would Jake go against her and patch up this monstrous man? He knew firsthand the pain Thomas had caused her. But, as she let that thought swim around in her mind, she watched Jake's lips move through a stream of words clearly meant for Thomas alone. And then she knew. Jake was protecting her. Again. He would not let Thomas bleed to death with her as the cause. No more than he would let Thomas leave without a single, choice threat to seal the deal.

She smiled in spite of herself. Because one threat from Jake would be more potent than a hundred assaults from Thomas.

Heavens, how she loved her gentle giant.

Jake swung the bandaged leg back into the footwell. He gave Thomas one last measured stare, slammed the door, and stood like a sentinel next to it.

The Rambler's engine fired up. With a terrified glance at Jake, Thomas spun the car on a dime and gunned it, spitting gravel and dirt over the onlookers. In a matter of seconds, Thomas was just a red and white dot on the road out of Harper Ranch—and Suzannah's life.

The rifle hit the ground, and before Suzannah followed it, Jake was there, wrapping her in his embrace. She began to shake uncontrollably. Jake scooped her into his arms and hurried toward the ranch house. Suzannah tightened her arms around his neck, trying to make her body stop trembling. "I'm sorry."

"Nae, lass. You've nothing to be sorry for. Hang on. I'll take you up to your room."

"Jake... I'm too heavy to carry up the stairs."

Jake ignored her, and seemed to have no trouble at all, even when he had to walk sideways to keep her feet from scraping the wall.

He placed her on the bed, atop Mary's beautiful quilt, and propped pillows behind her head. Jake sat on the edge of the bed and brushed the hair out of her face. "I'll get you some water."

"No, Jake. Please. Will you just hold me for a minute?"

Jake lifted her again, scooted under, and settled her in his lap. He sat with his back against the headboard and one booted foot on the floor. By slow degrees, she relaxed into the strength of his one-armed embrace, and the certainty of her love for him.

"Why did you bind his leg?" She thought she knew, but needed to hear it.

"Couldna leave the man to bleed to death, now could we? Much as it wouldna have bothered me one bit, I suspect you would have grieved killing a man."

A chill shot through her nerves. She pushed away from Jake's shoulder to look him in the eye. "I tried for a graze. Could he bleed to death?" As much as Thomas had harmed her, she would never have killed him. Not on purpose.

Jake chuckled. With one finger, he smoothed her furrowed forehead. "You just made my point, Kitten. You're not a killer."

"So, that's why you bound his leg. For me."

"Aye, and to remind him of a few things."

"What things?"

"He got the point. That's all you need to ken. You won't see the man again, lass."

Thank you, God, for that. "Oh, Jake. What would I do without you?"

He rubbed a thumb across her lower lip. "I dinna want you to find out." His gaze roved over every inch of her face with a warmth she could feel clear down to her bones.

She sighed deeply, content to be held. His gaze scooted up to her eyes. She stared back into his, so fathomless and full of expression these days. His brows were raised in question and she realized he'd meant more by his statement. "What?"

"Dinna ever try to find out what you'd do without me. You're mine. If you'll have me, Suzannah Marie Harper, I want to make you mine. Permanently."

Was he asking her to marry him? Could it be? She started to open her mouth to confirm what he'd meant when the bedroom door burst open.

Jake set her on the edge of the bed and was on his feet before she could say 'yes' to anything he'd meant.

It was Pete. "Jake. You need to come downstairs. There's... uh... someone—just come." Pete turned and pounded back down the stairs like his own herd of buffalo.

"Did Thomas come back?" Suzannah said on a constricted breath. "With the Sheriff?" The lump in her throat swelled by the second.

Jake put a hand on her shoulder. "Stay here. I'll find out."

She wasn't about to be left behind. She followed Jake's impressive three-leap jaunt down the stairs as fast as her short legs could go.

Jake flew out the front door with her on his tail.

A stranger waited at the bottom of the porch steps. Gray-haired with a ponch lapping over his belt, the man saw Jake and offered his hand. "Jake. Good to see you again."

The man knew Jake? Suzannah squinted at the visitor, trying to remember why he looked familiar. She stayed on the porch and watched the exchange.

Jake stiffened at the sight of the man. It seemed to take Jake several seconds before he thawed enough to climb down the steps to take the man's hand. "Harold."

Heavens! This was no stranger. This was Betty's father. Why was he here? Suzannah glanced over at the green Crestliner Ford, just like her grandpa's. An older woman—Harold's wife probably—sat stiffly in the passenger seat.

Once the men dropped each other's hand, they stood staring. Jake's stare was more of a scowl. Harold's, a look of contrition. Harold finally took his eyes off Jake and glanced at the gathered ranch hands. "You reckon you could send these fellas back to work?"

Jake glared at the men around him. It was the look of dark wrath Suzannah remembered seeing on Jake's face from her first days at Harper Ranch. Before he drove Rebecca and her to Wyoming. Before the news of Betty and the babe. Before their shared tears in a cramped pickup. Before Coo. Before their first kiss. Before his restoration back to life. Before.

The men scattered faster than pool balls after the break.

Jake's gaze landed back on the man before him. "Why are you here, Harold?"

"I... We—"

An instantly recognizable gurgling cry sounded from inside the car.

Jake's attention leapt to the woman in the car and caught on…

Was that a baby on her lap? Suzannah could hardly breathe.

"*Harold?*" Jake's voice seemed to skitter sideways out of his mouth as his jaw unhinged.

"Yours," Harold said.

Suzannah covered her own gaping mouth.

Harold couldn't look Jake in the eye. He looked wasted and withered beyond his years. After a shallow breath and weak smile, he trudged to the car door and opened it. The piercing wail of a hungry baby filled the open air. Harold helped the old woman out of the car with the little tyke in her arms.

This baby—this dark-haired, chubby child, could it be Jake's? If so, why had Harold lied to Jake? What did these people want?

Suzannah ached to run to the baby and grab the sweet thing out of the woman's hands. She wanted to soothe the baby's discomfort. Wipe the tears, kiss the top of the head, run a hand down the back. Boy? Girl?

Jake swayed on his feet. "Louise?" he said in faltering address.

The woman's whole countenance was beat. She managed to meet Jake's eyes briefly, then lowered her gaze to the bundle in her arms. "This"—she managed to lift the babe a few inches by way of introduction—"is Annabelle."

Instant tears filled Suzannah's eyes. *Annabelle*. Jake's precious baby girl.

Jake stood dumbfounded, not even a twitch of an eyelash to be seen. Harold stared at the crying child, misery on his face. The woman looked like her arms were ready to give out.

Suzannah ran down the stairs, then slowed enough to shuffle cautiously forward. "May I hold her?"

The woman nodded and sighed with relief.

Suzannah lifted her carefully from the woman's arms. She looked down at the baby, guessing her age to be around eight months. She jiggled Annabelle up and down in her arms, trying to soothe her, cooing as she stroked the little girl's silky hair. "Hi there, my princess."

Annabelle instantly stopped her tears and looked at Suzannah with curiosity. Suzannah brushed away the child's tears and mucus with her fingertips and wiped it on her own pants. Jake stared at her with a look of horror. She laughed, pure joy reaching into her soul simply from holding this baby.

As she inspected Annabelle's face, any doubt Suzannah may have harbored about Jake being the father fled. The little girl had a mop of wavy, sable-colored hair, and her large eyes were dark chocolate with gloriously long black lashes. She even had thin brown slashes for eyebrows, which a lot of little ones didn't even have at this age. And then, as if Suzannah needed any more evidence, Annabelle smiled at her. Two glorious dimples blazed back.

Suzannah instantly fell in love with the child. Jake's child. The more she ran that through her mind, the more excited she became. Jake had not lost his baby—his bairn—in the earthquake. She was here. Alive! And Jake could shed one more pound of guilt.

And then it hit her. If Jake's in-laws lied about this child perishing, did they also lie about Annabelle's mother. Was she alive?

Suzannah was too impatient to let things unfold. She turned to Louise—Annabelle's natural grandmother—and in a small voice, asked, "Betty?"

In an instant, Louise's blue eyes filled with tears. Her graying light brown hair lay limp around her sullen face. A face that had worked too hard—suffered too long. She shook her head. "She had Annabelle too early. She perished in childbirth." Louise glared at Jake then. "We hated him for so long. That he didn't want our daughter. That he'd got her pregnant but still didn't love her. That he didn't bother to look for her after the earthquake."

Suzannah shook her head. "But he did, he—"

"Suzannah!" Jake skirted around Harold and came to her side, resting a hand at the small of her back. The message was clear. He didn't care about Betty like he did about her. Part of her rejoiced, but the compassionate side mourned with these older people who had to live a lifetime without their daughter. "Dinna try to explain," Jake said. "They willna believe you, aye?" He looked first to Louise, and then to Harold.

Louise turned from him, closed herself into the car, and looked away.

Harold came closer and stroked the baby on her downy head. He took her out of Suzannah's hands and shoved her into Jake's chest. Automatically his arms wrapped around her. Harold had released her to her father.

Jake's own father slammed the ranch houses's front door open and bounded down the steps of the porch. "What's going on here, son?"

Harold's mouth gaped. He raked his gaze up and down Dodge. "This your father, Jake?"

"Aye."

"Yes, I'm his father. Who are you?" Dodge's words were curt, protective.

"I'm Harold Nichols. Jake's father-in-law."

Dodge looked to Jake. "You're *married?*"

"Aye. She…" Jake's Adam's apple dipped several times. Annabelle saw the movement and tried to catch it.

Suzannah came forward and placed her hand on Dodge's arm. "Betty was his wife. She was lost during the earthquake," she whispered for Dodge's ears only.

She glanced at Louise, then to Harold. "Jake tried *every day* since the earthquake to find her." Suzannah swallowed, piercing Harold with a fixed stare. Suzannah gestured to the baby. "Annabelle." She looked back to Harold. "How old? Eight, nine months?"

"Nearly ten. October 3rd." He glanced at Jake and said on a watery whisper, "That's her birthday."

And the day her mommy died. These poor folks must be hurting and hating. And Jake was the target of the hate.

Suzannah heard Jake whisper to himself, "October 3rd." Then he pulled Annabelle a little closer to his chest. Her heart broke all over again for him.

Annabelle looked comfortably dwarfed in Jake's bulky embrace as she sucked on one index finger. She had her eyes glued to Jake's Adam's Apple, as it slid up and down in unity with his strained emotions. She took that moment to pop out the finger and stick it in Jake's ear. He grimaced and pulled it out. She stuck it in again. Nonchalantly, he pulled it out a second time, so she stuck it in Jake's mouth. When he pulled the finger out with a pop from his lips this time, Annabelle giggled.

Jake turned his head from the adult conversation to watch the baby. He let her stick her finger back in his mouth. This time he sucked as she tugged it out, making it pop louder, dissolving the child into an adorable belly laugh. Jake was amazing with Annabelle now that the shock seemed to have dissipated a bit. Suzannah's heart swelled with love for him.

Everyone around was smiling now. Except Harold. "She's never laughed before," Harold said, amazement on his aged face. "In fact, we'd begun to think there's somethin' wrong with her." He smiled then, his grin so large, it crinkled his whole face.

Harold continued to watch, mesmerized, as Jake cooed and bounced and baby talked Annabelle into another angelic giggle. He was obviously studying how Jake treated her. But why? Were they planning on bringing Annabelle to visit her dad now? It would be healing for Jake, and so wonderful for the baby to get to know her dad. Suzannah felt love glow inside her, for the Lord, for Jake, for these good people who had chosen to let Jake back into their lives.

"Listen. Jake, my boy," Harold started.

He'd clearly surprised Jake with the title. Jake blinked, his full focus on Harold.

"We need to leave her with you."

"You want to—*What was that?*" Jake's eyes went wide and his brows shot up. "What do you mean, leave her? For the night?"

"She's too much for us old folk. Crawlin' everywhere. Startin' to walk around furniture now. Louise is wore out." He rubbed a hand over his mouth. "Seems Belle is taken with you." He gave Jake an apologetic smile.

Jake's eyes got huge. A funny, gurgly 'buh' came out Jake's mouth, leaving it agape. Annabelle was having the time of her life, poking her dad in every hole she could find on his face, smearing her saliva all over his cheeks. He didn't seem to notice. When he finally closed his mouth, his lips smashed together. Annabelle squealed in delight at two more holes showing up— Jake's dimples. While her little fingers dug into them with a fervor, Jake seemed to remain frozen.

Suzannah knew that look. He was completely overwhelmed.

"Uh, Harold?" Suzannah said.

The old man turned to her.

"Do you mean permanently? You're giving her dad complete custody?"

Harold rubbed a hand over his mouth again, clearly nervous. "Yes, young lady. It's what I mean. Uh… we have her stuff in the car. I'll get it."

That seemed to snap Jake out of his stupor. He put his legs in gear, following Harold to the trunk of the old Ford. "Harold. I canna take her. I have obligations here. I'm a working man, ye ken?" Jake scrubbed a hand down his face. "I bust bronc's. Not safe for me, so where does that leave her?"

Dodge strolled up just then, a huge smile on his face. "It'll be fine, son. We'll all pitch in." He slapped Jake on the back and absconded with Annabelle. Suzannah heard her giggling all the way to the house. Apparently she'd taken to her grandpa as quickly as her daddy. "Mabel's gonna love her," was the last thing Dodge said before entering the house. Suzannah knew that was true.

"Canna we talk about this, Harold?" Jake was still pleading his case.

Harold ignored him while he dug through the items in the trunk, haphazardly shoving what he could into Jake's arms. Jake was holding Annabelle's things without thought.

Suzannah drew closer to him, touched his arm. "It'll be okay, Jake."

That seemed to thrust Jake back into talking mode, like she'd hit an 'on' button with her encouragement.

"Harold! Stop and listen. I want to know my daughter, but—"

Jake stopped again, thrown off by the awareness the word 'daughter' brought, no doubt.

Finally Harold halted the thrusting of clothes and diapers and blankets at Jake. "Listen, son. We can't do it no more. You have no choice. I'm sorry. We'll visit. I promise." With that, he hastened to the driver's side and was about to crank open the door when he looked in the back seat. He opened the back door instead. "Oh, I forgot. We picked up these supplies at the road entrance, by the sign. Figured someone left them out there for you." He proceeded to pull boxes and sacks out of the backseat, leaving them on the ground by the door. Before they knew what was happening, Harold jumped in the driver's side and zoomed off. Louise never glanced at them and did not look back.

Suzannah stared at the boxes, bridles, bags stuffed full of who-knew-what, and four folded saddle blankets on the ground. Thomas had these things in his trunk? Stolen them? He'd been the only one on the ranch road before Harold and Lousie had shown up, so it had to be him. Terror must have really struck the heart of her nemesis for him to show his hand like this. He probably feared Jake would come after him for the theft. She wanted to laugh hysterically. For the first time in three long years, she felt free.

Instead, Suzannah breathed a lungful of fresh air and grabbed an armload of Annabelle's paraphernalia from Jake. She hurried into the house, dumped it by the front door, and flew back out, not wanting to leave Jake alone for more than a moment. She could hear Mabel tickling the baby in Dodge's arms. Annabelle was giggling breathlessly. She missed hearing the sound she had heard so often at the orphanage back in California.

When she returned to Jake's side, he was rigid as a board, still loaded up with so much stuff, all she could see was his grim face pointed toward the disappearing vehicle. Suzannah rested a hand at his back, the only place on him free of baby things. He peered down at her. She wanted to laugh at how cute he looked. Oh, he was going to make a great daddy, that was for sure. That is, if he could get past the shock of it.

She shifted to the front of him, still stroking a corner of his back. "Jake. Take a deep breath."

He did.

She smiled up at him, now. "You're a daddy, Jake! Your baby's alive," she said in a hoarse whisper. "We're going to be just fine, honey."

"*Honey...*" Jake repeated absentmindedly. Suzannah knew the actual word had sunk in when that fabulous dimpled smile obliterated his scowl. He opened his arms and reached out for her. Baby things dripped off him like he was a melting snowman, but he paid them no mind. With what little space he had left in his arms, he wrapped her up with him and the clothes and the blankets and the bottles and the diapers and Suzannah knew in that instant, the three of them would be fine. Better than fine.

CHAPTER 27

Jake awoke with a start, shaking the fog from his brain and blinking his eyes to adjust to the dim, predawn light filling his room. What woke him? A creaking floorboard? Since he and Annabelle had moved in, he'd noticed the ranch house was full of creaks and groans, especially during the chilly September nights. Did Annabelle cough? Was she breathing?

Jake shot to his feet and saw her wee bum stuck in the air, as it was every morning. Relief washed over him when he saw the usual index finger stuck in her mouth, and the intermittent sucking she usually did before she was fully awake. Staring down into the crib at the perfect creature God had blessed him with, he understood more everyday what a grand gift she was to him. And to Suzannah. Or, at least he thought so.

What once was a flood of pleasure when he thought of Suzannah now was a cloud of confusion. Suzannah had been distancing herself from him these last few weeks, and now she was doing the same with Annabelle. They'd had an exceptional past two months. As a family, they had enjoyed the Fourth of July celebration, in August they had designed a memorial to

Annabelle's mother at the location where her car had been abandoned during the earthquake. Suzannah and he had helped Coo begin the adjustment to life in the wild. He'd even easily borne the endless teasing the men gave him over his clean-shaven, ridiculously dimpled face.

Jake never thought he'd actually fall in love, let alone have that love grow so deep. But Suzannah had become his sustenance, the verra air he breathed. He didna ken how he could ever face a future that didna have her in it.

Yet, now he wasna at all sure she carried the same torch for him. She'd never told him she loved him, not that he'd ever voiced those three words to her, either. In the last few weeks, she'd stopped giving Jake those special smiles that always lit his. He felt the tether between him and Suzannah stretching, as if she were slowly pulling away, until one day he feared the bond would snap and she would be gone for good. The frantic feel of that reality made him take two steps toward her every time she took one step back.

He gave Annabelle a little pat on her raised bum, then turned away to pull on his blue jeans and denim shirt. There was no more room in his life for black clothes and all the bitterness they hid.

By the time he had dressed, Annabelle was standing in her crib with the one finger stuck in her mouth, holding her floppy rabbit around its neck in her other arm. She popped the finger out of her mouth and grinned with her four top and two bottom teeth, along with those two deep dimples that graced her chubby cheeks. A wave of pride swept through him. Jake grinned back at her, then tickled her neck. She bent her head into his fingers and giggled. The musical lilt lifted his flagging spirits. How could Suzannah want to see less of this wee squirt? Annabelle was getting cuter everyday. If only she'd call him dadda, then he'd be flying with the eagles.

Jake hoped when they reached the kitchen, Suzannah would be there to greet them. Though, she hadna been of late. If she was there, she would likely excuse herself from helping with Annabelle or from greeting Jake, and would scurry out of the house. Her sister Jessica had begun to notice, as had others. When Jessica questioned Jake about it, all he could do was shrug and shake his head. He didna ken.

He would soon need to confront her about her behavior, though he wasna at all sure he wanted to ken the reason for it. What she might tell him was playing havoc with his mind, and now his body. He'd been sleeping less, and the circles under his eyes revealed his anxiety to the whole Harper crew.

Jake changed Annabelle's diaper, put her in a red and white dress—Suzannah called it gingham—and wee white shoes and socks, then gathered her in one arm to walk to the kitchen and his babysitters for the day. Lately, Mabel, Mary, and Jessica took turns watching over the wee tyke. And Dodge, of course. Between his duties of doctoring anything alive on Harper Ranch, his chief pleasure had been his granddaughter. The bond Dodge had with Annabelle was slowly creating a union between her dad and grandpa as well.

But what of Suzannah? She'd been so intimately involved in his life, Jake had finally been able to con-template marriage again. On Annabelle's sudden arrival, Jake kent he must put aside all thought of marriage until he learned how to survive fatherhood.

Well, survive he did, with Suzannah. But now…

Jake had had enough of not sleeping, of eating even less, and of Suzannah's evasiveness. He and Suzannah were going to talk it out. Today.

"There's our girl." Mabel dropped her spatula onto the counter and rushed toward Jake and Annabelle. The bairn gave the squat little woman an open-mouthed grin. Mabel mirrored it with one of her own. Jake could hardly believe the change in Mabel. Old as the hills and irascible as a badger, Mabel had run her kitchen like a military installment until the wee angel in his arms softened the scowl right off her face. Now the poor cook was a puddle of melted butter in Annabelle's hands.

Annabelle was changing everyone for the better.

Mabel swept the bairn out of his hands and secured her in the wooden high chair. She affixed the tray, handed Annabelle a wooden spoon to beat on it, then waved a hand at Jake. "Go on now. You think you got all day hanging round the kitchen? You got things to do, bronc buster. Now git!"

"Aye. Sure. Let me eat first," Jake said with a half-hearted grin.

"No time. Pete says to tell you yer needed in the corral. Got a new mare givin' those tough cowboys fits." She pressed a banana in Jake's hand. "Come back later and I'll feed ya proper-like with the rest of 'em."

Jake scanned the kitchen and dining area. "Where's Suzannah this morning, lass?"

Mabel looked disgusted. "Don't know where that girl runs off to lately. Thought you might know."

"Nae. Wish I did," Jake mumbled, then strode out the door to go check on Coo before he helped the cowpokes with the wild mare.

When Jake entered the barn, he glanced around. No Suzannah waiting for him by Coo's cage. The coon was already sticking her paws out of the cage toward Jake, anxious for her time of escape. It was painful for Jake, separating himself from the raccoon. Especially since doing so reminded him of what Suzannah was doing with him.

It had to be done. Coo wasna far from mating age, and she clearly needed to be with her own kind if she were to have anything approaching a normal life. Last month, he and Suzannah had searched out release sites a quarter mile away from camp. It was just a matter of time now.

Jake tapped the bars of the enclosure, and said, "When Suzie shows up, we'll take you on your walk." He peeled the banana and stuck it through the thin bars. Coo grabbed it and scurried into the corner of the cage to enjoy her treat. She glanced up once to smile at him—if coons could smile, and he thought she did—before he headed to the corral.

Pete, Max, and another half dozen men were laboring over a jet black mare. Her coat shined blue-black in the bright sunlight, her black eyes flashed devilishly, and she squealed every time she dashed back and forth in front of the men. She could be kin to the black demon, what with that coloring and attitude. Jake prayed under his breath she wouldna be as incorrigible as that brute. He was still nursing a bruised shoulder from his latest dance with the devil.

When Jake reached the gate, he unlatched it and let himself into the corral. The other men had the mare contained in one corner, though they were careful to give her space. Pete handed Jake his usual crop with the leather strap at one end, and another rope.

"What's the word on this one?" Jake asked.

"Meaner 'n Demon, Jake. Be careful."

"What have you done so far?"

"Run around a lot."

"You or the horse?"

"Me."

Jake barked a laugh, then moved with purpose toward the black beauty, all the while whipping the rope at his side, digging chunks out of the turf with each circle round. The horse eyed Jake for a few seconds, then snorted and charged.

Jake didna wait for her to come upon him. He emitted a ferocious bellow, and sprang forward, increasing the whipping, pointing with the crop in the direction he wanted her to go. Stunned at his aggressive behavior, the mare veered to one side—not the side he'd chosen for her. He ran forward and whipped her on the rear with the leather strap at the crop's end. She wheeled around and galloped the correct direction. As was his usual training method, he kept this up for a half hour, until both he and the horse were dripping with sweat. The mare wasna submitting, but she was curbing her bad behavior a wee bit.

Handing off the tackle to Pete, Jake removed his hat, swiped his forehead with his arm, then settled the hat back in place. "You ken, Pete, you could do this yourself if you were nae so blamed lazy."

Pete snorted. "Not when yer willin' to do it. Think I'm crazy?"

"Aye. I do."

Pete guffawed, and turned back to the rest of the men who were milling around, jawing about Jake's efforts. They'd probably thought to see a show. In the past he would have mounted the stormy steed and given them one. Now, he had Annabelle to think of. And, Suzannah. He hoped.

Frowning at his last thought, he let himself into the barn through a gate, and headed straight for Coo.

"Nice work out their, Jake," Suzannah said, standing at Coo's cage. She smiled at him, but this time it didna trigger his own. Something wasna right with Suzannah, and the nae discerning was squeezing his heart.

He averted his gaze from her to Coo. "Gotta take Coo to her habitat." He busied himself getting Coo out of the cage. The minute she was free, she ran up Jake's arm to her favorite spot, wrapped around his neck with her nose in his collar.

"I know. I'm going with you as always."

Jake ignored her comment and headed for the barn door.

Suzannah skipped forward and grabbed Jake's forearm. He stopped but didna turn toward her. "What's wrong?" she asked.

Jake ground his jaw, breathing through impatience that she could read him so easily. "Aye. That's what I should be asking you." He looked down into her upturned face.

She dropped her gaze to her toes. "I'm…"

She looked so sad, Jake couldna help himself. He stroked her cheek with one finger, then used the same one to lift her chin. He searched her clear blue-green eyes for the answer before he said, "Everyone's worried. What's wrong, Kitten?"

* * *

Suzannah drew her brows into a frown. "Who's worried? Are you all talking about me behind my back?" she rasped.

"Nae, lass. Well… just Jessica… and mayhap Mabel."

"They should already know. They were there," she said, then walked over to the stall the gray mare was in.

She stroked the muzzle the mare lifted to her, hoping to find solace even when she knew there could be none, not since…

Jake peeled Coo off his neck and placed her back in her cage, then followed Suzannah. "What do you mean, they were there? Where?"

Suzannah closed her eyes, reliving that horrible afternoon over three weeks ago. She heaved a sigh, and opened her eyes. Jake was ready to listen, as he always did. He leaned his bulky body against the stall, hanging his elbow over the other side so he could have a good shot at her face. He swiped a hand down the mare's neck, then gave it a pat. Then he waited, as usual, until she squeezed the words out. "I almost got Annabelle killed."

She swung her gaze in Jake's direction to watch his reaction. The skin around his eyes tightened, but he said nothing. Averting her gaze back to the mare, she rubbed the soft muzzle and went on. "She got away from me, Jake. I had stopped to pick up her rabbit. She waddled too fast toward Patches. That darn dog took out toward her. You know how he is with her." She swallowed, tears welling. She could feel the heat of Jake's gaze on her face. Could feel his ire rising. Yet, he remained silent.

"I yelled. Nothing… *Nothing* came out." She tried to pull in a breath, but it sounded more like a sob. "I ran after her. Tried to holler. But all I could do was cough." She stopped, chancing a sidelong glance at Jake.

Jake's face was grim. His lips were pressed together, his jaw muscles flexing. He looked furious with her. As well he should. Still, he said nothing.

Suzannah's mind took a detour down the worn path of a tragic memory. Another two year old toddling across the park toward a young football player, his hands raised in the air to catch the ball, his cleats trampling the small body beneath him. The half dozen surgeries to put her face back together. And all on Suzannah's watch. Had her voice worked, it could have all been prevented.

She turned fully to face Jake. To face his wrath. She didn't deserve his mercy. It was his daughter. The one God had blessed him with when he'd thought her lost to him forever. "Max whistled and hollered. Stopped the dog. With those long legs of his… he caught up to Annabelle. Scooped her up. Saved her." Suzannah dropped her gaze from Jake's face, unable to cope with what she saw there. She coughed and sputtered. Talking this much always destroyed her voice for a long while. But Jake deserved the whole story. To know why, as damaged goods, she couldn't be a mother to Annabelle.

When she chanced another look at him, she saw it. The disappointment. The fury. The repulsion. True anguish was there, registered in his eyes, on his devastated face. All there on a face that usually stayed free of all that emotion. He agreed with her. She was a time bomb. In that moment she knew he'd never have forgiven her if the worst had happened, and she didn't blame him. She hadn't forgiven herself.

CHAPTER 28

Suzannah was near. He sensed her. Finally back from where she'd run off to—West Yellowstone and a friend, Jessica had assured him. She was on the other side of his bedroom door. Two small raps confirmed what he already kent. He slipped into his jeans, considered not opening the door. Having spent much of the evening in the kitchen with Clint and Jessica waiting for Suzannah to come home, it was now 11:30 at night, too late for this to be good news. But he could no more not open that door than he could give Suzannah up.

Jake rubbed his eyes hard and pinched the bridge of his nose. When she had detailed her story to him today, he hated that he'd let his inner agony become so transparent. She'd read that look in him, all right. And then she'd run off.

Him? He'd just stood there, stunned. Precisely when he should have been running after her instead.

The more he'd lived in her confession, the more he ached to be to her what she was to him—a confidant, a crusader. He'd let her down. And now she was here, on the other side of that door. Suffering her own agony all evening, making decisions about him… without him.

Fear gripped him. So hard he could feel his gut twist.

Having to force legs forward that didna want to go, he plodded to the door, twisted the knob, and slowly swung it in. There she stood, a lovely, sad waif. His heart gave a painful tug at the single wet streak on her cheek. The expression on Suzannah's face earlier today had told him everything, before she'd turned to quit the barn. Now, as he studied that same look, he thought to throw the door closed in her face. Better she be furious with him than to let her say her piece.

Before he could act on it, she started through the door toward him. "Stop right there, Kitten, before you say a thing." He grasped her wrist and dragged her forward, swinging the door shut behind her before he engulfed her in his arms. He felt her tremble. Squeezing her tighter, he prayed the whirlwind of guilt and fear and frustration inside her would go still. She struggled for breath, but if he could keep her from talking, mayhap they'd have a chance.

"Jake—"

"*Nae!*" He spoke too loudly, but thankfully Anna-belle didna stir in her crib. Breathing Suzannah in, he pressed his lips against her hair. "Dinna give up on us, Suze. Dinna do it," he whispered against the top of her head.

When she exhaled on a dry sob, his palm cradled the back of her head and pressed her cheek into his chest. They stayed that way, both of them breathing shallowly. He counted her breaths, praying each one would take her further away from her intent.

It didna work. She wrenched her head back, lifted her chin. He looked down into glistening eyes, and his heart fell. She blinked hard, holding back tears he'd only seen her shed once before. For him. But he feared it wouldna be long before she released them to fall to his shirt, killing the hope he held close to his heart.

"Jake. I have to go back to California—"

He turned her head up and smashed his mouth against hers, stopping up the words that would take his hope and rob him of the only woman he'd ever loved. He wrapped her in his arms, molded her softness into the hard crags of his body. His mouth moved over hers, adoring her lips, letting the passion build, praying his kiss would convince her their love was worth fighting for.

When the taste of her salty tears seeped between their lips and into his mouth, he broke the kiss and retreated a step. Grief weighted his arms. They dropped to his sides and hung there like heavy sacks of grain.

She backed two steps of her own, her gaze still locked to him. Her tear-filled eyes showed the same agony that was ripping through his heart. He reached out to grab her back, but she twisted to the side to avoid his hand.

"Please, sweetheart. Dinna do this," he begged. "We're in this thing together. Jessica told me of the wee lass back in California. It wasna your fault what happened there, or to Annabelle here. Toddlers get away from you."

She dropped her chin to her chest. "I should never be allowed to care for little ones."

"Hold it right there, Suzannah Harper." He advanced a step. "Look at me."

When she did, her face was twisted in misery. Only a few fat tears spilled from her eyes, dashing down those soft cheeks. He wanted to use the pads of his thumbs to erase them from her face, to say something that would stop her from leaving him. He racked his brain for the right words to make her stay. Nothing came.

They stood there, tormented, locked in a gaze that wouldna allow either to breathe.

She squeezed her eyes shut, inhaled, and broke the spell. It tore his heart in two. He would do anything to keep her from such suffering. Except the one thing he couldna do. Let her go. "Look at me," he said, more gruffly than he would have liked.

She raised her eyes back to him. Every visible muscle in her sweet body had tensed, but she remained in place.

He stretched out his hands, palms up, like she was a skittish filly. Kept his voice low, steady. "Suzie. What we've got is too good to give up on—a love of a lifetime. You have to fight for us. I'll be right by your side every step of the way. For life. Kitten. Love me, marry me, make a life with me, lass. God knows I love you with every living cell in my body. And, because of you, every cell is finally alive, you ken?"

Her eyes went wide, her mouth parted. She looked stricken. Shocked by his admission? Not wanting the same thing as him? He thought sure he'd read her right. That she wanted him as much as he wanted her.

She shook her head so imperceptibly that if Jake hadna been staring at her beautiful face with the focus of a sculptor, he might have missed it. Then she gulped, and seemed to draw on an invisible reserve. "Jake. You have a child to think of now. She deserves a mother who's not so damaged she could get her hurt, or even—"

He dove toward her, cutting off her words. Before she could flee, he wrapped her up in his arms again, crushing his lips to hers once more. For a moment she relented. Then she pushed against his chest to interrupt the kiss and pivoted to be let loose.

He let her move back, but not out of the enclosure of his arms. "Suzie…" he whispered, his voice sounding as broken as he felt.

"No, Jake. You don't understand. I have to go—"

"Suze! Dinna let us die." *If you do, I'll die.*

She broke free of his arms. The look on her face told him she craved a life with him as much as he wanted one with her.

He jammed his hands into the front pockets of his jeans, heat rising up his neck and hitting the top of his head with such velocity, he thought sure his hair would spark then blaze. "What is it, Suzannah? I'm not the kind of man you want? Such lousy husband stock that you dinna want me?"

She gulped in a breath, then gaped. "Don't say that! Don't you ever say that!" She glared, but suddenly looked agonized. She shook her head and turned to escape his room.

He pulled his hands out of his pants and flung them out. "Then fight for us, damn you! Fight for me!" he bellowed after her.

* * *

Jake's eyes cracked open to a stream of sunlight warming his face. What time was it? Had to be way past dawn. His body felt like lead. Boneless. Had he been drinking again last night, though he'd sworn to himself he'd never do that again? Jake lay in a stupor, blinking up at the ceiling. As the last remnants of sleep and nightmarish dreams dissipated, a new reality slid in. Suzannah had left him. He could feel it deep down in his gut. Last night's conversation had been it. She didna want him. The end.

Crushing sorrow flattened his verra soul. How would he face even one day without her in it? Annabelle. That's how he'd continue putting one step in front of the other. For the wee lass, his daughter.

Annabelle. Jake shot to his feet, rocking side to side as he found his footing and plowed toward the crib. One glimpse and he knew she wasna there. No bum sticking up in the air. He scrubbed his hand across his eyes, then down his scratchy face. Someone must have retrieved her. Had he been that dead to the world? He thought he hadna slept at all.

Jake dragged on his jeans, buttoning them as he raced out of his room and on down the stairs. Cowboys were already clinking forks on dishes and glasses on tables. By the looks of it, they were nearly done with breakfast. Amid the general racket of the meal, Jake heard Annabelle's giggling. His knotted heart started beating again. He slid to a stop at the doorway to the dining area and picked out the crowd of cowpokes who had lined up to blow raspberries and otherwise make fools of themselves for Annabelle's pleasure.

He smiled, but just as quickly the smile slid away. He kent better than to look, but he couldna help it. He scanned the tables, the kitchen, the front porch and road visible through the front window. No Suzannah.

Before his heart could tie itself into a new knot, he heard one of Annabelle's groupies say "Forebidder." Jake looked on, watching the fellow take his hand from her forehead and touch her left eye. "Eyewinker," he said. Then her other eye, "Tomtinker." Then her nose, "Nosedropper." Her mouth, "Moutheater." Her chin, "Chinchopper." His daughter was so attuned to touch that she didna seem a bit bothered by the loud noise clamoring all around her. And when the young cowboy finished by tickling her under her chin, they both burst into giggles. The game was Annabelle's favorite, and they all had learned it from Mabel. Who ken so many men were crazy about bairns?

"Whew-wee, now there's a rompin' good view," Mabel said, snapping Jake's attention from Annabelle to her. "You forget somethin', cowboy?" Her gaze skimmed his chest, and then his feet.

Jake actually felt a flush slide up his bare torso and into his face, but he ignored it. "Who took Annabelle out of her crib? Without telling me?"

"You were sleepin' like someone put laudanum in your soup last night. Couldn't wake you," Mabel spouted back.

Jake slid a hand up into his hair, smoothing it back off his forehead. He glanced around again, in case he'd missed her. But, nae, he'd been right. No Suzannah.

Jessica came through the back door, a basket of eggs in one hand, Clint trailing too close behind her. "Morning, Jake." She glanced over his body much the same way Mabel had done. "A new look for you, huh?" she teased.

Clint pinched her bum, and she squealed, eggs shifting as she spun around to smack him on the hand.

Clint scowled, though his eyes were dancing. "I'll not have you looking at other naked men, wife." Then he gave her a crooked smile just before leaning down to plant an affectionate kiss on her mouth.

Earsplitting whoops filled the kitchen. Jake jerked his gaze to Annabelle, and breathed a momentary sigh of relief she had not been scared by the sudden uproar.

Clint straightened to full height, scanned the crowd with a genuine scowl this time, and everyone shut up.

Jake growled his impatience, closing the distance to Jessica in spite of her hovering husband. "So, she's gone." The impact of his own words may as well have been a knife to his chest.

Jessica's smile dropped off. She skirted around him to set the eggs on the counter, then came back and searched his face.

What did she see there? An empty shell where a newly thriving soul once was?

Jessica tilted her head up to her husband and nodded. Clint nodded back in understanding. She gestured for Jake to follow her toward Roy and Mary's downstairs bedroom—empty now since the newlywed couple had taken off for a full week's honeymoon this time. Once Jessica was in the room, she turned to face Jake. Jake followed her in, closing the door behind him.

Jessica held up her hands as if pleading for someone's life. Problem was, Jake couldna tell if it was his own life she was trying to save.

"Promise you won't fly off the handle," she said.

He gave his best bullying look.

"Promise me."

She always was stubborn, this older sister of Suzannah's. And utterly unafraid. Figured. None of the Harper women could be intimidated. "Fine. I promise."

"Suzannah went back to California."

All the blood in his veins seemed to drain to his toes. So it was true.

"Before you get too upset, let me explain some things to you." She pushed him backward toward the bed. "Sit. You look like you might fall down."

He sat. Then trembled. How weak he must look. But he didna care. Grief hit him square in the chest. Right about heart area. He'd already started preparing himself for life without Suzannah, or so he thought. But the reality of it was so much greater.

"Jake, are you listening?" She touched his arm as she sat next to him.

So used to connecting his brain to Suzannah's words when she touched him like that, his body snapped to attention without hesitation. His eyes bore into hers, waiting.

"I'm sure her intention was *not* to leave you and Annabelle. I'm sure she loves you both."

She loved Annabelle, yeah. But him?

"She's gone back to her doctors in California with the idea Dodge had about her hyoid bone. She went to see if they could do anything for it. So she can get better. So she can be normal. She'll be back when…"

Did he believe it? That she'd be back? "She didna bother to say anything like that last night."

Jessica watched his face. Deciphering his thoughts like Suzannah could do? "She was afraid you'd stop her."

He jumped to his feet and glared down at Suzannah's older sister. "Why would I do that, lass? Does she ken me so little?"

Jessica rose to her feet, took hold of one of his hands, and held it in both of hers. "Jake. She's been suffering this affliction for a very long time. I don't think she knows what she's doing. Normal is what she's been striving for, for so long, it's become her reset. She always starts there when things go awry. This thing with Annabelle, it… it threw her. She hasn't been able to consider you three as a family since then. Not until she gets her part right."

Jake rubbed his free hand up his cheek, hearing the rasp of several days growth. Why didna she ken they could work anything out together? Wasna that what couples did?

"Have you told her how you feel about her, Jake?"

Why hadna he done that before last night, before it had sounded desperate and untrue? He yanked his hand out of Jessica's and jammed his fingers through his hair so hard, he found himself staring at the ceiling. Mayhap he wasna enough for Suzannah. He sure as Hades didna do right by his first wife. He dropped his hands to his sides like anvils and blew out a breath. "Leave it be, Jessica."

She saw his beaten expression. "Oh no you don't, Jacob Cooper. You will not give up on the two—the three—of you. I will stand in Suzannah's stead. I won't let you do it!"

He fired a scathing look at her. "I said, it doesna matter. I have work to do." He turned to go, but Jessica skated around to the front of him, halting his steps.

She smiled then. The wee imp. "We are sisters, you thick-headed Scot. I know a lot about you. I know you love her, want to fight for her."

Her smile nearly brought his. But it didna quite find his mouth.

"Give her time, Jake. God is in control. Pray about it." She patted him one more time on his shoulder before heading for the door.

"How long 'til she knows?"

She turned the knob, then said, "Two days."

Jake watched Jessica's back as she took her leave, feeling like she'd ripped out his heart rather than offered him wisdom. That was it, then. He had no say in the matter. Suzannah would ken what path she'd take within forty-eight hours. And then his own fate would be determined for him.

CHAPTER 29

Suzannah crossed her arms on the kitchen tabletop and nestled her forehead where they joined. No tears. Only hollowness.

Her father sat down next to her and stroked her hair. "I'm so sorry, sweetheart. The doctor did say you are getting better, though. That's something, right?"

She raised her head to look at him. He was such a dear man. It should have been her mom in the doctor's office with her today, but she was too busy with some community event to go with her. Oh well, that was Mom. It was helpful that Dad was self-employed.

"Thank you for going with me, Pop. But don't you need to get back to the Murphy project?" She needed to stop talking. Her throat hurt from all the probing the doctors did. The fact that Dodge had been right didn't help her cause. The x-rays had shown the hyoid had been fractured and now pressed into her larynx, hence the constant feeling of a lump in her throat. The pivotal blow came when the doctor stated in no uncertain terms it was too late to fix it.

"You have improved, and will continue to do so," her dad said. "Don't forget God in all this. He is a God of miracles."

Suzannah took a sip of the water her dad had brought her. "If He decides to heal me, Hallelujah. If not, I have to live with this." *But Jake and Annabelle don't.*

She rubbed her aching throat, got to her feet, and moved to the window above the sink. It overlooked the beautiful begonia garden her mother nurtured, still in full bloom. "Go back to work, Pop. I'm okay."

"Now, Suzannah. Don't start making such final decisions all by yourself. Your young man will want a say in this."

Her father always did that. He knew her so well. She twisted to face him. "He has no say. It's my problem, Pop. And, he's… he's not my young man." She needed to let Jake go. He didn't deserve this. He'd had enough to deal with in his difficult life, hadn't he? He sure as heck didn't need her as a liability to Annabelle's safety.

Her dad tilted his head down as he looked out from the tops of his eyes. She was always in trouble when he did that little move. "Suzannah—"

"No, Pop!" She suppressed the wince that such forceful words induced. I'm twenty-two years old, not fifteen. It's my decision." She forced a light-hearted look and the voice to go with it. "Besides, I'm glad to be back in California. With you… and Mom… the orphanage… No Thomas to fear." She pasted on a huge smile, gave her dad a kiss on the forehead, and trudged out of the kitchen, her smile instantly replaced by crushing despair.

Once she crossed the threshold to her bedroom, she closed the door, then leaned against it. A dry sob expelled on a breath, then a true one… along with a torrent of tears. They came too easily. But reality had finally hit today, and there was no more room for denial. She must find a way to live without Jake and Annabelle, even though doing so would destroy her.

The telephone in the kitchen rang. Suzannah cringed. That was probably Jessica. Suzannah had promised to call her, but hadn't found the strength to do so. Jessica would know something was wrong. Tears gushed down her cheeks.

Her heart sank at the sounds of her dad's footsteps coming down the hallway, knowing it was time to face her sister.

"Phone's for you, Suze. It's Jessica."

"Be right there." Her voice shook. She dashed to her dresser for kleenex. Before she could talk to Jessica, she needed a minute. She was hot and clammy and stuffed up and miserable, and her intuitive sister would pick up on all of that.

Her mind scrambled over what she could tell Jessica. Jake might be standing right next to her as well. Just the thought of the gentle giant made her heart ache so. She should have told Jake the real reason she was going to California, but he hadn't been listening that night. It was just as well. Having to face the doctors and the news that could change her life was overwhelming enough. To look in Jake's saddened face as he tried to convince her it didn't matter one way or the other, well… leaving his room had been easier. She was truly a coward. That was all there was to it.

Taking a steadying breath, she followed her dad back to the kitchen and picked up the receiver. Stretching the cord as far as it could go, she sat down in a kitchen chair, swiping at leftover tears. "Hi."

"Well? How'd it go?"

"Is Jake there with you?"

A pause. "No."

Why wasn't he there?

"Tell me what the doc said. *Please*. I've been praying all day," Jessica pleaded.

Now she was nervous. What was going on with Jake? "Dodge was right. My hyoid bone got fractured, but it's too late for surgery. I just have to live with it." She covered the receiver with a hand as a huge sob slipped out. More tears. *Come on, Suzannah. Straighten up, fly right.* Her dad's voice from her youth echoed in her head.

A long silence ensued. "Oh, Suzannah. I'm so sorry. But, you've been getting better. They can see improvement, right?"

"You sound just like Dad. Yes. Some improvement."

Another long silence. "What are you going to do, Suze?"

"I'm… I'm going to stay in California.

"No! Suzannah Harper, come to your senses. You have a man and little girl here who love you. You're not going to abandon them!"

Abandon. Was that what she was doing? "Stay out of it, Jessica. You don't know what you're talking about."

"I do. Jake and I have talked."

"*What?* Why? Why do you always do that?"

"Do what?"

"Involve yourself in my business." She coughed, then cleared her throat. "I have to go."

"No! Suzannah, don't hang up. Give me a minute. Please." Silence. "Are you there?"

She heaved a sigh. "Yes. I'm here."

"Suze. Go visit the family Mom has told you about a hundred times. Their situation is similar. Please. Go visit them. You deserve it. Jake deserves it."

Suzannah groaned loudly, hoping to give her sister a hint. "I'm not going to do that. It is so intrusive. I've told you all that... a hundred times as well."

"It's different now, Suzannah! You have Jake to consider. And Annabelle. It's not just you anymore. Quit being so selfish!"

"You think I'm selfish? I'm trying to be unselfish." Her throat hurt so bad, it crossed her mind she may ruin it for good. Well, maybe she should. She didn't care about herself anymore. "He deserves more than a chance. He deserves a happy, trauma-free life. I want to give him that." She stopped, her throat screaming at her. She swallowed hard as tears threatened again. "Annabelle needs a real mother. One who can keep her safe. You saw what happened. I nearly got Annabelle killed."

"*What?* You honestly think a one year old would have stopped if only you could have yelled? You're crazy if you think that. Any one of us would have had to run after her. From what I've seen, your legs work perfectly fine!"

Suzannah closed her eyes to the pain of it. To the broken bone in her throat, to losing Jake and Annabelle, to never being normal. *Why, God, do I have to live with this?*

"Jessica." Suzannah's voice was a mere whisper now. "You don't know what Jake's been through. I love him too much to saddle him with me. I must go. I love you." And she hung up.

* * *

Jake was standing at the sink listening to everything Jessica had said. She hung up the receiver and turned slowly, still deep in thought. She jumped when she saw him, a look of misery lining her face. A lump formed in his throat at the truth behind that expression.

"How long have you been there, Jake?"

"Heard everything."

"Oh my… I'm sorry. I didn't…"

"She's not coming back, is she?"

Jessica pressed her lips together and lowered her gaze, shaking her head no.

He inhaled sharply, exhaled raggedly. A kick in the chest by the demon horse would have been more welcome. In fact, that's just how he felt. What would he do without his Suzie? The one woman who made his sorry life worth living?

Jake grabbed his hat off the table, where he'd placed it before eavesdropping on Jessica's conversation, and stuffed it down to his brows. He stormed toward the back door. Clint was coming in right about then, and saw the look on his face. He stood in Jake's way, nose to nose, always able to read his men.

Just then, a chaos of hollering cowboys, rattled boards, billowing dust, and guttural squealing drew Jake's attention to the kitchen window.

"What's up, Jake?" Clint said, glancing at Jessica for answers.

"Got a demon to break." He shoved Clint out of his space, but the man was his size, so he didna move far. "What do you want, Clint? Let me by."

Clint's grim gaze shot to Jessica, but he didna move. "What's going on, hon?"

"Suzannah is what's going on," Jessica said on a sigh.

Clint rolled his jaw to one side and moved out of Jake's way.

Jake glanced back, seeing Clint take Jessica into his arms for a comforting hug. Sheer envy ripped through him, fueling his explosive mood.

He slammed out the back door. Max and four other cowboys were in the training corral, all trying different forms of Jake's method on the black stallion. All failing miserably.

Jake took in the scene at a glimpse. The horse bucked, trying to double barrel one of the nearby cowboys. The man leapt away, landed on his side, and rolled under the fence. Demon swung around, pure evil in his eyes. He charged another man, catching him by the shoulder, slamming him into the fence. Max yanked off his hat, waving it in the air so the others could cart off the limp man. Max hobbled along after them, then stood by the fence in case help was needed. The last one standing was spitting dust from his mouth as he eyed the horse. Then he began scanning the area for the best escape. His sweat-dampened shirt and dripping hair showed Jake how long they'd been at it. The demon had foam lining his coat. And still it looked like no one had gotten anywhere with the crazed horse.

Jake strode to the fence, stepped up to the second rung, and vaulted over, landing hard on the other side. That brought the attention of the remaining cowpokes.

Max trudged up, eyes narrowed. "What're you plannin' here, Jake?" Max's gaze tracked Jake from his split-leg stance to the fury in his face. "Yer lookin' as mean as Demon right about now."

Jake glared back at him. "Bring me the hackamore."

Max scrambled around to the front of Jake to slow his progress toward the horse. What was wrong with the men on this ranch. Didna they ken no man likes his space invaded by another man? "Get out of my way, Max."

"This black demon's not fit for riding yet. Didn't you get a taste of gettin' throwed on your head before? You need another lesson?"

Jake caught a glimpse of Pete coming over the fence. "Get out of the corral. Both of you," Jake snapped, glancing around him. The rest of the men were smart enough to stay out of his way and were already on the other side of the fence.

Pete sauntered forward. He got too close to Jake, yet another man in his space. Jake could feel his old wrathful self returning. Too many people, too much argument. Nae. He recognized it for what it was—too little Suzannah.

"Jake. What's this about?" Max asked. And for his ears only, he whispered, "I'm not going to let you ride this demon. Not today. The men already worked him into a lather. He's dangerous right now, buddy. More than usual."

"Good." Mayhap the demon would finish him, once and for all. "Get the hackamore, Pete. Now!"

Max got right in Jake's face. Though a hair shorter and leaner, he was formidable enough. "Think of Annabelle, Jake."

Annabelle was loved by everyone on this ranch. She'd be better off without a dad who would continually mourn the loss of the lass who'd brought sunshine to his soul, only to leave him and strip it from him. "She'll be fine." Then he thought how Max might take that, and said, "I'll be fine."

Pete showed up then with the headgear Jake had asked for. "About time," he grumbled.

Max lowered his chin and shook his head slowly "Jake…"

"I'll be fine, lad. Get out of the corral."

Max backed away, a look of defeat on his lean face. He climbed up on the fence, as did Pete. A row of cowboys sat the fence now, watching as Jake attempted to kill himself, or the demon horse. Only one of them would win today.

Pete scurried down the other side of the fence, and ran to the ranch house. Fool. He was off to tell Jessica, no doubt.

Jake turned back to the black monster who was huffing and plowing a hoof in the loose turf, reeking of confidence.

Jake's view tunneled in. It was only him and the demon now, head to head. He strode forward.

* * *

Jessica jerked her head up from the corn she was husking when Pete stormed in from the back porch, the screen door slamming hard behind him.

"My word, Peter! Scared the dickens out a me," Mabel hollered at him.

"Jessica, you gotta call Suzannah! Jake's gonna kill hisself."

"What?" Jessica came around the counter and gripped Pete by his shoulders. "Slow down, Pete. What's going on?"

"It's Jake. He don't seem like hisself, ya know? And Suzannah calms him. No. More than calms him… something… I don't know what. But, he's gonna get on that demon horse, and he shouldn't. Not after we prodded it into a frenzy already."

Jessica's hand went to her throat. "Even if I call her, she can't get here today! Go back out there and see what you can do. I'll bring Annabelle out. Maybe when he sees his girl, he'll behave."

Jessica scrambled over to the baby. Mabel was already cleaning her up and tugging her out of her highchair. "Here. Go fix that ornery varmint. Reckless bronc snapper!" Mabel said. "Tryin' to kill the babe's only pa," she mumbled to herself as she went back to work on supper.

Jessica plopped Annabelle on one hip and high-tailed it out the back door and around the side of the house to the corral. She saw Jake, his back to her. He had a bunch of tackle in his hands, a determined set to his shoulders, and his head slightly down like a charging bull. He strode purposefully toward the horse in the corner of the corral. From here, Jessica could see the fire in the animal's black eyes. Not the usual mix of fear and flight, but pure evil. No wonder they had nicknamed this animal Demon. She was sure if she could see Jake's black eyes right now, his would look the same. Was this going to be a battle between two enraged, wild things? She wished Clint hadn't just headed into town. He'd know what to do. Because Pete was right. Jake was not in his right mind.

Annabelle let out a wail. And then another. *Thank you, little girl. Perfect timing, Lord. As always.*

Jake's head came up. He halted, but remained fixed in place.

As if Annabelle knew what was about to happen, she screeched and stuck her pudgy arms out toward the corral. It was all Jessica could do to hang onto the wriggling toddler. "Daaaa," she wailed.

Jake's spine went rigid. He backed up slowly, never turning around. He retreated until his own back came up against the fence. "Why did you bring my daughter out here?" he practically growled at whoever was holding Annabelle.

"To see her father one last time!" Jessica bit back.

Jake dumped the gear on the ground, then turned and scaled the fence, dropping down in front of Jessica. "Take her back! Now!"

Annabelle held her arms out to her dad. He glanced at the flailing limbs, then back up at Jessica, ignoring the baby's request.

"No can do," Jessica said, staring into the violent, black eyes she knew she'd see. "I think she should watch as her dad kills himself, don't you? I mean, when will she ever see you again?"

"Stop smartin' off, Jessica! This has nothing to do with the lassie."

Annabelle had become strangely quiet. Out of the corner of her eye, Jessica watched the cowboys draw nearer. Not many people took on Jake Cooper. He seemed surprised himself.

"This. Has. Everything. To do with her, Jake! You're her father, and you're about to get yourself killed on that—that crazy beast out there." Jessica flung one hand toward Demon. "You should put him down, just like Uncle Roy wants. If it was between you and that horse, who do you think Roy would choose? And what of Suzannah? How do you think she would feel?"

She watched the high color in Jake's face drain, leaving him pasty. "Dinna think the lass would care," he muttered as he squeezed past her and Annabelle. "Take her back, I'm done here," he said over one shoulder. Then he disappeared into the barn.

The cowboys milled around Jessica. Some patted her on the back, others raised their eyebrows and nodded in respect. Most tickled Annabelle as she giggle, then dispersed one by one. Jessica didn't join them in their enjoyment of her back-talking Jake. He was unpredictable, and unstable right now. Suzannah would never forgive herself if something happened to Jake. She would blame herself, and regrettably, she would be right.

CHAPTER 30

Suzannah's hand seemed to have frozen to the telephone receiver as she tried to put it back in its cradle. Once she'd finally let go, she stared at it for long seconds.

"Who was on the phone, honey?" her mom asked.

"Jessica," Suzannah whispered back, staring at nothing.

"What is it? What's wrong?" Her mom grabbed hold of her arms, shifted her toward the kitchen table, and into a chair. "You're white as a sheet. Suzannah!" She gave Suzannah's shoulders a rough shake.

"It's Jake." Suzannah looked up from her stupor. "Oh Mom. Jake is going to do something rash. Jessica and some of the men at the ranch are worried about him. And now, so am I."

"Why? What's happening?"

She gazed into blue-green eyes, the color of her own, and decided to tell all. "I'm in love with Jake, Mom. And Annabelle."

Her mom gave her a warm smile. "No surprise there, honey. We know all about that. So, what's the problem?"

She jabbed a finger toward her throat. "This! This is the problem. I can't be a mother to Annabelle, Mom. I'm not mom material."

Her mom's frown spoke of confusion. "What do you mean?"

"I can't read to her for long enough to finish a book. I can't talk to her for long enough to have a conversation, without doing what's happening right now. My voice gets weaker and raspier." She swallowed painfully. "I can't yell after her if she wanders off."

"Oh, honey." Her mom rose up, gave her a hug around her head, kissing her hair, then stood over her. "A lot of moms don't have big voices, Suzannah. Many are deaf and mute. Some just mute. What I'm trying to say is, we're all flawed human beings. It shouldn't stop us from procreating."

Suzannah rolled her eyes. Mom was so weird sometimes, but Suzannah could see her point. She guessed. She covered both eyes with her hands, and rubbed for a second. "I don't know what to do, Mom. Jessica says Jake's even begun to ignore Annabelle. For over a week now. And he's getting worse. She says it's because of me." She coughed. Paused. " I thought I was doing the right thing, that he'd be better off, but now I don't know. I miss him so much."

Her mom marched to the phone and started dialing.

Suzannah watched the dial rotate back with each number. "Who are you calling?"

"You'll see." She waited. "Rex? It's Marie. Do you think I could bring Suzannah over for that short visit?" She listened for a few seconds. "That would be wonderful." Another silence, then she said, "We'll be right there." She hung up the phone.

"Is that the family you've all been wanting me to meet?"

"Yes. It's past time you see how a mute person can be a mom. Come on. We're going right now."

Suzannah's sense of urgency made her willing to try anything once. Or even twice. The hope of working out her relationship with Jake and Annabelle lifted her spirits.

Before she knew it, Suzannah found herself in her mom's car, parked in front of a charmingly painted Craftsman-style bungalow. With its toy-strewn lawn and trumpet vine trellis, it looked like the kind of cozy family sanctuary every woman dreamed of. She inhaled a breath of new hope and was about to climb out when her mom grabbed her arm. "Wait!"

Suzannah yelped, startled. "What's wrong?"

"I forgot to tell you something I thought you should know."

"Okaayy. About this family?"

"No actually. About Thomas's family."

The lump in Suzannah's throat doubled in size. She swallowed hard. Her mom being… well, her mom… didn't even notice her sudden apprehension.

"The word is, Thomas's father is dead."

A wave of dizziness came over her. "*What?* How?"

"They're investigating. Something about the grape jelly having cyanide in it? Or who knows what? They say Thomas's mom is not to be found. Disappeared. Since Thomas wasn't home when it happened, he's not a suspect. Moved up north, I hear." Mom grabbed Suzannah in a deep hug and whispered in her ear. "No more worries, honey. God's got your back."

Suzannah was stunned. By the information about Thomas, by the un-mom-like admission and hug, by the sudden need to see Jake.

She opened the car door numbly and at once heard young voices and loud laughter in the backyard. Sporadically, a loud whistle and clapping could be heard. Suzannah shook all thoughts of Thomas from her mind, because today was about her future, not her past. She followed her mom around the house toward the backyard.

"Rex said they'd all be in the back. Let's go," her mom said, seeming excited.

Suzannah stepped through a back gate and entered a beautiful backyard, trees all around, a large built-in swimming pool in the middle. Three little girls were in the pool even with the bite in the air, tossing a beach ball back and forth in the water, their squeals and giggles overriding any chance of normal talk.

Rex and a beautiful red-headed woman came toward them, a little girl about Annabelle's age in the woman's arms.

"Marie," Rex said, bending down to give her mom a kiss on the cheek. Then he looked at Suzannah. "This is my wife, Carol. Carol can hear, but she can't speak. Car accident. An injury to her larynx. And, this is our youngest, Connie." He patted the toddler on the head.

Suzannah was stunned. Jessica had told her Rex's wife didn't talk, but didn't say why. Yet, look how many children she had to manage—four little girls. Without a voice entirely. Hope spiraled up Suzannah's spine and centered in her heart. Could she and Jake actually become a family? Would she be able to handle Annabelle?

At once curious about how Carol managed this, she faced the woman head-on and asked, "How? How do you keep control of the children without a voice?" Realizing how out of bounds that question was, she blushed. "I'm sorry. That was kind of bold."

Carol threw her head back and laughed. Or, at least that's what it looked like since no sound escaped. Carol used some sort of sign language with Suzannah. She watched helplessly, then shrugged.

Rex spoke up. "She said, we all use sign language now. But, when they were too young yet... well, she'll show you what she did."

Suzannah understood implicitly. Carol needed her full attention. Suzannah stilled the whirl of her thoughts and nodded.

Carol winked, then handed Connie to her father and turned toward the girls in the pool. One loud whistle, and all activity stopped. Every head turned toward her. She clapped three times, and they all headed to the shallow end and hoisted themselves out of the pool. They scurried straight to her. "Yes, Mom?" the tallest one said as they all stood dripping and shivering.

Carol swung her hands in the direction of Suzannah and her mom. Then pointed at each girl one at a time. They followed their mother's lead and stated their names, each with a hand out. Suzannah shook one after the other. "How do you do?" they each said, then dropped their hands. "Happy to meet you girls. How old are you?"

"I'm seven," the littlest said.

"I'm nine," the middle one said.

"And I'm twelve, almost a teenager," the oldest one said with a grin, as her parents both groaned.

Their mother clapped twice, and they all scurried back to the pool with a boisterous splash from each.

"That's amazing. How about the toddler?" Suzannah asked, nodding toward Connie.

Rex set the child on the ground. She immediately ran off toward the pool where her sisters were happily playing, but not noticing her in the least. Carol whistled. All the girls stopped what they were doing—including the toddler, surprisingly—and faced Carol. The baby had to turn her chubby little body around in order to do it. Then, Carol clapped three times, and all four of them headed to their mom.

"It's okay, girls," Rex said to the ones in the pool. "You can stay there." He turned to Suzannah then. "Now, Connie is still learning, so she doesn't always do that well. But her sisters make sure she complies. If she doesn't, she has four mothers to contend with." They all laughed at that.

Watching how Rex overrode Carol's request made Suzannah realize that as the dad, he held the last say. Suzannah thought of Jake, and the control he enjoyed, though he always, *always* listened to her. The thought of the brooding, handsome cowboy she loved, on the tail of the hope she'd witnessed here, made her long for Jake. She had to get back. To throw her arms about his neck and cuddle him, as Coo loved to do. To hold tight, and never let him go.

* * *

Jake rounded up the tackle he'd need today and headed for the corral where half the Harper ranch hands were waiting. One of them was going to win. Would it be the demon or Jake?

It had been three weeks since Jake had seen Suzannah. Instead of forgetting about her, he ached more every day for even the sight of her. Overpowering dreams of her—in his arms, holding his daughter, soothing his brow, tasting his lips—had all but shattered his sleep. Anxiety built in him day by day, until he feared he was slipping back to that dark place he'd barely crawled out of the day Suzannah's sunshine arrived on Harper Ranch.

As he strolled through the barn toward the corral, thoughts of his past intruded. Even if he never loved Betty, he would always grieve his part in her death. And if she hadna perished, he would've honored his vows. But there wouldna have been sunshine in his life. Except for Annabelle.

If only Annabelle could pull him out of his mire.

Why wasna she enough?

Suzannah had been his hope. Without her he felt broken. Beyond mending. The kitten had soothed his soul, had given him a new love for life. And when he'd thought they might share that life together, well... he'd never felt such joy.

Now... now, he could no longer see the light. The sunshine was gone, and he didna ken how long it would be before he sank into the dark hopelessness forever.

Jake walked out of the barn and up to the corral gate. Cheers came from the tops of the fence, where two dozen cowboys perched. Some had there hats off and were whooping as they waved them in the air. They were only here to see him get his brains beat in. He ken that. Still, he'd get this over with, one way or another.

He stepped inside the gate and clicked it closed behind him, then faced the snorting black demon at the far fence. Jake inhaled a great breath, holding it inside for a few seconds, trying to gain an advantage somehow. Peace. Calm. Quiet. Composure. He needed all of it and had none of it since the day Suzannah had left him.

Out of the corner of his eye, he saw a dust cloud coming up the road. Someone was driving their direction at a pretty good clip. He grumbled, wishing he could go tear the head off whoever was driving so fast. Nae. Max would have to handle it. He needed to focus.

Forging his way across the soft dirt of the corral, Jake saw the demon's eyes widen and his nostrils flare. He was revving up for a good stomping, and Jake would be his stomping ground, whether he liked it or not. Holding his hands up with the crop in one and the rope in the other, Jake started his usual hollering. The black didna react. He swung the crop round and round. Chunks of turf flew from the place where the leather strap hit the ground, unsettling the horse a wee bit. Good. He wanted him off kilter. Treading forward a few more steps, he saw every muscle in the huge horse tense, poised to run at him. His shouts became louder, more sporadic, yet the animal would not turn to right or left. The massive stallion tossed his head up and down, trying his best to intimidate. Well, he'd met his match in Jake. Had he been a stallion himself, the fight would have been brutal, and probably to the death.

Jake was barely conscious of the sound of the vehicle skidding to a stop close by. He couldna risk a peek, knowing the horse watched for any advantage it could take.

Another step forward, another loud shout. Still no movement. A stalemate, lasting many long minutes.

Quite suddenly, the massive head rose up. Those evil black eyes softened as they shifted from piercing Jake's eyes to something over Jake's right shoulder. What in the world? Had he surrendered? Lost focus?

A shrill whistle reached Jake's ears. Loud. And familiar. His heart leapt in his chest in recogniton, and joy. *Suzannah!*

Still, Jake didna turn as he watched what the black was going to do. He was far too close to the horse now to give him his back as he exited the corral. He backed one step. Then another. Demon didna notice. He wasna looking at Jake at all. His gaze must've been locked on Suzannah. The stallion didna look angry anymore. More like... captivated. What an odd reaction for the horse who'd jumped a fence to harm her once before.

Jake's protective instinct surged through his veins, erasing his good sense. He turned, intent on sweeping Suzannah into his arms and away from Demon's line of sight. But the moment he pivoted, he froze at the sight of previously rowdy cowboys forming a perfect half circle at the fence. At the center of that crowd stood Suzannah... holding his daughter. Laird, but she looked good. Bright as sunshine, as if the clouds had parted and a stream straight from Heaven shone on her. Her eyes, blue as the Montana sky today, were wide with wonder, her skin soft as rose petals, her hair glimmering with beauty and health.

Just as his feet finally took heed of his brain and started forward, a look of horror spread to all the faces in front of him. Curses flew around in his head. Demon had found his edge. And there was nothing Jake could do about it.

Shouts, waving hats, whistles all came from every adult on the other side of the fence. Only one person was smiling, jumping up and down in Suzannah's embrace, and waving her wee arms to him. Annabelle.

Jake soaked them in, through his eyes, straight to his heart and soul. If this would be the last view of the treasures of his life, then he'd look his fill.

In a motion that seemed too slow, Jake twisted his body round to face his fate.

Then he saw it. The miracle. Everything in the massive horse had changed. Looking awakened rather than demon-possessed, he trotted toward Jake, every muscle alive by controlled strength. Lo and behold, the stallion did a wondrous thing. He ignored Jake. Instead, he darted around him for the other side of the corral. When he reached the fence, he skidded to a stop right in front of Suzannah and Annabelle.

Suzannah looked dumbfounded, her muscles stiffened solid to the spot while Annabelle jumped and squealed, delighted the big horse had come so close.

All shouting ceased. The silence was so immediate and so profound, Jake was sure he could have heard hummingbird wings whirling in the air. That is, except for his squealing daughter, who didna see any reason for fear.

The horse threw his head over the fence, and a collective gasp washed through the crowd.

Jake silently sped his way through the turf to one side of the horse, ready to use his own body to do what he could if need be. When he reached the fence, what he saw astounded him even more. The dark lids and long eyelashes of the steed had dropped to half, and a calming nicker escaped his mouth. If Jake didna ken better, by looking at him he'd think this was a docile pony ready to take the wee munchkin on a ride.

"Oh my goodness…" Suzannah whispered, but didna move.

The horse reached out his muzzle, and Suzannah jerked, but waited. Her head tilted to one side as she studied the steed. Then her eyes softened and her shoulders rounded.

Nae, Suzannah! Dinna let him get too close, Jake screamed in his head, but didna dare shout it out loud.

She let the demon snuffle them. Jake wanted to command that she back up. But she didna even look at him to see the message in his eyes. If he spoke, the demon horse might retaliate. So he bit his tongue and watched in silence.

When Annabelle reached out her wee hand to the horse, Jake's throat locked down.

"Move back," Jake said in a harsh whisper.

Still Suzannah didna move. The black moved one nostril to Annabelle's hand and inhaled. The motion brought the wee hand up tight against his nose, and Annabelle burst into giggles.

Everyone held their breath.

The horse nickered a pleasant sound, then stretched out to snuffle first Annabelle's hair, then Suzannah's. Jake felt terror along with an irrational jealousy. He had an absurd desire to shove the horse's head out of the way and do his own snuffling. In that instant he ken that's what he'd do the moment he leapt this fence and had them in his arms.

While the horse was distracted Jake bolted up two rungs and swung over the top rail before anyone had a chance to shift their gazes to him. Landing on the other side, he took a moment to interject his hand in the snuffling exercise, hoping to befriend the giant steed, but mostly to protect his lasses. *His lasses.*

Annabelle locked her gaze on Jake and squealed again. Without another thought to the crazy horse on the other side of the fence, Jake snatched Annabelle to one arm, and with the other, wrapped Suzannah up and bent in for a crushing kiss, all while backing them away from the fence a few paces.

Annabelle stuck her wet finger in Jake's ear and romped up and down in his arms, like she was riding her own steed. He ignored the wet ear, the bouncing wee lassie, and every cowpoke who had their eyes glued to them. "Kitten... welcome home, my lass," he whispered against her lips before he sank into a deeper kiss.

Suzannah reached one arm around his neck and the other around him and Annabelle, giving back all he gave. She momentarily broke the kiss and graced him with a promise that was sweeter still than the kiss they'd just shared.

"I'm home for good, my love," she whispered, and beamed a sunshine smile right back into his soul.

* * *

Jake followed Suzannah out the back door of the main house, the screen squeaking shut behind them. Joy filled his heart as he watched the woman he'd fallen hopelessly in love with carrying his wee bairn out to the newly sprouted grass. The day Suzannah returned, the sunshine had come flooding back to him. That day he ken he would have a good life. One that would be filled with love and laughter, and wee giggles from the miracle God had granted them—sweet Annabelle.

He was anxious to watch as Suzannah put into action what she'd witnessed with her mother's friend in California. She'd said it was a way someone such as herself could manage Annabelle, or a whole passel of bairns if they were graced with many.

Suzannah set Annabelle on the ground. As they'd both figured, off she went, as fast as her wee legs could carry her. First, Suzannah gave her whistle. Loud enough to beat any grown man in a contest. Annabelle didna turn, didna even flinch. Next Suzannah tried clapping, three times. Nothing. The wee bairn kept on running. The kitten caught up with her, scooped her up, and brought her back to try again. Off Annabelle ran, legs churning, feet smacking against the wee blades of grass, arms waving for balance. Suzannah clapped first, then placed two fingers to each side of her tongue against her teeth, and let out the shrillest whistle he'd ever heard in his life.

Jake held his ears, grinning with pride over the kitten's deafening noise. But Annabelle acted as if she'd not heard. A strange foreboding slithered up Jake's spine. What was this? How did she not react to that earsplitting sound?

Suzannah turned to catch his gaze with a similar thought bleeding through her expression. Frowning, she turned back. Running up behind Annabelle, she whistled again, right behind her head.

Nothing.

"Oh no... Jake!" Suzannah hissed, then stopped dead in her tracks. "It can't be."

Yet, it made sense. They'd all wondered why Annabelle hadna started saying words clearly. And there were other signs they'd all chosen to ignore.

Now he ken.

Annabelle was deaf.

Jake ran to scoop up the lassie in his arms. Then turned to Suzannah. Her face had blanched the color of a Montana snowcap. "Oh, Jake." She looked up into his face with tears in her eyes. Tears! Before he could blink twice, big round dots slid down Suzie's face, one by one, then dozens, until she knocked her forehead into his chest and sobbed with an intensity that shocked him. He put his free arm around her as she cried like he'd never heard her before, like he'd never heard anyone before. The sobs shuddered through her, breaking his own heart in half.

Would she leave them now for good? Was this too much for her? To care for a broken man and an impaired bairn when she fought with her own permanent affliction? Jake shook with grief for his Annabelle, and fear for an altered future with Suzannah.

Please, God. Help us. Make us a family in spite of our defects.

When finally Suzannah's sobs settled into sucking breaths, she raised her shattered face to his. Seeing streaks where tears had found their way down her cheeks, and pools of moisture still in her large eyes, he prayed again that God would answer his prayer.

"Jake," she rasped. "Our baby is deaf."

Our baby. And then he ken. God had answered his prayer. No matter how they forged ahead from here, they would always be a family.

EPILOGUE

There had been many a celebration at Harper Ranch, where friends, family, and crew all feasted together, but today was by far the best celebration ever had. Jake's heart was near to bursting at the love he shared with not just one lass, but two. As he stood to one side of the ranch house's massive green lawn, Jake locked his gaze onto his beautiful bride. Dressed in white lace with cowboy boots peeking out past the hem, Suzannah was radiant with her shiny hair glistening a dozen shades of sunshine as she laughed and visited with the many guests who'd poured in for yet another Harper wedding.

His and Suzannah's wedding just a few short hours ago had been perfect, and a ridiculous, sappy smile had lingered on Jake's face since then. Actually, ever since his Suzannah had come home to him, and agreed to marry him. Now she belonged to him, his wife, and he didna think a happier moment were possible.

Annabelle, his number two lass, was running from one cowboy to the next, chasing them like they were strays in the field. Someday he would watch her do that when she discovered a verra different reason for chasing men. He growled to himself, thinking of how he'd drill those men, until they didna ken which way was up. Grandpa Dodge couldna have agreed more with Jake. He'd laugh and remind anyone who would listen that he'd get the young men to behave by reciting the one warning only he could deliver with absolute honesty: "I don't mind going back to jail."

On top of that, it had been Jake's pleasure to tell Roy the black stallion had been saved... by a wee lass with a God-given gift with animals.

Then there was Coo. Aye, as a family, they'd taken the raccoon up to the hills daily for a month. Though she made a den for herself and had birthed her own family of kits, she still visited on occasion—for treats, and a few soothing words, though since she was part of the wild now, Jake didna allow anyone to touch her. It seemed fine by her as well. She had been coming less often now that she had a family, and that was a verra good thing.

Jake breathed in the mountain air, content to watch his beloved Kitten flit from person to person, saying little but smiling much. If she couldna say another word, but could only smile her way through life, he and all who came near would be the better for it.

Suzannah turned then and caught Jake's gaze. And like following a path to home she made her way toward him, her smile growing ever wider with each step. The white of her dress bespoke the purity of her nature. And she belonged to him.

She swayed up to him with the moves of an accomplished seductress, and Jake's mouth dropped open. He was more than ready to scoop her up from the crowd and plow a path toward their shared bedroom, to love her, to make her his, body and soul. His heart reached for hers as she drew near and he breathed her in.

She reached up to his face and smoothed her palm across the coarse stubble that showed up by this time everyday. "I love the feel of you," she said as she rasped her hand up and down his jaw. "I love your heart," she said as she placed her hand on his chest. "I love your mind," she said, sliding a hand into his hair. "I love your strength," she said as she rubbed a hand up and down a bicep. "I love—"

"You keep showing me what you love, and we'll not last out here much longer," Jake said, then bent in, wrapped his arms about Suzannah's waist, and lifted her into a victorious kiss.

The crowd hooted with joy.

Wham! Jake's knees nearly buckled from the impact. He released Suzannah's lips and looked down into the brown eyes that nearly swallowed Annabelle's face. The wee tyke had her chubby arms wrapped around one of Jake's legs. "Daaaa," she wailed.

He lowered Suzannah's feet to the ground, but kept one arm around her waist.

"She's adorable. Doesn't want to be left out," Suzannah said.

Jake reached down and scooped Annabelle up in one arm, then put his other back around Suzannah. He nuzzled Suzannah's neck, then breathed into her ear, "Well, my wife, she may have to feel left out for a while." Then he leaned back and grinned. "But I promise you, Kitten, we three are a family now. Mayhap we'll add more to our sporran soon, aye?" Then he growled and nibbled her neck.

Annabelle stuck the usual wet finger in Jake's ear. "Och! What is the interest in my ears, wee one?" Then, as if she understood his disgust, she moved on to his dimples, sticking that same wet finger into one of them. She giggled when he smiled, and stroked his dimple again.

Pete sauntered up, a dozen or so cowboys in their best duds following close behind.

He glanced around at his following as he often did, and turned back to Jake. "Yeah, who knew you had holes in your cheeks, my man." He laughed at his own joke. "Never seen 'em before with all that bush on your face." Another shout of laughter. "Kinda hard to get us to cringe anymore when you glare at us." Another round of laughter, though it was only his own. "Right, boys?"

No comments.

"Right?" he tried again.

No sound. From anyone in the yard.

Jake was having a hard time not joining him in laughter. He glanced around the yard, seeing happiness all around. Clint, dressed as Jake was, in black pants and boots, white shirt, silver vest, and string tie, was grinning at the scene Pete was creating. Jessica looked radiant as she leaned against Clint, who had one arm locked under her chest, and the other possessively over the growing baby they'd just announced. Another glance over and there were Roy and Mary, a few months married, Roy with one arm slung across Mary's shoulders, both beaming like teenagers after the prom. Then came Rebecca, Suzannah's maid-of-honor, perfectly poised and self-possessed, flanked by his only two amiable Cooper cousins. One couple over from them was Johnnie, also dressed like Jake, and his stunning wife, Rose Marie, who leaned back contentedly in her man's embrace. And, shyly smiling, in the far arc of the circle stood Harold and Louise. Jake hadna thought of inviting them, but of course his sweet bride had. Their presence this day closed yet another wound Jake hadna realized needed tending.

Now all eyes were locked on Pete, waiting to see what Jake would do.

Well, as much as he wanted to please the crowd by sucking in his cheeks, flattening his lips, and glaring black shards straight into Pete's eyes, he couldna quite rev up that kind of animosity anymore. Even in play. Instead, he cocked an eyebrow and stared at Pete, wanting more than anything to grin, or throw his head back and laugh aloud with the sheer happiness filling his heart. Pete saw the effort for what it was and played along, feigning his fear with wide eyes as he stepped back, straight into Max and his fiancée. Pete knocked the champagne glass out of Max's hand and onto a small serving table, shattering it all over the grass below.

In unison, everyone jumped back, startling an unsuspecting Annabelle. She let out a horrendous shriek and subsequent flood of tears.

"Oh, Belle, Da's sorry," Jake said, grabbing her wee cheek so she could see his apology.

She didna let up though, so Suzannah took her from his arms and jostled her back to bliss.

Pete took the three steps back to Suzannah and Annabelle. "Uncle Pete's sorry, too, little girl," he said, using hand signals along with his words. Annabelle stopped instantly and gave Pete a watery smile. He continued. "Do you want something to eat?" he said, giving the toddler the signal for eat with fingertips to his mouth.

"Is that sign language, Pete?" Suzannah asked. "I've seen this before."

"Yup. Been using it for my Aunt Hattie, lives in West Yellowstone. She lost her hearing a long while back, so when I visit we talk with our hands."

Pete went about talking to Annabelle as if it was no big mystery. The crowd gathered around, amazed that Pete ken such a thing.

"Can you teach it to us?" Suzannah asked Pete.

"'Course. We'll start tonight," Pete said.

Jake stepped forward then, grabbing Annabelle out of Suzannah's hands and placing her in Pete's. "Nae, *we* willna be starting tonight, Pete. Or anytime soon, ya ken?" He swung an arm around Suzannah's waist and grinned down at her. "My bride and me, well… we'll be a wee bit busy for the next few weeks."

Then Jake sobered, gazing about the crowd. "I want to thank everyone here at Harper Ranch. For taking me in—especially you, Roy—and for believing in me. For giving me my space at first, then a place to heal. For watching my back with the crazy broncs I bust. For bringing me my lass." He glanced down and smiled at Suzannah. "God bless you. Truly."

He spun himself and Suzannah around to head toward the house. As an afterthought, he turned back. "And if I so much as see one of your faces, or even hear one of your footsteps coming anywhere near my bride and me tonight… well, let's just say, the old Jake will return."

Jake and Suzannah waved at the crowd as the cowboys whooped and tossed hats in the air.

Then, with arms locked about each other as bride and groom, they strode away from their cherished Harper Ranch family and straight into their own bright future.

THE END

Did you enjoy this book?

I hope so!

Would you take a moment to leave a review and rating? It doesn't have to be lengthy. Just a sentence or two to share what you liked about the book.

Thank you!

* * *

Watch for the first book of the
Cooper Bar-Six Ranch Series,
coming in 2016.

Do you want to be one of the first to know when Book One of the Cooper series comes available?

Just go to my website at: www.janithhooper.com and fill out the get connected form. On the subject line, fill in: Cooper Ranch Series. In the message box, put your email address, and any other message you'd like to convey.

I would love to hear from you!

And, I promise to write back!

About the Author

Janith Hooper lives with her husband in Oakdale, California—Cowboy Capital of the World. She has four grown sons, Matthew, Nathan, Paul, and Benjamin; two daughters-in-love, April and Marisa, and one soon to be, Brooke; and three grandchildren, Abbie, Maddie, and Wyatt. So far.

Outside of spending time with her family, you'll find her reading a romance story on her Kindle, or writing up a storm, creating her own romance stories to offer to you, her beloved reader.

Ride With Me, Stay With Me, and Fight For Me complete her Quaking Hearts trilogy. Now available. All are stand alone novels, but are best when read in order.

Visit her website at: www.janithhooper.com

Email her at: janithhooper@gmail.com

Author's Note

Yes, the earthquake in this book was real.

Here is a link that will take you to sources of information about the Lake Hebgen, Montana, earthquake:
www.google.com/search?q=lake+hebgen+earthquake+and+tsunami=lake+hebgen+earthquake+and+tsunami

Below are statistics about the earthquake as documented by Wikipedia:

1959 Yellowstone earthquake

From Wikipedia

Date August 17, 1959

Magnitude 7.3-7.5

Depth Unknown

Epicenter location ~15 miles North of West Yellowstone, Montana

Countries or regions Southwestern Montana, Idaho, Wyoming

Casualties 28 plus, dead

The **1959 Yellowstone earthquake** also known as the **Hebgen Lake earthquake** was a powerful earthquake that occurred on August 17, 1959 at 11:37 pm (MST) in southwestern Montana. The earthquake was registered at magnitude 7.3 - 7.5 on the Richter scale. The quake caused a huge landslide that caused over 28 fatalities and left $11 million (1959 USD, $74.1 million 2006 USD) in damage. The quake-induced landslide also blocked the flow of the Madison River resulting in the creation of Quake Lake. Effects of the earthquake were also felt in Idaho and Wyoming.

The 1959 quake was the strongest and deadliest earthquake to hit Montana since the 1935-36 Helena earthquakes left 4 people dead and caused the worst landslides in the history of the Northwestern United States since 1927.